AN **UNLIKELY OPERATIVE** FOR THE **CIA**, BASED ON **TRUE EVENTS**

DEMARIS:
PROTOCOL

BRIAN DAVID RANDALL

Riptide Publishing
PO Box 1537
Burnsville, NC 28714
www.riptidepublishing.com

This is a work of fiction. Names, characters, places, and incidents are either the product of the author's imagination or are used fictitiously. Any resemblance to actual persons living or dead, business establishments, events, or locales is entirely coincidental. All person(s) depicted on the cover are model(s) used for illustrative purposes only.

Demaris: Protocol
Copyright © 2025 by Brian David Randall

Cover art: L.C. Chase
Editor: Grace Stack

All rights reserved. No part of this book may be reproduced or transmitted in any form or by any means, electronic or mechanical, including photocopying, recording, or by any information storage and retrieval system without the written permission of the publisher, and where permitted by law. Reviewers may quote brief passages in a review. To request permission and all other inquiries, contact Riptide Publishing at the mailing address above, at Riptidepublishing.com, or at marketing@riptidepublishing.com.

ISBN: 978-1-963773-18-7

First edition
June, 2025

Also available in ebook:
ISBN: 978-1-963773-17-0

AN **UNLIKELY OPERATIVE** FOR THE **CIA**, BASED ON **TRUE EVENTS**

DEMARIS:
PROTOCOL

BRIAN DAVID RANDALL

For Alex

TABLE OF CONTENTS

PREFACE

From 1981-92, the CIA developed and implemented a classified protocol that served as a dark ops support desk for counterintelligence where homosexual orientation could affect a successful recruitment. The protocol was designed in direct response to societal changes in parallel to the US gay rights movement. Officers were voluntarily recruited from the military when their sexual orientations were disclosed and dishonorable discharge was imminent. These recruits were trained to operate on the outer fringe of clandestine surveillance, where their specific skills and sexual orientation were an asset to US intelligence activities.

For more than a decade, the protocol operated in absolute secrecy at a time of the strictest ban on same-sex sexual orientation for both military and national security roles. The duality of these operations provided not only counterintelligence but deeper psychological insights into human conditioning, sexuality, recruitment, and coercion methods. These experimental recruitments incorporated unorthodox tactics—the results of which resembled Stockholm syndrome or, in present day, traumatic bonding (TB).

This is a fictional story based upon true events..

PART ONE:
RECRUITING

We can easily forgive a child who is afraid of the dark; the real tragedy of life is when men are afraid of the light.
— Plato

CHAPTER 1
BAIT

What am I doing? I shouldn't be here.

Trey Alan Carter inhaled slowly and forced another glance across the tree-lined street. The glow of dusk muted the neon lights above the darkened door of the seedy storefront. Growing up Baptist in Georgia, he had never seen the inside of an adult bookstore, never been to Germany, and definitely never been so far from home. He exhaled slowly and felt each thump of his heart.

"Trey?"

He swallowed hard at the sound of his assigned CIA officer whispering in the earpiece clogging his right ear.

"Trey?" the voice repeated.

"What?"

"You okay?"

"Yeah."

"What'd your PawPaw say about that dog—"

"*Can't catch a possum if ya dog's tied.*"

"I see our possum. You ready to untie the dog?"

"Yeah." Trey tightened his back. "Yeah." He stepped off the curb, crossed the street diagonally, but paused at the neon entrance. "Now what? Go in?"

"Not yet. He needs to clock you."

"Where's he?" Trey asked softly.

"By the cafe, but he's waffling."

"Did he see me?"

"Not sure. Hold up. He hasn't locked on you yet, remember a target must track."

"How do you get 'em to track?"

"Connection. Try again."

"Where?"

"Glance back—quickly. He's now on your six, toward the cafe."

"That's him?"

"That's our possum."

Trey met the man's eyes briefly and dissolved the one hundred and fifty feet between them. *Huh? He doesn't seem so old.*

"Gotcha. Target locked and tracking. Ready, Trey?"

"Now?" Trey couldn't help letting hope into his tone. Hope that the assignment would be canceled, that their target would not be lured, and he'd return to his normal life.

"We're green."

Two simple words punched Trey's gut and fizzled any shred of hope. His dark, familiar fear seeped back into his chest.

"Repeat, we're green. Trey?"

Trey stepped up and reached for the door, but his hand froze on the handle.

"Trey, acknowledge me. Now."

"I'm going. We're green." Trey exhaled and pushed the blackened door.

"Stay on cue, Trey. Every second matters now—we're not training anymore."

"I know, I know . . . *not a drill—this is real,*" Trey mimicked as the door closed behind him.

"So, you were listening to me these past few weeks. All right, get your bearings."

Trey squinted at the harsh fluorescent lights and the faint smell of floor cleaner. The cold air conditioning, combined with his nerves, rushed his senses.

Whoa! The array of images of bare flesh and fetish surrounded him. "Good lord, are you kidding me?"

"What?" Rick asked.

"Nothing, but a whole lotta buck nekkid."

"Don't enjoy it too much."

"Ha, ha," Trey mocked quietly.

"Crowded?"

"Nah, pretty empty." He nervously scanned the black wire racks. "Why's it so bright in here?"

"Empty? That's good," his officer acknowledged but ignored Trey's question.

"It feels different. You sure about our map?"

"Positive. Get your bearings. Remember: Stop, assess, and take a breath."

Trey breathed deeply and tried to fill the void in his gut. "It feels . . . real."

"I know. What song are you gonna use?"

"'99 Luftballons.'"

"Perfect, German."

"Yup. It's odd, not—" Trey did not finish his thought.

"Nerves are normal. Use them, Trey. Don't let 'em use you."

"Right. I'm gonna look around." Trey walked slowly through the racks of flesh and pretended to browse, but the door did not move. "Where's he?"

"Twenty yards out. You got this, Trey."

"You really think he'll buy it. I'm an airman on leave?"

"A hundred percent."

You better be right. Trey tugged at the scratchy unfamiliar shirt collar and glanced again at the entrance.

"All right, showtime. He's headed for the door. We're going dark. Ditch the earpiece but remember, I'm right here. Stay calm."

"Confirmed."

The radio went silent. Trey pulled out the earpiece, placed it in his shorts pocket, and focused on the VHS box in front of him.

Gang Bang III, Tina Takes on Tulsa.

I wonder if our parents know what we're both doing tonight, Tina? Suddenly he was bombarded with the Scriptures of his youth, *"Blessed is the man that walketh not in the council of the ungodly, nor standeth in the way of the sinner, nor . . ."*

Ding, ding.

As the door chimed, Trey turned his back on the person entering. *This is it. Game on.* A shiver shot down his spine; without turning back, his gut instinct affirmed his target had entered.

His newly acquired training now guided his actions and replayed in his thoughts.

"Take your time. Go to the back desk. Pay the fee. Enter the arcade."

Steadying himself, Trey handed the bookstore attendant the two-mark entry fee, then passed through the chrome turnstile with two clicks. As he entered the darkness of the arcade's back rooms, Trey paused to allow his eyes to adjust. The white piping on his shirt glowed strangely in the black light.

"Observe only—don't interact. Ignore everyone. Focus only on the target."

Trey quickly counted eight men lurking in the darkness. The seedy room was roughly thirty feet by twenty-five with the faint smell of sweat and antiseptic. It was somewhat like his training, but more real. Visceral. Light flashed from the video monitors as graphic images of naked men streamed overhead. Muted moans emanated from the maze of darkened corridors.

Trey ignored the other patrons and walked to the far wall without making eye contact. He steadied himself and tried to clear his head. His heart pounded louder and louder as he waited for several minutes until his target slipped into the room and locked eyes on him.

Trey sensed himself being ogled. He eased into a submissive lean against the wall and played into the fantasy as they had rehearsed, with both arms behind his back. Again he inhaled deeply and focused on his instructions.

"Tonight, you're not a tourist, not a shopper—you're an airman on leave."

But a single thought returned over and over: *What am I doing here? I shouldn't be here.*

His pounding heart nearly drowned out his opening lines he had memorized in German. His mind swirled with anxiety and all he could think was, *Come on, come over already.*

Trey broke his training and looked directly at the former Soviet nuclear engineer, who connected with Trey's eyes.

The eyes staring back at him were not menacing. Although his slight smile and hungry eyes were sexual, he gave no hint of the dark past that Trey had studied.

Huh, he doesn't seem so tough.

Trey broke his gaze but could sense the steps in his direction.

"Pretend to be nervous. It'll drive him to you."

There was no need to fake it. With each step, a growing chill washed over him. *What am I doing here?*

The question looped on endless repeat in his mind, but the souring ache in his gut held the answer.

I'm bait.

CHAPTER 2
ROPE

Monday, April 27, 1953
M-305 Quebec USSR Submarine - Baltic Sea

"Ivan."

Ivan grunted but remained asleep.

"Ivan."

Again, Ivan grunted but kept his eyes shut.

"Ivan . . . Ivan, get up," his fellow seaman, Uri, whispered, shaking him awake.

"What?"

"It's 0400. Your shift. My bunk."

Ivan nodded and stretched. He grabbed the bunk handles and quietly pulled himself from the middle one down to the deck without disturbing the sleeping crew above and below him.

Uri leaned in. "Officer Makar needs his breakfast . . . Oh, and don't forget his shirts from the laundry."

Ivan peeled off his T-shirt, leaving only his boxers on.

"And shower—our bunk smells like rotten cabbage."

Ivan shrugged and pretended to smell his T-shirt. "That's your own ass you smell."

"Bullshit," Uri hissed and play-punched Ivan.

Ivan winked and pinched Uri's ass as his only friend grabbed the handle and swung into the warm middle bunk.

Ivan tiptoed to his small locker. He pulled on his socks and boots, then made his way along the tight steel corridor to the head with his towel. As usual, the engines were humming and the dim overhead lights flickered. He passed the mess and nodded to the seaman already up prepping breakfast.

"Morning," Chef said, his gaze fixed on the potatoes he was peeling.

"Morning, gonna hit the head."

Ivan steadied himself in the small head and dabbed the warm washcloth over his naked body. *Four more days, and we get out of this tin can. Sunlight, fresh air, and a real shower.* He combed his hair, brushed his teeth, and pulled on his long-sleeve *telnyashka*, along with his black pants. His reflection told him he was ready, but flashes of Makar's stares made him hesitate. He closed his eyes. *Get in, get out. Don't look at him.* He again saw his own face in the mirror. Took a deep breath, and gave himself a forced smile. *Ready.* Ivan opened the small gray door and repeated his goal. *Get in, get out. Get in, get out.* His mantra repeated as he walked the twenty-three steps to the mess and found Captain Makar's breakfast tray. His smile faded. *Get in, get out.*

"You sleep?" Chef asked.

"Ya, you?" Ivan said.

"Not so good. Tell Makar I need sun . . . Been down here eight days already."

Ivan's stomach churned. "Where's his juice?"

"We're out," Chef said. Panic jolted through Ivan. "He wants juice. I need provisions." He continued to peel the potatoes as Ivan stared at the breakfast tray.

"Chef, please. He'll be pissed."

"There's no juice."

"Can you give me something else?"

The weathered man frowned.

"Please."

Chef sighed and pulled an object from his deep apron pocket. "I was saving this . . . last one."

Ivan placed the apple carefully on the tray. "Thank you." He took a breath, trying to quell the churning in his stomach.

"Ivan?"

"Yes, sir?"

"You fear Makar?"

Ivan shrugged.

"Don't. He can smell fear. Be strong." Chef raised his knife and circled widely as he spoke. "Down here, beneath the sea. We're all needed. He needs you. Understood?"

Ivan again nodded.

He steadied the tray and made his way down the long corridor to Makar's cabin. *Twenty-seven steps to go. Get in, get out. Twenty-five. Get in, get out. Twenty-four.* His stomach roiled. He forced his attention on the steam rising off the hot coffee, but the countdown wouldn't stop. *Nineteen, eighteen, seventeen . . .*

Get in, get out.

Thirteen, twelve . . .

Maybe it'll be okay this time.

Seven, six . . .

Maybe he'll let me leave.

Two . . . one.

He exhaled, then rapped twice on the gray cabin door before opening it.

Light entered the room as Makar stirred in his single officer's bed. *Just set the tray, turn and leave.* Ivan set the tray on the desk and clicked on the reading lamp.

As he turned to leave, he heard the dreaded three words.

"Close the door."

Ivan shuddered at the shadow on the ceiling, clenched his jaw, and closed the door. Then he stood quietly as Makar swung his legs over the edge of the bed and stretched.

"Come here, turn around. Good . . . untuck your shirt."

"I need to get your uniforms from the laundry . . ."

"It can wait," Makar said sternly, then glanced at the tray. "No juice?"

"No, sir. Chef ran out, but I got you an apple." Ivan shifted to his heels and stood rigid.

"Hmm. How are your studies?"

"Good, sir."

"You practice your knots?"

"Sir, I, uh—" Ivan stammered.

"Ivan, you must practice your knots. Do you have your rope?"

"No, sir."

"You can use my rope." Makar pulled back his sheet to expose his erection.

"Sir—"

"Come here."

Ivan took a deep breath before taking two steps to his officer. He knelt before him as Makar took the apple in his left hand while grabbing the back of Ivan's head in his right.

"Ah . . . easy."

When Ivan returned to the mess with the dirty tray, Chef frowned before taking it.

"Come here." He motioned after tossing it onto the metal counter. Ivan followed him toward the pantry. He slid back an empty box to reveal a bottle of vodka. "Our secret, okay?"

Ivan nodded but looked away.

"Take a sip. Wash away the taste." Chef sighed. "Stay out of his way and you'll be okay."

Ivan picked up the bottle and brought it to his lips. As the liquid burned his throat, a numbness oozed over him and began to dull his senses.

"You working on your knots?"

He shook his head.

"Why not?"

"I don't have rope."

"Here." Chef reached back into the storage and removed a small box. "For you, you keep it. Keep him happy. Okay? Our secret."

Ivan hesitated but then took the box, before heading back to his locker. Once there, he opened it. Tears filled his eyes at the sight of the small instruction book for nautical knots and the length of two feet of white cotton rope. *God, I don't want to practice.*

But he had no choice. He shook his head and swallowed his sadness. He began tying a knot.

One day, I'll be captain. My knot. My rope.

CHAPTER 3
BERLIN

Saturday, November 9, 1991
Bookstore Arcade - Berlin, Germany

Eight months prior to meeting Trey in Munich, a middle-aged Ivan Dimitri hunted in the shadows of a similar adult bookstore arcade in Berlin. He studied the other patrons as they slinked about in the darkness. He focused on one, then another—searching for his prey. A young sub to quench his thirst.

Two hours passed almost unnoticed in the maze of back rooms. Unfulfilled, he was about to surrender the hunt when the lights flickered at the neon entry. Ivan's blood pressure surged at the sight of the young blond man now rubbing his eyes, presumably trying to adjust to the black light of the arcade.

Yes, oh yes.

The man scanned the room before locking his eyes on Ivan standing rigid in his leather harness. Ivan registered his attention and reciprocated with a steely stare.

Ah, das böser Bub.

Ivan then ignored his target, who desperately tried to elicit a reaction from his stone-cold gaze. Ivan dismissed all the boy's impetus signals. He stood rigid but ignored the others in the room vying for his attention.

Come to me, böser Bub. Serve me.

Ivan adjusted his black leather codpiece with one hand and rubbed his jaw with the other, demonstrating his mastering dominance. His casual motion and rigid stance had been perfected by decades of secret encounters and dominating his prey. Now he saw his *böser Bub* shift his weight, round his shoulders, then cross his wrists in front of his waist.

That's right—come to me. Serve me, böser Bub. Ivan motioned his approval. The sub cautiously approached, passing the other hungry eyes in the dark room and leaving them disappointed with each step before stopping in front of Ivan.

Not here. Come with me.

Without words, Ivan guided him into an empty cubicle allowing his target to enter first. Once inside, Ivan locked the door.

In the silence, Ivan examined his *böser Bub*.

Ah, clean shaven. Youthful glow. He tugged the young man's shirt off revealing his naked chest.

Perfect, muscular yet boyish. Smooth. With deep cum gutters. Ivan traced the two opposing creases of ab muscles that disappeared into his pants on either side.

The *böser Bub* reached for Ivan, but he pressed him back against the wall. Ivan continued to survey him, then pointed his index finger out and moved it in a circle. The young man rotated slowly, allowing himself to be assessed. Ivan watched the *böser Bub*'s muscles contract as he breathed deeply and shifted his weight. Ivan delayed their pleasure with his ritual.

His prey finished a full rotation and tried to step forward.

Ivan shook his head and motioned again for a second rotation.

Patience.

Ivan paused once the muscular back was in full view. Without warning, Ivan grabbed and pressed him against the graffiti-marked wall. He deftly kicked his sub's feet apart. The *böser Bub* craned his neck to see Ivan had pulled out a five-foot nylon rope and looped a knot.

"Handgelenk," Ivan barked.

The young man widened his eyes and offered his wrists. Ivan looped the rope around the wrists and saw him bite his bottom lip.

Ah, you like it rough.

Ivan stared at him a moment, then jerked the knot tight. His sub gasped, closed his eyes, and licked his lips.

That's right, my naughty boy. Let's go further.

Ivan tied a noose on the opposite end of the rope and watched the wild eyes of his prey widen further as he slipped it around his young, sinewy neck.

"Was machst du?"

"Shh!" Ivan hissed and began to tighten the noose slowly as he pushed the man down to his knees. The fear seemed to soften in his sub's eyes as Ivan snapped off his codpiece, freeing himself. The *böser Bub* grinned slightly, then wildly engulfed Ivan's uncut muscle.

Tighter and tighter, Ivan gripped the rope and felt the warm mouth increasing the suction. *Yes, oh yes. Serve me, böser Bub.* In and out, he pumped his hips as he increased his grip. In, out. In, out. Ivan closed his eyes and saw the gray steel walls and endless thumping engine of their submarine. *Uri, ah, Uri. Fuck yeah.*

Ivan ignored the gags and gasps from below his waist and let himself fall back to his own youth, back to the *Quebec*—to Uri.

The gasps grew louder, but Ivan squeezed his eyes and grip. He continued thrusting into the warm, wet mouth—in cadence to his memory of the pulsating engines of the *Quebec*.

Suddenly, the rope ripped from Ivan's hands. The friction stung his palms, as he opened his eyes to see the panicked stare, bluish lips, and frantic struggle beneath his waist.

Not yet, I'm not done.

Ivan grabbed the blond hair and tried to force his way back to the rhythm, back to Uri. But the young man revolted and a violent surge of strength ripped them apart.

Crack.

Ivan slammed backward against the wall.

"Aaahh!" the raspy voice coughed and sputtered. "Hilfe—hilfe!"

"Halt die fresse," Ivan hissed and tried to grab him.

"Hilfe, hilfe!" the young man yelled and shoved Ivan. He tore open the door, dragging the dangling rope as he disappeared into the darkness.

Ivan shook his head and squinted to see the frightened sub burst through the exit and into the brightly lit bookstore. He followed and heard cubicle doors open and sensed a growing commotion. He peeked through the arcade door to see the store clerk approaching the young man and assessing the situation. The clerk then reached for his phone. Ivan closed the door but pressed his ear to hear the muffled voices.

"Hilfe!" The young man's voice was breathless yet clear.

"Ich rufe die Polizei?" the clerk asked as Ivan gripped the door handle but waited for a response.

After several seconds, came a reluctant "Nein, nein."

Ivan relaxed.

"Nein?" the clerk asked.

Ivan again cracked the door to see the young man loosen the rope from around his neck and discard it. He shook his head at the clerk and exited the bookstore into the night.

Ivan closed the door and returned to the cubicle.

Inside, he casually pulled on his long black duster, concealing his leather persona as euphoria bubbled up inside him like wine.

Run away, naughty boy. But I'll haunt you in your dreams.

Concealed in the shadows, CIA Special Officer Richard "Rick" Morgan studied Ivan from across the dark maze. He leaned out the fire escape and observed the former Soviet engineer climb down the ladder below, drop to the street, and walk briskly toward the train station.

Rick closed the fire exit door and turned to see the clerk standing before him.

The clerk asked if he'd seen the attacker.

"Nein," Rick answered in his best Frankfurt accent. "Haben Sie die Polizei gerufen?"

The clerk shook his head.

"Nein?"

"Nein. Er hat sich nicht geoutet. Seine Eltern wissen es nicht."

Rick motioned toward the exit. *I bet you're right. The kid's not out to his parents.*

"Er wird wegen der blauen Flecken an seinem Hals lügen müssen," the clerk added.

Yup, he'll have to lie about the bruises on his neck. Rick shrugged as the clerk returned to his desk. Rick exited the store. Outside, he glanced in either direction and breathed in the night air. Thirty feet ahead, a door flung open and four young people stumbled out of a bar in front of him—instinctively, Rick crossed the street and heard the young woman spilling her dinner into the gutter as her friends argued.

As he continued to the train station, Rick was lost in his thoughts of the scared young German.

The fucking closet is gonna get that kid killed. He'll concoct a story. Hide the bruises. Lie to his parents. But who am I to judge. We all lie. To our family, coworkers, friends—Hell, to ourselves. To protect, to hide, to survive.

CHAPTER 4
ENGINEER

CIA Deputy Director Dee Tibbins was not having a good morning. He was at his desk at 0620 rereading the classified top secret press release intercepted from its intended Czech Science Foundation.

Goddamn it, we don't need this bullshit. Nukes in an election year—we gotta shut this down. Do we tell him?

Dee swiveled his chair and stared out the large windows and reflected on the heightened reality pulsating the Beltway. *Like it or not—it's coming. Like goddamn cicadas crawling out of a hole. Every four years, this whole town fucking loses its mind.* His thoughts raced sensing the gyrating energy during the run up to presidential elections. Everything seemed to speed up in a town that somehow fed even more ravenously on paranoia and speculation. *No one's immune—POTUS, the Hill. Fuck not even us.*

He gripped the press release in his hand and resisted the urge to wad it up. *But this is different. He's one of us. When will we ever get another Former into the Oval?*

He turned to the headline emblazoned across *The Washington Post*: Conservatives Question Support for Bush as Reelection Looms.

Dee exhaled. *Great, now 41 has to fight his own party? Fucking self-righteous conservatives threatening to split the GOP.* He focused again on the press release. *Who the hell is this engineer? How do we bury this quickly? Loose Russian nukes—Goddamn Robert McGuire will eat this shit up.*

His office, large and imposing, suddenly felt small and confining. He turned and caught a glimpse of the 41st President of the United States of America grinning at him from the framed image. *Why did you put me here? You know damn well that I'm better in the field.* Unlike his friend and mentor, Dee spent years successfully avoiding beltway politics with much of his tenure spent on international assignment. He hated politics, hated DC, and hated sitting in traffic, which was why he commuted at 0500. As the first streaks of orange emerged in the black skies, he studied the release a third time, then let the single sheet fall atop his piled desktop. He ran his fingers over his desk's edges, and found the corners with both hands. He steadied himself, then released his grip, closed his eyes, and let out his breath slowly. Dee weighed his next action and tried to anticipate how the news would impact their daily White House briefing prep.

Do we include it or not? Time to find out.

He picked up the phone and hit speed dial 01. White House Chief of Staff Sam Tanner answered on the second ring.

"What?" Sam huffed.

"Good morning, Sam."

"You tell me. Is it a good morning?"

"Have you seen the Czech release I faxed over?"

"I'm looking at it now. Who else has seen this?"

Dee took a deep inhale. "We think only us."

"You *think*? Or you've verified?"

"Verifying, of course."

"Who?"

"Our contacts in Prague."

"Same ones you intercepted it from?"

Dee clenched his jaw. *Spare me your vast knowledge of counter intel you pencil-pushing prick.* "Yup, and our other sources."

"All right, when?"

"Last night, immediately as he sent it."

Sam grunted. "So who's this engineer?"

"Ivan Henryk Dimitri."

"Give me a second." Sam paused, presumably to scan the release. "What do we know about him?"

"Fifty-eight years of age. Married. Hana Machalek Dimitri."

"Where are they now? Where did they come from?"

"They moved to Prague from Leningrad now St. Petersburg about a year ago."

"Russians? Damn it, I thought we were done with containing all these Soviet nukes—were they not on our list of scientists?"

"No, not on any list, and technically, not Russian they're Czech."

"Same difference."

"Not entirely, but the point is they weren't on radar back in '88 or '89."

"Are they KGB or GRU?"

"No, we don't think so—"

"You don't *think* so or you don't know?"

Dee gripped the receiver tighter and stood up from his desk. "We *know* he works for a local start-up in Prague. On the surface it's legit—an energy brokerage in the former Soviet states of Eastern Europe."

"Like Enron in Texas?"

"Kinda, but—"

"But what, Dee?" Sam paused. "Tell me your gut, OTR."

"Way off the record?"

"Yes."

"They're not on any lists and I don't like his expertise."

"The nukes?"

"Yeah, and this white paper—the timing."

"What do you think he wants?"

"It's not just a publisher."

"What then?"

Dee exhaled deeply. "A calling card. He's fishing."

"To *sell* his intel?"

"Yeah."

"Jesus H. Christ."

"We caught it in time. We can—"

"We don't need this right now," Sam interrupted.

"We know and we'll handle it. Do we put it in today's PDB?"

"No."

"No?"

"No," Sam repeated. "For now, we keep this tight. It'll spook everyone till we know more. Can we stop the Czechs from publishing it—immediately?"

"Yes. Already done. The plan's in motion, but what about POTUS—"

"I'll worry about POTUS. We'll brief him when we know more. Dee, this stays tight. Our circle. Your team only—even Langley has ears. Got it?"

"Got it."

"Good. *Contain* this, Dee—I don't need to know how."

"Understood."

Dee hung up the phone. He closed his eyes and savored a last moment of quiet in his office on the third floor of the CIA headquarters. At fifty-four, he had enjoyed a long-storied career that others wished for, but only he and his cardiologist knew the price he had paid.

He glanced back to his side table at a photo of himself at thirty with the now forty-first president. *We were so young and stupid. I don't care what you say. I'm only two years from retirement—this fucking desk doesn't feel like a promotion. And you still owe me that whiskey.*

The neighboring photo immediately tugged at his private pain. His wife and late son were smiling back in the silver frame. *Why Demaris? Why?* He closed his eyes, swallowed his grief and squeezed his eyes to try to escape for a moment.

The sun shone on Dee's face. He squinted and saw his son's blond hair whipping and the blue jib flapping. The lanyards clanked on the metal mast as they sailed the Chesapeake in the warm summer wind. Demaris grinned.

Knock, knock.

The sharp raps jolted Dee back to his office. He shook his head. "Yeah?"

The door slowly opened as his two senior staffers entered his office. Senior Field Officer Claren E. Johnson and Dr. Carlos Martinez entered and stood rigid.

"Close the door. Have a seat." Dee motioned to the two chairs opposite his heavy oak desk. "Two months of surveillance—tell me we have *something* on this engineer."

"Yes, but it's tricky," Claren said calmly as she sat down.

"Let's hear it."

"Possible sexual deviation," Dr. Martinez said as he closed the door and took the chair beside Claren.

"He's a dom with extracurricular activities," she said. "His wife doesn't know."

"An affair?" Dee frowned.

"Not exactly, a bit darker. His appetite—" she paused "—same-sex."

"Homosexual?"

Claren nodded.

"And the wife really doesn't suspect?"

"No. We don't think so."

"Is that enough for your protocol?"

"Maybe."

Dee observed her tone. *Uncertain. Un-Claren.*

"You agree, Carlos?" Dee turned to their resident neuropsychologist.

"Perhaps. Closeted homosexual behavior is certainly an inroad, but our data isn't complete."

"Meaning?"

"Initially, Ivan presented as a quiet man, but now we're seeing overt actions at the same time he's soliciting his work to be published. Incongruent. As if he's running from or toward something."

"Incongruent?" Dee shook his head. "What's your point?"

"The point is, our instincts were right—he has darker secrets," Claren interceded while pulling several photos from a folder and laying them on the desk.

Dee relied on her ability to counter balance his and Carlos's egos to avoid loggerheads. He scanned the photos as she continued.

"Dark secrets coupled with bold actions."

"Precisely. His bold actions now indicate a need." Doc M paused. "A need we can exploit with highly *specialized* incentive."

"How specialized?"

"Quite. We've a theory based upon his excursions to Germany. He's bisexual or homosexual with latent traits of a sadist." Doc M pointed to a grainy black-and-white photo of Ivan and a young bound man.

"When were these taken?"

"Last week. At an adult bookstore. In Berlin," Claren said.

"Why now? What's his motive?"

"We have a couple of theories," she said, but paused.

Dee raised his eyebrows. *Damn it, spit it out, Claren. I don't need another lecture from the great Dr. Carlos Martinez.*

Doc M leaned forward and inhaled deeply. "He served for two decades at the Soviet's State Committee for the Utilization of Atomic Energy."

"But low ranking, right?"

"Yes, he was lower ranking, but his area of expertise is beyond nuclear fusion, maintenance or energy. It's a stretch in reading his paper that he clearly intends to parlay his expertise."

Get to the point. "Not reclamation—what then?"

"Reanimation."

Dee darted his eyes from Doc M to Claren.

Her lips pursed and brows lifted in affirmation.

"Fuck."

"Do we escalate? Today's PDB?" she asked.

Dee heard the stress in her tone as they were only an hour out from deadline on the president's daily briefing report. "No, I just got off the phone with Sam."

"And?" She leaned forward.

"We *contain* this." Dee picked up one of the photos. "Contain him. White House stays dark. They don't want to know. Do we have a plan?"

"We have a couple of options to consider." Doc M stared at Dee for a moment and dropped the thick file on his desk with a thud. He looked over his glasses. "Our assessment, while clinical, outlines verbatim a justification for a more *experimental* solution—"

"Before we dig in—you both realize that with all our technology, all our resources— How the hell did we not identify this fucker sooner?"

"Technically, we did," Claren calmly said.

Dee shook his head.

"He didn't make the cut. When we crossed tabs with Interpol. He was below threshold."

"How far below?"

"Seven assets to be exact. He was outranked by higher value targets."

Dee shrugged.

"You remember what it was like during the collapse. Our resources were tight, a call was made. We couldn't chase down everyone. Too little time, too many—"

"I know." Dee rubbed his neck. "Nearly a hundred displacements in twenty months from '88 to '90."

"Exactly," she said. "He fell below the markers. The focus was on more important scientists dispersing across Europe, Israel, and here. Missing this one doesn't mean our program wasn't successful."

"Won't matter in a Senate hearing. They'll only focus on this guy." Dee jabbed his finger into the photo. "We missed him."

"Essentially, yes," she said.

"Shit!" Dee turned his back and stared out his window. "I don't need to remind you two how we busted our asses identifying, tracking, and securing these targets. Hell, not only us." He turned back to them. "Mossad, MI-6—those final hours were chaos as the great USSR imploded and spilled its guts across Europe."

"You're right. We all thought they were secured," she said calmly.

"Or at least the KGB led us to think they were," Doc M added.

"Let's not dive down that KGB rabbit hole, Carlos," Dee said. "Let's move on. Who's most likely to target him? The usual suspects?"

"Of course. Most likely Iran, Syria, or Iraq—but we can't rule out several rogue North African states. They're all clamoring for this *type* of usable intel," Doc M said. "And the Soviets left dozens of exposed waste sites."

"Easy targets," Dee concluded.

"We're still assessing, but new ones pop up daily on our counter intel feeds," Claren said. "We have three full-time analysts searching geothermal surveillance imaging, but—"

"Are you shitting me?" Dee smacked his desk and stood.

"Dee, we've—"

"They'll fucking pay top dollar," Dee again interrupted. "Whatever he wants."

"Precisely." Doc M looked over his glasses. "That's why our incentive must be stronger. More enticing."

"We get to him first, turn him, and use him." Dee paused. "Risky but let's play out. The payoff could be huge."

Doc M confirmed and pushed his glasses back with a slight nod.

Claren shook her head. "It's more than risky. A huge gamble. Turning someone like him— We don't even know his true intention. We're guessing."

"Yes, but a calculated guess," Doc M countered. "And his intel would be both valuable and concerning." He turned to face Dee. "It's worth the risk. Even low-grade reanimation would be catastrophic."

"Dirty bomb." Dee's eyes widened as he deducted.

Doc M nodded slowly.

Dee exhaled deeply. "How's the Dimitri income?"

"A tiny pension and an equally small apartment in Prague," she said.

"Does Hana work?"

Claren nodded. "Yes, she took a job teaching language to the trainloads of ex-pats arriving daily. We're not sure that she's even aware or involved."

Doc M had lowered his chin at that, so Dee asked, "You don't agree, Carlos?"

"Perhaps," Doc M said. "But his paper suggests a level of detail and research that would be a heavy lift for one person."

"How sure are we on his theories? Are they legit?"

"Yes. Remarkably simple and highly valuable," Claren said.

"Completely solid," Doc M added. "We both agree it's actually intriguing and quite innovative. His theory could shatter claims about reclamation and the potential for reanimation."

"All from waste?" Dee widened his eyes.

"Yes, Claren and I agree on this point."

"Fine. How do we contain this quickly and quietly before the election?"

"We've run some scenarios; we'll need to decide soon but we have time," she said.

"Any chance he picked his timing purposely? Our election."

"What do you mean?" she asked.

"I mean why did he sit on this? He had all of '88 and '89. Why now?"

"Dee, we've analyzed every bit of intel. Carlos and I may disagree on the solution, but we agree we've arrived at a conclusion. He's playing a long game. But my gut says he knows exactly what he's doing." Claren sat forward in her chair. "We target and contain."

Doc M cleared his throat. "Perhaps. But maybe—my opinion—this immediate escalation from suspect to target has everyone a bit worked up. The daily intel feeds from both the Frankfurt and Prague field desks confirm that Ivan's brazenly soliciting to publish but remember . . . he's an unknown, former Soviet nuclear engineer."

"Meaning what?" Dee said.

"He's unknown. Maybe it's that simple. His motives were unclear at first, but could include a desire to step forward from obscurity. He's seen former colleagues get university positions across Europe, Israel, and here. A play for recognition, or simple misstep in his timing."

"Timing?" Dee asked.

"Yes. He stepped into our crosshairs as the election looms—could simply be bad timing."

"Bad timing?"

"Bullshit, he's playing his only cards to get back to a better way of life." Claren stared at Dee. "Money. Wealth. Power."

"Then why risk them by lurking in the back room of adult bookstores?" Dee challenged.

"While I will give you that, his needs do appear basic," Doc M said.

"Either way, he must be contained," Dee said. "We need a plan, which is exactly why it's not going in today's briefing. We need a resolution."

"We're really not including it?"

"No."

Claren shook her head. "Jesus, what if it leaks?"

"The White House will spin it as a possible solution to nuclear waste. Not as a nuclear intel threat. I've alerted Václav Havel at the Czech Science Foundation. He suppresses this immediately or his funding is cut. Either way, Ivan's our target," Dee concluded. "What's his next move?"

"We isolated a pattern to his movements," Doc M said. "Claren has the details."

"Every four to six weeks, he leaves Hana and the two cats in Prague to go on a 'business trip' to Germany." Claren unfolded a small map. "Berlin was his initial hunting grounds, but he's widening his circle to Frankfurt." She pointed to several red markings. "Usually it's an adult bookstore with video booths and darkened back rooms. He spends hours hunting and meeting men of all kinds, but his favorite are young men."

Dee raised his eyebrows.

"Several of our field officers have attempted to entice Ivan. He's never taken the bait in Czech or Germany." Claren's gaze darted toward Doc M.

"We've studied his routine," he said. "That's how we found the pattern. He's been consistent in Berlin, Frankfurt, and now . . . Munich."

"So Munich?"

"Adjacent, we think Nuremburg." Claren pointed to the red circles on the map. "We're not sure if it's because of cost or covering his tracks, but he never stays overnight in any of the cities. Once satiated, he hops a late-night train out to a small country inn."

"He's repeated this pattern for nearly four months," Doc M added. "We've tried to lure him with field officers—nothing. Our Frankfurt ops desk have tried to entice him using several male heterosexual agents."

"And?"

"Nothing. He's never once engaged."

"So what? You think he senses they're straight?" Dee asked.

"Yes," Claren said.

"So we need to use your team . . . the protocol?"

"Sort of, but this feels different," she said. "Our guys didn't work—not even Rick."

"So the protocol is now slipping?"

"Our agents failed—not our protocol." Carlos glared over his glasses at Dee. "This situation may call for some adjustments."

"How so?" Dee asked.

"Our unsuccessful recruitments did miss a fundamental principle in coercion and persuasion," Doc M said. "They failed to engage Ivan's darker needs. Officer Morgan's notes are correct. We need a young, closeted recruit. It's all outlined here." Doc M opened the file and pointed to the assessment.

Dee took the summary and quickly scanned the two-page document. "You've verified all of this?"

"Rick assessed the situation personally," she added.

"On the ground?" Dee asked.

Claren nodded. "We had to escalate. We added additional surveillance. Rick just got back from Berlin."

Dee stared back at the document.

"We have strong intel now. Rick observed Ivan for forty-eight hours. At first, simply blurred normality—but then in the shadows of that Berlin adult bookstore, Rick isolated it."

"Isolated what?"

"Ivan's true motive," Doc M said. "His actions were a tell. It focused to one clear conclusion. Desire."

"So all those weeks of surveillance?"

Claren shook her head. "The audio plants and bugs in the Dimitri apartment in Prague netted nothing. We had agents take language courses with Hana directly. We've reviewed the logs—useless intel."

"And you think luring him will be stronger than forcing an intake?"

"Yes. There's been talk of bringing him in but given his behavior and the situation—he's got no children to protect—only Hana. No real incentive that even off-record 'coercion' might not work," Doc M said.

"So what's our options—send Rick back?" Dee asked.

"No. He's thirty-six, and beyond the age of our engineer's tastes." Claren exhaled. "This is where we disagree."

"We need *specialized* incentive."

"How specialized?" Dee asked.

Claren shrugged.

"We need a young conservative, Caucasian, closeted homosexual male." Doc M's tone was flat and clinical.

"That's pretty specific—why Caucasian?"

"Racial bias. His specific profile is highly evolved. But the most important factor is youth," Doc M said.

Claren eyes widened.

"How young?"

"*Very* young." Claren pursed her lips, then added, "At least twenty-one years of age, but—"

"But what?" Dee noticed that she had now clenched her jaw slightly.

"The candidate needs to appear *much* younger," Doc M said.

"What are you suggesting? There are limits—"

"Of course, Dee. Nothing illegal. We simply need to modify the protocol to allow a more *experimental* intake." Doc M explained. "A young man like we've outlined who'll entice our engineer. If the pieces fit—we solve our puzzle."

"Puzzle?"

"Desire. Incentive. Containment."

"You know I don't like puzzles."

"This isn't the only tactic." Claren's tone grew stronger. "Carlos, you and I both know that he has other weaknesses that we can exploit."

"Sounds like you tried others." Dee stood and walked to the large windows to the left side of his office.

"And those other paths failed," Doc M said.

"Not all of them—"

"Claren, we're running out of time. We need to take action." Doc M stopped.

"So now I see where you guys disagree." Dee continued to stare out at the treetops of Virginia below. "It sounds very Russian, Carlos. You can use all the fancy jargon you want but all I'm hearing is that you want a fresh, young sparrow?"

"Precisely," Doc M said. "Think about it, Dee. Imagine beating Russians at their own game."

"It's tempting but how are we gonna find this sparrow? It's risky to go military again—Pentagon is snooping around too much. Which means OTR."

"We stumbled on a unique candidate in the McGuire probe—"

"That kid's a civilian. I don't like it," Claren said. "A sparrow? Honeytrap—we're not the KGB."

"And?" Dee said.

"And that's not us. We don't do that."

"Which is why he'll never even see it coming," Dee said.

Doc M nodded.

Claren shook her head. "But we've—"

"We've played too nice for too long, Claren," Dee interrupted.

"Precisely my point too."

"It's risky, but it's time we beat the Russians at their own game," Dee said. "We can't have this on our watch . . . especially during an election. We must *contain* this."

Claren raised her eyebrows. "Besides the civ there are other more qualified candidates."

"While a civilian does present unique challenges and risks, they could also open new areas of research and recruitment." Doc M turned to Claren. "Yes, it's a calculated risk. We'll need to modify the protocol to mitigate."

"A civ is not *any* risk," she said.

"Claren, there's always risks. Every assignment—everything we do." Dee stopped. *I hate when Carlos is right, but we've got to take the gamble. Contain this.* The two words echoed. "Show me the candidates?"

"We've narrowed it down to these four." Doc M laid the dossiers on the desk.

Dee returned to his chair.

"Two Navy, one Army, and . . . the civ," Claren said skeptically.

"How exactly did we come to know this civ?"

"Quite by accident. We uncovered him during the dig on Robert McGuire's American Seniors Initiative," Doc M said.

Dee flipped open the dossier and stared at the young blond man. "How old is this kid?"

"Turned twenty-one a month ago." Claren shook her head.

"Geez, he looks sixteen. He's gay?"

Doc M cleared his throat. "Yes. We've profiled him. A near perfect fit for the criteria: Conservative. Caucasian. Closeted. Grew up in Atlanta—quite unique, a Christian conservative homosexual civilian."

"Seriously?" Dee said, as he thumbed through the file.

"Graduated this year from Jerry Falwell's university," Claren said. "But the three other candidates are stronger."

Dee ignored the other three even as she outlined their extensive military service.

When she was done, Dee reverted back. "Tell me more about the civ."

"He's high risk," Claren said as she sat back and folded her arms. "What do you want to know?"

"Does McGuire know the kid's gay?"

"No, not yet," Doc M said. "The incentive will be strong."

She shook her head. "We've never turned a civ—"

"He has shown several markers that could make him receptive to the protocol." Doc M raised his tone slightly.

"It's uncharted."

"Uncharted?" Dee shook his hands. "We've put eighteen or nineteen candidates through your protocol."

"Yes, but they were all military, every one of them."

Dee nodded.

The three sat in silence.

"You want to call it off? Bring in the NSA or FBI?" Dee asked.

"A twenty-one-year-old civilian? Forty-five days to produce a civ-5 asset? Yeah—"

Doc M leaned forward, cutting Claren off. "That'd be a bad idea. We can modify the protocol. It will work and we'll create our first civ-5 asset. Think of the research, Claren. The intake and recruitment alone will be enriching to the program. Advance the protocol."

"Right, but you and I both know what happens if we fail—"

"That can't happen," Dee snapped and glanced to Doc M then back at Claren. "We go with the civilian."

Doc M nodded while Claren only shrugged.

"What's our timeline for the engineer, Claren?" Dee asked.

"The window on the target remains the last weekend in July. Munich."

Dee stood up from his desk walked around to join them.

Claren and Doc M stood. She faced Dee with pursed lips. "You know, for OTR my team will need additional support."

"Whatever you need." Dee glanced to Doc M. "Do what you need to do, but the kid has to be ready."

"He will be."

CHAPTER 5
POWER

Tuesday, January 7, 1992
Old Ebbitt Grill - Washington, DC

On the first Tuesday of 1992, at three o'clock, Robert McGuire followed a server to his favorite chair at his usual table at the Old Ebbitt. He glanced at his watch and scanned the room. *Good. Nobody important, only tourists.*

"May I take your coat, sir?"

"No," Robert said as he discarded his thick jacket over the back of his chair.

"It's a cold one . . ."

Robert's icy stare silenced any banter.

"Your usual?"

"No. Manhattan."

The waiter nodded and hurried away.

Robert sat rigid and again scanned the room, and gradually its familiar comforts sent ease rolling through his spine. He secretly relished the privilege that, as his party's staunch conservative, he publicly eschewed. Growing up on the dusty plains of Texas, he had longed to be a part of the power inside the beltway of DC and the inner circle of the GOP. Thirty years of politics had hardened him but given him his dream. He was by all accounts the leader of the conservative contingent of the Republican party.

As he waited, he tried to remember the first time he'd entered into this power den of Washington's elite.

'68 or '69. Nixon? 3:09 p.m., damn it, Sam! If he doesn't show, then who's he sending? Bet it'll be Jed. Better not be some junior staffer.

Robert again scanned the dining room and waited for Sam Tanner, the White House Chief of Staff. *Only a handful of diners, mostly tourists. No one of consequence to witness this meeting.* The crisp white tablecloths, richly paneled room, and hurried servers gave no hint of the bitter cold outside. Lost in his thoughts, Robert did not see his guest arrive. He suddenly looked up to see the blond liaison of the assistant deputy chief of staff smile at him.

"Sorry to keep you waiting, Robert," Tamara Lenox said as she approached. "No sit, sit. Please."

Robert tried to rise to greet the White House liaison as she immediately pulled off her red coat and casually placed it on her own chair. She sat down across from him before he could sit back down.

"Where's Sam?"

"Sorry, he's in meetings and asked me to meet with you. Cold day, huh?"

Robert did not speak.

"Did you have a good holiday?"

"Why did Jed send his pretty young intern?" Robert smirked.

Tamara seemed to ignore him. She motioned to the nearby server. "Coffee, please." She turned back to Robert. "Manhattan? That's early even for you."

"So, they sent you to do their bidding."

"How's your wife?"

Robert narrowed his eyes and forced a slight smile. "She's fine. I was expecting—"

"Listen, I can't stay long. You clearly don't want chitchat. Can we dismiss the formalities here?"

Robert nodded.

"We know, Robert."

"What do you think you know?"

"Cut the shit—we know about your book."

Robert did not budge.

"We even laughed about the title. *Read My Lips.* Really? Ridiculous, a bit on the nose—even for you. Did Steve write it?"

Robert bristled but did not answer. *I'm not taking your bait, missy.*

Their silence hung in the air until the waiter cautiously approached the table with her coffee. "Cream, ma'am?"

"No, thank you." She cupped the warm mug with both her hands as the waiter scurried away.

Robert picked up his cut-glass drink, feigned a toast, and took a sip. "What book?"

"Are we doing this?" she said with a slight shift in her seat.

Robert sat still.

"Fine. Forget the book, I'm sure it's a real page-turner." She brought her mug to her lips. "We know about your plans. Perot."

Robert clenched his jaw as his right eye tightened ever so slightly.

She returned her mug to the table and leveled her gaze to punctuate her statement. "Ross?"

Robert took a drink from his glass and did not answer.

"POTUS is pissed."

"He should be—"

"Did you think we wouldn't find out?"

"Your boss knew full well that we'd stick to our guns," Robert snapped.

"And do what exactly? Split the ticket? Split your party?"

"Conservatives put him in and we can take him out."

"How long's your arm, Robert?"

Robert leaned forward and hissed, "We're serious. We have the votes."

"Do you now? Just saying that you of all people shoulda known who you're picking a fight with."

"He swung first."

"He's not Reagan. Not your puppet."

"No, he is *not* Reagan."

"He's the president, and your party's leader . . . and supposedly your friend."

Robert did not respond.

"JJ knows all about your fundraising."

Robert took another sip of his drink. "JJ's inquiry? That was you? I should have known."

"He seemed pretty interested—"

"We've nothing to hide."

"Then I hope you enjoy the House investigation of your senior citizen brigade."

"Is that why you go running to the great JJ Pickle?"

"The enemy of my enemy." Tamara again raised her mug.

"JJ will burn you—"

"No, unlike you, he's smart. He knows how this town works and he knows exactly who wields power . . . real power. Unlike you—"

"He's a goddamn Democrat." Robert clenched his jaw and narrowed his eyes.

"Yes, he is and you used to be a Republican."

"I *am* the Republican party."

"No, you were back in '80 but it's 1992—"

"You listen to me, I've suits older than you, missy. I've—"

She stood instantly and leaned over the table. Her blond hair cascaded forward as she spoke a foot from his face. Robert scanned the room quickly and saw the other patrons turning toward them.

"Sit yo' ass down," he hissed.

"Thatta boy. That's the asshole I've heard so much about. Listen to me carefully, you misogynistic, political-has-been, prick. You think I'd be here if we didn't already anticipate all your pathetic moves? We. Know. Everything."

"What do you want?" Robert said softly.

"We're past that but if you want to step foot in the OEOB again—I suggest you kill that book."

Tamara took a final sip of her coffee and breathed deeply. She sat down the cup and picked up her coat. "Thanks for the coffee."

Robert stood from the table and she turned to leave. Suddenly, she turned back and leaned close. Uncomfortably close, he could smell her perfumed skin.

"One word of advice? Next time, do your homework."

What is she getting at? Steve? Robert's mind raced.

He could sense Tamara studying his facial expressions. "Next time tell your boss to meet me man-to-man."

"A simple background check. You're slipping, Robert. You of all people should know who you're playing ball with—you don't have friends in Langley."

"So you're a former spook like your boss."

Tamara only smiled. "Order the Cobb. It's great." And with that she walked to the door.

Robert waited until he saw her cross the street, her red coat in sharp contrast to the white frosty paladin windows. Then he turned back to his server, handed him a twenty dollar bill, and walked out without finishing his drink.

Alone in his car a minute later, Robert gripped his steering wheel. He was locked on one thought.

Who leaked the book?

He pulled out his mobile phone and hit 003 on his speed dial.

"American Senior's Initiative, this is Trey—"

"Get me Steve, now."

CHAPTER 6
GREEN

Saturday, May 9, 1992
CIA Headquarters - Langley, VA

Claren sat in her conference room alone waiting for her ops team to call into the speaker phone. Her intuition gnawed at her nerves as she replayed over and over the details of their plan. After four months of planning and arguing, she'd yielded to Dee and Doc M. The intake team was in place. *This kid better take the bait. This better work.*

"Claren?" Doc M said, appearing in the doorway.

"I thought you were dialing in?"

"I wanted to be here with you."

Claren smiled slightly and motioned to the chair opposite her.

"Well, it's a hot summer day—that pool should be tempting. Are we ready?" he asked.

"You tell me. This was your idea."

"Claren, it will work, but your team must follow the protocol."

"They will. We're in position now. We should be green in thirty-five minutes—assuming the civ's on time."

"I thought you quit drinking coffee?" he asked.

"You know what's at stake," she said. "This has to work."

"It will."

"I'd rather be the one lying by that pool today—instead of stuck in here."

Ring, ring.

"Claren, ops is in place. Standing by for your signal for Operation Wet Willy."

Claren rolled her eyes. She hit Mute and the mic lights turned red. "The team nicknamed it."

Doc M shook his head.

"A bit of levity, Carlos," she added, sensing her analytical colleague's serious nature—ever-present, even on a Saturday afternoon. "But they fully understand the risk of our exposure. We have to execute this flawlessly."

Doc M lowered his chin.

Claren unmuted and the lights turned green. "All right, everyone. Huddle up. Remember, we do not exist. We do not operate on US soil much less in the heart of DC. Today, each of you must bring your A game. Zero mistakes. No deviation from any procedure. For the next four hours, we are one unit. One ops plan." Her words hung in the air. "Are we clear? Acknowledge."

"*Affirmative*," rang out in unison from the speaker.

"Officer Farro?"

"Yes, Claren."

"You are Todd today. We need this kid. Take things as far as you're comfortable, but we must get it on camera."

"Understood."

"When you flip, it must feel real."

"The punch?"

"Yes. Don't hold back."

"I won't."

Doc M and Claren sat in silence for the next eight minutes. Then Claren unmuted again. "Standing by for update. Do we see the kid?"

"Affirmative. Target is pulling up now."

Claren switched on the television monitor at the end of the conference table. The naïve target, Trey Carter, hurried to the elevator. They observed him enter and push the button marked RT for rooftop pool of the Apolline Condominiums. The elevator doors shut with the grainy black-and-white image on Claren's monitor of Trey in his board shorts, T-shirt, flip-flops, and with a beach towel on his shoulder.

"Target is here. Our target's on deck," the voice echoed on the speaker.

Claren raised chin and looked at Doc M.

He nodded.

She leaned into the mic. "All right people, we're green. Repeat, we're green."

CHAPTER 7
POOL

Saturday, May 9, 1992
DuPont Circle - Washington, D

As the doors opened, the bright afternoon sun poured into the small elevator. Trey squinted, and then pulled on his sunglasses. *This is going to be such a cool party.* Still, nerves made his heart thrum as he stepped out into the crowd of sunbathers and scanned the roof deck for his acquaintances from Worldgate Athletic Club.

"Hey, Trey!" Abby shouted over the crowd. "So glad you made it," she greeted him with a warm smile after she and her boyfriend Jake zigzagged their way through the crowd of bikinis and board shorts.

Jake grinned. "'Bout time, we thought you might not show up."

"Hey, guys. Yeah, sorry I'm late. I had to coach my rug rats."

Abby frowned. "Rug rats?"

"Yeah, my boys . . . I coach gymnastics on Saturdays in Chantilly."

"A gymnast, huh?" Jake asked.

"Yeah, I was. Now I only coach."

"Cool. I'm glad you made it." Abby shifted a little, and gave him an awkward smile. "Listen, we gotta go, but you should stay."

"What? Are y'all leaving?"

"Yeah, man, but you should stay—hang out. Enjoy the pool," Jake added.

"No, I can go . . ."

"Relax. Stay." Abby grinned.

"But I don't know anyone—"

"Hold on. Hey, Todd. Take care of our friend."

A dark-haired frat boy grinned wide and raised his beer from across the pool.

Trey frowned. "Seriously?"

"Seriously. That's Todd. He's cool. Loosen up. Stay. Have fun!"

"Okay, well thanks again for inviting me."

Abby smiled as they turned toward the elevator. Jake hollered back, "Have fun! See you at the gym."

Trey nodded as the only familiar faces disappeared into the elevator. He was suddenly stranded in a sea of strangers at the rooftop pool in DuPont Circle.

He would remember this moment, a simple decision to stay, for the rest of his life. Over and over during the next eight months, he would vividly replay the next two hours and ask one simple question.

What if I had just left?

"Beer?" Todd asked as he approached Trey.

"Um, yeah, okay. Thanks," Trey said, taking the beer.

"I'm Todd."

"Trey." He shook Todd's outreached hand.

Trey's Baptist upbringing had graced him with a strong character but exactly zero tolerance for alcohol. Alcohol had been forbidden growing up in his fundamentalist church back home in Georgia.

One beer won't hurt.

After a few swigs, he tried to relax and talk with Todd under the glow of the late-afternoon sun. The cold liquid tingled his tongue and warmed his hands and face. His first beer buzz heightened his senses while lowering his apprehension.

"Where you from, Trey?" Todd asked after a few minutes. "I'm guessing down South?"

"Yeah, I grew up in Atlanta. You?"

"All over, but mostly Arlington—my dad was Army," Todd said, motioning across the treetops toward Virginia. "Is this pool awesome, or what?"

"Yeah."

"How do you know Abby and Jake?"

"What?" Trey was puzzled by the non sequitur.

Todd shrugged and smiled.

"Worldgate. My gym, but I don't know them that well. They invited me yesterday. Do you live here?"

"No. I'm kinda crashing too— Ha! Here's to crashing a cool pool on a fucking hot day." Todd held up his beer and they clinked cans.

The two young men laughed and talked about their colleges, DC, and the Redskins as the afternoon sun sank lower toward the horizon and the crowd thinned.

"Another beer?" Todd offered, about ninety minutes later.

"I better not."

"Trey, you've had like one beer in an hour. Come on, don't make me drink alone."

Trey reached for the second one as the last few guests started to pack up.

"Looks like we're closing the place down," Todd said with a grin. They were alone as Todd continued to tell stories about his college frat house at UVA in Charlottesville. "You can't imagine how crazy it was on Friday nights. There'd be like ten or twelve kegs. WahooWa!"

Trey laughed. "Well, we couldn't have had more different experiences. Liberty's a Christian college. No smoking. No sex. No beer."

"Are you shitting me?"

"No, I'm serious. This one can would get me expelled."

"You'd get kicked out of school for one beer?"

"Yup. This is the most I've ever drank in my life."

Todd grinned and raised his beer. "Damn, well cheers to that."

The sun was barely a sliver on the horizon in the dark blue summer night. The air was warm. Suddenly, the pool lights turned on and shimmered indigo below their waists.

Twenty minutes later, Trey sat in the shallow end on the white glowing concrete steps watching his new friend. Todd, already having done a lap or two, swam close, before grinning and peeling off his trunks beneath the water. Standing naked with them in his hand, he dared Trey to join him.

"Ha! C'mon, nobody's here now—only us. Geez, loosen up and live a little."

Trey was confused but curious. Todd's tone and demeanor had led Trey to sense he was straight. But now standing naked, Todd's grin and dare gave Trey an odd feeling. Heat started to rise in his chest, fueled by adrenaline and beer. He took Todd's dare and shed his own bathing suit.

"Is this cool?"

Todd grinned.

Trey stole a few glances of his well-defined biceps, abs, and exposed flaccid dick. "You work out."

"Yeah. You like what you see?"

Trey nodded and bit his lip. Emboldened by Todd's statement, Trey stared at the wet skin and muscles.

Todd again smiled.

Suddenly Trey turned his gaze and looked away at the night sky.

"What's wrong?" Todd said.

"A bit nervous."

"Don't be. Hey?" He motioned for Trey to move closer.

Trey frowned—something felt off here—but it was hard to resist this masculine man naked in front of him when heat was radiating through his body.

Trey moved closer. Todd looked up at the night sky. They sat inches from one another quietly. Todd lightly splashed at the warm blue water in front of them and allowed his left leg to graze Trey.

Trey looked around and scanned the empty pool deck. He reached over to touch a part of Todd that should have never been uncovered in a public pool.

Suddenly Todd's fist slammed into his lip, shattering his fantasy forever.

Trey tasted blood. His head swam. *What—*

Then he was being yanked from the water. But not by Todd. Hands, several of them, dragging him out of the pool. *Who are they? What's happening? Am I being arrested?* "No!" he yelled and strained against the grips of the hands with all his might as a black hood was shoved over his head.

Complete darkness enveloped Trey. "Help me! Help!" But the thick fabric muffled his screams.

Trey panicked and began swinging blindly with his arms. Strong hands grasped his wrists, forcing them together, where they were bound tightly with thin cold strips. Suddenly he was lifted off the ground.

"What? Stop!" Trey writhed and struggled to catch his breath while kicking wildly in the darkness. Sharp pains pulsated from the tops of his feet as he realized they were scraping the rough, concrete pool deck as he was dragged off the roof and down the stairs by the unknown attackers.

What's happening? Who are you people? Oh God, help me!
"HELP!"

CHAPTER 8
TEAM

Saturday, May 9, 1992
Classified Field Ops 23rd/M Streets NW - Washington, DC

"He's scared shitless," CIA rookie officer John Farro said as he toweled his black hair dry and pulled on a T-shirt.

"Of course he is," Special Officer Darius Morris said.

"Look at him—shak'n like a . . ."

"You would be too—he's got no clue what's going on," Darius said.

"He thinks he's been arrested for indecent exposure and groping a hot dude . . . me!"

"Yeah? You ain't that hot, 'Todd'!" Darius mocked. "Saturday night in the *Hole*—damn it. We were supposed to be at Cafe Atlantico with friends." He turned to the other officers in the small, dimly lit room.

"I hear ya. My eight-year-old had a little league game," Chris said. "Is this normal for you guys to pull an assignment on the weekend?"

"Normal? No, not how we usually spend a Saturday night," Special Operations Officer Jeni Yoon said.

"Which division are you?" Darius asked Chris.

"National Resources."

Jeni and Darius glanced at one another.

"What?" Chris asked, but neither Jeni nor Darius offered a comment.

"So do we wait?" Chris eventually asked.

"Yup," Jeni said. "She's on her way."

"Who?" John interrupted.

"Claren," Darius said.

Chris and John nodded.

"She'll be here any minute." Jeni turned back to Darius. "How's your shoulder?"

"Sore. Kid's stronger than he looks." He stretched out his left arm and walked over to the coffee machine as the final gurgles hissed and the ready light flashed red.

Chris asked, "Is he really a civ? I mean, what are we doing here?"

Jeni shot Chris a look and offered one word. "Yes."

Claren pulled into her parking spot in the underground parking deck and turned off her Audi. She flipped down the visor, applied a fresh hue to her lips, smacked her lips twice, and breathed out deeply. *Well, we got him. That's a start. Why the hell did we agree to this timeline? Forty-five days to live, fully operational. How the hell is my team supposed to produce a civ-5 in little more than a month?*

She exhaled and returned the tube to the side door pocket. Dee's instructions echoed in her mind. She had been struck at how unusually clear and direct he'd been on their last call.

"The recruitment must be spotless—no redshirts, Claren."

She exited her car, walked the long interior hallway, and swiped her badge to enter the classified underground bunker at 23rd and M Streets. The room fell silent as she entered.

"Good evening. Thank you all for giving up a Saturday night."

She walked to the table and sat her bag down, then looked through the two-way mirror at Trey. "How's he?"

"Well, he showed his 'propensity toward action,'" Darius said. "He struggled a helluva lot harder than we thought, but we got him. He seems disoriented and scared, but that's to be expected, obviously."

Claren nodded and stared at Trey's wet skin, glistening in stark contrast at the white walls and bright fluorescent lights of the ops room.

"I almost feel bad. The kid looks sixteen," Darius said.

"Yeah, but he's twenty-one," said Chris Ryder, a CIA officer on loan from Langley. Chris and John were not part of the protocol team but on temporary support for the risky intake.

The team watched Trey sitting motionless in the stark ops room, which seemed to swallow the naked young man. Claren noticed that his hands covered his genitals, and his shoulders shook slightly from the cold air pumping into the underground bunker.

"What's he thinking right now?" John asked the room.

"The usual. 'Where am I? Who are these guys? Why am I here?'" Darius said.

"How do we know he'll go along with it? 'Cause he's gay?"

Claren turned, pursed her lips at the rookie, but held her thoughts.

"We don't," Jeni explained. "But his profile's strong. He's not being voluntarily recruited. So he needs *incentive.*"

"Precisely, Jeni. John, this kid is not volunteering at this point of the intake," Claren said. "Being a closeted gay isn't enough—strength and vulnerability. An involuntary civ-5 is an entirely different intake. We must set the stage and persuade him."

"Persuade him?" John frowned.

"At this moment, he's not coming to us willingly. We need him," Darius said.

"Okay, but what makes us so sure that he's right for this one?" John asked. "I mean, why him? Go down to Tracks or Badlands any Saturday night—we'd find a dozen pumped-up, closet-case faggots shaking their asses."

Rick flinched, but remained silent.

Claren darted her eyes to Rick in the back of the room, but then turned to John. "We've analyzed him. He fits the need for the target." She pulled the thick file from her bag and laid it on the table. "Beyond his sexual orientation, his profile also indicates that propensity toward action you guys dealt with."

"Right, the profile," John said.

"Besides, that kid's a beast. He benches 285—I spotted him at Worldgate."

"Oh, Chris, you've been eyeing him at your fancy gym . . . huh?" Darius chided.

"I gave him a spot, you asshole," Chris said. "He's a former gymnast. He's wicked strong, Claren. He'll breeze through phase two."

She silently observed her team.

Claren had grown to hate this part of recruitment—the waiting. The part where the young, cocky officers jockeyed for the point position to groom a recruit.

"Still, we need the photos from the pool."

"Civ-5s always need incentive," Chris said. "Looks like the pics are coming in now."

John walked over to the fax as the light turned green and the machine began to hum. The thermo paper rolled, and the smell of burnt ink filtered into the room.

"Hot off the press—incriminating incentive," John said delivering the faxed images to Claren.

"Incentive is only our key to unlock him," she said shuffling through the grainy images before selecting one. "Fear is an entry point. Opens the door to his head." She held up the image. "Then and only then is when our real work begins."

CHAPTER 9
CHOICE

Claren felt the weight of her tenure on her shoulders. She tried to tune out the chatter of her team and stared at the photo of their target: Ivan Henryk Dimitri. *One more former Soviet nuclear engineer. How did we miss this one? One more assignment, one more turn. One more choice.* Her decision could determine the outcome—operational success or failure. She'd stood at this type of moment many times in her twenty-four years at the Agency where one choice, one decision seemed to predetermine the outcome of the assignment. She scanned the room of the team assembled.

One more choice. Who can guide this kid? Roll the dice.

She weighed her options and the stakes.

The Agency and the White House were pushing her team to gamble. The involuntary intake of Trey Alan Carter was high risk, but small and calculated compared to a potential nuclear threat in an already heated election. *Contain him. We don't need to douse gasoline on this election.*

"Who's he?" John's question interrupted her thoughts as he pointed to the photo.

"Ivan Henryk Dimitri," she answered.

"What's he done?"

Claren did not answer but glanced to her right at Darius.

"Not what he's *done*. What he's about to do." Darius turned to Claren for approval.

She nodded.

Darius continued. "Dimitri's trying to publish a scientific white paper on the reclamation of spent nuclear waste. On the surface it's a white paper, but it ain't just a theory."

"No?"

"It's an advertisement of services. He wants to sell his expertise," she said.

"His paper was supposedly for the environmental science community, but international intelligence saw through the façade," Chris added.

"Nukes?" John asked.

"Re-fucking-animation intel to the highest bidder," Darius confirmed.

"Jesus. Have we approached him?" John asked.

"Several times. All failed. And now the White House with the reelection campaign has increased the pressure." Masking her stress, Claren breathed deeply, sat back in her chair, and crossed her legs while staring through the mirror at Trey. "We got a lot riding on this kid. You're right, Chris. He does look sixteen."

"I told you. He looks like a teenager."

Jeni or Rick? Why is he lurking in the back of the room? He'll get this kid on our team. Claren glanced at Rick still standing in the shadows. *But at what price? Can he handle it? We cannot afford another Mexico City.*

Claren was haunted by Mexico City 1988 where they had lost two officers on her watch. The incident had nearly blown the lid internally off their dark ops desk. Containment and discretion were essential to the protocol.

She alone knew the secrets of her assembled team. Echoing in her mind, Claren heard the raspy voice of her late mother-in-law. *"Most folk don't know a simple truth about DC. This is a very small town with a very long memory."*

Claren had observed early at the Agency that secrets were not only spoken. They could be seen if you were watching. They were the powerful currency of intelligence work at Langley or in the field. Secrets pumped through the veins of Washington, DC. From each agency to the Capitol to the White House—they were the lifeblood of the dirty business of politics. They could be as powerful as steel or brittle as glass. For nine years, her ops desk was a pivotal keeper of secrets for Director Tibbins and the White House.

At forty-nine, Claren was growing sick of the chase, sick of banter, sick of sexism, and sick of the games. She had never got her station in Costa Rica, never got the pleasure of watching her ex-husband squirm when he lost the divorce settlement. She was working, always working. *Twenty-four years and for what? Saturday night as senior officer, in the Hole.* Instead of going to the movies or dinner with her friends, she was stuck in a basement in Foggy Bottom.

Focus, Claren, focus. She scanned her team, letting her gaze settle on her two most experienced officers. *So Jeni or Rick? Why's Rick so damn quiet? Jeni's always quiet during these intakes but why's Rick not gunning to take lead on this turn?*

"Hmm . . . good shots, Darius," Claren said as she looked at the freshly printed black-and-white images of John and the young man naked at the pool.

She sat back and folded her arms over her Talbots navy blazer.

The officers gathered in the small operations room were posturing for the leadership role—vying for who would lead the intake and recruitment. Who would build the trust and guide—

"Poor little boy caught nekked in da' pool," Darius mocked.

Not to be outdone, John mustered a Southern drawl. "What would his football buddies say back in Stone Mountain, Georgia? Hell, does Falwell know he's got a fag grad?"

"I'm guessing Mama and Daddy don't know he sucks cock," Chris added.

Claren remained silent as muffled laughter erupted as the group bantered about the recruit. In the corner, she could see Rick clenching his jaw. She waited and allowed the officers to act like jocks in a locker room. Joking about this assignment and this kid's life as though he were subhuman.

Rick began to pace and stare at the young man in the next room. "You guys are fucking amateurs. Claren, why do we need to speed up the turn?"

"Why, Rick—nice of you to join us," Claren said.

"Why are we speeding up the turn?"

"The timeline is tight and that's the plan."

"Give me a day or so . . . let me get in his head."

"Why? Is your gaydar going off?" She hated herself for busting on Rick in front of these pricks, but knew her deflection would have the counter effect and shield his secret. It perhaps wasn't her duty, but she wanted to protect him if she could. As a woman of color at the agency, she knew what it was to deal with prejudice and hatred. Rick would have to face it too if his truth were known.

Before the team could respond with another joke or jab—like dogs lunging for the bone—Claren shut down the banter. "Listen up, we don't have time. Tibbins sped up the timeline. We have to be fully operational in forty-five days. Forty-five days, people!"

The team bristled back into ops mode as her words hung in the air. Their quick recoil was no doubt due to their respect of her ability to allow some free rein but then to pull it in when needed. She was smart and drew her team in with not only her intelligence but her utter command of language and presence. Her team knew that Senior Field Officer Claren E. Johnson only repeated herself when displeased. Repeating a phrase in crisp diction was nearly the only emotion that allowed her team to sense the stress of a deadline or decision. Cool, confident, concise—Claren.

Jeni leaned into Rick's right ear and whispered.

You know I'm picking him, you little Miss Know It All. Always a step ahead.

Rick did not move.

"Claren, do you still need me?"

"No, thanks, Jeni. Great work tonight."

Jeni shrugged.

Clearly she'd anticipated Rick would be the choice. *I bet she wants to get home to Kristin and be done with this night.* "See you, tomorrow."

Jeni turned to Rick and punched his left shoulder playfully. "Later, handsome."

She grabbed her bag and exited through the service door leading to the long hallway and the parking deck below the small, artsy Cineplex Odeon. As Jeni left, Claren observed the team. Rick seemed in deep thought. He moved to within inches of the mirror and stared at the kid in the next room. He thumbed his chin thoughtfully.

"Okay, Rick."

With two words, her statement confirmed the decision. She faced the other three officers and said firmly, "You'll ride point on his intake. You three will support."

All eyes turned to Rick.

Claren stood from the table.

"Establish trust. Hold the line. Let's engage phase one."

CHAPTER 10
SURVIVAL

One single word had distinguished Rick Morgan in the first "class" of recruits for the dark ops protocol, code name Demaris: *survival*. It started with twenty, then fourteen, then five, but only three recruits passed the initial protocol in December 1981. Three had advanced to the field. Rick was assigned in Ankara, Turkey. After a decade, he alone survived. Twenty-six missions. Four continents. Eleven years.

Rick had survived the Reagan administration and now Bush. The fall of the Soviet Union. The AIDS pandemic. His survival skills were honed by eighteen years on a cold New Hampshire dairy farm with an alcoholic widower of a father. At twelve-years-old, Rick alone had survived the car crash that killed his mother, brother, and nearly all the love left in Cecil.

Rick graduated from college and went into the Marines as a closeted elite officer. Now a decade into his clandestine career in the uncertain post-Soviet world, he stood at the door of his first lead assignment to groom a high-value asset, and not just any recruit—a gay civ-5. Even in a world that had seemingly transformed overnight, this was new territory.

I guess things are changing faster than they seem. Rick was closely following the news reports of outed Navy pilot Tracy Thorne, Colonel Margarethe Cammermeyer, and dozens of others hitting the front pages. The media played into the witch hunts as dozens of service men and women were being outed. Like thousands before them, these men and women were being robbed of their military careers, pensions, and privacy. Offered up as fodder to a white-hot media frenzy.

The Agency had taken note and deviated from their proven recruitment path of voluntary service members on the verge of court martial. The media was an unwitting contributor to the experimental intake of a civilian recruit, but the question remained.

Can a civilian survive our protocol?

From the shadows of the monitoring room, Rick stepped forward to within an inch of the mirror. The twenty-one-year-old sitting bound and terrified in the next room now appeared not as a muscular young man, but as a puzzle to be solved.

Eleven years ago, it was me. Another group of officers staring at me through the glass, probably wondering what the US government could want with a faggot Marine.

To those who did not know his secret, Rick seemed damned near perfect—rising like a rocket from military to intelligence to dark ops. Only a few knew the price he paid and his constant fear. The fear of being outed created a duality in his mind, a bifurcation of sorts that allowed him to excel at counterintelligence work. Meticulously, he groomed his demeanor and switched the pronouns of his lovers. He limited those whom he trusted, which included a small circle and professionally now only his ops team—but not the ever-widening circle of agents, like John and Chris, vying for assignment to the protocol.

John handed Rick a small bundle of light-blue cotton scrubs, tightly folded. Darius sat at the computer and television monitors while Chris divided up the tasks and timeline for the phases. As he turned to leave the monitoring room, Rick gripped the cotton scrubs like a football. Claren stepped toward him and squeezed his left elbow. He leaned in.

"I know you've got this, but be careful . . . candy's hard to resist," she whispered quickly and turned back with one last piece of advice for all the team to hear. "Earn his trust, but remember: hold the line."

Rick nodded and looked back at his recruit. *Hold the line. What the fuck, Claren? This kid's not military. Not trained. He's a Southern, evangelical kid caught skinny-dipping with a guy at a rooftop pool. The setup was easy—too easy.*

Rick recognized the pain in Trey's eyes. He had to get close yet keep a distance. Get in the recruit's head and heart but not reciprocate. In all of his work to date, it had been much easier, one-sided.

Six months earlier, Rick had observed their target nearly strangle a similar young German national. Given Ivan's tastes, Rick knew he would find this similar blond American kid irresistible. Rick left the monitoring room, but something felt different.

Earn his trust—the words reverberated in his mind as he stepped into the short hallway of the Hole.

Alone now, a rush hit him. *Shit, I guess this is a promotion of sorts. I'm leading our first-ever civ-5 intake.*

He walked the three steps, reached for the door to the adjacent ops room, and paused to wait for the buzzer indicating it had unlocked. He rolled his shoulders back twice and turned his head left, then right. *Relax. You got this. Just focus on the intake steps.* His gut was a flutter. *Just nerves, let it go.* He swallowed hard yet sensed he was about to confront his own fears, desires, and fate.

Captor, confidant, mentor, coach but never friend. Hold the line.

Turning the handle, Rick entered the ops room.

CHAPTER 11
ROOM

What's going on? Where am I? Who are these people?

Trey shivered as he tried to recall the moments prior to being yanked out of the pool. The air vents above him showered his damp hair and body with cold air. As minutes passed, the panic in his gut cemented his fears.

Is this DCPD? Am I going to jail?

He closed his eyes and tried to remember details in the darkness. Strong hands had gripped him and held him on both sides. His hands had been bound tightly by what felt like thin plastic.

He opened his eyes and inspected the black zip ties on his wrists.

Why did I give in? I shouldn't have groped Todd. But he started it—he led me on. He dared me. Oh, God—please forgive me.

Trey tasted the blood in his mouth. He opened his eyes and saw his own reflection in the mirror.

Where's my car? My trunks? Did anyone see this go down and call the police? Are these guys the police? Oh God, am I going to jail? Dear Lord, please. I am so sorry. I gave in. I need you, Lord Jesus.

Again, Trey closed his eyes and relived the struggle with his captors. They dragged him down the stairs, into a van, then a long hallway, and then shoved him into this metal chair. Blinding light as the hood was yanked off. When his sight had adjusted, he was alone.

Trey again studied his reflection, his disheveled damp hair and dried blood on his lip and chin. He raised his bound hands and rubbed the dried blood from his chin. Suddenly, a thought shocked him from his reflection.

I'm not alone. Someone's watching me from behind the glass.

Trey immediately covered his genitals.

He tried to remain motionless and stared at the mirror. *I don't want to be here. Oh God help me.*

Trey allowed his mind to go beyond the image, back to his childhood in the suburbs of Atlanta. He heard singing in his head.

I heard an old, old story . . . of a Savior came from glory.

It was a trick he had learned during the thousands of hours of Bible-thumping, pulpit-beating sermons at his independent, fundamental Baptist church. He was no longer bound in this room, naked, and in trouble. He was strong, in his football uniform with his helmet on his lap. He was on an old school bus with his teammates. They were headed to the stadium and singing their pregame tradition.

I heard about His moaning and His precious blood's atoning . . . then I repented of my sins and won the victory. Oh victory in Jesus . . . my Savior forever.

The door opened, scattering his memories. Trey's gut wrenched with fear as a tall, dark-haired man entered. Before Trey could muster the courage to speak, demand to know where he was, demand a lawyer—the man's green eyes pierced him, and he froze.

CHAPTER 12
PHASE ONE

"How in the world did you manage to get in so much trouble tonight?" Rick said approaching Trey.

"What? I'm sorry. Am I under arrest?"

"What do you think? This isn't Disneyland." Rick motioned around the room then stepped closer to Trey. He could almost smell the fear emanating from him. Rick stopped and waited for Trey's eyes to connect. Rick allowed the corners of his mouth to tighten slightly, then extended his hand, tossing the scrubs on the table. He drew out his long blade and without speaking, he motioned, indicating his intention to free Trey from the zip ties.

Trey recoiled but slowly held up his wrists. Rick cut him loose, and the blade disappeared again.

"Get dressed." Rick turned his back and faced the mirror where his colleagues in the adjacent room studied his every move.

In his peripheral vision, he observed Trey quickly stand, pull on the scrubs, and return to his chair.

Rick turned back to Trey.

"Thank you, sir."

Seated. Called me "sir"—huh maybe this will be easier than I thought.

Rick locked eyes and extended his hand.

"I'm Special Officer Rick Morgan."

Trey stood again and offered his hand. "Trey Carter."

He gripped Rick's hand.

Confident. Warm. Firm grip. What? You're not scared now?

Rick may have underestimated the assignment. In an instant, he saw Trey's greatest strength and weakness. A familiar electricity reverberating up his arm to his chest.

What the hell? Damn, somebody did their homework. Yes, he's hot but he's in over his head. This isn't right. Damn it—don't let him know. Let go of his hand already. Rick knew his initial feelings weren't real, not physical. Yet he felt them. If he held Trey's hand a second longer, Trey might sense he was gay.

Not yet.

Rick let go of Trey, but locked the moment in his memory.

Rick then paced slowly around the room as he outlined the events from the pool to Trey. Each sentence and gesture on point with his phase one training.

"See what I mean?" Claren said proudly. Both Chris and John were watching intently as Rick deftly controlled his cadence and posture while addressing the potential recruit.

"Utter confidence. He makes it look so easy," John said.

Claren nodded.

"Look how he just lays out the situation," John said, seemingly absorbing Rick's tone, stance, and fluid manner.

"The trick is to be natural and use the situation as your framework," she said. "He's hitting all the major points of the intake: dominance, doubt, trust, and authority—but all the kid thinks is that he's recalling the events of the last two hours."

Claren watched her team study the intake. She breathed deeply. Her instincts had not failed her.

Rick's the right choice but he better hold the line. There's tough work ahead of us. How the hell we gonna pull this off? In forty-five days.

She watched Rick pace around the room, questioning Trey, whose face grew tense as though he sensed that his every reaction was being assessed. Rick recounted detail after detail.

"Trey, did you coach this morning?"

"Yes, sir."

"At the Chantilly Academy of Gymnastics?"

Trey's eyes widened and he nodded.

"How did you know Todd?"

"I didn't—Abby and Jake introduced me."

"And you know them from where? Your gym?"

"Yes, sir. Worldgate."

"Why did you go alone? Where's your friend . . . Mark. Mark Trenton?"

Claren leaned into the mic, pressed the unmute, and softly said, "Good, Rick. Turn up the pressure."

Rick nodded slightly.

"Wait, how do you know Mark?"

Rick stared at Trey. "You don't ask the questions here. Answer me. Why did you go alone?"

"Mark's at school. UVA. I don't know a lot of people—"

"So did you know Todd prior to today?"

"No. Are you DCPD?"

Rick did not answer. Trey's eyes started to dart around the room again, his breathing speeding up.

Claren pressed the mic button and whispered, "Use the photos now, Rick."

Rick reached into his back pocket and pulled out the photos. He shuffled them and took his time as he scanned them and seemed to rearrange their order. He stepped forward to the opposite side of the table and slapped them down one by one.

"Public intoxication. Indecent exposure. Sexual assault."

Trey stared at the naked images.

"At best—you're facing probation. But if the guy presses charges . . ."

Trey looked up from the photos and locked eyes with Rick.

"Could be two to five years depending on the judge."

Trey buried his face into his hands.

The agents chuckled behind the soundproof glass.

"Two to five . . . geez, Rick's laying it on thick," Chris said.

"Ha! The kid's freaking out," John said.

Claren ordered, "Quiet. He's gonna talk?"

Darius turned up the speaker to hear Trey request, "May I please use the restroom, sir?"

Rick held his gaze for an uncomfortable moment before consenting. "Second door on the right—make it quick."

Trey sat frozen.

Claren leaned into the mic. "Rick, back off the gas."

He studied Trey for a moment.

"Trey, the door will unlock. You're not currently under arrest. Your presence here is voluntary, despite initial appearances."

Trey nodded and stood. He exited the room barefoot in the scrubs.

Darius whispered into Rick's earpiece, "He's choosing the second urinal, center one. Confident."

Every detail was used to analyze potential, and assessment was constant during these first few hours of an intake—especially with an involuntary recruit.

"He shook, pulled up, and washed not only his hands but his face too. He looked in the mirror. For a minute, it looked like he might lose his shit. He didn't. He took a deep breath, and he's now returning to the room." Darius finished his play-by-play as the recruit returned.

"The kid's tough," Chris said, breaking the silence in the monitoring room.

Claren turned to John.

"Developing dominance and trust is essential to phase one. Dominance is easy. Trust, real trust, is much harder. Regardless of how high or low a recruit's value, trust is essential. It's the bond between the handler and recruit. Captor and captive. It's literally the difference between success or failure in the field."

John nodded.

Claren turned back to the mirror and breathed deeply. She knew Rick was the right choice, but she needed him to step forward. Now she was relieved to observe Trey leaning in, looking Rick in the eye and willing to respond. Trust markers that the potential civ-5 was demonstrating. It seemed things were going smoothly.

"Have a seat," Rick said.

Trey walked toward his chair but hesitated when he noticed the new objects in the stark room. There was now another chair on the opposite side of the table, and in the middle of the table beside the photos was a large manila folder inscribed with red ink. As he sat, Trey tensed up when he seemed to register the words clearly.

Trey Alan Carter.

That's right, young man—we've got a whole file on you. She watched Trey sink into the folding chair as fear apparently doubled-down deep in his gut. "This is it, Rick. Stay calm. Stay on point," Claren said into the mic. *Stay on point, tighten the pressure—one turn at a time.*

Rick waited for Trey to sit back in his chair, then took the new chair opposite, with his back to the mirror. He opened the folder, looked up, and cleared his throat for effect.

"Trey, let's begin."

For forty minutes, Rick reviewed the young man's file. There were notes from his teachers, school transcripts, and lists of classmates, coaches, ministers, and employers—along with the photos of him naked in the pool with "Todd."

"Why go so deep into the details?" John asked.

"To narrow his choices," Darius said.

John pursed his lips.

"The recruit needs to feel like we know everything about him. Even things that his family and closest friends don't know," Claren outlined.

At the end of the session, defeat was settling on Trey's shoulders, yet he had not buckled under the increasing pressure until Rick pulled out the last photo and laid it in front of Trey.

"This your brother?"

Trey only nodded.

"Career US Air Force. A staff sergeant at Shepherd in Texas. Does he know about you? That you're gay?"

Trey shook his head, even as he welled up and bit his lip, clearly defeated. His shame was palpable with his older brother now staring back at him.

I hate this part. This is fucked up. Hold the line.

Rick sat across from the young man, keeping his face stoic. He could feel the acid welling up in his throat and fought the urge to comfort this kid. Finally, after two long minutes of silence, he again cleared his throat.

"Trey, look at me. I have a question for you."

Trey raised his red, moist eyes.

"Would you be willing to serve your country?"

"I don't understand."

"Instead of arrest, charges, and filing all this on your record. There's a program that we are considering for you. We've never allowed in someone without military training—a civ, civilian—but your background is intriguing and possibly of use to us."

Rick paused, studied Trey's face for a moment. Trey furrowed his brow and stared at the table in front of him.

"Trey, if you would like to hear more, I must ask for verbal consent," he said, nodding his head to the left, acknowledging for the first time his colleagues in the next room beyond the mirror.

Oh god—it's not just him. Other people are watching this. Trey lowered his head in a crush of embarrassment due to the larger audience, now confirmed, that had seen him broken and on the verge of crying.

"Men don't cry!" Suddenly in a flash, there in front of Trey was Coach Harper, a ruddy, hardened Marine with tattooed forearms. They were at spring training in the hot Georgia sun. Trey's friend had broken an unspoken Southern rule when, after getting drilled by an upperclassman and cutting his arm, he'd cried. Trey's temper had flared, and he dove in after the play, hitting the upperclassman to defend his friend. Coach had been furious. He'd screamed for several minutes but ended with the phrase that now echoed in Trey's embarrassment.

"Men don't cry!"

Rick cleared his throat,

What do I do? Can I trust this guy?

"Trey?"

He seems to know me. How?

"Do you want to hear more?"

"Yes, sir."

CHAPTER 13
INTAKE

"Trey, you need to sign here, here, and here."

Rick collected and sorted the various forms one by one as Trey signed them.

"What's all this for?" Trey asked.

"Consent." Rick did not elaborate.

As Trey scribbled his name on each form, Rick outlined the next forty-eight hours to him clearly and succinctly as though he was interviewing Trey for a job.

"You're going to need to stay here tonight, Trey. Is there someone that you need to call?"

"No, sir. I live alone, but I would like to call my brother—"

"No," Rick interrupted. "I meant friends, anyone from work or gym?"

"No, sir. But my brother—"

"There will be time to speak with your brother—the staff sergeant—later, once we know where all this is headed. He's military. He'll understand."

Trey tensed his back at the mention of Robby's rank. The thick file of all Trey's data cemented the gravity of the night. Trey was in over his head but was intrigued with what his service might be. *What do they want from me? Serve my country? How? By trusting this guy?*

"Trey?"

"You'll call Robby? But what will you say?"

"Let that to me."

"Thank you, Officer Morgan."

"Look, we grabbed some toiletries at Walgreens for you. Basics but did you need anything specific?" Rick offered. Trey shook his head. "We have a cot for you and some blankets in your bunk room. This is going to be home for the next few days. You know your way around now?"

Trey was surprised, "Here? But I have to be at work on Monday. What about my car? My job? I also coach gymnastics . . ."

"We'll take care of all that and handle your work excuse due to an 'illness.' Just focus on getting through the assessment."

"Yes, sir."

During the past ninety minutes, the haze had begun to lift, and Trey had started wondering if he had been selected not in spite of his secret but because of it. The fear that gripped him eased a bit. Despite his fear, a new feeling emerged from this green-eyed agent. Trust.

Did they pick me 'cause I'm gay? Why? And all this spy bullshit. Officer Morgan seems to understand even though his moods are hard to read when he turns on a dime. Can I trust him?

Trey felt an odd attraction to the situation and Officer Morgan. *This is nuts! Why am I crushing on him?*

Claren studied her officers as they observed the intake from behind the glass.

"Why is he just going along with it?" John asked.

"He's not just going along with it . . . He's reacting to the incentive. The incentive is fear. We use it to persuade."

"I get it, but Trey seems to be trusting Rick now. How?"

Claren turned to face him. "Traumatic bonding. It's similar to Stockholm syndrome. We use TB and amplify it during an involuntary phase one. Doc M writes every detail of the protocol to reinforce the bond between our officer and the recruit. Urges, roles, games, and feelings will develop, but for now Rick will focus the recruit on the assessment. It's far from simple. That's a decade of training you witnessed in the last forty minutes. Every detail. Every action."

"Wow, I had no idea. It's a lot to learn. Thanks, Claren," John said.

"We're always learning. Now, gentlemen, I'm going to head out. We begin at 0700. Keep me posted."

Claren felt the civ-5 recruit's intake went like textbook. She was relieved when she left the Hole for her drive back over the bridge to her home in Falls Church at just before midnight.

The kid's starting to trust Rick. Maybe this will work, she thought to herself as she turned by the Kennedy Center to head over the Potomac.

Trey stared at the mirror as Rick further outlined the assessment and tomorrow's meetings. Presumably someone was behind the mirror and watching his every action. The whole situation seemed both frightening yet exciting.

Rick led Trey across the hall to a small bunk room with only a desk, lamp, cot with bedding, and a chair—it was less James Bond and more bad dorm room. As Rick turned to leave the room, Trey sat down on the twin-size cot. Rick seemed to sense the anxiety in his head.

Rick placed a hand on Trey's shoulder.

"Sleep well, Tiger."

Trey froze. *Oh my god! How does he know my PawPaw's nickname for me? He knows everything about me. How?*

Rick switched off the lights and closed the door. In the darkness, the lock *clicked*. Trey was alone, imprisoned, and felt the full weight of the situation. His evangelical family was in jeopardy of learning their son was gay, but could they also be in danger?

I want out of here. Should I demand a lawyer? Try to escape? What's happening? God, please help me. I'm in so much trouble.

Trey lay on his back for several minutes in the dark. The tiny red light in the upper corner of the room came into his focus.

They're watching.

Just as he had done his first few nights at boarding school, Trey flipped over and concealed his sobbing in the pillow.

Wonder if they saw me break protocol by touching him? Fuck it. My hand on his shoulder cemented the "Tiger." Rick entered the dimly lit monitoring room.

"Where did 'Tiger' come from?" Darius asked.

"From his files—an interview with his grandfather. Was it too much?" Rick asked.

"No, but from the look on his face— It shook him."

"Yeah?"

Darius motioned to the grainy TV monitor. In eerie green backlight, Trey's shoulders shook. The CIA officers fell silent at the sight of the young man breaking via the monitor.

After a minute, Chris broke the silence. "Rick, I'm supposed to remind you that we're not at touch yet . . . but you got him."

"I know—just went with my instinct . . ."

"No worries," Chris said. "Here's my notes, Darius."

"Thanks, Chris. Rick, what time you back on?" Darius asked as John and Chris headed to the exit.

"Seven-thirty, but I'll be up late if you need me, Darius," Rick said.

"We'll be fine. Good work, Rick. You got him."

John, Chris, and Rick headed to the parking garage, where they parted. John offered a quick "Great work, Rick," as he left.

Rick nodded and got into his BMW M3. He watched both sets of taillights head up the ramp to the 23rd Street exit. Rick started his own engine but remained in park.

What are we doing here? This kid is not military. I shouldn't be doing this . . . Why do I feel sad?

Rick knew why when he looked in the rearview mirror and saw concern on his face. He cleared his throat.

"Hold the line."

CHAPTER 14
GOD

An hour later Rick popped open a beer and sank into the couch at his apartment in Silver Spring.

Wonder if he's asleep?

He picked up the remote, turned on CNN, but hit Mute. He tossed the remote on the coffee table, grabbed the file folder, and stretched out his legs as he again opened Trey's dossier.

Damn, somebody did their homework. Why the hell is there so much background on a civilian intended for only one assignment?

His phone rang. "Rick Morgan."

"Hey, handsome. How'd it go?"

"Good. He agreed and signed on. Jeni, why's his dossier so thick?"

"What do you mean?"

"I'm reviewing it and—I don't know. It seems odd to dig this deep for a civ on a one-and-done."

"How deep can it be? The kid's only twenty-one."

"Yeah, but they really dug in. Notes from teachers, youth ministers. What do we care about his church?"

"You know as well as I do, the deeper we go, the more we can use. It'll amplify the incentive. Keep him in line."

"I get it, but this isn't—" Rick stopped.

"What?"

"He didn't ask for this."

"I know. It feels different . . . strange, but look, Trey has us."

Rick frowned. "What do you mean?"

"You and me. We watch out for him."

"Whoa, did you see this part about his job?"

"Yes, crazy right-winger."

"Who is Robert McGuire?" Rick asked.

"Trey's boss."

"You did the intel. Give me the cliff notes."

She sighed. "He's a beltway bandit. Ran for vice president in '76. Hates Bush—wrote a book about it."

"Why would Trey be working for him?"

"He's naive. There's no way he knew how conservative and extreme McGuire's American Seniors Initiative is."

"Probably not—just like they don't know he's gay."

"Exactly. I bet he was excited to land his first job and to move to DC. They called. He jumped."

"That's a bit convenient."

"What's that?"

"We're all supposed to believe finding this kid is just a fluke?"

"I hear ya, but ... who knows. I guess it could be coincidence?"

"Bullshit. Nothing in this scheming town is a *coincidence*."

"It's DC, baby."

"It's all games and politics."

"Yeah, but there's a bright side."

"Enlighten me," Rick said with a laugh.

"We watch out for the kid, plus we also get to nail this homophobic prick, McGuire. Did you see the tax stuff?"

"Yeah?"

"They're dancing on a razor-thin line between fundraising and politics. Taking full advantage of tax laws to fund McGuire's political ambitions and appetite. They churn out direct mailers begging for donations to 'keep America safe.'"

"Yeah, more like 'keep America White and Christian.'"

"Exactly."

"So, they're scaring the shit out of old people to fuel his campaigns of hate?"

"Exactly."

"Is this for real about a possible House Investigation?"

"Rumor has it. The point is Trey was in deep even before us, Rick."

"So this is about McGuire too and pumping Trey for intel?"

"Maybe. I bet Trey doesn't even know what he knows."

"Nope. He's in over his head. I mean reading his background in Atlanta—growing up in some Christian fundamentalist microcosm."

"Yup. McGuire probably thought the kid was one of their own. That's why they recruited him from Jerry Falwell university."

"You think they know Trey's gay?"

"Hell no!" she blurted. "And that's why he's scared out of his mind."

Rick felt the hairs tingle on the back of his neck. "I hate this one, Jeni."

"I know—it's fucked up. Just get through it best you can. And remember, at least he has us. Right?"

"Right."

Jeni sighed softly. "You sound tired, don't study too late."

"I'm gonna review it one more time. Good night."

"See you tomorrow, handsome."

Rick popped open another beer and skimmed the dossier. Trey had spent his first twenty-one years in churches, youth groups, and private Christian schools. When his father was transferred to North Alabama, his parents had shipped their youngest off at fifteen from his home in Atlanta to an ultra-conservative Christian boarding school in Pensacola, cutting him off from his childhood friends for his final two years of high school.

Isolation, we can poke into that in phase one.

Trey had started university at the co-located religious Pensacola Christian College, but by the end of his freshman year, he had been eighteen, free to leave the confines of the religious extremist world.

So, why jump from the frying pan to the fire? Why Liberty? Rick picked up the copy of a handwritten letter from Trey's close friend, Mark Trenton, a missionary kid from Brazil. Mark had transferred from Pensacola to Liberty University and had reached back to Trey.

"Trey, you have to transfer here. It's so much better than Pensacola. Tell your parents to call me. I will tell them it's okay."

Trey must have had to persuade his parents to allow him to attend Liberty as they felt Rev. Falwell was too liberal.

Rick shook his head in disbelief.

You gotta be kidding me . . . Falwell too liberal?

As Rick pieced together the intel, he saw that Trey's parents' religious beliefs, dictated by their pastor, had extended from clothing, entertainment, and politics to food and drink. There had been rules for everything, with much of their lives spent separated from the larger world around them. Rick pulled out a pen and jotted down the dates of schools and jobs for Trey.

Aha—that's a gap. Rick's instincts were razor-sharp and now on alert.

Five full months. Where did you go after Pensacola but before Liberty? What made your parents relent and compromise? Something happened. What happened in those five months of '88?

On paper, Trey had excelled both academically and athletically. At 5'8" and 160 pounds, he had been fit but a bit too small to play college football as Liberty was a Division 1 school. With no men's gymnastics team there, Trey had used his skills as a college cheerleader for two years on scholarship.

I see you, Trey. You project on the outside that everything's great. But internally . . . constant fear of being outed. So your cheerleading team becomes your world—your team. We can use that.

Rick studied the photos of Trey alongside the young women and men in acrobatic stunts, tumbling, and halftime routines.

You graduate in May '91 smack dab in the middle of the recession. So no jobs, but you interviewed and interviewed. That shows determination. You're running, escaping the world of your parents' fundamentalism. We can use that too. McGuire comes calling with American Seniors, and you jumped. Never asking how high? You aced your interviews, and the conservative pricks embraced you as one of their own. Or they used your naivety. Damn it, am I missing something. Fuck, Claren—this is too easy. Something doesn't add up. How did we find you, Trey?

Rick closed the dossier and took a long swig of beer. He thought about his own naivety eleven years ago. Moving through heterosexual-male dominated circles most of his life, Rick had hid his true self. He had mastered separating his mind, as he had done his entire life to hide his secret.

He related to Trey moving to the suburbs of DC in Fairfax, Virginia. Rick closed his eyes and envisioned Trey with all his possessions loaded in his car and moving into his small apartment at the Hermitage by Fair Oaks Mall. Rick pulled out a map and circled the milestones in Trey's last year. *So your apartment is expensive but allowed you to live alone for the first time in your life. Freedom. Two miles from your office in Fair Lakes and to make ends meet, you got a part-time job at night and weekends coaching gymnastics.*

Rick opened the file again to Trey's interview for the fictitious aviation PR job that the Agency had covertly created. He re-read Trey's quote. *"I played football and basketball growing up in Atlanta but gymnastics was my passion. I started late though 'cause my folks felt it wasn't masculine enough. I shocked them though at Liberty when I tried out and made the varsity cheerleading team. They did not approve but never complained about the money. My athletic scholarship removed the burden of tuition. In two years they only came to one game. My dad said 'Don't drop any girls.'"*

So, you're trying to get your old man's approval. We can use that need to please.

For a year, Trey worked as a production coordinator at American Seniors, and away from the office he coached. Rick thought about Trey's newfound freedom to watch television without censorship, to go to the movies, which had been forbidden to him for twenty-one years, and to listen to rock music. Rick closed his eyes again and envisioned Trey dancing around his one-bedroom apartment to Madonna, the B-52s, and the Red Hot Chili Peppers.

So by February '92, you're emboldened and we see you dash into Lamba Rising on DuPont circle. But you don't buy a gay porno—no, you buy a book about a gay umpire who's been outed—Behind the Mask. *So is this really your first time peeking outside your closet?*

Rick grabbed his laptop and waited for the screen to renew its glow. He entered his long security encryption just below the seal of the CIA. A moment later his login restored his portal and he began typing his assessment for Doc M and Claren.

Our potential civ-5, Trey Alan Carter, has feelings of isolation, difference, and a strong need to please. Although he was athletic, had strong leadership skills—there appears to be something beyond his reach. No doubt he tried to live up to the ideal of a Southern young man through his church, schooling, and sports. We can poke into this feeling of difference. His teachers noted that Trey had something driving him that they "could not fully understand." Some of the clergy thought he might enter the ministry as a preacher or an evangelist. I suspect that Trey always knew otherwise. He had been taught that his secret was damning. Enduring thousands of hours of preaching, he had been told that his immortal soul would spend an eternity in hell for his "perversion." Bottom line, we have more than enough insights to reinforce his incentive. He will turn quickly, but I am concerned about his—

Rick lifted his fingers from the keyboard and tried to think of the right way to document his thought.

Goddamn it. So this kid begs God to change him. His parents force him into Christian, psycho-babble counseling, and *an ex-gay reparative therapy in Exodus ministries.* Rick's blood boiled as he re-read a section of the file. A surge hit him as his thoughts focused on a singular trigger. *Trey feels damaged.* Rick rubbed his neck before deleting his preceding sentence.

He will turn quickly as he thinks God made a mistake. I am concerned about his deeply held belief. We will need to tread lightly and monitor carefully. He's seems strong but could break.

Rick allowed the cursor to blink for several seconds. He hit Enter and closed his laptop. *This is fucked-up. Way bigger than Doc M or Claren get. They're straight—they'll never fully understand. If Trey gets outed, he could lose everything—his job, his family, his friends. Fuck it, Falwell might even revoke his college degree.*

Rick crawl into bed and tried not to think about Trey, but as he closed his eyes he saw him. Wet. Scared.

What are we doing? We are way beyond incentive.

CHAPTER 15
WHY

I don't get it . . . the kid doesn't look gay. If this is how young gay guys are now, then how will we know someone's gay? Back in the day, it was easier to spot 'em. Light in the loafers. Weeks prior, Special Officer Chris Ryder was lost in his thoughts when he had an unauthorized encounter with their target at the Worldgate Athletic Club in Herndon, Virginia.

"Excuse me, sir. Could I get a spot?" Trey asked confidently.

"Huh?"

"A quick spot?"

"Sure. Two hundred and eighty-five pounds . . . you got that?"

"Yeah." Trey grinned and did six reps effortlessly.

Chris nodded and walked back to the locker room. He was impressed not only with Trey's fitness level but also with his discipline. Chris had been profiling Trey for a week. He took special notes on Trey's routine.

He works out every night after leaving work and coaching at the gymnastics center. He's a fit kid, Claren. Geez, most kids his age would be drunk in Georgetown by 9 p.m., not working out at Worldgate. He throws up big weight for such a little guy. This kid will breeze through phase two.

Chris had been a Navy intelligence officer prior to joining the CIA and was on loan to the dark ops desk. Though not fully briefed, he was earning Claren's trust. He was thirty-seven, heterosexual, and considered the unofficial expert on phase two of training, the physically demanding breakdown and rebuilding of the recruit.

Trey had no idea that the same guy who'd been re-racking the bar for him at Worldgate in May was planning to break him down in just a few weeks.

Trey's thoughts swirled through his mind in the darkness of that first night in the Hole.

I wished I could rewind this day. Never stay at the pool. I'd be home right now at my apartment in Fair Oaks.

"Get up, Trey!" barked a freshly shaven Special Officer Rick Morgan.

The recruit jumped from the bed shirtless, in his hospital scrub pants. His bulge pitched a partial tent before subsiding.

From his earpiece, Rick heard Darius's lame joke about "morning wood" followed by Jeni's sarcastic "that joke's as stale as these bagels."

Rick did not react to the banter echoing in his ear but stole a glance at Trey. He then took control of the situation. "Drop and give me twenty."

"What?" Trey asked groggily.

"Push-ups. Twenty. Now."

"Are you serious?"

"Fuck yes, I'm serious, civ."

Trey did not move. Rick noticed his furrowed brow.

"Now make it thirty, maggot."

"What did you just call me?"

"Thirty now—"

From nowhere, Trey seemed to explode with rage. "Motherfucker, don't you ever call me *faggot* again!" The young man lunged at Rick.

Rick shoved Trey back onto the cot and leaned down into his flushed face. "I called you *maggot*, not *faggot* . . . and if you want to live, you'll never address me as anything other than *sir*."

Silence.

Rick leaned in closer.

"Are we clear!"

"Yes, sir," Trey said, his voice barely above a whisper.

Tears began to well in Trey's eyes as Rick attempted to tone down the Marine in his voice.

"I see you've got a temper. That will either burn you or serve you. Depends *if* you learn to control it." He paused. "Now give me my thirty so we can start our day."

Trey dropped and easily banged out the thirty push-ups as if he were a ten-year Marine. Rick was impressed with the rigid posture yet effortless way he moved his body.

"Damn, he moves like a grunt," Darius said in the earpiece. "His form is nearly perfect. Intel says he started weight training at the age of twelve."

Rick glanced up to the camera in the far corner of the small room. "Well, Tiger, you got an obvious advantage for phase two, but we need to get through phase one."

"Ha, no shit," Darius said. "Well, propensity to action duly noted. Faggot-maggot. I am going offline and handing over to Jeni, Rick."

Rick nodded slightly as Trey stood up to face him.

"Trey, today you'll be briefed on our ops team, your volunteer role if selected, and an outline of the next few days. There are three phases to the assessment. Today, we'll focus on phase one. Understood?"

"Yes, sir," Trey said.

"Grab a shower, get cleaned up, and meet me in the ops room in ten minutes. You'll find what you need in here."

Rick kicked a duffel to his feet. "Here's your gear for the next few days: white briefs, blue T-shirt, gray sweatpants, a pair of Nike low-cut cross trainers, socks, a towel, toothbrush, and various toiletry basics. You good?"

Trey nodded.

"Shower up and meet me in the ops room in ten."

After showering, Trey made up his cot and placed the items on the small shelf in the room. He walked across the hall and reached for the ops room door. For a split second, he thought that he had heard voices, but they were already gone. All he could hear now was his own heartbeat and the hum of the overhead vents in the stark white drop ceiling. Fear gripped him as he opened the door to the room where he had been held captive the previous night. Rick was seated at the table with his back once again to the mirror.

"Let's go, Trey. Have a seat," Rick said with a simple nod.

For two hours, Rick asked question after question after question. His back was to the mirror, so Trey could see his own reflection.

"He seems tense," Jeni noted. "Look at his body. He's rigid and his tone." She flipped the switch for Rick's earpiece and whispered, "Rick, he needs to relax."

Rick nodded slightly to acknowledge Jeni.

"Trey, are you okay? This is just a conversation . . . there's no right or wrong answers. Try to relax."

Relax? Are you kidding me? I just want to get out of here. "Yes, sir," Trey said but kept his thoughts to himself.

Little by little he relaxed into a normal conversational style.

Rick repeated several questions within the series of inquiries.

"Tell us about a time when you were challenged to do something that you had never done before. How did you feel? Were you afraid? Why did you play football? Tell us about your first summer job."

Then suddenly an odd question emerged.

"Do you believe in God?"

"Yes, sir."

"What God?"

Trey was puzzled, but before Rick could ask another question, he answered. "I believe in one God, the Father Almighty, the maker of heaven and earth, of things visible and invisible . . ."

Jeni, in the next room, chuckled and whispered into the microphone: "He's quoting the Nicene Creed, Rick."

Rick touched his left ear and tapped twice to signal that he heard her.

"So you're a biblical scholar and a homosexual?" Rick joked after Trey finished reciting the creed.

Trey tried to respond, but Rick cut him off. "Let's break for five."

He left the room, entered the monitoring room, and greeted by Jeni. "How are you doing? He's showing good trust markers."

"Yeah, but what do you make of the creed? Who recites a fucking creed?"

"A kid conditioned for twenty-one years in an extremist faith."

Rick nodded.

"You ready to turn up the heat, handsome? Signal if you need me."

Rick again nodded and returned to the ops room. He looked the recruit in the eyes and smiled slightly.

"Ready, Trey?"

Trey stared at Rick.

"You okay, Tiger?"

"Yeah . . . I'm a bit confused."

"They're simple questions. Ready?"

Trey nodded.

Rick spent several minutes in rapid fire of questions.

"Have you ever stolen anything?"

He repeated some and jumped to many aspects of Trey's life.

"What was the angriest you ever were with your mom and dad?"

"Why did you leave Atlanta?"

Then Rick turned his attention to Trey's sexual orientation. "How did you survive Liberty knowing you were a homosexual?"

An hour and forty minutes into the second questioning session, Rick put down his notepad and pen. He stared at Trey without speaking for a long moment, and the young man squirmed and shifted slightly in his seat.

Finally, Rick broke the silence. "Why did you not tell your parents that you were being molested?"

Trey froze.

"What? How do you know..." He stammered, stopped, and tried to start again. "No, I never—"

Rick pulled a piece of paper from the file and read aloud the therapy notes from a Christian counselor, the evangelical answer to therapy that Trey's parents had made him attend at the age of fifteen.

As though he were once again naked and damp, Trey instinctively covered his genitals.

Rick placed his fingertips on the notes and the file. "See, we know a lot of details about your life, but we don't know you, Trey. You're the only person that can tell us who you are."

Where did you get that? How? Oh God, please help me.

"If we're to continue into phase two, you have to let go and let us in," Rick said calmly, pointing to his temple.

Trey took a deep breath, wiped his face with both hands. "You wouldn't understand."

"Help me understand."

Trey sat frozen for a moment before he whispered, "I was scared. I was thirteen."

Rick leaned forward. "It's okay, Trey."

"Our whole lives were that church and school. Nobody would have believed me, and I ... I didn't want to disappoint my family. I was ashamed ... that I caused it ... that I didn't fight back. You don't understand ... I felt ..."

"Alone?"

Trey nodded.

"You felt alone but not scared?" Rick asked.

"No, but yeah—I mean," Trey stammered. "It was a sin. I was afraid that people would know that, that I—"

"That what?"

Physically shaking now as if cold, Trey seemed to struggle to find his words.

"You were afraid that people would know what?"

"That I liked it," Trey whispered, staring downward.

"What do you mean—you liked it? You didn't want it to happen."

"No but . . . it was confusing. There were times it felt good—but no. I didn't want it to happen."

For the next few minutes, Rick listened as Trey confessed his "sins." The level of specificity was uncanny. When he finished, Trey's eyes were moist, and even Rick was a bit shaken.

Jeni whispered into Rick's earpiece. "Take a break. Claren's on the phone."

"Trey?" Rick stared at the recruit until their eyes again connected. "Good job." He left the room. The lock *click*ed.

Jeni handed Rick the phone as he entered the monitoring room.

"Yeah?"

"I hear it's going well?"

"Pretty much textbook. I need to get him down again after lunch, maybe see some waterworks, and then turn him toward our agenda. I plan to start initiation tactics later today, so we should be good to go by Tuesday to transition to phase two with Chris."

"Good," Claren said. "And how are *you* doing?"

"I'm fine. It is no big deal . . ."

"No big deal? Rick, we are interrupting this kid's life. Big deal? If I felt you didn't see that—"

"I know, I know. I'm holding the line. Okay? But it's different with a civ."

"I know." Claren paused. "You got this. All right?"

"Yeah." Rick nodded slowly.

"Call me if you need to. Otherwise I will see you tomorrow at 0800. I have to be back on campus with Tibbins in Langley by noon for the briefing."

"We're good here. See you tomorrow."

Top secret protocol was in effect, so all communications were being recorded. Rick knew this, and although he wanted to say more, he held back. Claren also knew this as she hung up. They could talk candidly tomorrow offline. She wanted nothing in the transcriptions that could give fodder to rumors or innuendo about Rick.

He hung up the phone. Jeni had gone up to sign for the takeout from the café three floors above them. He glanced up at the clock as he stood alone in the monitoring room. It was 1228—a long day already and not near over. He stared at Trey in the ops room seated at the table. *Why would you be so ashamed as to protect your molester? Why didn't you tell your parents the fucker's name? Why did you think you'd caused it?*

His questions swirled, but Rick knew the answer. He, too, was alone. Different. He'd felt like an outsider most of his life.

He pulled out his notepad from his back pocket and wrote three words. *Different. Alone. Shame.*

Then under the three words a single word.

Protect.

CHAPTER 16
LIP

Friday, June 3, 1966
Marriage Palace - Leningrad, Russia USSR

Ivan Dimitri paced back and forth on the plush, hand-knotted carpets. He had never seen such opulence, and the weight of his marital obligation bore down upon him. He wanted a cigarette, but the attendants had made it clear that no smoking was allowed within the hallowed halls of the marriage palace.

He looked down again at the chandelier's reflection on his polished black loafers as he waited for his former lover now best man to help him get through the next two hours.

"Ivan?"

"Thank you for coming," Ivan grabbed Uri. He firmly kissed him and parted his lips in hopes of tasting Uri again.

Uri shoved away.

"What?"

"Stop."

"Why?"

"Not here. People will see."

"You like it, though."

"Yes, but . . ." Uri flinched as Ivan tried to grab his ass. "Stop. Your bride is waiting."

"Let her wait."

"Ivan . . ."

"What if I don't sign the marriage document?"

"You must."

"What if . . . we ran away? Just you and me."

"Where?"

"I don't know . . . Yugoslavia?"

"And then what?"

"Uri, we could do it. Leave."

"Right . . . two grown men living together. One call, one gesture seen . . ."

"No one will know."

"We'd end up in a gulag or the psikhushka, like your sister."

Ivan stepped back, and turned away. He restarted his pacing as if the rehearsed motion could turn back time. Ivan abruptly stopped and shook his head. "I know, I know but . . ."

"But nothing. She's waiting."

"I wished it was you."

"We don't get that choice."

Ivan shrugged in defeat and resigned to the moment. "What if."

Uri raised his eyebrows and mustered a slight smile.

"We'd dance till dawn." Ivan pretended to move about the room and then spun toward Uri. He grabbed Uri in a bear hug.

Over his shoulder, he heard the voice of his bride.

"Ready, Ivan?"

"Be right there, sweetheart—just saying goodbye to Uri."

Tatyana nodded but did not leave. Ivan squeezed Uri tighter and his eyes grew narrow. He turned and faced her.

"Out. Now!"

Tatyana closed the door most of the way, but lingered for a moment to peek through the crack. She saw Ivan turn Uri and forcefully kiss him, and she jerked away, aghast. A second later there was the smack of fist to flesh. Tatyana spied again to see Uri bleeding from his mouth. She shuddered seeing Ivan had a strange smile as if proud of the pain he had inflicted.

"Tatyana?" her mother interrupted behind her. "We're ready."

"Okay." She turned to her mother and tried to swallow her fear.

"What's wrong? Cold feet?"

Tatyana nodded.

"It will be okay. You know, after the war, when I married your father, I was scared. We were so young, but look—it turned out fine."

Tatyana nodded again, her eyes on the floor.

They walked back to the marriage license hall of the former czarist, Baroque grand hall.

"Sweetie, don't worry. You will learn in marriage. There are good days and well . . . you get by. Ivan is a good catch. He has a good job."

"What if he doesn't like me or want me?"

"Nonsense . . . Tatyana. Look at me."

Tatyana stared at her mother's brown, kind eyes.

"He's a man. Men only want two things, and one of those things is vodka." She raised her eyebrows knowingly.

Tatyana forced a smile before hearing footsteps behind her. She flashed back to the image of Ivan and Uri in an embrace. *Just friends?*

"Anna, good to see you," Ivan said as he quickly approached the two women.

"Speak of the devil," Tatyana's mother said.

"Devil? I'm soon to be your son."

"Yes, my new son, the handsome devil," Anna said, nudging Tatyana into Ivan's embrace.

"Anna, you remember Uri?" Ivan said as he tilted his head toward his friend.

"Of course. Uri, what happened to your lip?"

"Hello, Anna. Clumsy. I fell," Uri said.

Tatyana stood rigid.

"What a lovely dress. All set?" Ivan asked.

She nodded.

"Dimitri and Smyrnoi?" bellowed the short, round woman with a clipboard.

"Ready or not," Ivan said as he turned her toward the heavy, sixteen-foot-tall doors of the ornate hall. She glanced at her mother, who was beaming with pride, and away from Uri's sad eyes and jealous stares. Ivan hurried her along into the hall and up to the four women seated at an oak table.

"Ivan Dimitri and Tatyana Smyrnoi?" the woman asked again.

"Yes. Here are our papers," Ivan said.

Five minutes, four signatures, a hundred rubles, and several forced smiles later, the Dimitris were married.

The four made their way to the small pub near the corner of their apartment building.

"Vodka!" Ivan shouted as he entered, all but dragging with him his new bride, mother-in-law, and now-former lover.

The local men drank round after round with Ivan and Uri as Tatyana and her mother spoke about her dress, the women at the marriage hall, and her daughter's new life with Ivan. Smoke billowed from the tables as the men laughed and catcalled the two waitresses.

"Tatyana, I must go catch my train. Be good to him. I will come and see you in two weeks," Anna said as she stood to leave.

"Goodbye, Mother. I will try and call you next weekend."

"Don't worry so much. You and Ivan will figure it out. Just keep him happy. Here. For you." Anna pressed a thin gold ring into her palm quickly to conceal the exchange from the men.

"No, mother, it was grandmama's. You should keep it. Sell it."

"Never, Tatyana! You must never be without it. Keep it . . . for luck."

Tatyana nodded and hugged her mother. She felt eyes on her and turned to see Ivan staring at her. She tried to smile, but he did not return it.

An hour later, she was pulling the two drunk men out of the pub and toward the entry to their building. Uri and Ivan stumbled as Tatyana hailed a cab.

"Goodbye, Uri," she said as the cab stopped. He looked at her and then back at Ivan. Then he nodded and fell into the back seat of the taxi.

As the cab left as quickly as it appeared, Ivan grabbed her shoulder. They labored up five floors in the hot summer night.

"Draw me a bath," Ivan said.

"Ivan, you're drunk. Go to bed."

Ivan slapped her hard across the face. She tasted blood in her mouth and instantly thought of Uri.

"Draw me my bath, bitch!"

Tatyana rushed to the bathroom and closed the door. As the water in the bathtub ran, she pulled the ring from her pocket and stared at it, then looked up at herself in the mirror. Her hair still held the beautiful curls that her mother set, but her lip was now puffy and stained red. She dabbed her lip with a wet rag.

Tatyana would remember the day not as her wedding day but as *krovavaya guba*—bloody lip, the first of many.

CHAPTER 17
FOOTBALL

Why's *he watching me eat?* Trey enjoyed the warm chicken soup while ignoring Rick's stare. *Say something already.*

Finally, Rick broke the silence. "How's the soup?"

"Good."

"There's some interesting stuff in your file. Can you tell me more about you?

Trey shrugged.

"How about football? Your high school coach?"

"High school? It was all right."

"Did you enjoy playing?"

"Yeah." Trey reached into the corners of his mind and was transported back.

Oh Victory in Jesus, my Savior, forever. He sought me and bought me with His redeeming blood. He loved me 'ere I knew him and all my love is due him.

He plunged me to VICTORY!

Beneath the cleansing blood.

The old bus was vibrating with the yells and voices of the thirty-eight young men singing and screaming the song, "Victory in Jesus." The hymn was a pregame tradition at their Christian school. Trey felt the rumble and then the brakes, his coach would stand up and lead his young champions in a brief prayer before yelling his familiar, "Whose field is this?"

"Our field, sir!"

"Whose victory is this?"

"Our victory, sir!"

"Go, go, go, go."

"Go, go, go, go."

They'd run off the bus and through the cheerleaders' paper sign, which would be emblazoned with Philippians 4:13 or another verse.

A crisp, fall Friday night meant one thing: football. Especially for the private Christian schools in the seventies and eighties. Like his brother before him, Trey had played football not because he'd loved the game but because you were supposed to. It was a rite of passage. So, weekly games, practices, bruises, blood, and his second concussion had all been on the football fields.

Trey had vivid memories of spring trainings where his coach had forced two-a-day practices in the blistering Georgia sun. Inevitably by late afternoon, those guys who had guzzled Gatorade and ate honey buns or hotdogs would be puking their guts up on the sidelines in the humid, suffocating heat. Practice was intense and in full pads, even at ninety-plus degrees. Only at a hundred degrees would coach relent and let them practice touch-only with no pads or helmets. It was on that field that Trey had learned two things: determination and difference.

On the practice fields, Trey learned determination to take all Coach Harper could dish out. *Never quit.* Trey was not a quitter. Bruised, skinned, and bloody, he had returned to the scrimmage line over and over again.

But it was also on the gridiron, Trey learned difference. He knew in his heart that he was different from the rest of the guys. Beyond being gay, he did not understand the sense of pummeling his pigeon-toed friend in practice. Coach had once realized that Trey had allowed his friend to tackle him out of compassion to keep him from getting extra laps. The old Marine blew up at Trey and made him tackle his friend five more times till the young man couldn't get up.

"Over and over." Trey squeezed his eyes shut. He left practice that day determined to never hurt someone else to prove anything. From that day on, he had not cared what coach thought of him.

Trey paused his memory.

"So you were pissed that your coach wanted you to do your job?" Rick said.

"No, I didn't think it was right to make me—"

"Oh, I see. You thought you knew better than your coach at fourteen. That you knew more. That you . . . fuck you, Trey. Your job is not to think, goddamn it! If I were to say jump, you jump. Got it?"

"Yes, sir," Trey said, shocked. He was confused by Rick's mood swings.

"Easy, Drill Sergeant," whispered Jeni via the earpiece. "This ain't Parris Island."

Rick paused, stood up, and turned toward the mirror. For two hours, he had lowered his tone and stance to create a closeness with Trey as instructed by phase one, but now the protocol required dominance.

"Before we end this session, I have just one more question." He swung around, picking up the table, and then slamming it down as if shaking a rope. Paper flew through the air. He pulled his Sig Sauer P220 from his back waistband and pressed it coldly to Trey's right temple.

"Do *you* want to live?" Rick asked flatly.

Without hesitation, Trey said only two words. "Yes, sir."

Rick held the gun to his head for several seconds before pulling back and placing the weapon on the table. Rick alone knew that it was not loaded.

"You want to pick it up?"

"Sir?" Trey hesitated only for a second. "No."

"Why not?"

"I don't know this gun."

"Do you want to learn?"

Rick was taken with Trey's precise tone and calm demeanor. Before he could think, he repeated his own brother's last words as a question. "Do you want to make the team?"

Trey locked eyes with Rick. "Yes, sir."

Rick glanced downward at the dark circle on Trey groin and leg. *He pissed himself. Don't laugh—don't hug him either. He's scared.* Rick turned his back and headed to the door. "You did well, Trey. Most recruits shit themselves, civ or not. Now, go get cleaned up. Dinner will be in this room at 1800."

Rick spun around.

"Tomorrow's tougher. You better get some rest tonight." Rick winked his right eye at Trey and gave a half smile, breaking phase one protocol. Reassurance could cancel dominance.

Cameras couldn't catch that. Even if they did—Jeni won't rat me out to Doc M. They don't need to know. That was for Trey and me only.

Trey heard the double *clicks* of the locks and walked over to his bunk room. He stripped off the soiled clothes and grabbed his towel. After a shower, he lay down on the cot. He was sleepy—and then darkness.

The lights turned on, and he returned to the ops room alone. There was only the table, one chair, and a small television/VCR along with his dinner. He ate his dinner quietly, not knowing that Rick and Jeni sat on the other side of the mirror intently watching.

Abruptly, the television in the room turned on. The seal was instantly recognizable but not the man in the blue suit who faced into the camera.

"Good evening, Trey. Let me be the first to welcome you. Our team tells me you are progressing well. We have a lot riding on you, young man. Please watch this short video and know that we all appreciate your service to our country."

The screen went dark. Trey knew it was prerecorded. *Who was he? When was it recorded?* Then the music started, and Whitney Houston sang: "Oh say can you see . . . by the dawn's early light . . . what so proudly we hailed at the twilight's last gleaming . . ."

Images of DC were scrolling across the screen. The Lincoln, the Jefferson, the Whitehouse. Vietnam Memorial. Then Gulf War images. Then a familiar set of faces. Suddenly his parents, grandparents, football team, college cheerleading team, and friends scrolled across the screen. The photo montage ended with his brother in his dress blue USAF uniform.

These are my pictures. They've been in my apartment. How? When?

Rattled at the images, a new worry seeped in as he scanned the room for a clock. There was not one.

What time is it? What day is it?

Trey felt panicked and crossed the hall inspecting the bathroom and then back to his bunk room. *No clocks.* The door at the end of the hall was locked. The door to the left of the ops room, presumably on the other side of the mirror, was also locked.

Back inside the ops room, he saw a built-in VCR at the bottom of the TV. He rewound the tape and watched the video again. Then the tape ended, and after a second, the TV switched from VCR to a static white-noise screen. Then before he could reach to turn it off—the TV turned off. *Who switched it off? Someone over there.* He stared at the mirror.

From across the hall, he heard a door shut. Trey returned to the bunk room and found a notebook and pen on the bed.

He opened the notebook. It held blank pages except for the first page, which held one handwritten sentence.

Write down what you want to know.

CHAPTER 18
QUESTIONS

"**G**et up! Get up!" Rick shouted in the darkness before flooding Trey's room with the bright fluorescent lights. "Let's go!"

Trey jumped out of bed in his white briefs. Rick stole a quick glance at the recruit's morning bulge, but kept a stone face. He knew the team next door was recording the interaction.

"Give me thirty, recruit!"

Without hesitation, Trey dropped and banged out thirty push-ups.

"Where's your notebook?"

"Right here, sir."

Trey bent over and picked up the notebook from the floor. Rick enjoyed another glance before taking the notebook.

"Shower, get dressed, clean up this room, and meet me in the ops room in fifteen."

"Yes, sir."

No argument. He's falling in line. This could work. Rick took the notebook, left the room, and returned to the monitoring room.

Immediately Jeni met him at the door. "Let's see. What does he want to know?"

"I don't know."

Suddenly, the back service door opened, and Claren entered. "Good morning. How did he do last night? What did Darius report?"

"He said uneventful," Rick answered and opened the notebook.

"Are those his questions?" Claren said, motioning to Rick.

He nodded.

"Let's hear them."

Rick read aloud.

"Five questions, geez and he numbered them.

"1) Are you the DC police, FBI, or CIA?

"2) Are you training me for an assignment?

"3) Will I be able to return to my normal life?

"4) If I do this assignment, will you clean my record?

"5) Why me?"

Claren took the notebook from Rick and reviewed it again quietly.

"Wow, good questions. Common sense." Jeni returned to setting up the equipment and monitors.

"Simple and direct. I like this kid," Claren said. "Shoot straight with him, Rick. No bullshit. He's passed day one, but at civ-5, I think we can turn it up. Let's expedite the assessment."

"How fast—I mean what if he breaks?" Rick asked.

"Use your judgment. Get physical. If he starts to crack, ease off the gas. Guys, I have to leave in about two hours to meet Tibbins on campus. Jeni, I want to be inside," she said, pointing to her ear.

Rick shot back a look, *Inside? That's not typical of you, Claren. You only observe. Never get your hands dirty. Why? Don't you trust me?*

"Stop worrying, Rick. Don't get paranoid," Claren said. "I'm navigating but you're still driving,"

Rick grabbed the notebook and headed for the door. He paused and looked through the mirror at a fresh, clean-shaven recruit now seated in the farthest chair, focused on the ops room.

Only two choices and you picked the one facing the mirror. Smart. Luck or good instincts. We'll find out.

Rick stepped into the hallway.

Today, there would be no table. No barriers. It was time to begin the physical connection.

CHAPTER 19
TOUCH

Rick entered and walked over to his recruit without saying a word. He tamped down the doubt in his gut, and let his face settle into stone.

Time to turn the dial.

He took the notebook and smacked Trey upside his left temple, not hard but in a demeaning manner. Trey sat stunned for a moment, then bent down to retrieve the notebook.

"Leave it!" Rick barked and stepped closer into Trey's face. "You think *we* owe *you* answers?"

"What? You said to—"

"You think you *deserve* answers?"

Trey only shrugged.

Rick studied his recruit, then pulled out four black-and-white photos of Trey naked at the pool. The angles made it look as if Trey was groping "Todd." Rick laid them in Trey's hands. Trey's eyes widened as his posture stiffened. One by one the photos floated past his frozen hands to the floor. Rick observed Trey's eyes narrow and his brow tighten.

That's right. It's all on camera. Feel the fear. Give into me.

"We could make a call or send a fax. You'd be facing multiple felonies: indecency, alcohol, and sexual assault. If he pressed charges, you'd be branded a sexual predator."

Rick paused for effect, then continued.

"You lose, Trey." He leaned in closer. "Your job. Your family. Your career. Your coaching. Gone." He snapped his fingers on cue in Trey's left ear.

Trey stared at the strewn photos on the floor.

"Jesus, he's good at 'bad cop,'" Jeni said to Claren, who said nothing, but a faint smile came over her plum lips. They observed through the glass. The silence hung heavy in both rooms. Their recruit stared at the floor. Rick focused unflinchingly on the defeated young man. Then Rick turned, glanced into the mirror, and seemed to await instructions. Claren offered none.

She allowed the silence for another agonizing minute. "Now, let's begin."

He nodded and walked over to the second chair.

"Pick up the notebook, Trey."

"Yes, sir."

Trey picked it up. Rick inched his chair closer and now sat less than arm's length from him.

Rick saw Trey squirm and shift in his seat. *Uncomfortable, good.*

"Am I CIA? Only civs call it that."

Trey looked up with wide eyes.

"We simply say the Agency." Rick continued, "Will I be training you for an assignment? Maybe, if you don't wash out or I don't put a bullet in your head." Rick glanced down at his visible P220 on his shoulder holster.

"Will you return to a *normal* life? No, but you don't want a normal, boring life. Do you, Trey?"

The next question irritated Rick and he clenched his jaw. "Cleaning your record?"

Rick took a long pause, then blew out a deep breath so that the young man could feel the air on his face. "Our ops team doesn't exist, and we damn sure don't negotiate with a civ. We're dark ops, not sanctioned." He gestured around the room. "All this and you could be gone tomorrow morning."

Rick saw Trey's eye twitch and his legs slightly shift in his seat.

"Why you?" Rick picked up one of the photos. He looked at the image, then held it up for Trey. He leaned forward, pointing a finger just inches from Trey's chest.

Trey looked away and his body went rigid.

"*Why you?*" Rick repeated sarcastically.

Rick's adrenaline surged as he tightened his abdomen.

Now.

Without warning, he thrust his flattened palm squarely on Trey's sternum, launching the young man backward off the chair and crashing onto his back.

Rick tossed the chair aside and delivered a powerful kick to Trey's left femur.

Secure him now.

Rick lunged and straddled Trey, pinning both arms and legs down with his knees and body weight. Rick was 6'2", 210. Trey was 5'8", 160, and seemingly no match. Still he struggled and flailed.

Oh you wanna fight? Let's turn it up some more.

Rick grabbed Trey's throat. The shortness of breath and futile struggle sent the recruit further into panic. In one last gasp for air, Trey snarled at his captor, "Get off! Stop!"

Want me to stop, then stop fighting. Break. Submit already. Geez, you're stronger than I thought. One more push then.

"You begging for your life?" Rick hissed.

"Get. Off. Me." Trey's strained voice echoed in the stark room but he intensified his struggle.

"You want to know why you?" Rick eased off his chokehold. "Why you?" He repeated mockingly.

"That's enough, Rick." Claren whispered into his earpiece. "Careful. You got him."

Bullshit, he's resisting submission. Phase one states we must gain physical submission to reinforce psychological dependence. Give and take.

Rick turned to the mirror and saw himself straddling Trey. He then looked down to see a tear trickled down Trey's reddened face.

"Back off, Rick." Her tone was stern.

Fine. I guess I took it too far.

He removed his right hand and placed it over Trey's mouth and chin, leaving only his left in a loose grip on his neck.

Claren said softly, "Love is stronger than fear."

Love? What the hell?

Rick took a deep breath and connected with Trey's eyes, which were wild.

"Aargh! Get off me."

"Calm down."

Trey stopped resisting.

"Look at me, it's okay."

Trey narrowed his eyes, seeming confused as Rick moved from captor to consoler, and once again struggled frantically.

"Aaah!" Trey yelled as Rick deftly pressed down into pain-inducing pressure points.

"I can do this all day, Trey. Come on, let it go. Give in to me."

After several minutes and grunts, Trey relented.

Rick removed his hand.

"Good. I'm going to stand up now. This is part of the assessment. Look at me. Look . . . at . . . me." Rick paused until the young man's watering eyes locked with his.

"I'm going to stand up. You're okay, Tiger. Do you understand?"

Trey did not speak. Seething anger contorted his face. Rick stood, and no sooner did he let go, the recruit recoiled to his back with this legs high, then catapulted forward to his feet, using a powerful gymnastic maneuver.

Later, the team would watch it over and over again on tape.

In one motion, he popped to his feet and immediately lunged at Rick's midsection, slamming them both against the wall. Rick instantly widened his stance, surged his upper body, and grabbed Trey's shoulders in a vice-grip.

Then the cold metal of his P220 jabbed into Rick's rib.

Thatta boy. Damn, he does have balls.

"Get your hands off me!" Trey yelled, holding Rick's gun awkwardly.

Rick let go and backed away slowly with his hands raised.

"Trey, listen to me—"

"You don't understand, I didn't mean to do this—"

"I know, Trey—"

"I can't be here."

"Trey, listen—"

"These photos—you don't understand."

"I know but you are here," Rick said calmly.

"Nobody knows—you don't get it."

"What don't I get?"

"That," Trey whispered, and motioned to the scattered photos.

"I do get it. Now, give me the gun."

"No, you don't get it—no one knows. If they find out—"

"What?" Rick probed.

"It's a sin—I'm an abomination." Trey shook.

"Is that what you think?"

Trey shrugged. "If y'all tell—my life will be over."

"Your life is not over. Now give me the gun, Trey."

"Nobody can know," Trey whispered. His face contorted. Slowly his arm moved the gun from Rick toward his own temple.

"Here we go. Be ready, Rick," Claren whispered.

"No, Trey." Rick narrowed his eyes and held up his hands. "Put the gun down!"

"I'll lose everything—my job, my friends, my church. My family." Trey pressed the muzzle to his temple with a slight tremble in his hand. "Everything."

"No, Trey!"

Trey tightened his grip.

"Let me help you. Don't do this!"

"No one can help me." Tears now trickled down his face.

"Listen to me—I will help you." Rick stood rigid. "Let me help you!"

"You don't get it—I've tried everything to not be gay." His hoarse voice was barely a whisper.

"I know that—"

"No, you don't know me—" Trey looked up.

"Let me help. Let me know you. Nobody will know, if you listen to me—it will be our secret. I promise. Look at me." Rick reached out.

Trey closed his eyes tightly. "Lord Jesus, please forgive me."

"No, Trey!"

Trey squeezed the trigger.

Click.

Click.

Again, Trey pulled the trigger.

Holy fuck, he did it. I can't believe this kid. A civ, damn, Doc M was right.

After several seconds, Trey's eyes opened and his face hardened.

"You got him," Claren said softly. "But give it a moment, Rick."

Rick nodded slightly.

Trey lowered the gun into both hands and stared at it.

Surprise, Tiger. That's right. Did you really think it was going to be that easy? Come on. Look at me.

Trey shook his head and stared at the P220 in his hand.

Don't give in. It's for his own good. Be like steel.

"I thought you wanted to live?" Rick asked coldly.

"What?"

"Did you think that I'd bring a loaded gun in this room and allow you to take it from me?"

Trey whispered, "Why?"

"Simple, really. We train for hours to do this."

"What?"

"It's part of the process."

Trey frowned and tightened his stance.

"Not the answer you wanted?" Rick motioned to the mirror. "We're studying you, Tiger."

"Don't call me that—"

"Why not? Isn't that what your PawPaw calls you?" Rick said in a Southern drawl.

"You don't know me," Trey hissed.

"Calm down," Rick barked.

Here we go again. Damn, this kid's temper.

"Why?"

"I will tell you, but only if you calm the fuck down!"

One Mississippi, two Mississippi, three . . .

"Aaargh!" Trey ignited and threw the gun at Rick's head.

Rick ducked but felt the metal graze his hair as it flew across the room.

Trey again lunged at Rick.

Rick deftly grabbed Trey and used the momentum into a twisting pull, turning them both and slamming Trey against the wall at full force. Rick plastered Trey to the wall, rendering him immobile by firmly placing his right knee to Trey's groin, shoulder to his chest, and pinning his arms overhead. He pressed his shoulder harder to the sternum, nailing Trey against the wall with his powerful frame.

Shit! Where's my earpiece?

Claren sat motionless watching the scene. *Don't let this get away from us, Rick.*

"Why do you always push a hair too far?" She turned to Jeni who seemed glued to the thick, bulletproof glass in front of them.

"Oh my fucking god!" Jeni threw up her hands. "That's more than any military recruit. What the actual fuck—you said this kid was a civ, Claren."

"He is. But—"

"But what?"

"It's involuntary. I hate when I'm right. We're no longer textbook here," Claren said.

Damn it, Carlos. I knew this was too risky.

Claren and Jeni watched in horror as the assignment now seemed to teeter.

"Nothing about this is textbook." Jeni shook her head. "No, one or both of them could end up at GW's emergency room."

Claren pursed her lips and turned back to the scene before them. "Rick?"

"Good thing it's only a few blocks away."

"Rick? Look at me. Rick?" Claren repeated.

"He can't hear you, Claren. Look." Jeni pointed to the tiny device lying near the corner of the room. "He's lost his earpiece. We're flying blind."

"Shit! Well, he can do this." Claren stared intently at Rick. "Talk him down."

"How? This kid is not responding like—"

"We don't have a backup recruit. It would take a month to pull one." Claren shot Jeni a tense look. "We have to make this work."

"Fine. I'll go in." Jeni stood and pulled her Glock 17 from her waistband. She'd taken two steps toward the door when Claren interrupted.

"Hold on, hold on. Let's give Rick a minute."

Jeni turned back and exhaled deeply when she saw an exchange between the two men. "They're talking."

Claren leaned forward and turned up the volume on their speaker.

Come on, Rick—you can do this. Talk. Him. Down. Use your training.

Suddenly, Trey's lips parted slightly and expression softened a bit. Clearly, Rick was speaking to him.

"Good. Keep talking, Rick," Claren said.

"Thatta boy, handsome." Jeni returned to her seat and put her gun away. "That's it—reel him in."

"Say his name, Rick. Say his fucking name," Claren repeated.

"Why? Repetition? Break him out of his state?"

"Exactly, at this point he's running on instinct."

"Fight or flight," Jeni said.

Claren nodded and let out a deep breath.

Inside the room, Rick had struggled several minutes to keep Trey pinned against the wall. He felt the strain as beads of sweat began to appear on his forehead. In the silence, his training kicked in.

"Trey Alan Carter, I need you to calm down. Breathe, Trey. You're okay, let's calm down. We'll sit down, Trey, and talk this out . . ." Rick said softly to the recruit inches from his face.

It was then he felt it. At first he thought it was the waistband of the recruit's sweatpants, but as it grew, it became undeniable.

What the hell? This is turning you on? All right, let's play rough. Rick leaned down, allowing his lips to graze Trey's right ear as he softly whispered, "Trey, we're not alone. Not yet. Let me explain." Rick softened his hold as Trey's muscles eased. "Trust me, Trey. Give me a chance."

Rick then pressed himself hard into the young man, then abruptly pushed off, quickly freeing Trey. He took three steps back and assumed a defensive stance in case Trey tried once again to attack.

Trey was panting but stood rigid. He squeezed both fists.

"What did he say to him?" Claren asked. "What the hell did he say?"

"I don't know," Jeni said. "But oh my god. Look. He's breaking."

"I'll be damned. Rick got him." Claren nodded slowly.

All right, Rick—we do it your way, but you better keep it in line.

The air in the ops room was thick as both men regained their breathing. Rick stared at Trey, who eased his stance and then slowly slid down the wall. He curled his legs, lowered his face into his hands, with elbows on his knees.

Defeat. I hate this part but I did it. Rick resisted the urge to go to him and hold him. *Look at him, this doesn't feel like a win. Hold the line.*

Doc M's voice echoed in his training, *"It is essential that the recruit feels completely alienated and turns toward the solution on his own."*

He had already bent his training, but knew not to break this final line of the protocol.

Rick knew from his training the next few steps, but his heart ached to see the isolation in the young man's posture.

Don't get involved. This is just a job. Stay focused. Where's my earpiece?

Rick scanned the room and saw it just three feet away. He strode a few steps and picked up his unloaded gun, the earpiece, and the chairs that had been flung during the struggle. He placed both chairs on the red tape markers on the floor in front of the mirror again. Without saying a word, he walked over to the broken young man and extended his hand.

Trey looked up. Rick held out his hand and waited for his recruit's choice.

Come on. Take my hand. Trust me.

Trey wiped his face and grabbed Rick's right hand. He stood up, put his shoulders back, and looked deeply into Rick's eyes.

"I'm sorry, Officer Morgan."

Uh-huh, I bet you are—you moody little Tiger. God, grunts are so much easier than this. Oh and now you're gonna give me those sad eyes. Don't give me those—damn they are beautiful. Blue? Gray? Shit. Fun's over. Here comes the harder part.

"Have a seat, Trey. I'm gonna get us some water."

Trey sat.

Rick exited the room. Jeni and Claren were waiting on the other side of the glass.

"You got him," Claren said with a hint of surprise. "We were worried there for a minute. His *propensity to action* didn't take long to grab your gun."

"No way did I think he would turn that quickly," Jeni blurted out. "Chris was right; that kid's a beast. Glad he didn't get the best of you, Rick."

Rick smirked and opened his left hand to reveal the earpiece. Jeni immediately went to work on the equipment. Rick had seconds to get back in the room and continue the session to keep up the momentum. He and Trey were far from over, but they were over a tough hurdle.

"Did you say something to him?" Claren asked. "In the scuffle, when you pinned him—we couldn't hear." Her question provided an out.

She's always a step ahead. Rick looked back at Claren as she pulled two bottles of water from the mini fridge.

"Yeah, I, uh . . . just repeated his name."

"Of course, great work. You better get back in there. We need to get him to phase two by tomorrow, but he needs to be solid. No redshirts," Claren stated, handing Rick the waters.

"I know. I got this," Rick said, holding them up.

Jeni traded the waters for a new earpiece and quipped, "Good luck, bad cop." She clicked on the mic. "Testing, testing, testes, balls," laughing as she did her best Rick imitation.

Rick gave Jeni a thumbs-up and turned to Claren, who rolled her eyes but did not acknowledge the lame joke.

"How about some good cop now, Officer Morgan?"

He softened his face and exited.

For Rick, this was the hard part. Being tough was always easier for him—more natural to his persona. It was far harder to hold the line when you were also comforting a recruit.

Rick walked the few steps to the ops room and paused. *Okay, he's just a recruit. Civ or not, keep him at arm's length. Just talk. Be calm. Build his trust.*

Rick let out a deep breath and turned the handle.

"Here you go," he said casually as he entered the room. He held up the water bottle, then tossed it.

Trey caught it with one hand. "Thank you, sir."

Rick crossed the room and sat down in the chair directly opposite Trey. He swigged his water, and the young man followed suit. They did not speak for a couple of minutes, but just drank the water quietly as the overhead fluorescent lights buzzed.

"Listen to me, Trey. You're smart. Based on what you know now, I want you to answer your questions for me." Rick scooped up the notebook and offered it to Trey.

He relaxed his shoulders and took the notebook.

Claren narrowed her eyes.

"I'll be damned. See that. Eye contact, passive shoulders, open legs—"

"Yeah?" Jeni asked.

"He's crushing on his captor." Claren turned to Jeni. "Classic TB markers."

"Traumatic bonding?" Jeni asked.

"Yes, Doc M will be pleased," Claren said. "But I'll have to admit to him that I was a skeptic—it worked on an involuntary civ. I'll be damned."

Trey cleared his throat and began as if in a college class.

"Are you CIA?" Trey nodded slightly. "You're Agency, but I thought you guys only operated outside the US?"

"Usually. We're dark ops—we work *globally*." Rick nodded.

"Are you training me for an assignment? If I pass, you'll train me."

"Yes, if you'll trust me." Rick shrugged.

"Will I be able to return to my normal life? No, I guess not."

Rick did not gesture.

"If I do this assignment, can we please clean my record? You don't understand—please . . ."

"Stop, no one's going to find out unless we want them to, Trey." Rick motioned for him to continue.

"Why me? Honestly, I don't know," Trey said. "Did you pick me? Do you believe in me?"

The last statement came out more as a plea. Without hesitating, Rick took the notebook from Trey, placed a hand on his knee, and motioned to the mirror. "We picked you because we do *believe* in you, Trey, but *not* your temper. There's a lot of work ahead. Are we good?"

"Yes, sir."

Rick turned back to the mirror.

"Good. That part's over. He's crushing on you, Rick. It's working," Claren said softly in his earpiece.

Rick rubbed his right ear lobe to confirm.

"Well, we can use the attraction to our advantage," she said. "Let's get into it, then."

Rick turned back to Trey. "Ready for our next part?"

Trey rubbed his chest and nodded cautiously.

As Claren guided, Rick returned to the assessment questions, asking about his coaching, his friends, and then more in depth about his work.

"Tell me about your job. Specifically, Robert McGuire. Do you like working for him?" Rick asked while opening the notebook to a fresh page and pulling out a pen for effect.

"I guess."

"I'm guessing he doesn't suspect you're—"

"No, he doesn't— Sir . . . please . . ."

"Stay calm, Trey. Tell me about your job."

"If I still have a job. I haven't called in sick today."

"Stop. We will be calling McGuire directly, and you'll be fine. Now tell me about a typical day. What do you do at American Seniors Initiative?"

Trey talked about his role, coworkers, Robert McGuire, and many details about the organization. He talked about disagreeing with much of their politics. He told of a CBS news crew with Bob Schieffer showing up unannounced the month before and his reactions.

"No shit, Bob Schieffer from *60 Minutes*?" Rick raised his eyebrows.

"Yeah, they've been focusing on these allegations. Tax stuff."

"That Robert's using fundraising from the organization to fund his endless political attacks?"

"I guess so. That's why Congress has jumped in. Everybody at the office is worried it's gonna turn into, like, a full-blown investigation."

"So it's not just a rumor?" Rick asked.

"No, they're worried. The fight's spearheaded by this Democrat from Texas?"

"JJ Pickle?"

"Yea, he and Robert can't stand each other. I heard Robert screaming at him on a call a few weeks ago. JJ's pushing for American Seniors to be reviewed by the House and IRS for abusing their tax-exempt status. Or something like that."

Something like that, huh. Rick shot a look at the mirror.

"Yes, Rick. There is a *possible* House Investigation," Claren said.

Rick cleared his throat.

"We didn't target it—it's not us. Just a coincidence," she said emphatically.

Coincidence my ass, Claren. This is exactly why you targeted this kid.

"Let's continue," she said into his earpiece.

Their dialogue progressed for nearly an hour with several follow-ups. Rick would touch his left ear from time to time as Claren pressed him to ask more questions.

God, Claren. How much more digging on this? The kid is going to get crucified by McGuire. No doubt this is all going into tomorrow's Oval briefing.

He followed instructions and repeated her questions. Trey answered them all.

"Okay, let's wrap." Claren paused. "Ready to head into his trigger—you ready, Rick?"

Rick glanced at the mirror and then turned back to Trey.

"Do you find me attractive, Trey?"

"What?" Trey stammered, and frowned.

"Do *you* find *me* attractive?" Rick repeated more sternly.

The young man squirmed. "Officer Morgan, I don't understand . . ."

"You found *Todd* attractive in the pool the other night."

Trey stared away, seemingly embarrassed.

"Look at me. Do *you* find *me* attractive?"

"Yes, sir . . . a lot."

"Good. Now push him," Claren whispered in Rick's earpiece.

"Get on your knees," barked Rick.

"On my knees?" Trey asked, aghast.

Rick just spread his legs wider and adjusted himself in one fluid movement.

What the— Is he gonna ask me to blow him? Here—in front of whoever's behind that mirror?

Trey complied, though; he never looked away and dropped to his knees in front of Rick. Their eyes locked for what felt like several minutes. Trey feared some sort of sexual request was about to be made, when for a split second he thought he saw a flicker of kindness in the agent's expression.

"Stand up," Rick ordered. Trey stood but broke the gaze, staring up, beyond the corner of the room.

"Now take off your clothes," Rick said.

Trey looked down and then back at Rick. "Sir?"

"Take off your clothes."

Trey kicked off his shoes, shirt, socks, and sweats. He was standing in his briefs when he glanced back at Rick.

Rick nodded and pointed to his briefs.

"Everything?"

"Now," Rick said.

"Please don't. What are you gonna do—"

"Stop. Do as I tell you. Now."

Trey dropped his briefs. Rick stood and ordered him to spread his arms to a T and legs shoulder-width apart. He walked around Trey slowly counterclockwise, pausing, and making statements as though he were taking an inventory.

"No tattoos. No piercings. Circumcised. Two-inch scar above the navel. Large lateral scar above the pubic below the waist. Mole on right upper thigh. Slight scar on left inside knee. Mole in right armpit. Vertical scar on left temple."

Rick paused and glanced back at the mirror.

"Trey, turn ninety degrees to the right. Again . . . again . . . again."

Trey pivoted as directed.

"Now get dressed, Trey, and have a seat," Rick said. "I'm going to step out and get our team physician. She's the nice one. We're going to do the medical exam now."

Trey nodded and pulled on his briefs.

Rick turned to leave the room, taking his chair and the notebook.

"Try not to take a piss, Tiger—she'll need a urine sample. You okay?"

"Yes, sir," he responded, with a hint of relief.

Rick gave Trey a nod and a wink, then exited.

Now you're nice. Back and forth. Jekyll and Hyde. I don't get it. Is he gay too? What's happening? Is it really just a physical?

He bit his lip.

I've got to get out of here.

CHAPTER 20
PHYSICAL

"**H**e looks so young," Dr. Chulpa Patel said as Rick entered the monitoring room.

"He's twenty-one," Jeni confirmed. "Good job, handsome. He seems calm now."

Rick nodded.

"Calm now?" Chulpa asked. "What did I miss?"

"Well he's confirmed his *propensity toward action* a few times now. Doc M warned us but it got tense. Be careful in there," Jeni cautioned.

"I've got my bodyguard. Ready, Rick?" she asked.

"Chulpa, stay alert. You should be fine but keep the exam routine."

"Of course," she said.

"Be careful," Claren added as Rick and Chulpa left the monitoring room.

Trey looked up as Rick entered along with a woman in a white medical coat. She was quite striking at 5'6" with tan skin and long brown hair. She smiled at Trey, and a warm feeling seemed to dim the harsh lighting and volatile emotions of Officer Morgan.

"Hello, I'm Dr. Chulpa Patel. I'm the physician for our protocol team," she said, extending her hand.

"Trey Carter." *Finally someone who smiles.* Trey smiled.

"Nice to meet you, Trey. So this is pretty routine. We're going to conduct a complete physical with you now. Okay?"

He darted his eyes to Rick as his smile faded.

"It's SOP," Rick assured. "Standard ops."

"Totally, routine. First things first." She pulled from her coat pocket a white plastic cup with a bright yellow lid. "Urine sample. Have you done drugs recently?"

"Never."

"Good. Don't." She smiled again and handed him the cup. "Officer Morgan will escort you to the bathroom across the hall. Okay?"

Trey walked slowly to the door.

"Rick, can you give me a few minutes to get set up? I'll knock when we're ready."

"Got it. Come on, Trey."

Rick, huh. Trey saw Rick smile at her but resisted asking him about her as they walked to the bathroom.

"Here." Rick took the cup from him and popped the top off, then handed it back. "Filler 'er up."

Never any privacy with you. Trey stepped up to his familiar second urinal and began to fill the cup. A few seconds later, a steady flow started to his right and he nearly dropped the cup.

Holy crap! Rick's taking a piss right beside me. There's no dividers. Oh my god, don't look, but damn—if I just turn slightly, just a quick peek.

Tilting down, Trey bit his bottom lip at the sight of the black hair, shaft, and uncircumcised head. He saw the center vein and the distinct plaid boxers. He turned back and did not say a word.

After filling his cup, Trey finished emptying his bladder into the urinal. He then faced the challenge of pulling up, not dropping the cup, and flushing the metal top handle of the urinal.

"Here." Rick took the cup and walked to the sink. "You know it's okay, right?"

"What?"

"We all sneak a peek every now and then. Comparing; it's totally normal."

Busted. Oh my god, he saw me. Trey mouth opened but he could not voice his embarrassment. *Ignore it. Don't say anything. Wash your hands.* He scrubbed his hands a bit harder.

"Don't stress out, Trey; Dr. Patel is cool. Be one hundred percent honest with her, okay? Everything here is all classified."

"Secret?"

"Yes. One hundred percent. Just answer her questions. You want to make the team, right?"

"Yes, sir."

"Great—help us, help you. Don't hold back."

Rick's warm tone soothed Trey, even as it unnerved him. Maybe because of the showers, stalls, and urinals—the bathroom felt a bit like a locker room. A place familiar to Trey all through high school and college, though also a place where he'd had to hide his true self. His sexual orientation had haunted him at times, as he'd felt his football teammates would never understand. He'd just wanted to belong.

As if reading his thoughts, Rick broke the silence. "So what was your position? Football?"

"How did you guess what I was thinking?"

"It's my job."

Trey frowned.

"It's not hard. I'm trained to observe. What position?"

"QB in eighth and ninth. Running back and safety on varsity. What about you?" Trey asked.

"What about me?"

"Did you play?"

Rick did not respond for moment.

Geez, I don't know anything about you.

Before Rick could respond, Claren whispered into his earpiece, "Give in a bit, Rick. Build rapport."

Kinda stating the obvious now. This ain't my first rodeo, Claren.

Rick turned to Trey. "No, I ran track and wrestled in high school. Then wrestled in college."

"You're a wrestler. So earlier . . . in there?"

Rick raised his eyes.

"Guess I should say sorry about that." Trey paused.

"Let it go."

"But . . ."

"But nothing. Lesson one: stop apologizing. You were scared and defended yourself. That's entirely reasonable. Learn to use your temper—don't let it use you. Control it—re-channel it. Got it?"

Before he could stop himself, Rick again winked and cocked a smile.

Trey immediately softened.

Shit. Bet Claren will get me for that—screw it. "We'll do the physical, eat a late lunch. Then just the psych. test before dinner. Do exactly what I tell you—maybe tomorrow, we go for a run. Outside."

"Tomorrow. Okay, but what about my job?"

"We've contacted them. Told 'em you had an accident but you're okay—you'll be out until Thursday."

"Thursday. Really?"

Rick nodded.

Knock, knock.

"You guys ready?" Chulpa's voice echoed.

Whoa, guess she's serious. Trey scanned the room and saw the folding table was now back but partially draped with a white cloth, along with two crates on wheels sitting by the wall. A well-worn black leather bag sat on the table, and on the floor, there was a simple bathroom scale.

Rick stood by the door as Dr. Patel pulled a needle and various instruments from her bag. She turned to Trey. "Let's get started. Can you undress for me and step up on the scale?"

Even though he had been naked several times in the ops room, Trey flashed a look at Rick as Dr. Patel pulled on a pair of latex gloves.

Rick gave his familiar wink and nod. Guess this is all part of it, then. Trey took a deep breath, then tugged off his shirt.

For the next hour and a half, the exam was routine: Weight, height, hearing, and reflexes. She asked dozens of questions about scars, illnesses, and past surgeries.

"And what about this one." She pointed to a scar above his navel.

"Doubleback."

She raised her eyebrows.

"Double-backflip on floor. I was trying to do one and ripped my intestinal wall."

"Did you land it?"

"Yeah, in the resin pit."

"The what?"

"The foam pits we use in the gym when trying new tricks. Hurts a lot less if you miss."

"I bet, and what about this one?" She lowered her latex-covered index finger to a long lateral scar just above his pubic hair and genitals. "This one also from gymnastics?"

"No, bladder reconstruction surgery when I was five." Trey explained that he had been born with a partially collapsed bladder. The doctors at Crawford Long Children's Hospital in Atlanta had cut him hip bone to hip bone for the experimental surgery. She was seemingly about to ask further questions when he continued in a softer voice.

"It's why I have to pee a lot, and it left me—" He glanced at Rick.

"Did it damage your ability to have an erection?" Dr. Patel asked flatly.

What? Trey again glanced at Rick. "No, ma'am, I get hard . . . but I'm not able to cum."

She nodded and wrote a note. "But do you climax?"

"Yes, ma'am, but nothing comes out."

"Retrograde ejaculation," she said clinically. She turned to Rick. "You know because of the assignment, we may need to confirm."

Confirm? What the hell, Chulpa. Rick shook his head but Claren's voice interrupted.

"She's right, Rick. Jeni will take it from here. I'm headed to campus in Langley but will circle back tonight."

He tapped his ear and gave a slight nod.

Chulpa continued her exam.

Rick's mind raced. *How am I going to confirm his inability to ejaculate? Am I supposed to help him in a circle jerk? Jesus, this assignment gets crazier and crazier. Huh, well, it could be kinda hot. But— Fuck it. Hold the damn line.*

Trey watched as her hand raised to his left temple.

"Was this one from the incident in Albany, Georgia?"

What does it matter? Why are you asking about all this? "How?" Trey did not offer an answer.

"Medical records. You were admitted but never filed a report according to the police."

He nodded.

A few stitches but no fracture to your orbital rim, correct?"

"Yes, ma'am." *If you knew already—why ask me?*

She smiled and looked down at her notes.

"Is that it?" Trey softly asked.

"Almost." She turned and opened one of the larger cases, then flipped a switch. "You can put your briefs and sweatpants back on. We're now going to do a modified EKG and EEG."

"I've heard of EKG but what's an EEG?"

"Neurological scan. It's totally painless, but you have to be very still. Rick, can you give me a hand?"

For several minutes, Dr. Patel and Rick applied sticky nodes to Trey. He felt trapped by the wires and nodes on his scalp, chest, temples, and right arm. He closed his eyes and tried to relax as he lay awkwardly on the table with only a small sheet covering the cold surface. The lights overhead were blinding when Rick leaned over him.

"I am going to place this last one on your femoral artery. Be still, okay?"

Trey nodded as Rick pulled open the sweats and shoved his hand down his pants. He placed the node and began to slide his hand back when he grazed Trey's tip through his briefs.

Whoa. Trey shot a look at Rick.

"Easy, Tiger. Good thing you're smooth or it'd hurt later when we rip these off."

Trey lay still, attached by dozens of wires to both machines. The EKG scrolled and ticked with the occasional beeps. As instructed he relaxed and breathed.

Dr. Patel interrupted the silence a few times with "Good," "You're doing great," and "Almost done."

Done? What time is it? Hell what day is it? He had no real sense of time as he had not seen the sky since Saturday night from the rooftop pool. The windowless rooms, bright lights, and lack of clocks frustrated him. *I bet it's Monday afternoon.*

"I am going to draw a few blood samples, and then we can get you some lunch." Dr. Patel was polite but kind. She drew four vials of his blood and then taped a cotton ball to his arm. Rick then removed all the nodes, including the one on his inner thigh, which stung a bit. Trey sat up and pulled on his cotton T-shirt.

"Dr. Patel, what time is it?"

She looked at Trey, then to Rick, then she held up her empty left wrist. "Sorry, I didn't wear my watch today." She smiled. "Good luck, Trey." She exited and Rick packed up the cases and wheeled them out.

The door closed with a familiar click. Trey sat alone on the chair by the table, not looking at the mirror for the first time.

She was the first normal person in all this. So confusing, after slamming me to the floor—now they care about my health? Back and forth, maybe they're testing me. Keeping me guessing. Geez, am I really doing this? Joining the CIA? Holy crap.

A couple of minutes later, Rick returned. "Chow time. In your bunk room." He motioned. As Trey walked back, he handed him a wrapped sandwich and bottle of water.

"Thanks."

"I'll be back in an hour."

As Trey entered the bunk room, Rick placed a hand on his shoulder.

"Make sure you shit and shower, soldier. I want you squeaky clean wearing these." Rick tossed a clean pair of gray gym shorts on his bunk. "Only these."

Trey nodded.

"This afternoon will be intense—no breaks. See you in an hour."

He walked out. The door shut, but the lock did not click. *He's not barking at me anymore. Is this for real? Can I trust him? Make the team. His team.*

The opening and closing of the five doors had become so orchestrated with the buzzing clicks of locks and no locks that it now felt somehow familiar. Trey could tell the slight differences between the ops-room door, his bunk room door, the monitoring-room door, and the squeak of the bathroom door, but not the door at the end of the hall. Never in three days had he heard it open or close.

In captivity, even the mundane becomes important in setting the routine. Setting these routines create an environment, which over the past hundred years of modern warfare and intelligence has led to a complete study in human conditioning. From these conditionings comes protocol.

CHAPTER 21
PAST

Thursday, July 9, 1981
CIA HQ - Langley, Virginia

"You must be Richard Morgan?"

"Yes, sir, but it's Rick."

"Rick it is then." Dr. Carlos Martinez motioned. "And you can call me Doc M."

Rick entered but stood rigid for a moment. *Fuck, more psycho bullshit. Just be cool—keep your head.* He exhaled and glanced between the couch and two side chairs. "Where do I—"

"Anywhere you like."

Rick hesitated.

"Relax, Rick. Choosing a seat isn't part of your evaluation. Please." Dr. Martinez motioned to the couch and took one of the adjacent side chairs. "I've reviewed your family history. New Hampshire."

Rick nodded.

"I very much like New England. Tell me about Thomas?"

"Who?"

"Your brother?"

"Oh, sorry. We never called him that."

"No?"

"We always called him 'Bear.'"

As the first born to Barbara and Cecil Morgan, Bear had been named Thomas after his grandfather, but no one ever called him that except on the first day of school. It was always Bear.

Bear had been four years older than Rick. He'd been a fun kid and had always encouraged Rick to break the rules and "find the fun."

He had taught his little brother swear words and introduced him to comic books and an old Playboy magazine hidden in the hay barn.

Their home had been lively before, but now it was just Cecil and Rick. Life was never the same since 1970.

"Tell me about the accident," Doc M said.

"We'd been at Mount Sunapee skiing all day with our friends. Mom was in her green Volvo station wagon and running late." Rick turned toward the large windows and stared at the treetops. "She pulled in and saw us sitting on the curb with our gear." Rick closed his eyes. "We were laughing. Bear used to do these Mad Libs. He was always writing and making up stuff. Mom was—"

Rick tightened his eyes and saw his last memory of her. *"Come on, guys. How was the mountain?"*

"She was what, Rick?"

"She asked us about our day. 'How was the mountain?' Bear was in the front. I was in the back. I watched him turn to her and say, 'Great . . . I made the team.'" Rick opened his eyes and looked at Doc M.

"And then?"

"Then—darkness. Nothing was ever the same. He made the ski team. Those were the last words I ever heard him say."

"What happened?"

"Logging truck split the car in two. No time to react." Rick turned back to the windows.

"What do you remember?"

"Bits and pieces."

"Shards of memory is consistent with TBI." Doc M looked over his glasses. "Any flashbacks?"

Rick shook his head. "Only in my dreams."

Doc M opened his file. "You spent three weeks at Dartmouth-Hitchcock Hospital. What do you remember?"

"White walls, antiseptic, strangers—I felt . . . abandoned." Rick rubbed his face. *Dad shoulda stayed with me?*

"Then what?"

"Dad came and took me home. But, the house . . . so empty."

"Did you talk about it with him?"

"Cecil Morgan's not much for small talk."

"Nothing?"

"No. That next Saturday, we got up, dressed, and visited them."

"The graves of your mother and brother?"

"Only time we visited them *together*. I'd missed the funeral and the service while I was in . . ." Rick turned back to Doc M. "We never spoke about it again."

"That's a lot to take on at twelve. Did you keep skiing?"

"No. Too many chores. Running a farm isn't easy with just the two of us. Dad never remarried."

"No more skiing?"

"No. No more skiing. No more Mad Libs. Only the basics. School, chores, running track, and wrestling."

Doc M nodded thoughtfully, then glanced down at the open file. "Cecil must be proud of you, Rick?"

"I guess but Bear was his favorite."

"Top of your class, ROTC, University of New Hampshire, and a decorated Marine—"

"Was." Rick shrugged. "But then—Okinawa."

"No one will know about that as long as you're one of us."

Rick clenched his jaw but nodded slightly.

"So making our team is *important* to you?" Doc M peered over his glasses.

"Yes, sir."

"Good. One more question. You never go back to the farm?"

"No, we sold it."

"Where's your dad?"

"Concord. But you must know that." Rick motioned to the file.

"Is he okay?"

"He's fine. I visit once a year but things aren't the same—too many secrets. He's kinda stuck."

"Stuck?"

"In 1970."

Doc M nodded and closed his folder. "Our process is intense."

Rick stretched both arms over head. "I've been through worse—so now what?"

"Yes, you have. Are you okay?"

"Did I make the team?"

"Yes."

"Then I'm okay."

CHAPTER 22
HAZE

A simple sandwich from a local deli was a welcome sight for Trey—something normal, no matter how small. Trey was running on empty. Beyond the hunger, spending three days underground away from his life was beginning to disassociate Trey from his work, his coaching, and his routine. Rick had explained that they would contact his work with news of an "accident," buying them three days of explained absence.

As Trey finished the sandwich, he wondered what life would be like after all this.

Two more days, and they will have to let me out. Right?

The bunk room door opened, and Rick walked in. Gone were his usual dress slacks, black loafers, and crisp Oxford shirt, replaced by a white V-neck T-shirt and navy sweatpants. He was barefoot.

Trey scanned his thick neck and the crease of his collarbone, the veins and hair on Rick's well-defined arms—but halted when his eyes fell on the metal object in Rick's hand.

"Our team is not like other assignments. It calls upon all parts of the recruit to engage, and no one is ever prepared for this final session of phase one. If you pass, tonight I will explain tomorrow's phase two. If you don't . . ." Rick stared at Trey for a moment. "Each of us on the team have walked through this same door." Rick held up the syringe. "Do you want to move forward?"

Trey nodded cautiously.

"Sorry, but I need an audible response."

What if I say no? They'll out me. Lose my job, my coaching. Trey closed his eyes. He saw the faces of his friends, family, and brother all scowling and shaking their heads. *Not really much of a choice.*

"Trey?"

Trey opened his eyes and stared at Rick.

"Do you want to move forward?"

"Can I trust you?"

"What—"

"I've got no one if this falls apart," Trey whispered. "No one."

"I know—"

"No, you don't."

"Yes, I do. We've all walked through this."

Trey stood silently.

"Now, do you—"

"Wait, I have one condition."

Rick glanced upward and paused. "What?"

"You."

"Me?"

"Will you help me through . . . whatever this is?"

"Yes." Rick narrowed his eyes. "Every step."

"Promise?"

Rick nodded.

Trey took a deep breath. "Okay, let's do this."

Rick gave a slight smile and motioned toward the ops room. "Let's go, then."

Geez, every time it's always different. How? Each time, Trey had entered and observed the new configuration. *No chairs, no table, no equipment, nothing, but I know these mats—like the ones at my gymnastics gym.* He stepped up onto the large blue training mats covering nearly the whole space. He walked to the center of the room, looked up. *Plenty of height.* He gave a glance to the mirror. *Watch this.* Trey launched upward into a backflip. He landed with a light thud.

Rick placed the syringe in his mouth and gave three slow, sarcastic claps.

"Showing off?" he asked, taking the syringe back.

I shouldn't have done that. Heat rushed to Trey's face. He suddenly felt small compared to Rick's larger frame. Trey again looked around the room.

Oh god, he's a wrestler—his cauliflower ear. Oh my god, I'm in this small room on the mat with a Division One college wrestler. He's gonna kick my ass.

Rick studied Trey's expression. "No, we're not wrestling. This session is about actions and reactions." He held up the needle.

"What's it for?" Trey grimaced.

"You scared of needles?"

"No."

"You scared of me?"

"A little bit."

"Good." Rick grinned and pulled him closer. "Hold still."

The sting was sharp as the needle entered Trey's neck, and instantly the substance warmed his blood. *What is that? It's hot, tastes like metal.* After a few seconds, the room became fuzzy as the lights now had halos.

Whoa, everything's spinning. Am I melting?

Trey slumped as Rick's arms reached for him.

He's so strong. Safe.

Rick slid down the wall with Trey. He ended up lying between Rick's legs like a rag doll. He caught a glimpse himself in the mirror, and at Trey limp in his arms and between his legs. He gave a thumbs-up.

"That didn't take long." Chulpa said in his earpiece. "Wow, how cool was that backflip."

Rick rolled his eyes and shook his head slightly. His right arm was wrapped around Trey while his left hand, now free of the syringe, rested on his own knee.

"We need a few more minutes for the drug to take full effect, and then we'll leave so Doc M can begin."

Rick folded both arms around Trey and waited. *I hate this part.* When he told the recruit that this session would be tough, he'd meant for both of them. Mentor and recruit. Captor and captive. He detested the psychological methods of the protocol. So called charging sessions. Rick was haunted by his own session.

He closed his eyes, and deliberately relaxed the muscles in his shoulders. He allowed his breathing to sync with the warm, young man in his arms.

God, he smells good—feels good.

"Where— Are we flying?" Trey's voice was slurred.

"Yeah, Trey, we're flying." Rick smirked.

"Ha!" Chulpa's laugh echoed in his ear. "Well, I guess it kicked in. Rick, can we pulse check?"

He gently moved his hand down Trey's arm and stopped at his wrist. Rick glanced to the mirror.

Chulpa continued, "Great, counting in three, two, one . . ."

"Count?"

"Forty-two," Rick said aloud.

"Got it. Thanks, Rick. It was great to see you. I'm transferring to Doc M and stepping out now. Good luck."

Rick smiled at the mirror.

"Good evening, Rick. We'll begin in a moment. Everyone is now leaving. We'll begin the charging session momentarily."

"Charging session" my ass—more like on-camera confessional. Rick closed his eyes and held his guard.

Doc M was legendary at the Agency, having published volumes of classified and declassified papers on the neurological and psychological effects of traumatic bonding. The now graying doctor had personally trained, observed, and mentored all of the protocol officers and operatives throughout Rick's tenure. But after a decade, Rick could never fully figure out the good doctor or his intentions.

Besides Jeni and despite reservations, there was no one at the Agency that Rick trusted more. As much as he loathed it, Doc M's tone and demeanor anchored these sessions for Rick with some sort of sanity or purpose.

Fucking walking contradiction but if we have to do this—he'll get me through it.

"Ready Rick?"

Do I have a choice? He opened his eyes. "Let's get it done."

"Thank you. Recording now, this is Dr. Carlos Martinez of the CIA classified support desk code name: Demaris. Today is Monday, June 12, 1992. We are conducting a modified charging session of the contracted civilian operative, Trey Alan Carter, who has volunteered."

Volunteered? Are you fucking kidding me?

"I am supported with the interaction of Special Officer Rick Morgan at a classified operations training center within the District of Columbia. Rick, can you acknowledge."

"Affirmative, this is Special Officer Rick Morgan."

"We'll begin with a series of questions about his sexual history and your mutual attraction," Doc M said flatly as if ordering a cup of coffee.

Mutual, huh? Rick nodded.

"First question. Are you a homosexual?" Doc M asked.

No warmup.

"Trey. Trey, you ready?" Rick lightly squeezed him.

"Yeah, what?" Trey yawned.

"Are you a homosexual?"

"What?"

"Are you a homosexual?"

"Yeah," the recruit said drunkenly.

"Does Robert McGuire know you are homosexual?"

"No, don't tell—" Trey tensed his shoulders.

"It's okay, relax."

Trey softened and closed his eyes.

"You like it when a man holds you like this?"

"Yes. I—I love it." Trey's voice was a whisper.

Doc M's voice sounded slightly higher. "Did he say 'love'? Please confirm, Rick."

"Yes, that is correct," Rick confirmed.

"Interesting."

What's that supposed to mean? Always so cryptic.

"Can you confirm your sexuality to the recruit, Rick?"

"I'm gay too, Trey."

"Really?"

"Yeah."

"Oh, I thought so."

"You like me, don't you?"

"Yesss," Trey slurred.

"You think I'm attractive?"

"Yeah. You're super-hot."

Rick grinned and rolled his eyes.

Doc M clear his throat. "Rick, ask him if he wants to be on the team—"

What? This is about him not me—not Bear.

"*Your* team."

Rick breathed deep. "Tiger, you want to be on the team? You want to be on *my* team?"

"I do. Will you let me?" Trey tried to turn in Rick's embrace.

Rick squeezed Trey so he couldn't. "Yes, but sit still. I got you."

"Let's continue with his sexual history." Doc M prompted.

"Tell me about your first time—having sex. Did you enjoy it?"

"No."

"No? Why?"

"I don't want to talk about it. It wasn't supposed to happen."

"Who was he?"

"My youth minister. You can't tell nobody—"

Oh fuck, that's right. Shit. Reassure and push pass. "Shh . . . it's okay, Trey. What about in college? Did you have a girlfriend?"

"Yeah."

"How many girlfriends?"

"A few."

"Ever have sex with 'em?"

"Yeah."

"Did you like having sex with women?"

"Yeah, kinda."

"Kinda? Didn't you enjoy it?"

"I guess. It's complicated."

"Rick, press him on his retrograde ejaculation," Doc M clinically instructed.

"You like shooting your load? Cumming?"

"I can't cum," Trey said softly.

"You don't want me now, do you?"

"We'll figure it out." Again, Rick squeezed the young man in his arms.

"Ask about his same-sex experiences. Masturbation, fellatio, anal—"

Whoa, whoa—I get it, Doc M. Only you can suck the sexy outta sex.

"What about boyfriends? Have you had sex with guys?"

"Yeah."

"What's your favorite position?"

"I don't understand."

"In bed, Trey, having sex with a guy—do you pitch or catch? Give or receive?"

"I haven't gone all the way yet with a guy."

"Never?"

"No, but I want to . . ."

Are you shitting me? This kid's a virgin with men. Rick shot a look at the mirror.

"Okay, this is a bit uncharted, Rick," Doc M said. "But not a deal-breaker. In fact, it may heighten the allure with our engineer."

Rick widened his eyes.

"I know, I know—most of our service recruits rattle off their conquests or favorite sexual experiences. But the drug does elicit candid responses. He's been reared in such a conservative, religious manner—honestly, it does makes sense."

Before Doc M could prompt him with another question, Rick asked one of his own.

"What's your fantasy, Trey?"

"You."

Rick grinned slightly. "Don't you have a boyfriend?"

"No."

Rick took a deep breath. A twinge of guilt seeped into this chest. *Damn, it's never felt like this—not with any of the military recruits. Why? Because we're dragging him into this—he didn't ask for this shit.*

Rick felt Trey gently massaging his leg. He looked down and saw Trey's growing bulge. Trey was at full attention in his cotton shorts. Rick was too but concealed in his confining jock. Hopefully it did not seep through to his sweatpants. He was just inches from his desire. Pressing against the young man's back, he was nearly lost in his arousal when Claren's words rang in his memory.

"Candy's hard to resist. Hold the line."

Doc M cleared his throat politely. "Excellent, Rick. I believe we've covered everything. Do you need a moment?"

Rick glanced at the mirror. "No, I'm good."

"Good. We're at thirty-eight minutes from injection, so he will be returning soon." Doc M paused for several minutes before returning. "Forty-two minutes now, can you check in with him?"

"Trey? You okay?" Rick said as he adjusted himself and then shoved Trey up to a seated position. He tossed a white T-shirt onto Trey's lap. They sat for a couple of minutes without saying a word. Then Trey pulled on the shirt and shook his head.

Doc M gave his prompt into the earpiece.

"Let's begin. Remember, Rick, he needs to fear you now."

CHAPTER 23
HUSTLER

For twenty minutes, Rick forced the focus on Trey's inexperience with sex. Both he and Doc M behind the mirror analyzed Trey's discomfort in his flushed face, stammered responses, rigid posture, and deflecting tone.

Come on. This is bullshit. Let's turn up the heat and get this over with.

"When did you start jerking off?"

"What?"

"We all jerk off, Tiger. Every man on earth. When did you start?"

"I don't know . . . I guess when I was twelve."

Rick motioned for him to continue. *Come on already.*

"Old Man Taylor had the farm next door to my uncle's. My cousin and I were playing in the woods. We found some *Hustler* magazines. There were three or four of them. He would look at the women, but I would secretly . . ."

"Look at the men," Rick said.

"Yeah, I memorized them. Then back home, my neighbor and I started messing around in front of each other. Nothing major, just touching and stuff. He moved away when his parents divorced."

"What about high school?"

"I tried really hard to be 'straight' in high school and college. Prayed a lot."

"Really? And no guys?"

"No, only girlfriends. But—"

"But what?"

Trey bit his bottom lip, then said, "I had to fantasize about men to—you know."

"Get hard. Okay, I get it. Geez." Rick stretched his legs and glared at the mirror.

"Yes, Rick, he's deflecting, and you want to speed up the session," Doc M whispered in the mic.

Rick raised his eyebrows.

"Okay, we should have enough then. Well, transition. Ready when you are, Rick, but be careful. His religious beliefs seem to run deeper than we've encountered."

No shit. Rick stood up and stared downward at Trey seated on the floor. "You know that we're not playing around here?" Rick used a deeper tone.

"What? Why does all this matter?"

"Because it does. We need to know everything about you."

"You already know everything?" Trey shook his head.

Rick pursed his lips. "Again, tell about the girls in college."

"What—"

"Again," Rick barked.

Trey shrugged but repeated his escapades in college, He went further and described fumbling with bras, panties, and finding the clitoris.

Rick observed Trey relax a bit just as Doc M's voice interjected.

"Now, Rick, time to turn it up."

"Shut up," Rick interrupted. "Sit up."

What? Trey's eyes focused on Rick's hands as he took cloth out of his back pocket. His powerful hands pulled the fabric taunt.

"Sit up, now."

Trey sat up immediately as Rick strode around him. *What is he doing?* Trey saw their reflection in the mirror as Rick squatted behind and pulled the cloth within inches from his face. Trey saw a stone-cold look in Rick and his own terror.

Oh my god, he's going to strangle me!

Blinding darkness enveloped him.

His head pounded as Rick tightened the now blindfold. Trey's breathing rapidly increased—the drug's presence had dissipated. *What tha'?*

Trey's hatred of blindfolds stemmed from a peculiar childhood experience. He'd been playing in the barn on his uncle's farm as a kid. His cousins had accidentally left him in the dark barn at the end of a long game of blind hide-and-go-seek. When he'd finally realized they were not coming back to get him, he'd panicked and pulled off the blindfold. Less than a foot from his face, a large, black king snake observed him. Its tongue darted in and out as Trey sat frozen. Uncertain as to whether he should move for what felt like hours . . . suddenly the snake had shifted and slithered past him and into the hay bales.

The barn door had flown open, and Trey's older brother yelled.

"Come on."

"Where were—"

"Come on. Granny made ice cream."

"Listen to me," Rick said just inches from his right ear, snapping him back from his memory.

"Stop with the basic facts—we want to know how you feel. What excites you? What—"

How I feel? Scared as hell but now I'm pissed. I've been here for god knows how long getting pushed, poked, and punished—for what?

"I don't like being blindfolded," Trey blurted out.

"I don't give a shit what you like. You're wasting my time. We don't care who touched you first," Rick barked.

"What?" Trey swung his heard from side to side trying to determine the direction of the voice.

"Your preacher? Cousin? Neighbor? Who cares!" Rick yelled. "Fuck 'em."

"Fuck them? What?" Trey ripped off the blindfold and hissed. "Fuck you, Rick!" Trey bolted to the locked door and tried in vain to yank it open.

"Really, where you gonna go?"

"Outta here."

"Where?"

"I had a life before all this. I have a life!" Trey shouted over his shoulder and continued to yank at the immovable door.

"Shut up, Trey."

"This isn't for me."

"So that's it? You quit?"

Trey turned to Rick. "What do you want from me? Why me?"

"Not this pansy-assed tantrum." Rick stood rigid. "Fine. Fucking quit! Stop wasting my time and my team!" Rick pointed to the mirror.

Doc M's voice rang in Rick's earpiece. "Get ready. He's nearly there."

Rick instantly looked back to see Trey flex his back muscles. *Okay, buddy—here we go.*

"Rick, we don't have to do this physically—try a conversate approach," Doc M said.

Rick shot a skeptical look at the mirror.

"Fine, we'll do it your way, but you must either talk him down or dominate him now . . . physically."

Rick assumed his combat stance.

Trey turned from the door, red and seething. He narrowed his eyes at Rick. "Open the door!"

"Trey Alan Carter, listen to me—"

"Open the door—"

Rick squeezed two fists as Trey lunged.

Rick grabbed and slammed the young man to the mat and spun like a matador, but his stubborn bull did not stand down.

You want more, huh?

Trey again lunged at Rick.

Wanna fight? I'll give you a real taste. Instinct took over, and Rick's first kick landed squarely on Trey's right hip, but his next kick missed the upper thigh. Rick attempted a one, two kick punch, but Trey deflected and again lunged. *Oh shit.* Rick intended his kick to force Trey's momentum backward so his fist would only graze him. As his fist exploded forward, Rick knew he'd fucked up.

Crack!

Rick winced at the sound of the impact squarely to Trey's face. Hard. Too hard.

Oh fuck! Rick saw the first spurt of red hang in the air as Trey launched backward.

Thud!

The lifeless body hit the mat, and then deafening silence.

Oh my god. "Trey?"

Trey did not move.

Rick stared at his motionless body. *Shit, shit, shit.*

"Rick?" Doc M shattered the silence.

Rick turned to the mirror.

"I'm getting the first-aid kit ready. Assess the situation."

Rick dropped to his knees beside Trey and immediately rolled him onto his side so the blood gushing from his nose wouldn't choke him.

"Trey?" *Come on, buddy, please be okay.* "Trey, can you hear me? Give me a grunt."

The young man lay motionless.

Rick frantically checked his pulse and breath for any sign of life.

"Is he breathing, Rick?" Doc M entered the room and laid the kit next to Rick.

"I think so—I don't know." Rick paused. "Yes."

"Keep his airway clear."

He nodded and then opened Trey's right eye. "He's concussed."

Doc M pulled out two white towels and a compression chemical ice pack.

"Can you handle this? I can stay but . . ."

Rick turned to Doc M. "But then we're blown."

Doc M shrugged.

"No, he can't see—I got this." Rick shook his head. "Shit, this is my fault."

Doc M laid a hand on his shoulder. "Keep your head. There's adrenaline in there as well." He motioned to the black bag. "You sure?"

Rick nodded, and Doc M exited the room.

Rick took out the antiseptic wipes, gauze, and the adrenaline stick. He grabbed the ice pack to puncture the reactive chemicals. He snapped the stick to activate and waved it under Trey's nostrils.

"Argh," Trey moaned a few seconds later.

"Trey?"

"Ooouch." Trey tried to rise.

"No, lie still." Rick placed the now-cold ice pack on his face for several seconds. "I got you, Trey. Don't move." Rick laid his free hand on Trey's chest.

Shit! I am so sorry, Trey.

After a few minutes of compress, Rick spoke up. "I need to take a look. Okay, Trey?"

"Uh-huh," Trey grunted.

Rick removed the pack and knelt closer. He assessed Trey's fingers, toes, and neck. "You're good." He then quietly wiped up the blood, turned Trey to his other side, and then applied the ice for several minutes. Rick sat back down on the mat, spread his legs, and pulled Trey into his lap. The recruit was pliable and simply held the icepack to his face.

"I didn't mean to hit you so hard, Trey," Rick said. "Please let me look at your nose."

Trey removed the icepack and squinted at the overhead lights. "I'm done. If I'm gonna to die tonight, then—" he whispered.

"You're not gonna die. Not on my watch."

"Why—"

"Shhh. Let me finish."

Trey closed his eyes and visibly relaxed. After several minutes examining Trey's nose, cheekbones, eye sockets, and neck, Rick finished his assessment.

"Looks like nothing's broken, except your nose. You're gonna be fine, but this is going to hurt. I need to set your nose."

"Right now?"

"Yes. Let's stand up, okay?"

Trey opened his eyes and sat up.

"Come here." Rick stood over Trey with arms outstretched.

Trey took hold as Rick helped him up. He did not immediately let go of Rick, taking a moment to steady himself. The two men stood for a moment, hands clasped, facing one another. Energy pulsed between them. If it weren't for the blood smeared on their shirts and down to Trey's shorts, the scene would have seemed, to anyone looking in, like a more intimate moment. Eventually, Rick released Trey's hands and placed his on Trey's face. Trey in turn grabbed hold to Rick's forearms.

Crack!

Trey's legs buckled, but Rick managed to grab him, tightening his grip as Trey's head rolled back.

"Easy, just breathe." Rick squeezed his grip fearing that Trey might pass out. Blood again gushed downward, covering any remaining white of the T-shirt.

"Trey?"

"Ahhh."

"You okay? Talk to me."

"Yeah, think so—man, that hurt." Tears flowed down his face.

"You're going to be okay. Come here." Rick tended to Trey with the small cotton towel with one hand while keeping the other on the back of his neck.

They stood for several minutes in this position with Trey's hands on Rick's forearm.

"It's like you're baptizing me," Trey said.

"What do you mean?"

"Baptism, like my pastor at church in Atlanta." Trey glanced down at his shirt. "But this ain't water."

"No, I guess more like a baptism of blood."

Trey gave a slight smile.

"Let me see. How did I do?" Rick inspected the alignment and winked at Trey. "Looks good, Tiger. Chulpa's gonna be impressed. You're definitely gonna be sore, and you'll probably have a set of double shiners." He hugged him and softly said, "You know that was an accident. Right?"

Trey sank deeper into Rick's embrace.

"I'm sorry, Trey. That wasn't supposed to happen."

After a minute, Rick was about to push back, but Doc M whispered into his earpiece. "Keep holding him, Rick."

Then shortly after, two more words. "You won."

Trey squeezed Rick's muscular frame and took a deep breath. He tasted blood and sweat. *I'm guessing that this wasn't normal? He seems genuinely sorry.* The room smelled of sweat and blood. "What's next?"

Rick spoke softly, "Well, we're a bit bruised and battered, but tomorrow we'll begin phase two."

Trey pulled back from Rick's chest and looked up. "So, that was an accident?"

"Yes, I'm really sorry."

Trey nodded. "I have to pee."

"Well, let's go pee." Rick grinned and helped Trey to the bathroom, then to his bunk. Trey sat down. Rick returned quickly with the black bag from the ops room. He cleaned the abrasions and remaining blood.

Trey was amazed as Rick tended to his wounds as if he were a seasoned ER nurse or doctor. "Are you a doctor too?"

"No, but I trained as a medic in the Marines."

Geez. He really knows what he's doing.

Rick broke the silence. "Almost done, but now we have to pack it. This is going to sting a bit. You good?"

"Yeah."

Again, fire burned Trey's face as Rick stuffed both nostrils with cotton.

"Let's get these off," Rick said, as he then pulled off the T-shirt and tossed it in the pile of clothes by the door. He turned to Trey. "I'm guessing you normally don't sleep in clothes. Am I right?"

"No. I didn't sleep too well the last two nights here." Trey laughed and tried to smile.

Rick grinned as Trey pulled off his blood-stained shorts. Trey slipped under the sheet and blanket as he watched Rick pull out another syringe.

"You're going to sleep well tonight."

"What is it?"

"Just a little something to help you sleep." He injected the shot. "Dr. Patel will be checking in on you, and the team is here all night. If you need anything, just yell."

Rick scooped up the clothes and bloody towels from the floor and switched off the lights.

Trey nodded groggily. "G'night."

"Goodnight, Trey."

Rick returned to the monitoring room and stuffed the soiled clothing into a laundry bag in the corner. He peeled off and added his own bloody T-shirt. As he pulled on a clean T-shirt, he turned to Doc M, who was typing on his laptop.

"I should've tried to talk more. It was an accident . . . I just didn't expect it to go down like that."

Doc M remained focused on his screen. "Rick, life never happens according to plan. I've already spoken to Claren. He'll be fine. Chulpa will reexamine him in the morning. You did a *great* job in there tonight. Go home and get some rest now. I will wait for the night team, but I need you back here at 0700. I am recommending you to also lead phase two."

"Phase two? But that was supposed to be Chris. He's the expert on the physical assessment—"

"Things changed here tonight." Doc M looked up from his laptop and pulled off his reading glasses. "We all agree. He *trusts* you now. Deeply. The markers from the tape, his actions, and reactions—we're in new territory. Quite exciting stuff. Here." He handed Rick a blue notebook. "Phase two."

"You think he's still up for it now?"

"He's banged up but will be fine. You need to get out of here and get some rest. You have a big day tomorrow."

"Okay, thanks." Rick shoved the notebook into his duffel. "See you tomorrow."

Rick waited for the service door to shut behind him before he exhaled. *Holy shit, I'm leading this now. Wow.*

Rick walked the long service corridor and to his car. He cranked the BMW and drove home to his apartment up Sixteenth Street to Silver Spring without music—lost in his thoughts.

As he entered, he glanced at the glowing red *0* on his answering machine. *Guess they didn't change their mind. Phase two. Holy shit.*

He stripped down and tossed his clothes into the hamper, turned on his shower, and stood for a moment in front of his vanity, waiting for the water to warm. *Blood. His blood.* He wiped off the remaining spots of blood on his cheek and neck with his first two fingers and before thinking, held them to his nose. His thick muscle was again growing and in need of attention.

In the shower, he let the water run down his body as he stroked himself with lather. He closed his eyes and thought of the young man as he shot against the tiles once, twice, and a third time. He lathered his whole body again and grabbed the shower wand, rinsing himself thoroughly.

Rick walked into his kitchen naked and still damp. He grabbed the carton of lo mein and quickly ate while thumbing through the phase two protocol in his manual. He was always studying and always preparing. He did not want to screw up this opportunity.

Trey was *his* recruit.

CHAPTER 24
PHASE TWO

R ick entered the Hole at 0620. Jeni was packing up as Darius made a pot of coffee, and the rooms were still quiet. Jeni mustered a smile at Rick but was clearly exhausted from her night shift. Darius looked over his shoulder.

"Morning, Rick," Darius said.

"Morning. He's still asleep?"

"Yeah. Rough night I heard. You good?"

"Yeah, it was an accident . . . I—"

"Totally, Rick. He leaned in—you couldn't pull your punch," Jeni interrupted. "Doc M showed us only the fight. Total accident, we saw."

Rick nodded.

"Tough lil son-a-bitch. That temper." Darius took a sip of coffee. "He ain't gonna make this easy, is he?"

"No," Rick said.

"He'll be fine. I'm headed home. Bye, guys." Jeni exited as Rick poured a cup of coffee. He joined Darius at the monitors. There in the green glow of the night-vision camera, his recruit slept.

"I think we should do it in the bathroom," Rick said as he reviewed the day's ops plan.

"The buzz cut?"

"Yeah." Rick made a quick note.

"Fine by me, easier to clean up too."

Behind them the service door opened as Chris walked in at precisely six thirty. "Morning, guys."

"Morning, Chris. Look—" Rick turned.

"Rick, I already heard and completely agreed . . . you've got phase two. I will be in your ear if you need me. Given the situation and condensed timeline—this is on point. Forty-one days, and this kid's got a temper. But he's a hoss. Phase two should be a breeze."

Rick nodded, relieved that Chris was on board with the switch. "Why exactly does a civ need the buzz cut?"

Chris poured a cup of coffee and took a seat beside Rick. "Physical appearance and maintaining a personal style distracts. You know it's SOP in all five branches of military."

"I know, but him being a civ and this being involuntary—I don't know."

"I get it—but even though he's civ, the effects are real. I suggested this and Doc M agrees. It'll speed the plow. Help him shed the past and step forward."

Rick nodded. *Yeah, but he's not straight—I don't know if he might freak out at the thought of losing his hair. We can sometimes take things differently. We— That's it.*

"Chris, what if I buzz too?"

"Really?"

"Yeah, show him we're a team."

"Excellent. I could call it in, but I think it's brilliant. One team, one dream."

"Exactly. Come on, buzz me now before I wake him or change my mind."

"Let's go, cowboy," Chris said.

At seven thirty, Rick was sporting a new clean cut and felt fully prepped for the offsite morning run. Chris and Darius would drive, acting as backup. Claren had phoned in and was en route to pick up Doc M. All was set. As he stood outside the bunk room, Rick took a deep breath and turned the handle.

"Seven thirty, Tiger. Get up! Get up!"

Trey startled, got up, and stood naked at his cot. His face was a mess: two black eyes and a swollen nose.

"Dirty thirty, sunshine." Rick gestured to the floor. "Let's go!"

Trey frowned. Rick widened his eyes.

The young man dropped to the floor and banged out thirty push-ups. As he rose, he got a better look at Rick. "Whoa, you buzzed your hair."

"Yup, you like it?"

"Yeah." He then noticed Rick was wearing shorts, running shoes, and a white T-shirt. "Are we going running?"

"Hopefully. Dr. Patel will be here shortly to check you out, and if she clears you, then we'll go for a run." Rick paused. "Outside."

Outside. Finally, some fresh air. Yes. The thought of getting out of the three underground rooms brought a crooked smile to Trey's face. He grabbed his towel and draped it around his waist. "Let's do this."

As he walked to the bathroom, he realized Rick was following. "What's up?"

Rick motioned for him to enter. As he entered, he saw the chair and hair clippers plugged in and lying on the sink. "Wait, why am I getting buzzed too?"

"We're a team, right?" Rick walked to the sink and grabbed the clippers.

Buzz!

"Have a seat, Tiger."

Oh my god. Trey sat silently as chunks of hair fell into his lap. Over and over the razor buzzed by his eyes methodically, then suddenly it was over. Throughout his first twenty-one years, his church had dictated the part in his hair, left or right only. He had been forbidden to part his hair in the middle, as it was considered effeminate, and according to his pastor only homosexuals did so. His hair had been a bit longer for the first time in his life, touching his ears and back collar.

Trey gave up a bit more of his new freedom. But he wanted to join his coach and make the team.

"Take a look," Rick said as he stood in front of the large mirror above the two sinks.

"I look like a POW with this swollen nose, black eyes, and buzz cut."

"Nah, I think you look tough." Rick moved closer. "I think we look hot."

Trey turned and stared at Rick—and suddenly hugged him.

"All right, all right . . . now get cleaned up. Leave the cotton in, and I'll lay out some clothes for you," Rick said, pulling and guiding Trey toward the showers.

Rick exited and walked back to the monitoring room. He scooped up the running clothes for Trey. "Any word from Chulpa?" he asked Chris.

"She should be here in five or ten minutes," Chris said. "You may need to stall a bit."

Rick nodded.

"You know the kid's crushing on you?" Chris raised his eyebrows.

Rick shrugged and stared blankly. "Whatever."

Don't make this a thing, Chris. Rick knew that none of the other agents had or would see the moments that led up to the fight on the tape from last night's session. Doc M, Claren, and Tibbins only— Rick had learned early whom to trust at the protocol. Doubt could lead to a crack and showing your hand.

Rick refilled his cup of coffee and flipped through the notes. He glanced up at the monitors and saw that Trey was now out of the shower and drying off at the mirror. As Trey turned and walked back toward the bathroom door. Rick left his coffee and exited quickly.

In the bunk room, Rick watched Trey slip on the briefs, shorts, T-shirt and then sit on the bed to put on his socks and running shoes.

"Where we running this morning?" Trey asked.

"I have a route for us. I cut it back to three miles to see how you'd do," Rick said, pointing to his nose. "Dr. Patel will be here shortly. It's really her call, Trey. She is going to take a look, and we only go if she clears you."

Trey shrugged. "Can I ask you something?"

"Shoot."

"I know y'all got coffee over there. I smell it. Please, can I have some?"

Damn it, simple request but off protocol. No doubt smelling it through the vents sucks as he's only had small rations and water.

Before Rick responded, Chris spoke into the earpiece. "Easy incentive. Make him work for it today."

"Here's the deal. Give me one hundred percent today on the run, the endurance test, and the limits assessment," Rick said counting with his right thumb, index finger, then second finger. "No whining, no temper, no tears. Tomorrow morning, you'll get coffee."

"Promise?"

Rick grinned and extended his right hand. "I'll pour it myself."

The young man smiled, stood, and grabbed Rick's hand. "Deal."

"Rick, Chulpa's here and will knock on the door in two," Chris informed Rick via the earpiece.

"Ready for Dr. Patel?" Rick motioned for Trey to sit on the cot.

Knock, knock.

The door opened, and Dr. Patel walked in wearing her white coat and carrying a purple and white tackle box.

"Good morning, guys." Chulpa's smile was like sunshine in the windowless basement. Rick saw the growing smile on Trey as she blurted, "Oh. My. God. Rick Morgan! What the hell did you do to my beautiful boy?"

Rick shook his head as she immediately walked to Trey and cupped his chin with her warm hand.

"It was an accident—"

"Men and your *accidents*." She opened her toolkit and pulled out a new pair of latex gloves, a small white towel, and several packets and tools. She turned to Rick. "No more accidents. Can you go get me a cup of warm water?"

Rick took the cup and rolled his eyes as he exited the room.

She's awesome. Love how she yelled at Rick.

"Now, tilt your head back," she instructed before gently pressing and inspecting his forehead, eye sockets, temples, cheeks, and jaw, asking periodically, "Does this hurt?"

"You're gonna be sore for a few days, but you're fine. What did you do to cause this accident?"

"Got mad."

"Anger is a choice." She shook her head. "Now let me clean and re-dress this. Did you sleep well?"

"Yes, ma'am."

"Good. You're quite the athlete I hear."

He shrugged.

"I saw that backflip yesterday. Cool. How long have you been a gymnast?"

"About eight or nine years. I coach part-time now—or did before this ..."

"You are going to ace phase two today and be back to your coaching before you know it." She crossed her arms. "Can I give you some advice?"

Trey nodded.

"Rick is one of the best at the Agency. You could learn so much from him. Instead of igniting in anger, try pausing and listening?"

Trey nodded again in silence.

"My grandmother would always say, 'Chulpa, the gods have given you two ears and only the one mouth.'" Her perfect Punjabi accent reinforced the wisdom.

Trey smiled.

"Now tilt your head back again, stubborn man."

Rick rejoined them in the room with the warm water. For the next several minutes, she unpacked, cleaned, and redressed his nose. Trey breathed through the pain. As Dr. Patel was snapping off her gloves, she turned to Rick.

"Not bad for a med tech grunt!"

"Good excuse to use my training," Rick shot back.

Trey could sense the connection between them.

"All right, he's going to be fine." She turned to Trey. "Some additional bruising and bleeding is totally normal. After your run, shower and lightly wash around it. Rick will re-dress it."

"Thanks, ma'am."

"Good luck, Trey, and remember my grammy's advice."

"I will."

"Good." She and Rick left the room.

Click.

The door locked. Trey got up and started stretching.

Oh my god—I'm finally getting outta here.

CHAPTER 25
RUN

"Ready, Trey?"

"What's that for?"

Rick saw the panic fill Trey's eyes as he stared at the hood.

"Why? I've done everything you've asked. I really hate those things."

"I know, I know. But it's just for security. And I'm sorry, but we also need to use these," Rick said, pulling out two black zip ties. "I am going to be by your side the entire time. You can do this."

Trey stood from his cot. "Fine." He held out his hand. "But at least I'm getting out of here."

Rick gave him the hood. Something about Trey putting it on himself was not only a great marker for progress—Rick felt a swelling of pride.

In the darkness of the hood, Trey put out his hands in two fists. Rick put on the zip ties, careful not to tighten them too much, and led Trey out the door, down the hallway, and through the monitoring room. In the darkness, Trey's hearing grew heightened. He heard the buzzing of electronics, and a door open and close. They walked twenty-five steps. The sound of the van door opening was easily recognizable, along with the echo of an engine and the smell of exhaust. He deduced that they were in a parking garage.

"We are going to step up into the van now," Rick said. "Lower your head, okay?"

The van door shut, and they were off. Rick was on his right, and the van sidewall was on his left. They drove for several minutes—starting and stopping in the early-morning DC traffic.

After several minutes, Rick leaned toward him. "We're almost there."

A minute after that, the van stopped, and they exited.

"Stay here. I'll be right back," Rick instructed.

Trey heard the van pull away, and there was just the sound of the wind and birds. He felt the morning dew on his skin and gave a deep sigh.

Rick pulled off the hood. Blinding sunshine hit Trey for the first time in four days. He squinted as Rick came into view in front of him, knife in hand.

"I'm going to cut these now. Are we good?" Rick asked.

"Yes."

"Hold still." Rick cut the zip ties from Trey's wrists.

"Ahh." Trey immediately reached to scratch his back. Rick grinned and shook his head. Rick dropped the zip ties and hood, then motioned to the nearby van.

Trey could not see the two people in it clearly. "We're never alone—are we?"

Rick shot him a grin. "Not yet. Ready?"

Who's watching us? How many people? He probably can't tell me.

"So how does this work? You timing me?"

"No, we're just gonna run at a normal pace," Rick said. "When we finish, I'll record your pulse and explain more about the day. For now, breathe it in, enjoy, and try to keep up!"

He gave one of his familiar side nods with a grin, then started down the trail. Trey immediately followed. For a while, Trey trailed Rick, unable to match his longer strides. He then caught up and settled into his own pace. It was a warm and bright sunny morning.

At the first signpost, Mile 1, Rick turned. "You good?"

"Yeah. But it's harder with all this stuff up my nose."

"Ha! No doubt. You're doing great."

They kept running, passing the Mile 2 signpost. They rounded a bend, and Trey saw in the distance a pond with the rooftops of a modern, sleek set of office buildings. Trey was reminded of Fair Lakes, the corporate center in nearby Fairfax where he worked. He briefly wondered where they were, but then dismissed the thought. He was so happy to be outside and exercising with Officer Morgan.

Just ahead of the Mile 3 signpost at the far edge of the lake, Trey saw the two people sitting on a bench. *Wonder if they are Agency too?*

Rick lightly punched him in the arm.

"Race you to the sign!" Rick took off—full sprint. Trey's competitive edge took over, and he sprinted for all his might. He gained on Rick as they reached the bench, but Rick turned it up and passed the signpost first.

Rick clicked the timer on his black wristwatch, then turned and raised his fists in the air for a little Rocky Balboa victory strut.

Trey grinned.

"Not bad, Tiger," Rick said. "Come here. Hold still." He placed two fingers on Trey's neck and held up his own wristwatch to take his pulse.

They were cooling down walking back toward the pond when the two strangers approached them. "Good morning," Trey said as they passed. The woman nodded and smiled.

Rick glanced back at the two people and nodded slightly to the woman, who returned his gesture with a faint smile.

Tiger has no idea, he met the grand dame of CIA field operations, Claren E. Johnson, and the insufferably correct Dr. Carlos Martinez.

"Now what?" Trey asked as Rick laid a hand on his shoulder.

"Over here." Rick guided him to the wooden outdoor-fitness setup.

"Looks like a jungle gym for adults."

Rick did not respond but stopped at the first station. He reached into the awaiting black duffel and pulled out a clipboard along with a black, bulky stopwatch with a long nylon strap. He clicked the pen and recorded the run.

"Nice run, Tiger. You broke sevens: 06:52 average."

"Thanks. Did I pass?"

"Ha! It's not pass or fail. You did fine. Just keep doing your best, okay?"

"Yes, sir."

"We're going to go through a basic series of fitness drills and agility tests. First, grab a drink." Rick motioned to the old, green water fountain twenty feet to their left on the side of the trail.

Trey drank for a while with his head over the flowing stream. Rick watched as he stood back and paused, breathing in the morning and sunshine. *Bet Chris is right. He's going to ace this.*

After a minute, Trey bounded back to Rick eagerly and stood waiting.

"Tilt your head back," Rick instructed. "No bleeding. Good. How do you feel? You good?"

"Yeah. A little sore, but I'm good."

"All right, first up—chin-ups. Twelve."

When Rick stopped Trey at fifteen, he knew that Chris had been right. The recruit's fitness level was better than most of the recruits he had seen in the last few years.

Shit, we may bang this out in an hour.

"All right, box jumps, balance, sit-ups, and the rope ladder," he said.

Trey's breathing was heavy, but other than his challenge of having to mouth-breathe, he was sailing through the test. All eights, highest bubble on the scale, as Rick checked off the assessment sheet. Then he pulled out a brown leather, wooden-handled Everlast jump rope and passed it to Trey.

"Five minutes straight, no stopping," he instructed.

Trey grinned curiously when he took the rope, as if he had a secret. Rick heard him start jumping but still counted him down to start the stopwatch, "Let's go five minutes in three, two, one."

Click.

Rick glanced up and saw Trey jumping like a pro, but instead of the rope coming over his head and under his feet forward, he was jumping backward. Fast and effortless, as though he were a prizefighter.

What the hell? Who is this kid? Rick tried not to register any pride or other emotion as Trey furiously commanded the rope, shuffled his feet in various steps and cadences that made it seem as though he was dancing—not exercising at seventy plus rotations per minute.

"All right, in five, four, three, two, one, done," Rick said as he clicked the timer and then recorded his assessment. "Highest tier, good job." He returned his fingers to the recruit's neck and without glancing up from his watch, asked, "Where did you learn that?"

"What?"

"Jumping backward."

"Oh, I grew up jumping rope with my brother for basketball. But at my gym, I took a class in doing it backward. It felt odd at first, but it's a more natural motion and easier on your shoulders. You just got to trust the rope and let it do its thing."

"Nice."

Trey smiled.

Damn, even bruised he's cute as hell. Rick grinned slightly.

"Now what?"

"Just a few stretches, and we're done." Rick rolled out a large towel on the grass and motioned for Trey. "On your back." He flipped the page on the clipboard and laid it beside Trey. Then he nudged the recruit's legs apart, took a knee, and placed Trey's right leg up onto his shoulder.

"Straight leg," Rick said as he pressed inward and assessed his flexibility of his hip and hamstring. Rick saw Trey was sweating lightly and looking away. *He's feeling more than just the stretch—he's avoiding eye contact.*

"How long you been a gymnast?" Rick asked after a minute, breaking the silence.

"I don't know—guess about seven or eight years."

Rick nodded. "Switch legs."

As they repositioned for the other leg, Rick felt the tension. *New topic, what? Weather.*

"It's nice out but it's gonna get hot later. Good thing we got an early start." He continued to stretch and assess Trey's hamstrings, hip flexors, ankles, and calves in a series of precise moves. After five minutes or so of assessments, Rick picked up the clipboard and made notes.

"How'd I do?"

"You aced it, Trey. No doubt your gymnastics gave you a solid base. When this is over, you gotta show me that jump-rope thing. That's pretty cool." Rick smiled.

Trey blushed and bit his lower lip.

Damn, Tiger. He's really gotta ease off—stop distracting me, or we'll never get through this. Twisting away, Rick made a few more notes, though he barely knew what he was writing.

"Can I grab some water?"

"Yeah, sure," Rick said.

When he returned, Trey motioned to the woods. "I need to water a tree."

"Yeah, me too." Rick followed Trey to the tree line. They walked in about ten paces and stood only a few feet apart. When Trey stole a glance, Rick shot his stream just inches from Trey's shoe.

"Hey!"

"Ha, serves you right, peeping tom."

"Whatever, old man." Trey grinned and turned to leave.

A joke and a smirk, that is a damn good marker. Rick felt a growing warmth. *He gets me and my humor. See—I'm not a total asshole.*

As they packed up the duffel, Rick saw the crude outdoor parallel bars, nudged Trey, and went off protocol. "Show me some moves, Tiger?"

"All right."

Trey jumped up and in two graceful glides came to a perfect handstand and then lowered to a V-straddle. He then flipped over the bars backward to the ground and pretended to salute a set of imaginary panel of judges.

"No shit, that's impressive— Fuck."

Trey's shirt had gained several red spots.

"What?"

Rick winced and pointed. "Your nose is bleeding again."

"Oh, man." Trey cupped his hands under his nose.

"Here." Rick gently pulled off Trey's T-shirt and then deftly ripped it in two pieces. "Use this—hold it to your nose." Rick handed back one half of the shirt.

He walked over to the water fountain and doused the other remnant in water. As he did, he caught a hit of black and gray in his periphery. He glanced up to see two women in business clothing and tennis shoes walking along the trail. *Perfect. With any luck they'll be able to help me out.*

Rick returned to Trey. "Here, use this to clean up. Stay here."

Trey watched Rick approach the women and talk with them. One of them looked over at him, nodded, and then pulled something out of her bag. They all nodded to one another as Rick ran back. The women continued walking down the path toward the pond.

Rick approached with a wide smile. "Success." He opened the package and pulled out a tampon.

"Are you serious?" Trey started to laugh.

Rick laughed as well as they cleaned up, and then he repacked Trey's nose with two halves of the tampon. Rick waited a moment, then inspected his nose. "No blood."

"Great." Trey rolled his eyes.

"First rule in an assignment: focus on the goal but be flexible. Adaptability can get you out of a pinch." Rick winked.

Trey smiled.

Rick rolled up the rags in the beach towel and shoved it all into the duffel. They walked casually back toward the large gray-mirrored building and to the left-side parking lot. There in the parking lot was the black van with blacked-out windows from the start of the trail. They hopped into it and sat in the second row of seats.

Rick handed Trey the now-familiar hood.

"Didn't I pass?" Trey frowned.

"Of course. Look, it's just SOP, for security. Yours and ours. I would like to go off the books a bit too, but we have rules that even I can't break."

Trey nodded and pulled it on.

"Hands," Rick said as he once again zip tied Trey's wrists. Then Rick shifted.

Click.

"Guys, we're green."

Through the hood, Trey could barely hear the muffled response.

"Roger, we're walking back now," the strange voice said.

"Roger," Rick said.

They sound like military—must have been watching us from a distance.

Trey tried to relax. Rick's presence oddly made him feel safe— even though he was bound and blindfolded. Being sensory deprived, Trey felt a tingle each time their bare legs would graze one another. Trey pushed his leg and connected with Rick's fully. Skin on skin. Calves, knees, thighs.

Rick pulled away.

Rick watched Trey lower his head slightly when he removed his leg. *Shit, dejected. Not yet, Tiger. Believe me, I just want to grab you and hold. Taste that ripe sweaty, tight ass. Fuck. Hold the line.*

Rick studied him. *Still, I wished I could do this my way. I should just hold him. He's finally starting to trust me. Doc M doesn't get it— 'cause he's never been the one bound in the blindfold.*

Trey heard the van side door slide shut and heard the two front doors open and close. Once again they were moving. After several minutes hooded in the van, Trey lost track of the time. He stopped wondering where they were. After four days of detainment, he'd surrendered. His panic about his job, coworkers, apartment, and family had subsided. In the darkness, he reached over and found Rick's arm. He held on to the muscular bicep and slowly laid his head on Rick's shoulder.

Rick did not pull away.

They rode in silence until the van stopped, the doors opened, and again Trey was guided once more.

Rick pulled off the hood. Trey's eyes adjusted, and he saw they were alone in the hallway of the bunker in front of the open door to his bunk room. The room had been cleaned, and there was a faint smell of disinfectant. He turned to Rick, who again pulled out his knife and freed his hands.

"Can I hit the head?" Trey asked.

"Yeah, we're just gonna get cleaned up, eat some lunch, and then I will explain the afternoon session."

Rick kicked off his shoes, and it was then that the word *we're* registered to Trey. He turned to the cot and saw two sets of towels, T-shirts, and sweats.

Oh my god . . . we're? We're going to shower. Together? Just be cool— don't freak out.

Rick peeled off his sweaty shorts and socks. Trey tried to mimic his casual manner. *Damn, his body is unbelievable. Hairy muscles. Stop staring.*

Rick grabbed a towel and tossed the other one to Trey.

They walked the few steps to the bathroom, hung their towels on the wall hooks, and entered the shower. After four days, Trey knew every inch of the three rooms. The warm spray splashed as Rick took the far right and turned on the water. Trey took his usual one on the far left.

"Toss me the soap?" Rick said.

Trey turned and handed him the bar.

They lathered and showered, stealing glances.

He is so hot. Stop looking. Is he looking at me too? Don't get hard. Don't. Get. Hard. Dead puppies, dead puppies, dead puppies.

After a few minutes, Rick turned off his shower and walked out.

Trey lingered and looked down at his half-erect muscle. *Phew. I don't think he saw it. Just hide it. No big deal.*

Trey turned off his shower and gave his face a final wipe. He opened his eyes to find Rick staring at him, then he looked away.

Was he checking me out?

Rick grabbed Trey's towel. Trey tried to scurry over to his towel, concealing his growing muscle. Rick's eyes widened.

"Well now . . . here." Rick tossed him his towel.

"Sorry, just daydreaming."

"Stop apologizing, Tiger." Rick raised his eyebrows. "Must have been a good dream."

Trey bit his lip. They dried off and dressed in the bunk room. With their new buzz cuts, the two nearly looked like brothers in the matching outfits.

"We need to re-dress your nose." Rick pulled out the black first-aid kit. "How does it feel?"

"Not too bad now."

"Ready? This may sting a bit." Rick pulled out the halved tampons and could not resist the obvious. "Looks like you popped your cherry."

Trey rolled his eyes.

"Seriously, you did great out there today," Rick said.

"Really?"

"Yes—even for a civ." Rick winked.

"Thanks."

Trey recoiled as he heard a woman's voice from the round white speaker in the ceiling above them.

"Rick, when you're ready."

Who's that? It was one thing to know in the theory that your every move was being watched, yet another thing to have that knowledge confirmed.

Rick pointed to the ceiling. "Like I said—we're not alone. Not yet."

Trey widened his eyes.

"Wait here for the buzz and then head over to the ops room." Rick walked to the door. "We have lunch for you. Phase three will begin after lunch."

"What's phase three?"

"Psych evaluation. You'll be fine. First, let's eat." Rick disappeared.

Well, I've passed phases one and two. I can do this. Trey was only alone with his thoughts for a moment.

Buzz.

He entered the room and again the configuration was different. The mats were gone, and the folding table was back but parallel and close to the mirror. There was only one large, odd chair at the table where there was a sandwich, turkey and Swiss cheese with mustard; a bag of SunChips; and instead of water, a large orange Gatorade.

Awesome. Distracted by the food, Trey barely noticed the seatbelt-like straps on the black chair. He quickly ate and was satiated for the first time in four days. The single bland energy bars and water for breakfast that morning had not been enough for his metabolism. He had lost weight and was quite hungry.

After eating, Trey sat quietly and studied the room again. The two cameras in opposite corners with tiny red lights, the two overhead air vents in the drop ceiling tiles—eighteen tiles if you counted the small quarter ones on the end of the rectangular room.

Trey looked back at the mirror and studied his new aerodynamic haircut. The blue-black bruising under each eye was almost symmetrical.

So, phase three's a pysch eval—as if this whole thing hasn't been psychotic. CIA. I wonder if this is the final test. Are they over there right now—checking me out?

"Did you guys save me something?" Rick asked as he entered to see the whole team eating.

"Cool haircut, handsome." Jeni motioned to the remaining sandwich on the back table.

"No roast beef? Did our budget get cut again, Claren?"

"You were right on, Chris. He did well," Claren said, ignoring Rick's comment.

"Here." Jeni offered her opened bag of SunChips to Rick. "That jump-rope routine is cool." She nodded to the lower left monitor. There on the screen the video was playing out the endurance and agility tests.

"Great intel, Chris and Rick." Claren held up the phase-two report. She shifted the team's focus. "But what about his temper?"

Rick shrugged and ate. No one seemed to volunteer an answer. After a moment, Chris broke the silence.

"I hear ya, but look at him." Chris pointed to Trey in the next room seated calmly. "Gay or not, I've seen grunts double his size cry like a baby and wash out after phase one alone." Chris paused. "And look at his skills." He then motioned to the small video screen replaying Trey on the p-bars. "If he's coachable, that could be his advantage. He's stronger than he looks."

Thanks, Chris, but are you kissing up to Claren to join our desk or are you for real defending this gay kid? Rick only nodded though, and kept eating.

Jeni placed her Diet Coke down. "I know what Doc M says about the tears and temper, but I think it just shows he's got heart. We've pushed him hard and he hasn't broken. Shit, now he likes you." She turned to Rick. "And trusts you—"

"What?" Rick muffled with a mouth full of food.

"We've all seen the footage. He's crushing on you, handsome, but his emotional markers are in range." Jeni turned back to Claren.

"And his physical markers are off the fucking charts," Darius added. "Right, Chris?"

Chris agreed, "Exactly. He's taken a lot of shit in the past four days, and look at him. Calm, trusting, we could even push him harder. Who knows? Doc M said we could be looking at a whole new kind of asset. A civ-5."

"Doc M can sometimes get ahead of himself. We've never put a civ through a phase three," Claren cautioned.

Rick devoured his sandwich as she spoke. He studied Claren as she intently focused on each member in the room and then paused intentionally. *Damn, she's good. She's pulling us together around Trey. She's always pushing us in new ways. Must be why Tibbins gave her this challenge. Getting him through phase three. And then what? We're nowhere near done yet.*

Claren turned back to Rick, who was now eating Jeni's SunChips.

"Can you handle more, Rick? He's gonna be a handful in an offsite."

Rick looked up at Trey through the mirror and then back at Claren. "What? We're not doing this at the Farm?"

"No. Too risky. We're dark. He's civ," Claren added. "Tibbins and I talked it through: has to be offsite, with constant tracking and surveillance."

"Where?"

"His apartment in Fair Oaks."

"Who?"

She pursed her lips. "You. With Jeni and Darius made so we'll have backup. But you'll move in with him at his apartment. He'll go back to work. You'll train him nights and weekends."

"Great. Now I'm a babysitter? And we're doing this *part-time*?"

"We'll all support you. Jeni and Darius are running phase three today. He'll meet them like I said so you'll get some breaks, or if this is all too much for you—"

"Bullshit, you know I can handle it."

"We're counting on that. Besides, it's only forty days."

"Only, huh?" Rick said. "Offsite?"

Claren nodded.

"What about his coaching?"

"He can coach Saturdays, but he'll have to cut back to two nights a week."

Rick shook his head.

"Do you have concerns about blurring the protocol or intimacy?"

"Hell no, it's just . . ."

"What then?"

"He's our first gay civ-5, we have a month, training is offsite, and the target's high-profile. That's all."

"Yes, it's high stakes and a bit unorthodox, but . . ." She looked around at her team. "I assembled the best team. We can do this, people—but I need everyone's A game. We follow the protocol, execute flawlessly, and hold the line."

If I say no, my ass is shipped back on the line in the field. Russia, Germany, or fucking Turkey. If I say yes, I can spend the better part of summer here in DC and stay close to him. Protect him.

"Fine, but I want cable, two bedrooms, and two baths, Claren," Rick shot back. "I'm serious. Not that rat hole you put me into in New York in '89."

Claren sighed. "Anything else?"

He turned back at the bruised young man staring blankly at them all through the glass.

"I got this, but I will pummel my new roommate if he messes with my junk."

Jeni rolled her eyes.

Claren nodded. "Don't have too much fun."

Geez, not subtle. But Rick nodded too.

"I'll have the apartment set up later today—starting in the one bedroom, Rick."

"You already got an ops team at my apartment in Silver Spring as we speak—don't you?"

"No, by now they're dropping your stuff off at his apartment in Fair Oaks." She lowered her voice to a more serious tone. "You can break the news to him tomorrow morning once you've assessed the setup tonight. But in the meantime." She stood. "We're ready for phase three."

CHAPTER 26
PHASE THREE

T rey was startled to see a tall, muscular African-American man enter into the ops room without saying a word.

"Hello," Trey offered.

The man ignored him and walked to the table, carrying a square black suitcase that he set on the end of the table with a thud. An Asian-American woman entered behind him and immediately approached Trey with a smile.

"Hi, I'm Special Officer Jeni Yoon, and this badass is Special Officer Darius Morris." She motioned to the tall officer looking sternly at Trey.

"Hi, I'm Trey Carter." He stood and extended his hand to Jeni, who had a surprisingly strong grip. Then he turned to Darius, who was busy with setting up the polygraph. Darius ignored Trey's hand and stared down from his 6'4" hulking frame.

"Sit down, recruit," he barked.

Trey immediately sat.

Jeni set up the two folding chairs she'd carried into the room and sat them on either side of him.

"Congratulations, Trey. You've passed phases one and two. So this is phase three. We're going to hook you up, strap you in, and ask a few questions. Rick and the team are over there." She pointed to the mirror.

Trey nodded and relaxed a bit when she mentioned Rick was watching from the next room.

"Have you taken one of these before? A polygraph?"

"No, ma'am."

"Okay. Well, there's no right or wrong answer. You just need to remain calm and answer the questions truthfully. Don't over think, okay?"

"Yes, ma'am."

Jeni smiled and stood. "Now, arms up."

She tugged Trey's shirt off and tossed it on the floor, then buckled him into the chair with two shoulder straps, a chest strap, two forearm straps, and one lap belt. Finally, she bent down and clasped both leg restraints tightly at the ankles.

"I can't move—"

"That's the idea. Stay calm, Trey." She pulled a set of wires from the case. "Now these might be a bit cold."

"What are they?"

"Sensing nodes." She started applying the nodes to his chest, three of his fingers, and right wrist. After several minutes of adjusting and reapplying the nodes, she added, "All righty, just two more." She leaned over him and gently placed the final two nodes on either side of his temples. She smiled inches from his face and adjusted the wires.

"Double shiners. Damn, Rick, why didn't you just shoot the poor boy?" she said toward the mirror and then turned back to Trey and gave a slight wink.

Trey grinned.

Darius interrupted, brusque and cool, as though he were reading from a technical manual. "You need to sit still during the test, recruit. Both Officer Yoon and I will be asking questions. There are no right or wrong answers. Answer each question in a clear, audible voice. If you don't understand, tell us so that we can rephrase or repeat it. Do you understand?"

Trey nodded.

"Clear, audible voice," Darius repeated flatly. "Do you understand?"

"Yes, sir."

Jeni cleaned up the lunch wrappers and the empty bottle of Gatorade, then took her seat next to Trey.

I can barely move. Rick, are you really over there?

Trey looked in the mirror that they all three now faced. He caught Jeni's eye. She smiled. "You'll be fine." But the restraints, sensing nodes, unknown audience behind the mirror, and Darius's scowl said otherwise.

This is does not feel fine.

Claren switched on the microphone feeding both Darius's and Jeni's earpieces.

"Let's begin."

"Today is Tuesday, June 9, 1992. I am Officer Darius Morris, and with me is Officer Jeni Yoon. We are here in an undisclosed location within the District of Columbia for the phase-three assessment of this civilian voluntary recruit for classification level five." He stopped and turned to Trey. "Please state your full name."

"Trey Alan Carter."

"The recruit is a twenty-one-year-old male residing currently in Fairfax, Virginia. Correct?

"Yes, sir."

Darius stared into Trey's eyes via the large mirror in front of them as he recited the instructions. "Please do not attempt to raise your right hand at any time during this session. Remember to breathe and simply provide clear audible answers. Do you understand?"

"Yes, sir."

"We start easy then dial it up on my cue," Claren said. "Jeni, you start."

Jeni nodded slightly. "Where were you born, Trey?"

"Atlanta."

"Be more specific," Darius snapped.

What is the point of this? You already know my life history. Just stay calm—get through it.

"Georgia Baptist Hospital in Atlanta, Georgia."

"Good," Jeni assured. "We're going to do a series of questions. Let's start with your education. Where did you attend elementary?"

"Atherton in Decatur."

"Middle—"

"Forest Lawn Christian Day School for grades 4 through 11."

"Oh, okay. Then your last two years of high school?"

"Boarding school—Pensacola Christian High in Florida."

"And college?"

"Pensacola Christian College for my freshman year, then I transferred to Liberty University in Lynchburg, Virginia."

"Jerry fucking Falwell's school," Darius barked.

"Yes, sir."

"So you stated that you grew up in Atlanta, but then your address was Decatur. Can you explain?" Darius pressed.

"Yes, sir. Decatur is just a suburb next to Stone Mountain."

"In the Atlanta area?" Jeni said.

"Yes, ma'am." *You've already asked me that like five times—geez.*

The questions were mundane and repetitive. After an hour, just when Trey had been lulled into believing the entire test would be annoying and easy, like a sniper, Darius interjected from nowhere, "Why were you naked at a public rooftop pool on Saturday, June 6, 1992?"

"What?"

Darius repeated his question.

"I was swimming."

"Why were you there?"

"Friends invited me. They left. I stayed—met that guy."

"But why were you naked?" Darius asked sternly.

"No one was around."

"So, you just removed your clothing?"

"Sir, he started it, the skinny-dip."

"I didn't ask *who* started it," Darius said. "Why did *you* remove *your* clothing?"

"He dared me. I shouldn't have but I did."

"Is that when you decided to sexually assault him?"

Sexual assault? Oh my god—they're gonna charge me. This isn't a psych evaluation. This is an interrogation. Panic contorted his face and the straps seemed to grow tighter.

"Answer me, civ. Why did you sexually assault him?"

"I—I thought it was mutual."

"Mutual? Did he grab you?"

"No."

"Why did you think it was going to be mutual, Trey?" Jeni asked.

"I don't know, ma'am. He was staring at me and—"

Darius interrupted, "Are you a homosexual?"

Trey nodded.

Darius cleared his throat pointedly.

"Sorry—yes, sir."

"So as a homosexual, some would simply say gay, right?" Jeni asked.

"Yes, ma'am."

"Did you think that the undercover intelligence officer that you referred to as 'Todd' was also a homosexual?" Darius asked.

"Yes. Wait, Todd?"

"And did you—"

"You set me up?" *Oh my god, I knew it.*

"That's our Tiger—keep your foot on the gas," Claren instructed to both Jeni and Darius. "Press in, Darius."

"Did you think he was also a homosexual?" Darius repeated.

"You set me up. You set me up. Why?" Trey snapped.

Darius barked, "You do not ask the questions here. We do! Am I clear?"

Trey did not answer.

"Heart rate is 126 and climbing. Goal is 180," Claren whispered.

"AM. I. CLEAR?" Darius shouted.

Trey shook the chair and wrestled wildly against the restraints.

"Okay, good cop. Nice but not too nice," Claren said.

"Trey, just answer the question. Did you think Todd was also gay?" Jeni placed her hand on his shoulder.

"Yes, I guess so," Trey shouted. "I don't know—besides, you—"

"Do you think that everyone is gay?" Darius hissed.

"What? No."

"Then why did you think the officer was a *homosexual*?"

"I don't know. I had drank a few beers, and wasn't sure—"

Jeni interjected, "So you were a bit buzzed and you thought what? This guy's hot? We're alone? Naked?"

"Yes, ma'am, no. Well, sort of . . . I misread the situation."

"Do you think I'm a homosexual?" Darius said flatly.

"No, sir."

"How do you know that to be true?" Darius retorted.

"You just know. It's hard to explain to straight people."

"Hmm. Which is the very reason we need him," Chris said.

"Exactly," Claren replied.

"So you modify the charging session to harness trust?" Chris asked.

"Doc M has refined the charging session to achieve the breaking—"

"To heighten the TB?"

Claren nodded.

"TB?" John asked.

"Traumatic Bonding," Chris answered.

"Wow, so the restraint chair, lighting, tone, good cop, bad cop, temperature, the monitors—every single element is to what? Break him?" John further asked.

"Yes, Doc M outlines every detail," she said.

"But it's never been applied to a civ," Rick interrupted.

"No?" Chris asked.

Claren glanced back at Rick. "No, it hasn't, but it's based upon hours of research and application with our team."

"So, you've been through this?" Chris turned to Rick.

Rick clenched his jaw and nodded slowly.

"Shit," John blurted with wide eyes.

Claren turned back to the mirror. "Okay, we're at forty-eight minutes and his heart rate is 132. Let's turn it up, dig back into McGuire, and go legal."

"You work in the Commonwealth of Virginia, correct?" Darius asked Trey.

"Yes, sir."

"Are you aware that you can and likely will be terminated from your employment if American Seniors is made aware of your homosexual orientation?"

"I don't know. Yes, sir, I guess."

"Have you told them that you are gay?" Jeni asked.

"No, ma'am," Trey said.

"Then you lied on your interview. There's no way that the leader of the GOP conservatives, Robert fucking McGuire would have knowingly hired a *homosexual*. No way." Darius gave a disgusted snort. "You knew this as well as I do. So you lied. Didn't you, Trey?"

"Yes, I guess, but . . ." Trey said, his eyes brimming suddenly with tears.

I fucking hate this. Look at the kid—he is terrified. I bet I could have recruited him without all this psycho bullshit. Still not as bad as mine back in '81 but pressing the fear factor. Rick got up from the table and went to the small refrigerator in the darkest corner of the monitoring room. *He already trusts me—we don't need this extra shit.* He grabbed a water bottle and paced back and forth for several minutes. *What if this breaks him? Really breaks him. How am I supposed to rebuild him if he truly snaps? Like that guy in '87—what was his name? Alfonso—he fucking killed himself.*

The Agency had experimented with many techniques for breaking recruits: sleep deprivation, food deprivation, sunlight deprivation, repeated emotional highs and lows. Restraint. Limited freedom. Clothing. Nakedness. The analysis of the data indicated that the lack of control enabled the protocol to have its greatest impact.

This kid is not *military. What are we doing here, Claren? And on a condensed timeline. We usually spread this over nine or ten days. We're barely at four.* Rick stopped his pacing. He turned to Claren to see her looking back at him.

"It's SOP, I know, but—" Rick held up his hand.

She raised her eyebrows.

"Alfonso."

Claren nodded slightly and turned back to the window.

Trey squirmed in the confines of the straps. "May I please use the restroom—"

"Not this time. You asked the same thing that first night. I was sitting right over there." Darius nodded to the mirror.

"Please, I got to go—"

"This is an active interrogation. I don't give a good goddamn if you piss yourself right here, right now, faggot." Darius leaned in. "I will release you when we're done!"

Trey grimaced and started violently shaking the heavy restraint chair to no avail.

"Keep going," Claren whispered.

"When were you going to tell your parents about your *sexual orientation*?" Darius continued.

"Aargh!" Trey yelled and struggled against the straps.

Jeni interjected on cue, placing her hand on Trey's left forearm above the tight restraint. "We have a ways to go, Trey, if you have to—just let it go. We'll clean it up later. Focus."

She then stood and began to pace behind the recruit.

Claren whispered, "Good, Jeni. Pull back."

You better be right, Carlos—this civ better be fine after this. Jesus, she and Rick think I'm some callous bitch. Like I don't see Alfonso's face in my own regrets? She breathed deeply. *Stay calm, stay focused. You set the tone—you set the tone. Calm.* The stress visible on her only two gay officers had not been lost on her— "Darius, he's bleeding again, hold back until his bladder releases. Then go for it. Ask about Rick."

He motioned to the mirror. "Recruit, you're bleeding on my chair."

Trey faced the mirror as blood seeped from his left nostril and dripped to his chin and chest.

"Must be hard to breathe with all that stuff up your nose. Huh?" Jeni said from behind.

Trey nodded slowly.

"Now that we have your attention, tell me." Darius cleared his throat. "What do you think of Officer Morgan?"

"What?"

"Do you find Officer Morgan attractive?"

Trey shrugged.

"No? You don't find him *handsome*?" Darius asked mockingly.

Trey stared at the mirror. Then he closed his eyes and renewed his struggles against the straps.

"Answer me." Darius stood and stepped back from the table beside Jeni.

"What!?"

Good, we have our pressure point. Claren interjected, "Repeat and press harder."

Darius barked, "Do. You. Find. Officer Morgan. Attractive?"

"Yes!" Trey squeezed his eyes shut.

"Do you think he's a homosexual?"

A look of fear passed over Trey's face.

Darius repeated, "Do *you think* Officer Morgan is a *homosexual*?"

"I don't know—I don't—"

"Oh, I think you do."

"Nooo!"

"Do you beat off to him? Fantasize about him?"

"NOOO!"

"I bet that's why he beat the shit out you, faggot."

"Aahhhh!!" Trey writhed, jerking back and forth. The cotton in both nostrils dislodged, sending blood down his chin, neck, and chest.

"Did you try and grope him?"

"Nooo!" Trey spasmed as his bladder released, drenching his sweatpants and the chair.

"Faggot, I bet you tried to sexually assault him too."

Trey writhed and yanked at the restraints.

"I have seen enough, you piece-of-shit faggot. And you think Officer Morgan wants you on his team? Our team?"

Trey convulsed and shook violently.

"Answer me, faggot!"

"No!"

"Oh, so you do want him."

"No!"

"He's at 180. Last push, but make him see it," Claren said.

Darius grabbed Trey's hair and raised his face toward the mirror. "I bet you dream about him. Don'tcha? You want him to fuck you?"

Trey screamed incoherently. He lowered his head, chin to chest, and sobbed.

Darius turned to Jeni, who shook her head slightly. He stood took two steps from Trey.

"Standby, final counts are registering," Claren instructed and paused before adding one final word.

"Done."

Rick walked briskly to the monitoring-room door but glanced back at the glass. He grimaced at Trey's swollen eyes, blood, and shivering soaked body now slumped in the restraint chair. *Fucking horrific—for what? Force him into submission for what—for them?*

A minute later, he was alone in the quiet bathroom, staring at the hot water pouring over the white washcloth as he gripped both sides of the sink. *What are you doing? This shit's real—he'll remember that for the rest of this life.* Rick shut his eyes but still saw Trey writhing. He squeezed his grip tighter as his legs weakened.

"Faaaggot!!!" The screams echoed louder. Rain pelted his face as one by one his platoon took turns screaming and hitting him. Then like Trey, he was naked in a room, strapped to a chair cutting into his arms as the screams grew louder.

Gunfire. Darkness. Screams.

"Rick, Rick?" Claren's voice through his earpiece forced him from his flashbacks.

"Yeah?"

"Are you ready?"

"Yeah."

He opened his eyes— *Shit.* The water was overflowing the small sink. He shut off the valve and wrung out the cloth. *Hold the fucking line. Don't go back there. Leave it.* Rick saw the water forming in his eyes. He turned the faucet back on and splashed his face.

He's not you. But that's just it—he's civ. What if we took this too far? What if he's broken. Fuck—how am I gonna do this?

Rick grabbed a towel and tried to wipe away his guilt, his memory, and his growing feelings.

He's a job. Hold the line.

Claren flipped the switch and whispered, "Now, Jeni."

Jeni step forward and placed her hand on Trey's shoulder. She stared into the mirror seeming to wait for his eyes to rise to meet hers.

Good instincts, Jeni. Claren stared at the young man.

Slowly, Trey raised his head.

"Still want to join our team, Trey?"

Trey had a vacant look.

"Now you, Darius—gently," Claren instructed. Darius stepped forward and in a completely different tone from the last two hours, asked, "You're okay, Trey?"

Trey still did not speak but breathed deeply.

"No regression—he seems calm. You're done," Claren whispered. "Come on back—Rick's ready."

Darius headed to the door. Jeni paused and squeezed Trey's shoulder. She gave a slight smile, then left the room.

Claren watched Trey isolated now in the ops room. He stared at the door, then back to the mirror. "Rick, he's at 110. I think we're good. You're green."

Rick entered. Trey's posture tightened.

"Easy, easy. Give him his space," Claren guided.

Rick did not speak as he approached Trey. He held up the washcloth.

Trey nodded but again his tears reappeared. Rick gently wiped his face, neck, and chest. He then began detaching each of the nodes from his head, chest, and arms. Rick glanced at the mirror.

"Okay, here we go. Be careful—remember work from the bottom up," she said.

Rick knelt down and began to unbuckle each restraint from Trey's ankles, then his legs.

He skipped the lap belt and advanced to the buckles on Trey's arms, chest, and shoulders, both rooms remained eerily quiet.

"Good, last one. Be careful, be ready," Claren cautioned.

All right, here goes. Rick unbuckled the two remaining lap belts that crisscrossed. Rick stood and took a step back, expecting Trey to rouse, speak or stand up. The young man remained motionless—still staring downward.

Nothing. Shit, I knew it—they took this took far. They don't know how this feels—but I do.

"Trey?"

Trey turned and caught Rick's eyes, then lowered his head.

"It's okay—"

"I'm sorry, I'm so sorry," escaped Trey's lips as new tears trickled down his cheeks.

"Shh, come on. Let's stand up." Rick eased him up from the chair. They stood in silence for a moment. *I know what this feels like.* Suddenly, Rick pulled Trey into his embrace.

"Rick?" Claren cautioned but stopped.

He held him tightly for several minutes until Trey pulled back and faced Rick.

"I failed, didn't I?"

"No." Rick slid both his hands to Trey's shoulders.

"But I—"

"You made it through."

"But—"

"No buts, I've seen many guys flunk."

Trey's eyes narrowed.

"Not again." Rick squeezed his shoulders. "Not on my watch. You're on *my* team." Rick's voice cracked.

"Really?"

"My team."

Trey hugged Rick.

"My team," Rick repeated.

Trey sank deeper into Rick's embrace.

"I'll be damned—a bit off-script—but you got him," Claren whispered.

Rick held him for a moment and then asked, "Let's get you cleaned up?"

Trey nodded.

They walked arm in arm out of the ops room.

In the bathroom, Trey stripped off his wet, bloody clothes as Rick started the shower for him.

"I'll go grab you a towel. Be right back. You going to be okay?"

Trey only nodded but stepped into the shower.

Rick returned to the monitoring room, and Jeni handed him a towel along with the black first aid kit. She did not speak but nodded to him. He glanced at the team, and Chris gave him a thumbs-up.

Rick turned to Claren. "I—I went with my gut—"

"Stick to the routine, but—he leaned in. Doc M will be impressed. You got this?" Claren asked.

"Yeah." Rick left the room and quickly re-entered the bathroom. He silently watched Trey finish his shower. *You're gonna be okay—if I have my way, you're gonna be better than okay. I'm going to teach you everything I know. Stuff I wished that I had known. Nothing is going to hurt you. Not on my watch.*

Trey turned off the shower. Rick appeared in the opening.

"Here you go." Rick handed him the towel.

As Trey dried himself, Rick sensed his unease.

"You okay?"

"I guess—why?"

"It's part of it."

"You went through that?"

Rick nodded.

"So why me? Y'all picked me. Why?"

"Limited intel, Rick. Stick to the—" Claren tried to caution.

Rick pulled out his earpiece and turned on the shower closest to him. He turned back to Trey. "Yes, we picked you. Look, I know this won't make sense now, but, Trey, if you just trust—I will get you through this."

"So, you think I can do this—"

"I know you can."

Trey wrapped the towel around his waist, then shook his head. "I don't get it?"

"You don't have to—it's confusing as hell." Rick returned his earpiece and turned off the shower. "I know how you feel."

"Really?"

"Yup. And I know you have questions, but let's talk about it later after you rest—when we're alone." Rick raised glanced upward to the speaker overhead.

Trey nodded.

Rick smiled and unzipped the kit. "Now, let me take care of that nose again."

For the third time in twenty-four hours, he re-dressed Trey's injured nose. The time was only 1700, but in the basement without clocks, Trey did not know. The emotional drain was overwhelming, and now he only wanted to rest. Rick helped him to his bunk and once again helped him sleep with a syringe.

Trey lay quietly and closed his eyes. He was already asleep when Rick kissed his forehead.

Sleep well, Tiger. Rick turned out the bunk room lights and walked back to the monitoring room. *Geez, I'm covered in his blood.*

The team stopped talking as he entered. Rick ignored them as he rooted through his duffel for a fresh T-shirt. He stripped off his shirt and dropped it along with Trey's soiled clothes to the floor. As he pulled on the clean shirt, he was grateful to catch Jeni slipping across and snagging the dirty clothes. She threw him a small smile as she shoved them into their soiled laundry bag.

"Is he okay?" she asked in a low voice.

"Yeah, I think so." Rick turned to Claren. "Is Doc M on his way?"

"Yes, he's ten minutes out," Claren said.

Rick watched as the others cleaned up the workstations. *Busy work—like straightening up makes all this normal.*

"Want to grab a beer?" Jeni asked.

Rick shook his head. "I don't know—I think I'm good. I need to sit with this and get settled into the new place."

"Okay then, fine, asshole. Kristin and I are knocking on your door at 19:00 sharp with pizza and beer. We'll help christen your new digs."

He forced a grin. She smiled.

But little of the unease in his chest dissipated. "I'm not good at asking for help—"

"No shit, handsome. Like that time in Tel Aviv?"

"You know me—"

"Better than you think."

He smiled. "Thank you. What the hell would I do without you? No, I don't want to be alone at that kid's apartment tonight."

Claren interrupted the banter in the room. "Huddle up, people."

The group stopped and turned to form a circle.

"What we do is hard. What we do is tough. What we do is sometimes ugly. Exposing and using raw emotions requires discipline. Anger. Lust. Fear. Terror. These are not simple. No, there is nothing simple about them. Nothing simple about what we are called to do. Our training supports our assignments but that is only half of it. In the moment, it requires us to do one thing—act decisively. On point. But it doesn't mean we aren't human. We feel things even if we can't act on them." She paused and glanced around the circle. "Are we using that civ—bending the rules? Yes. But our engineer doesn't play by the rules. There are no rules to a rogue regime getting their hands on nukes. So, yes our tactics may seem unorthodox. But remember, what we do is always in the gray. Never the easy black-and-white. And in the gray, we save lives."

Claren cleared her throat and took a deep breath.

"I know this has been an intense four days, not just for him. Us too. We still have a long way to go in getting him ready."

Claren was careful to lock eyes with each team member. "We are a team. Each one of you matters in this challenging assignment—forty-five days for a civ-5. Some even said impossible. But here we are intake completed. Now we train as one team, one assignment."

Everyone nodded as she again looked around—even Rick.

"Darius, you're on duty for the night. Right?" Claren asked.

"Yes."

"Good. Support team is here at 1800. But as for the rest of you, get out of here. Rest up. Tomorrow, we take it to the field."

PART TWO:
TRAINING

The purpose of training is to tighten up the slack, toughen the body, and polish the spirit.
— Morihei Ueshiba

CHAPTER 27
ROOMMATES

An hour later Rick found the white envelope under the new welcome mat at 4224 Hunt Club Circle, apartment 813. He turned the key and the alarm beat rhythmically as he punched in the code he had been given. He turned on the lights to reveal a modest, post-college apartment with the basics.

On the kitchen counter was a six-pack of Sam Adams lager, his favorite, along with a note.

Welcome home, Rick! - CEJ

Huh, not Claren's handwriting—bet it's Jennifer—still though, nice touch. He placed the six-pack in the refrigerator and walked through the apartment, taking inventory: Football and basketball trophies from high school were on Trey's small dresser in the bedroom. A large press photo with Trey surrounded by his cheerleading teammates hung on the bedroom wall. He walked back to the living room, where there was one small, lonely plant along with a TV in a simple oak cabinet, one couch, and a matching chair covered in southwestern flame stitch with overstuffed pillows. *Not great but not too bad.*

He returned to the bedroom and spotted a leather-bound book on the small bedside. Geez, a Bible by the bed. King James Version. *God, Trey, what you must have endured growing up in a cult.* He picked it up and ran his finger over the engraving of gold block letters . . . *Trey Alan Carter.* He flipped open the first page and saw a handwritten dedication of sorts: *This book will keep you from sin, or sin will keep you from this book. Love, Mom and Dad.*

Whoa! Jesus, is that passive-aggressive or what?

The whole apartment was basically three rooms: a kitchen/living room with a large gray island and two stools separating the space;

bedroom with queen-size bed, dresser, and nightstand; and bathroom with a large walk-in closet—*and there's my shit. No, please feel free to break into my condo and pack up my stuff.* Rick left his clothes now hanging on the right side and walked back to the kitchen with a small pantry and tucked in the left side a stacked washer and dryer. *Well, at least no need for a laundromat.*

Rick returned to the three black duffels in the middle of the living room and opened the first bag. *Let's see what kind of equipment we get to play with.* First up was a simple surveillance kit. Rick then unpacked and assembled a set of bugs, which were programmable by remote. *Geez, three listening bugs for a tiny apartment—Doc M always overdoing it. Fine, in the kitchen, living room, and bedroom. But not the bathroom—at least we'll have privacy there.* He installed phone devices on both the wall-mounted one in the kitchen and the bedside phone.

After completing the equipment setup, he walked back to the kitchen and surveyed the whole. *Well, it's small but clean—at least there's a pool and a gym to take advantage of while the kid's at work.*

Rick packed up the empty duffels and additional equipment. He packed them away in the trunk of his BMW parked directly adjacent in the covered parking deck. *1833—Jeni and Kristin will be here in twenty—damn, why do lesbians always have to be on time. Still have time for a cat nap.* He hopped on the couch, turned on CNN for background noise, and closed his eyes.

"How are you going to tell Trey?" Jeni asked.

They stood around the island eating pizza and having a few beers. She'd come alone, as Kristin, her girlfriend of three years, was stuck home grading papers. Rick was grateful for the company, and the food.

"I don't know. This could either go really well, or be an assignment from Hell," Rick said. "I was thinking that I was just gonna tell him straight up, first thing, but then—"

"Offsite, out of the Hole?" Jeni finished his thought.

He nodded.

"It's risky but stronger. Really, what's the risk? If he redshirts, you go back to the Hole and reassess. But if he's green . . . you got him."

Rick nodded. *Redshirt* was their term for unprepared recruits that needed more time to be ready for the "varsity" team.

They talked as he showed her around. They walked the grounds of the apartment complex. To an untrained eye, they appeared a couple looking at the amenities, but essential to their work was verifying strategic drops and evac routes. Tactics and training that Rick would lead Trey through over the next month.

"Shit." Jeni glanced at her watch.

"What time is it?"

"2200." Jeni punched his arm and winked. "Later, handsome!"

"Thanks again for the pizza."

Rick closed the door. He brushed his teeth and glanced at his folder for training. *Not tonight—I'm exhausted.* Rick grabbed his pillow from one of the duffels, along with his New England Patriots throw blanket. He lay down on the couch.

Geez, it's too quiet out here in the burbs.

He flicked on CNN. *Forty fucking days, a civ and stateside—guess this is a test for me too.*

CHAPTER 28
EXIT

Wednesday, June 10, 1992
23rd & M Streets NW - Washington, DC

"I will survive!" Rick sang aloud as he drove, blasting Gloria Gaynor's hit song. He pulled into the parking deck and walked the long hall to the service door. When he swiped his ID card to enter the Hole, Doc M was sipping his coffee and typing on his laptop.

The rookie officer, John, was at the monitor table making some notes. "Morning, Rick."

Doc M glanced up and offered a silent greeting.

"Morning, guys. How's our boy?" Rick poured a cup of coffee.

"Still sleeping."

"How was last night?"

"Fine, he only got up once and peed at 0315," John reported. "But on his way back he stopped and stared at the ops door for like three or four minutes. I thought he might regress, but he crawled back in bed at 0322."

"Last night was rather intense." Doc M looked at Rick. "If he regressed, we'd have to delay the exit but it'd be completely understandable."

"Good thing he didn't," Rick said.

"Yes, I am quite pleased at his progress so far."

"Yeah? That's good." Rick sipped his coffee. "Anything else?"

"When he got back in bed, he, uh . . . relieved some stress." John grinned.

Rick widened his eyes, but before he could add a joke, Doc M returned the moment to a more serious tone.

"It's perfectly healthy, gentlemen. In this situation, it's actually a positive marker." He peered at Rick over his reading glasses. "Are you ready for the offsite and today's exit?"

"Yeah, Jeni came over last night. We're ready. It's a small setup, but the layout works. Several concealed drop spots. I feel good about it," Rick said confidently.

"Good." Doc M gave a quick smile and returned to his laptop.

What's that supposed to mean? You're always analyzing shit. Rick grabbed a chair in the back of the room as one by one the team trickled in. By 0700, they were assembled and tightly jammed into the small monitoring room.

Claren conferred with Doc M, then interrupted the morning banter. "Huddle up." She reviewed the planned final session at the Hole and their coordinated exit. "Darius and Chris will drive Rick and our civ-5 in our ops transport. John and Jeni, you'll follow in Rick's car. Doc M and I will hold back and return to campus." Director Tibbins had called them to a meeting in Langley. "We do this by the book, which means you'll be back to the Nest in Fair Oaks by noon."

The Nest . . . his apartment—always with the jargon. Rick turned to Jeni, whose eyes were clearly urging him to share his idea with Claren.

"Any questions?" Claren concluded.

"Yeah, Jeni and I had a thought last night."

Claren turned to Rick.

"What if I take him offsite first . . . for breakfast. We green-light him in a more relaxed, neutral setting?"

Claren pursed her lip. "Where?"

"There's a cop diner in Southeast, Dootsie's. It'll be quiet on a Wednesday. Darius and Jeni could sit a few booths away. It would give me a chance to lay out the offsite, the Nest, our training."

"What's your strategy?"

"Give him a bit of choice in all this." Rick shrugged.

Doc M raised his eyebrows and shot a glance at Claren.

"Choice." She tilted her head. "The risk is minimal. If he regresses, you'll fake an arrest and come back here?"

Rick nodded.

"A perceived choice would be good. It could deepen the bond," Doc M said.

Perceived, huh? Rick bit his tongue.

"I like it. Good recommendation. All right. Dootsie's," Claren said.

Immediately, the team rearranged the details of the exit.

"I have an asset in the DCPD. Want me to call her and set up the diner in advance with just the basics?" Jeni asked.

"Yes—minimal intel, though," Claren said. "Okay. Chris and John will support the exit but stay back here on standby in case Trey regresses. Rick, you drive him in your car. We'll monitor from here. Jeni and Darius will follow in the support van. Everyone good, then." Claren paused and turned to Rick. "Time for you to wake our sleeping prince."

Damn, she's good, Rick thought as he grabbed the clothes he'd brought from Trey's apartment. He started to walk to the bunk room. She must have known her fairy-tale reference would land with him. *Wake him gently . . . maybe a kiss.*

Rick propped open the bunk room door to allow in the light to cascade over the muscular young man asleep. *Damn, he looks good. Hope this goes well—we've got a lot riding on you, Trey.*

"Good morning, Trey."

Trey stirred slightly, but before he could lunge to attention, Rick had already crossed the room and placed a palm on his chest.

Rick smiled and pressed a firm kiss to Trey's forehead. "Want to go grab some coffee, Tiger?"

Trey hesitated. After a moment, he stretched and yawned, enjoying the simple courtesy of being awakened and talked to like a human being.

"Yes, sir!"

Jeni and Darius broke away from the monitors to fist-bump.

"Yes!" Jeni exclaimed.

Everyone in the room was smiling and taking deep breaths at the positive marker.

He seems different. Nicer. Trey got up.

Rick turned on the lights.

Trey squinted and tried to shake off his grogginess.

"Stop giving everyone a show. Here." Rick tossed a towel to him.

Trey wrapped his waist. "No push-ups?"

"No, you can grab a shower. But first let's see that nose," Rick said, inspecting the dressing.

Trey leaned his head back as Rick unpacked his nose and removed the bandage.

"Not bad, not bad. Now get cleaned up so we can get out of here." Rick playfully slapped Trey's butt as he hurried to the shower.

When he got back, clothes were laying out on the cot. *That's my stuff. I'm for real getting outta here finally.*

"I hope you don't mind, but I used your keys and brought you some things from home."

"No. That's awesome. Thanks, Officer Morgan."

"How about just Rick?" Claren whispered into Rick's earpiece.

"From now on—" Rick smiled and put out his right hand. "—how about just Rick?"

The effect was instant. On the monitors the team saw Trey grab Rick's hand and lean in for a bro-hug.

"So far, so good." Jeni turned to Darius.

"Yeah but the hood—"

"What about it?" John asked. Darius turned to Doc M.

"Articles of clothing, smells, and noises can remind recruits of our intake, their time here—all can be triggers for regression," Doc M said.

"How do we avoid the hood triggering him?"

"Rick will need to explain—maybe even provide choice," Darius said and pointed to the monitor. "But we're about to find out."

Rick had rehearsed in his mind how he would present the hood this morning, which he'd tucked in his back pocket. Trey had pulled on his jeans, green polo, and was slipping on his docksides when Rick started his final speech in the bunker.

"Look, I want you to hear me when I tell you that *everyone* in that room believes in you. We all know firsthand how tough these past five days have been, but here you are, Trey. This part's done, but we've a lot of work ahead of us. Little over a month. But this—" Rick motioned around the room "—this part is done for now. There's only one small thing left. I know you hate it, and it sucks, but we have to . . . SOP."

Trey winced. "The hood, right?"

Rick nodded. "But no restraints."

The recruit lowered his head slightly but then stood up with an outstretched hand as Rick handed him the dreaded hood.

"All right, but I am ordering a *large* coffee."

"Large coffee it is." Rick grinned.

Trey slipped on the hood, and Rick guided him through the short walk out of the Hole.

In the darkness, as Trey walked through the monitoring room, he felt several pats on his back along with a few muffled voices as his new team encouraged him.

"Good job, Trey."

"You got this."

"Great job, little man."

So many unseen voices had the intended effect. *Whoa, Rick wasn't kidding—there's a whole group behind this. I got through it. I'm not alone . . . I'm on a team again—like my squad in college.*

As Rick guided Trey into a car, he smelled leather, then heard Rick get in the driver's seat.

Varoom.

Trey heard the engine rev. "Is this your car, Rick?"

"Yeah."

"It's nice."

"You're hooded, Trey."

"Well, it smells nice."

Suddenly, the tape deck blared, "I will survive!"

"Shit." Rick quickly shut off the tape.

Trey burst out laughing.

"What, you don't like Gloria Gaynor?"

"No, she's great—it's just . . ."

"Just what?"

"Don't get mad."

"I won't. What?"

"'I Will Survive'—kinda the gay national anthem."

"Ha! I guess it is—that stays between us, Trey."

"Okay, but can we please listen to it? It's awesome!"

"Sure, why not."

Gloria Gaynor sang their anthem as Trey sat in darkness and hummed along. He sensed that they drove for several miles until suddenly Rick stopped and turned off the car.

"Wait here."

The car door shut and Rick did not return for several minutes. *Ummm . . . I'm hooded and don't have a clue where I am—should I peek?* Then Trey felt his passenger door open, and Rick took his arm as he stepped out into what smelled like fresh air. *We're outside.*

Rick removed the hood and sunlight blurred Trey's vision. As it dissipated, hulking iron statues and a massive flag came into focus.

Iwo Jima.

They stood in silence in front of the sacred site with its four US Marines representing thousands of fallen heroes as they anchored Arlington National Cemetery.

No one's here but us. Can the CIA empty out parks?

The only sounds were the chirping of birds and flapping of the large flag waving high overhead.

"Trey, I'm not going to apologize for our tactics—your intake, but I do want to explain some things."

Trey shrugged.

"I'm not going to bullshit you—like they bullshitted me. Some stuff I have to do by the book but where I can—I'm gonna do it my way."

Trey nodded. *Don't talk—let him get this out.*

"I asked my director if I could offer you a choice. But first, I wanted to bring you here. Tell you some things. I'm gay too, Trey."

Trey again nodded.

"For guys like us—we don't get to serve out in the open. Not like these Marines or the ones I served with as my brothers." Rick never turned his gaze from the monument. "I didn't get to really make a choice, Trey. When my platoon found a private note— Well, they figured it out. We were in Okinawa. It was pure hell. My commander marched me back and forth nearly all night in front of the entire squadron—in the rain. They spit on me. Called me faggot. Nearly beat the shit out of me."

Rick paused.

"Then what?"

"My ass was on the next C-130 cargo flight back Stateside. Threw me in the brig. Three days. They were going to court-martial me. Sentence me to three to five."

"I'm sorry."

"My director bailed me out and made me an offer—kinda like the one we made to you."

"Get outed?"

"Yup, lose everything. My career, maybe jail time. Or . . . the Agency."

"And you chose this?"

Rick turned to Trey. "Yes. Guys like us, if we get to serve at all— it's different, in the shadows. Our government thinks we're weak, that we can't serve side by side. They don't know any better. But the protocol gave me a second chance. And what I learned is that serving your country doesn't just mean putting on a uniform, picking up a gun, and being out in the open. Maybe one day, but for now, we're dark ops."

Trey nodded.

"I decided last night. I'm not gonna force you. If you don't want to serve, then walk away. There's five hundred bucks in your pocket."

Trey put his hand into his right pocket and felt the bills. *He's for real—this is real.*

"What about them?" Trey motioned to the van parked thirty yards away.

"My team? They'll all freak, and I can't promise the Agency won't come after you—out you, all the stuff we talked about, but I can give you a head start. It's your choice."

Trey gripped the bills in his pocket. *He's serious. Then what, I run? To who?* "What about you?"

"I'll catch hell—but don't worry 'bout me. If you move forward, it doesn't get any easier."

Trey nodded. "How long have you done this?"

"Twelve years, I've known every day could be my last. Our team, we have to be stronger, fight harder. And there won't be a monument for us. Only a simple, anonymous star on the wall at Langley."

"One day things may change. They can't keep kicking every gay service member out."

"Maybe. I do believe one day things will get better, but not today. People don't like change—it takes time. Look, the job isn't easy, but we make our choices. And now it's your turn. What do you want to do? Are you willing to serve your country with me?"

Trey stood taller and more rigid. "Yes."

"We have a lot of work ahead. The training is intense—I won't let up. But it'll be for your own good," Rick said as Trey again nodded. "You ready?"

Rick extended his hand to Trey, who gripped it in his own.

"Let's do it."

Headlights flashed on the van behind them.

"Is that the rest of the team?" Trey asked.

"Yup. Let's go."

"Where?"

"Breakfast. But you're paying—I hear you got cash." Rick smiled. They returned to the BMW.

"Can I ditch this now?"

"Yeah."

Trey tossed the hood in the back seat as they drove silently to Dootsie's in Southwest near the Anacostia River. Both men were lost in their thoughts.

Southwest DC was rough in '92 but not unfamiliar to Trey. He had gone a few times to Tracks, a large gay dance bar in an area where drugs and gangs had ravaged the once-thriving neighborhood.

They parked and went inside the diner.

"Morning. I'm Marnelle—I'll take care of y'all. Sugar, take that booth over there," the bubbly waitress said to Rick as they entered.

Trey could not take his eyes off Marnelle. *If Dootsie's was a stage, she would most definitely be the star. Look at the way she's handling all these cops, pouring coffee, barking orders, and doling out advice.*

"She's incredible," Trey said.

"Who?" Rick asked.

"Her. Marnelle. Bet that's why the cops love it here."

"Maybe. Or for the bacon and eggs. You hungry?"

"Starving."

Marnelle approached the table. "Y'all gonna eat?" she said, slapping down two thick white mugs and pouring coffee without asking whether they wanted any.

"Yeah, we'll take two large breakfast plates with an extra side of bacon."

She nodded and walked off.

"She doesn't even write anything down."

"Nope."

Trey watched Darius and Jeni come in and settle into the booth directly across the room and closer to the door. *What? I thought it was just breakfast.*

"Why are they here, Rick?"

Rick tilted his head and raised his eyebrows.

Heat flooded Trey's face. *He hates dumb questions. I better step up my game.*

"So what's next?"

"Next we drink this coffee. Eat breakfast."

"That's it?"

"Yeah, I want to just talk. Off the record, no wires," Rick said, pulling and popping his white Oxford's buttons to show they weren't being listened to.

"So why did y'all pick me? What is it that you need me to do? And when is it?"

"You're not gonna make this easy, are you?"

"I just want—"

"Trey, it's one assignment, but we only have forty days to get you ready."

"That's a long time—"

"Not really. The training, assessment, a field test or two—and we only get to work part-time. You'll be training early mornings and at night side by side with me."

"I'm going back to the office tomorrow?" Trey asked.

"Yeah."

"What'd you think? Five days in, and you're our new gay James Bond?"

"I don't know what to think. So will I be an officer after this training?"

"No."

"What then?"

"Technically, a civ-5 operative. But don't worry about that. It's a one-and-done assignment."

Trey frowned. "So what's it like? Are you 007?"

"Hell no. The Agency's not like that. I don't drive an Aston Martin. I don't own a fucking tuxedo. I live out of a suitcase. Eat a lot of takeout. I drink beer, not martinis."

"Yeah, but you got a sweet Beemer."

"Yup, and I'm reminded of that fact every month when I make the car payment. Look, Tiger, here's the deal. What we do is keep secrets. Seriously, I am not shooting bad guys every day or jetting off to Rio. *Yes*, my passport *is* thick, but I've spent a lot of time in some crazy places like Budapest, Ankara, and Kuwait. I just want to get off on the right foot here as we are going to be spending a lot of time together over the next few weeks. You'll have plenty of time to get to know me. I want to learn more about you."

"You have an entire file on me."

"Yeah, but I want to hear it from you. The real story."

Trey shook his head. "Okay, but you first?"

Rick frowned.

"I don't know anything about you."

"What do you want to know?"

"Where are you from?"

"New Hampshire."

"In a city?"

"No, a dairy farm."

"Brothers or sisters?"

"No sisters. Had a brother."

"Had? What happened?"

Rick took a deep breath and said in a low voice, "He died when I was twelve."

"I'm sorry."

Rick rotated his coffee mug.

"How old are you?"

"Thirty-four."

For the next hour at the diner, the two men shared their lives. Rick talked about growing up on a New England dairy farm, wrestling, and his love of art museums. Trey talked about his love of gymnastics, the South, and his ultra-religious upbringing.

He's avoiding these past five days and his work. Bet he needs a break. Just go with it.

Marnelle checked in from time to time. Finally, Rick motioned for the check.

"Sugar, that fine-ass cop over there got you covered." Marnelle pointed at Darius.

"All righty, thanks, Marnelle." Rick turned to Trey. "You ready to go?"

As they walked to the door, Trey nodded to Jeni and Darius.

Jeni smiled. "You look good, Trey. Good to see you out of the Hole."

Trey returned a smile.

Darius stood and offer his hand to Trey, who took it.

"I should be mad at you," Trey said.

"For what? Doing my job?" Darius squeezed his hand.

Trey met his eyes warily. "Well, you're maybe a little too good at your job."

"That's why they pay me the big bucks. Hey, you did good too, Trey."

Trey smiled and swallowed a bit of his apprehension. "Thanks, I guess. Hey, I think Marnelle may want your phone number."

"Boy, they *all* want my number." Without missing a beat, Darius grinned and playfully grabbed Trey's neck as they walked out.

They all got into their separate vehicles and headed toward Fourteenth Street, beside Arlington National Cemetery. As he turned onto 66 West, Rick broke the silence.

"Trey, we have a lot of work ahead of us to get you ready. The assignment for you is in forty days. But before we even think about it, first we have to train you up to be what we call a civ-5."

"A what five?"

"Civ-5. A civilian asset, an operative. You won't be an officer in the Agency."

"So not like you?"

"Technically, no. It's complicated right now, but if you pass our training, do the assignment—you may not want to join even if you could."

"So who knows?"

"What do you mean?"

"I mean like—does your dad know what you do?"

"No, our team is dark ops. Do you know what that means?"

"It's secret?"

"Even above top secret to be exact. This is our first rule. Most people even within the Agency don't know we exist. Do you understand?"

"Yeah, I think so—if your dad doesn't know then I can't even tell my brother?"

"No. No one, Trey."

"Will we be training at Langley?"

"No, and being on our team and a civ-5 asset means you'll probably never step foot on Campus in Langley or at the Farm."

"The Farm?"

"Camp Peary. We operate in the shadow of the shadows."

Trey nodded.

"Trey, it will all be clearer soon, but for now—just know that I've got your back."

"But if I tell—you guys will out me?"

Rick took a deep breath. "Yes. They will make sure that everyone in your life will know."

"Everyone?"

"And there's nothing to tell as we don't exist. Look. I could sit here and sugarcoat this situation. But I'm not gonna do that. I'm not gonna lie to you."

"Promise."

Rick nodded.

"So I train with you, do this assignment and then—" Trey stopped.

"And then what? Things just go back to normal. How? I mean everything is crazy now. Right?"

Trey nodded.

"No, your world has changed, but tomorrow morning, you'll get up, and go to work."

"How do you always seem to know what I'm thinking? How?"

"It's my job to read body language. Situations. Besides, you forget—I've sat in your chair. You'll go to work, coach, train with me and in time, things will even out."

"Right. It will be odd to go back tomorrow."

"Yup, but you'll reinforce the car-accident story. Did you memorize it yet?"

"Yeah."

"Let's hear it."

"I was driving on Frying Pan Road last Saturday night at ten thirty, I was on the way home from Worldgate and swerved to miss a deer but hit the guard rail," Trey recited.

"Where did you go to the ER?"

"Fair Oaks."

"How's your car? How are you getting to work?"

"My friend, Rick, is picking me up and dropping me off for the next week or so until Jessup's Repairs can get my car fixed."

Rick nodded. "Lucky for us your black eyes give you the perfect alibi. One look, your coworkers are gonna gush with sympathy. They won't suspect a thing. No one will."

Trey nodded, then brought a hand up to his now fuzzy scalp. "What about this buzz cut?"

"ER did it when they performed the CT and MRI. They wanted to make sure you didn't have a concussion."

"Is that normal for a scan?"

"Not really. It's a stretch, but they'll buy it."

Trey nodded.

They reviewed the story a couple more times, and then Trey repeated it back to Rick until they were both confident he had it.

On 66 just past Falls Church, Rick again broke the silence. "So we thought about having you stay at my condo up in Silver Spring, but it's too far from your office and gymnastics gym. We looked at renting something, but it wasn't feasible for only a few weeks. If you're open to it, I think it's best if I bunk in with you at your apartment."

Oh my god, just be cool. Trey turned to his window, away from Rick, as he felt a rush of energy. "Yeah sure, you're welcome to stay with me. My place is small, but then you saw it already, right?"

"Great. So, we're roomies, Tiger." Rick held out his fist. Trey mimicked his fist but didn't get the whole fist-bump thing. Rick tapped top and then on the bottom. Trey again turned to look out the window, as if lost in thought, but secretly he was just hiding a grin.

I can't believe we're gonna live together for the next month. Wow, we won't have much privacy. Where are we both gonna sleep? Oh my god, look at him. He is so fucking hot.

Why am I crushing on this guy? He kidnapped me, broke my nose, threatened to out me—if they tell, I'll lose my job. Mom and Dad will disown me. Rob. Oh god, my brother will freak out.

The closer they got to his exit and old life—the stronger the fear gripped his gut. Trey felt his eyes welling up. *Rick is one of the best; instead of getting upset, ask for help.* He took a chance and Chulpa's advice.

"Rick, please don't think I'm a wuss, but—I'm kinda freaking out. I'm really—" *Don't say scared. He'll think you're weak.* "—overwhelmed."

"Hey, look at me."

Trey turned to Rick's caring eyes.

"You'd be stupid not to be scared. Let's get *home*, and we'll talk it out, okay?" Rick laid his hand on Trey's knee.

Trey smiled and turned away.

"That's good. Did you hear that, Claren? The recruit was stressed and voiced it to his handler. That's a validating marker. Just as we planned. Textbook." Doc M got up from the table within the monitoring room as they listened to the audio plant in Rick's car.

"I would not call it textbook, but it was positive."

Doc M raised his eyebrows.

"What? Yes, it does sounds like the protocol is working."

"You seem skeptical. I assure you that the TB will work—an impenetrable cement both to one another."

"No doubt, Carlos. I don't like playing god. Can the kid handle it? Hell, can Rick handle it?"

"They can and they will. But Rick has to stick to the protocol."

"I know. I will speak to him later about going offline at Iwo Jima, but off the record—I liked that he trusted his gut."

"Trusting one's gut is a tactic not a strategy. If we had made Rick get wired, we'd know what he said."

Claren stood. "I don't like forcing a wire on my team; it's bad enough we bugged his car. No, we don't know what was said between them at the memorial, but whatever it was—it worked."

"You're right. No regress."

"Not at the diner or in the car. He expressed his feeling," she outlined.

"Yes. Overwhelmed—interesting word choice."

"Don't go overboard. He voiced that to his captor—"

"Not captor. Now Rick is his coach," he interjected.

"Well, either way it's extremely positive. Whatever Rick did is working."

"The TB is working."

You never give an inch do you?

They packed up their bags and turned the lights off. They walked the hallway in silence. They stood behind their cars.

"I'll report the good news. The recruit passed the intake—the initial test," Doc M said.

"Yeah, but the real test is in the field. Forty days."

"One day at a time. Get some rest."

"See you back at Campus," Claren said opening her car door.

"Claren?"

She turned back.

"Our protocol will work." They stood for a moment and then he got into his car.

Claren waited for his taillights to head up the ramp before putting her car in reverse.

She breathed out deeply.

Forty days—Carlos, you better be right.

CHAPTER 29
SPACE

"**R**ick, *in an offsite training, you must assert alpha dominance quickly with the recruit. He must know upon entry that it's no longer his space.*" As Rick drove to Trey's apartment, he recalled Doc M's instruction. "*The close proximity, intimacy—you must be firm. The recruit will challenge your dominance. You must hold the line.*"

Rick sensed the line would be thin. He and Trey training intensely and bunking in the small one-bedroom apartment would require strict discipline and clear boundaries.

Sexual intimacy was not forbidden; on the contrary, it was inevitable, and an essential part of the protocol. However, Rick had to follow his training. Trey could be confused about what the intimacy meant—and what it didn't—but Rick did not have that luxury.

Hold the line.

A moment later, Trey and Rick entered the apartment. The alarm began its countdown. *Wait for it. Lead him in.*

Trey instinctively punched in his old four digits repeatedly. The alarm continued more rapidly and was about to go off when Rick leaned over him and quickly entered the new set of numbers.

"Oh, yeah, I changed it," Rick said.

"Why would you change my alarm?"

"Have a seat, Trey."

"Why?"

"Now."

Trey sat on the barstool.

"Look, Trey, while I'm here, this will be *my* house, and you will go by *my* rules," Rick said sternly. He pulled out a list that he had printed and slapped it on the island in front of his recruit.

THE RULES

1) You're grounded: no calls, no friends, no TV, no car—only Officer Morgan Taxi.

2) Contact with your parents and family will be limited and monitored by Officer Morgan.

3) Control your temper.

THE CHORES

Cleaning Bathroom—Recruit
Laundry—Recruit
Dusting, Vacuuming—Recruit
Dishes, Cleaning Kitchen—Recruit
Cooking—Officer Morgan

THE SCHEDULE

Monday-Friday:
Exercise 0600-0730
Breakfast 0730-0800
Get Ready 0800-0830
Work 0845-1700
Training 1700-1930
(Exception Tues./Thurs.—Coaching 1700-1930)
Dinner 1930-2030
Clean up 2030-2100
Training 2100-2200
Sleep 2200-0600
Saturday-Sunday: Officer Morgan Discretion

Rick pointed to the fridge. All of the recruit's magnets and photos had been removed. Instead just three items were attached: the rules, the chores, and the schedule. All three were duplicated, laminated, and stuck to the door with four black magnets each. Rick then pointed to the back of the front door where the rules were yet again posted directly below the peephole.

Trey's face reddened. "Rick, I'm an adult. You're welcome here, but this is my—"

"Close your mouth."

"Where's my stuff—"

"Trey Alan Carter, we're doing this my way!"

Rick stood silently and watched Trey's face go from anger to fear to defeat. But he stood rigid. *Come on. Give in to me. Let go.*

The stare down lasted for several seconds until Rick saw the slight tremble in the bottom lip.

"Come here," Rick said softly, extending his arms, but Trey did not budge. "Come here."

Trey folded his arms and did not move.

You're not gonna make this easy are you? You have to come to me willingly. I can't force this part. Wait it out.

"Why?" Trey said.

"You will know soon. Come here." Rick guided him over to the couch and kept his arms around Trey but did not speak.

"I just don't get it. Sometimes you are so stern and other times..." Trey bristled at, then melted into Rick's strong grip.

"I know it seems confusing but just let go. I got you." Rick squeezed tighter and thought about Doc M's guidance. "*Remember Rick, seeing his surroundings is going to be tricky. He could get quite emotional, which is fine but we don't want a regress. Support him.*"

"Why me? I don't understand. How am I—"

"Shh—doesn't matter. Let it go." Rick kissed the top of Trey's head and then relaxed his grip.

Only then, Trey crumbled. As if he had stored up his tears for twenty-one years, the dam was finally breaking.

"That's it—let it out. You've been brave these past five days. I know how strange it is to drop back into your life. But I'm here. I got you. We'll get through it—together."

"Sorry, Rick—I just feel so—"

"Shh... it's okay. I've got you."

I've seen guys bigger than you break. Marines sobbing. You can do this, Tiger. Rick kept his thoughts and simply held Trey. *I'm gonna do this different, Trey. The way I'd wished mine had gone.*

His recruit was broken, but Rick would rebuild him to be stronger and more resilient. He needed Trey to emerge as iron.

Rick laid him out on the couch, removing his shoes. Rick returned with his own New England Patriots throw blanket. *It smells like me and will reinforce our bond. For the next forty days—you're mine, Trey.*

The young man slept for an hour as Rick sat at the kitchen island and quietly recorded their exit, breakfast, and initial re-entry on his laptop via the Agency's encripted VPN. *Too early for beer. What's he got here?* Rick found herbal tea in Trey's pantry and put a kettle on.

Twenty minutes later at 1245, the phone let out two fast, odd rings. *The Agency never sleeps. Geez, I just hit Enter and they're already calling?* Rick grabbed the phone quickly, but Trey sat up, stretched, and looked around the apartment.

"Rick Morgan."

"Hey, handsome. Why are you whispering—is he asleep?"

"Hey, Jeni. Yeah, he was—"

Trey listened to Rick, his face hardening as he scanned his living room and kitchen area. *Where's my TV? What's the machine in the black case? Are the two duffels by the glass slider Rick's stuff?* He got up and motioned to Rick that he was going to the bathroom. Rick nodded but continued his call.

Passing through the bedroom, Trey saw the door had been removed along with both the closet and bathroom doors. *What the hell? I kinda get the no-TV rule but why'd he take off the doors? This is nuts. Damn, now my head's starting to ache.*

Trey peed, flushed, and then washed his face in the sink, examining his shiners and nose, which wasn't as swollen as the day before. A zit was starting on his forehead—*damn it—no doubt from all the stress.* He opened the medicine cabinet and in place of his Tylenol found a Post-It note that read: *Let me know if you want an aspirin. RM*

Trey shut the cabinet and was startled to see Rick standing over his shoulder in the mirror.

"I need my aspirin. Where'd you put it?"

"The pain means your nose's healing. That's actually good, Trey." Rick ducked out but quickly returned with two chewable kid's aspirins.

"What's this? Baby aspirin? Seriously. Why? 'Cause I'm a *cry baby*?"

"No. Chill the fuck out. It's SOP. We use them in the field. You don't need water, and they taste better."

"What else did you mess with?" Trey said, irritated.

"Stop. This is what I am talking about, Tiger. The temper. I have stronger stuff if you need it, but let's start with these first."

"Where's my TV and all the doors?"

"Along with your car—in storage. You'll get them back when you earn 'em, maybe in two, three weeks. This . . ." Rick motioned back and forth. "This will go a lot easier if you chill out and trust me. If I wanted to hurt you, I would have."

"Like what you did here?" Trey pointed to his nose and blackened eyes.

"That was an accident."

"So they ain't SOP?" Trey said sarcastically.

"No. But they're gonna give you a great story for work tomorrow."

Returning to the living room, Trey sat on the couch while Rick went to the kitchen and poured two mugs. Handing him a hot herbal tea, Rick sat across from him in the large chair.

"So now what?" Trey took a sip of the tea.

"Let's get some things straight. Jeni's headed over with some groceries for us. She'll be here in about an hour. The rules, chores, and schedule—it's no joke. Every infraction will have consequences. Discipline is an integral part of training. Understood?"

"Yes, sir." Trey nodded.

"We aren't playing house. I've got forty days to get you ready. Football, your parents, Christian schools—God knows they gave you a strong foundation, but they also fucked you up. We need to strip down to what's core. Only keep what's solid, and ditch the confusing, religious shit."

"Why?"

"To strengthen your instinct. All that conflicting mumbo jumbo clouds your mind. We need you mentally, not just physically, tough. That's the purpose of the rules—and they don't end when you walk out that door. Out in the field, discipline is your friend."

"How so?"

"Keeping your cool, observing your opponent can save your life. But temper—it's just your ego. It'll get you hurt. You've got to let it go."

Trey nodded.

"In your world, there were minor consequences with minor discipline. In my world—well, if you listen to me and learn, hopefully there won't be major consequences. Those come with major discipline." Rick pulled out his gun and laid it on the coffee table between them.

"I get it, Rick." Trey stared at the gun. "Is what you're gonna train me for dangerous?"

"Minimally. But by the time we're done, you'll be ready."

Trey nodded.

"Listen to me." Rick took Trey's hand. "My job isn't just to train you. I'm here to protect you."

Trey sat back and exhaled deeply. "Can I ask you something—personal?"

"Sure."

"Y'all kept asking me if I found *you* attractive. But do you—" Trey stopped.

"Let me guess. Do I find you attractive too?"

Trey nodded silently.

Damn it, why is Doc M always right?

Instantly, Trey's expression validated the good doctor's warning.

"Rick, the mutual attraction will be a distraction. Even though healthy, you must deal with it quickly. Diffuse and set the right tone."

"Trey, we're gonna be here together in close quarters for the next few weeks."

Trey's eyes widened a bit and his jaw tightened.

Shit, don't fuck this up. Rick nodded. "Look, we've been clocking each other a bit for the past few days—"

"Clocking?"

"Stealing glances."

Trey nodded.

"Let's talk this out. Okay?" Rick stood. "There's only one way to make this less awkward." Rick crossed the room and closed the vertical blinds covering the glass slider, the lone window to the outside. The room darkened with only the back lighting from the kitchen sink, but he could see Trey's posture become rigid and his knees pulled closer.

Be cool. He doesn't have a lot of experience. Slow down. Rick walked over and motioned to the space beside Trey on the couch.

Trey again nodded but pressed his lips together.

Rick sat just inches from the young man, kicked off his shoes, and pulled off his socks. "I'm going to get undressed. I want you to as well but it's up to you. Okay?"

"Yeah," Trey whispered.

Rick unbuttoned and removed his Oxford shirt. Then in one motion, tugged off his white T-shirt.

Trey sat motionless for a moment.

Come on, Trey. Trust me.

Trey untucked his polo, grabbed the back collar, and took it off.

Rick smiled. "You okay?"

Trey nodded but stared downward at the gray carpeting.

Rick stood, unbuckled his belt, and dropped them to the floor, kicking them over to join their shirts. He slid his plaid boxers to his shins and sat down naked by Trey on the couch.

Rick watched Trey's gaze slowly move from his chest down to his abs, navel, then widened a bit, stopping at his groin. Rick pulsed his half-erect muscle. *Come on, Tiger. I can feel the tension. Trust me.*

Silently, Trey stood. He unbuttoned his jeans and pulled them off along with his white briefs. He sat back down. His breathing had become shallower and faster.

"Trey?"

He cranked his rigid posture toward Rick.

"Try to relax. We're alone now." Rick took hold of his own fully erect cock. "We are not going to touch one another yet. Just ourselves—okay?" Rick said softly and slowly began to massage himself.

Trey stared at the motion of Rick's hand, then melted back in to the cushions. He took hold of his erection and found a similar motion.

Yes, go for it. Relax.

They continued to masturbate, a foot apart in the dim light. Trey accelerated his rhythm.

Start the lesson—pump the brakes. Rick interrupted. "Stop. Hands off."

"What . . . why?" Trey stopped.

"Close your eyes," Rick instructed. "Part of training, we'll have to get you comfortable in this type of situation. Breathe. Relax. Imagine you're in the field on an assignment. It's a bit awkward sexual situation. You'll need to be able to think clearly on the edge. You'll want to blast one. Climax. But you won't be able to. You've got to be able to keep your head. It'll take practice. The trick is to shut it off—turn down the juice. Control the situation. There could be times when your safety might depend on it. Now open your eyes. Look at me."

They were both at half-mast. Rick scanned the room. Trey's body suddenly went rigid.

The young man leaped up and blurted, "I can't do this. You don't understand."

"What?"

"Are there cameras in here? Rick, please, please, don't tell anyone. I'd lose my job, my coaching, my family . . ."

"No one can see us. It's just you and me." *What the hell? Talk him down.* Rick raised both hands. "Trey, it's just us here. No one else."

"Swear?"

"I swear. Look, you're right—I don't fully get these panics, but I do understand feeling threatened. Being outed."

"My church, my parents." Trey rubbed the back of his neck.

"I know. You were taught that this was wrong, immoral, perverted."

Trey nodded.

"But you're not a total virgin."

Trey frowned.

"Easy, don't take offense. We both know you've had some experiences."

"Yeah, not like this."

"Come here." Rick patted the couch beside him. Trey stood rigid. "Please?"

Trey breathed deeply and returned to the couch.

"Part of what we use to our advantage in the field is up here." Rick gently tapped Trey's temple. "Despite what they preached, sex isn't evil, Trey."

"I know but . . ."

"But what?"

"I was taught wanting this, wanting a man was wrong."

Rick motioned between them. "These desires are not wrong. Tell me how you feel when you look at me?"

"Like electricity is shooting through my body."

Rick smiled. "So that's a good feeling, right?"

"Yeah."

"Give me your hand."

Rick took Trey's hand and pressed it on his own temple. "Sex, especially for men, happens in our minds. If you can learn to control your mind, you can control nearly any situation."

Trey nodded.

"All that stuff you were taught—that this is sin. Perversion. That was by people trying to control you. Your mind." Rick widened his eyes and let go of Trey's hand. He placed his own palm firmly but gently on Trey's stomach above the navel and just below the sternum.

"Listen, we're not going to have sex right now. Not because I don't want to but because when or if we do, I want you to . . ."

Trey dropped his head to his hands. "You don't understand. I can't—"

"Talk to me, Tiger. What do I not get?"

"How I was raised. My church. No, I'm not a virgin. I'm supposed to be married or in love to do this."

"I know you were *taught* that. I get it. Trey, look at me."

Trey sat up. His eyes couldn't conceal his worry.

Jesus, what did all that preaching do to you? Rick connected with him. "That's what they said, but is that what *you* really *believe*?"

"Yes. No. I don't know. I guess, but— This is all happening so fast."

Damn, he's right. Take your time. We're not in a hurry here. "Listen to me. We go at your pace. No one touches your body unless you invite them. You hear me?"

"Yeah."

"That includes me, Trey."

Trey nodded but his eyes were back on the gray floor.

"I know we've pushed hard these past five days." Rick shook his head. "I don't know. I thought— I misjudged you." He sank into the cushions, relaxed, and placed both arms on the back of the couch.

Trey took a deep breath and slowly eased against Rick's chest and arm.

"You're different than men I've known."

"I don't like being different."

"Don't say that, Tiger." Rick kissed his forehead. "You're incredibly special. That's why we picked you."

"How am I different?"

"Most young gay guys would've jumped on me in a heartbeat for sex but would have freaked out at the first hint of fists, guns, or blood—not you. Not you, Tiger." Rick gave him a squeeze. "We'll take this part slowly," he whispered. "I promise."

"Thank you." Trey relaxed deeper into his cradle.

"No worries. Just do me one favor, Trey. Don't ignite that panic or temper so fast. Talk to me first, okay?"

"It just feels like I've been hiding and fighting my whole life."

"I know exactly how that feels." Rick exhaled. "It's exhausting. With me, you can let go."

"Really?"

"Yes." Trey laid his head on Rick's shoulder. *God damn, he's trusting me. He's so different yet familiar. Smells so great—like candy. Damn it, hold the line. So this is what you meant, Claren. How is she always a step ahead? Focus.* Rick broke the silence of their breathing. "Talk to me?"

"I just need some time. I can't change overnight."

"No one's asking you to."

"If I flunk out of this, you're still you, Rick, but I still have to be me."

"You're right—just be you, Tiger."

A couple of minutes passed as they sat quietly. Rick breathed in the smell of Trey and allowed his erection to harden. Trey was also back at full attention. He sat up, shifting to be next to Rick. Their legs fully connected from hip to ankle.

"Can we?" Trey whispered.

"Go for it."

Trey lay back and began stroking himself. He squeezed his eyes closed as Rick joined his primal motion and rhythm. Rick did not close his eyes but soaked in Trey's pale smooth skin, taunt youthful muscle. Rick bit his lip. *I want to taste him. Oh god, I want him.*

Trey's eyes opened and startled Rick's fantasy. *Busted. Don't spook him. Check in.* "You close?"

"Yeah." Trey again closed his eyes and bit his bottom lip.

"Go for it," Rick repeated and continued to pump himself. He watched the muscles ripple in Trey's abs and become more rigid.

Trey jerked backward into the couch once. Twice. And a third time. "Oh god, yeah. Yeah." Trey tensed and stopped his motion. His body relaxed.

Fuck yeah, Tiger. You weren't lying. Dry as a bone, but damn. You are hot as fuck. Rick closed his eyes and lay back. He moved his arm faster and more rhythmically. "Yeah. Ahhh." The thick liquid shot up onto his neck, chin, and chest. "Ahhh!" he said as he shook. "Fuck, ahhhh."

Rick exhaled deeply and melted into the sofa.

The couch creaked as he felt Trey lean forward. "Rick, can I touch it?"

"What?"

"Your cum."

Rick opened his eyes and grinned. "Of course."

Trey lightly tapped a puddle just above Rick's navel.

He watched Trey wipe his finger but hold it to his nose. "You like that?"

Trey nodded. "Can I— Is it safe?"

"You wanna taste it?"

Trey nodded.

Rick scooped up a droplet on his index finger and held it out.

Trey closed his eyes as he opened his mouth.

Trey's warm mouth squeezed around his finger and the tip of his tongue tickled Rick's fingertip.

Don't say anything, just let him explore.

Trey released Rick's finger and opened his eyes. "Sorry."

"For what?"

"You think I'm weird?"

"No, I think you're sexy." Rick pulled Trey back into his cradle. "How'd it taste?"

"Salty but good."

"Good, 'cause that was fun." Rick narrowed his eyes. "How 'bout for you? It seemed intense."

"It was. But—"

"What? The retrograde?"

"Yeah."

"What are you worried about?"

"That I'm not good at this."

"What? You're hot as hell. Look what you made me do." Rick smiled and pointed to his chest.

Trey's worried look softened.

"I mean really—you're kinda lucky."

"I don't feel lucky."

"I can tell by your breathing and spasms that you feel it deeply. Right?"

"Yeah, but I can't do that." Trey nodded to his splattered chest.

"So what? It's less mess." Rick smiled. "Different is good. Different is sexy, Trey. It's just another thing that makes you unique. So very special." Rick softly caressed Trey's chin.

"I hate having to tell someone before we . . ."

"I could see that, but when you're older and meet the right guy, he's not gonna care. In fact, I bet he'll like it," he said with a grin and stretched out wide with his limbs.

"I'll get you a washcloth." Trey got up.

Rick studied the silhouette of the young man. *Damn, he doesn't even know how special and beautiful he is. My Tiger.*

"Do you think bad of me?" Trey asked as he returned and handed Rick the warm, wet cloth.

"Bad of you? No." Rick mopped up his chest. "But I don't think that's the real question, is it? Come here." Rick grabbed him and pulled him down into his embrace. "The real question is, do *you* think bad of *you*?"

"I don't know, I guess—"

"Stop. It's only sex, Trey. And believe it or not, it can be quite fun. So don't beat yourself up." Rick smiled warmly. "Besides, beating you up is my job not yours." He gently kissed Trey's nose.

Trey smiled but then frowned. "I just have to be safe."

"You were and you are. Safe. I'm negative. The Agency tests me monthly. You tested negative too. Part of the training will be on safety. With HIV . . . it's not just about dodging bullets."

"I know, but . . ."

"Look at me." Rick waited for Trey to connect. "You're not crazy. This situation will feel a bit strange at times. Listen to me. Okay? I promise I'll get you through this. Are we good?"

"Yeah—I find it hard to talk when I get pissed or overwhelmed. Scared."

"Of course. Let's agree on a safeword?"

"A what?"

"A word you can use with me when things get too fast or you're overwhelmed during our training."

"Any word?"

"You pick."

"How about . . . *takedown*?" Trey smiled slightly.

"Takedown. Wrestling—you remembered. I like it." Rick grinned.

Worry seemed to wipe Trey's smile away as his lips pursed and eyebrows tightened.

"What? Talk to me." Rick lightly rocked Trey's knee.

"I want to survive this . . ."

"You will. You just got to listen to me and stop overthinking it. Deal?"

"Deal."

Rick kissed his forehead and playfully pushed his knee.

"Now it's laundry time, grunt."

Half an hour later, Rick and Trey were relaxed in shorts and T-shirts.

Knock, knock.

Jeni rapped on the door but used her key to barge in with two bags of groceries. "Hey, hey, handsome boys. Give me a hand with these."

"Finally, I'm starving." Rick took the groceries.

"You're always hungry. Hey, Trey. Great to see you out of the Hole. How are you?" She plopped down on the stool as the guys put away the provisions.

"I'm good, but hungry too."

"Well, lucky for you, you got Chef Morgan here. Rick can cook. Seriously, you might have starved with any of the others."

Rick saw Trey relax and laugh with her. *She's laying it on thick and he's already charmed by her.* "Did you get the shallots?"

"Yes, Chef Morgan. Look in the bag."

"Oh, got it, thanks."

"And the red pepper flakes in the white label."

Rick saw her roll her eyes at Trey. "They're the best—"

"That's what you said . . . ten times."

Rick caught Trey's eyes. "See, I get no respect."

"Shit, I've got to go pick up Kristin. We're having dinner tonight with her dikey softball friends. I wish I could stay, but my wifey waits for no one." She flashed a smile to Trey and winked.

Trey smiled and nodded.

She headed for the door. "Bye, boys. Don't kill each other."

The door shut.

"She's awesome," Trey said.

"She is a beautiful pain in the ass. But she actually listened and got me everything on my list." Rick started prepping dinner.

"Well, I think she's awesome."

"Yes, but still a pain in the ass. Someday I'll tell you about spending ten days with her on a boat in the South China Sea," Rick said, chopping an onion.

Trey grinned and returned to folding the laundry. They ate dinner at the island as Rick explained their next few days. Without prodding, Trey started clearing the dishes and cleaning up.

"You got this? It's been a long day," Rick said.

"Yeah, I'm good." Trey started loading the dishwasher.

Rick headed to the bathroom, presumably to shower before bed.

As he dried off, Trey joined him in the small bathroom.

"What if I have to . . . you know—"

"What? Take a shit, drop a load, drop the 'kids' off at the pool . . ." Rick joked. "Turn on the sink, have a seat, and flush often. You think this is bad, try Parris Island. Five shitters across with no dividers."

Trey followed the instructions, and took a quick shower. When he came back to the bedroom, Rick was lying naked on the bed with his laptop over his legs. The glow of the screen illuminated his face.

"So you get the bed, then. Where do I sleep?"

"Right here with me or on the couch. It's your call."

"I'll, uh, take the couch. I need to get used to all this."

"Okay." Rick tossed a pillow from the bed.

"Good night, Tiger."

"Good night, Rick."

Click, click.

Rick typed and waited for a response.

The cursor blinked as Claren typed. *How did he do?*

Rick: *Good. Calling it a night.*

Claren: *Jeni's on watch tonight. Parking deck.*

Rick: *Got it.*

Claren: *Supposed to ask where he's sleeping but knowing you. Beside you?*

Rick: *Nope. Couch.*

Claren: *Huh, so you ARE holding the line.* ☺

Rick: *Yup.* ☹

Claren: *OTR?*

Rick: *Yeah?*

Claren: *Think we'll get to civ-5 in 40?*

Rick: *Do we have choice?*

Claren: *Nope.*

Rick: *Then you'll get your civ-5.*

Claren: *What did you say at the monument? OTR.*

Rick: *Told him how I joined.*

Claren: *Good call.*

Rick: *Doc mad?*
Claren: *No worries. Night, Rick.*
Rick: *Night.*
Rick closed the laptop and stared at the empty bed.

Wish he was here and not out there. How the hell am I gonna do this? One down. Thirty-nine to go.

CHAPTER 30
OFFICE

"Let's go! Let's go! Let's go! Get up, get down, get the hell outta that nightgown."

"What?" Trey jumped off the couch to find Rick naked and clearing the floor for push-ups.

"Dirty thirty, Tiger!"

"What time is it?"

"Six o'clock, sunshine." Rick shoved the coffee table to the far wall. "Thirty, now."

They dropped and banged out thirty push-ups, matching pace.

Rick leaped up from the floor and ripped open the blinds. "Look at that sun."

"You know you're naked, right?"

"Yeah. So what?"

"Neighbors?"

"Let 'em see." Rick walked around the apartment completely at ease. "Go time. Grab your runners." He pulled on shorts and his running shoes lying on the island but no shirt.

Trey went into his closet and returned with shorts, a shirt, and running shoes.

"Come on," Rick said.

Trey shook his head at the drill instructor.

They ran three miles each morning that first week, then four, five, and then six. Trey would always try to beat Rick on the inevitable last sprint back to the trailhead at the end of the street.

After the run, Rick guided his student through a series of strength and endurance exercises. Returning to the apartment, Rick would strip down and jump in the shower, while Trey would make a pot of coffee. Then Trey would join Rick in the bathroom, shaving as Rick finished showering, then switching places with him, often leaving the shower running.

Thursday, the first morning back, Trey dressed as Rick made breakfast.

"Hurry up, Trey. Eggs are getting cold."

"Be right there."

"Child, sit cho ass down . . .you 'bout to get the best eggs ever," Rick attempted a Yankee version of a Southern accent but fell silent when Trey emerged from the bedroom. It was the first time he'd seen Trey in dress pants and a dress shirt. "Wow, you clean up."

"Yeah?"

"You look great, Tiger. Have a seat."

They ate and read the paper. Then Trey cleaned up as Rick got dressed and grabbed his keys.

"Ready?" Rick asked.

"Guess so."

As they drove to Trey's office, Rick saw Trey rubbing his fingers individually and tensing his shoulders. "What's on your mind?"

"Nothing." Trey turned to his side window.

"Talk to me?"

"What if they don't buy my story?"

"Trust me. They will."

Trey sighed and nodded.

"Here we are. Meet you back here at 1700 sharp. You good?"

"Yeah." Trey got out of the car and disappeared into the glass atrium of his office building.

He's got this. Time to check in with Claren. Rick reached into the glove box and pulled out his Comsat encrypted phone. He punched in his passcode. The buttons illuminated and he dialed Langley.

"How did it go, Rick?" Claren said.

"Good. Just dropped him off."

"If he regresses, then we'll know soon. Chris is there playing janitor."

"Wait. You put eyes on him?"

"We have a lot riding on this kid."

"Fine but why not read me in? I don't like surprises and nobody said anything about Chris hanging around."

"Relax, Rick. I added it last minute. For the first few days; till we know he's solid."

Damn it, why doesn't she simply trust me? "Any other surprises?"

"No. Got to go. Enjoy that pool."

Rick hung up and shook his head. *Always a curveball.* He drove back to the apartment and reviewed the outline of the training. At 1400, he threw on his trunks, grabbed an Anne Rice paperback of *The Vampire Lestat,* and headed to the pool. *This is not too bad. My day's free. Pooltime. I'm stateside. Not bad at all.*

At 1700, Rick stopped in front of the office building. A minute later, Trey walked out of the atrium and got into the BMW. "Well?" Rick asked.

"What?"

"How'd it go?" Rick widened his eyes.

"Great. You were right. They were like 'Oh my god, your eyes. Are you okay?'"

"Wait can you please repeat that?"

"What?"

"That first part—"

"Yes, you were right."

"Ha! I'm always right, Tiger. Buckle up."

Rick sped out of the parking lot to chauffeur him to his coaching gig.

"Did you call your gym and scale back your coaching hours?"

"Yeah, they were cool."

"Is this good here?" Rick asked as he pulled up to the large industrial building.

"Yeah, right here. I'll be done by seven—"

"You mean 1900?"

Trey smirked. "Right, 1900 but make it 1915 some parents are always late."

"I'll be here."

Two hours later Rick picked him up. They ate dinner and finished the first day by working through body language signals or "tells" as Rick described.

Each night, Rick picked a different topic for training.

"We're not military, Rick, so why do I need to know military time and insignias for all five branches?"

"You need to be at ease around service personnel. We hop Macs and do base drops all the time."

"Macs?"

"Military airlifts. Again, what is this?"

"Easy, like my brother. US Air Force. Staff Sargent."

"Ding, ding, ding . . . we have a winner." Rick smiled and tried to make training fun.

It was not secretive and was sometimes boring. Assessing room setups using blocks at the kitchen table. Military time, military insignias for all five branches, observation skills, drops, pick-ups, listening and retention tricks, and etiquette—always dinner etiquette. It wasn't anything like a Hollywood spy film. Except for the handgun training, it was more like a Psyche 101 meets Boy Scouts meets an Emily Post class.

"Rick, why do I need to know all this?"

"Because a gentleman does. Again, salad fork, soup spoon."

By the end of the first ten days, Trey could take apart the Glock 17 and reassemble the unloaded gun in under two minutes *and* tell the difference between salad and dinner forks by counting their tines.

In the mornings, Rick pushed him physically, and at night mentally. The sexual tension between them would ebb and flow. Except for the occasional banter and a few mutual masturbation sessions, the situation wasn't unlike roommates. But Rick had to maintain a careful balance. Where he could he interjected humor, but maintained discipline as it was still an offsite basic training. Each day required check in with Claren and the team.

"Ten days in. How's our boy?" Claren asked.

"Good. He's picking it all up as if he's been doing it his whole life. Ops, observation, drops, listening—even the Glock."

"Glock? That's a bit out of scope."

"I know. I— Look I need some breathing room here." Rick paused before adding, "You know that I'm on task—but I'm doing a few things my way."

"Okay, but keep me posted—only me. Doc M doesn't need more gray hairs."

Rick held the phone back and breathed deeply. "Thanks."

"Of course. You got this. Okay final question—don't make me ask it every day."

"Ha! He's still on the couch, Claren. Seriously, why does Doc M care about where he's sleeping?"

"You know why. Keep me posted."

"Will do."

She's not telling me everything, but at least she didn't freak out about the Glock. My methods. Where's he sleeping? Geez. Why does Doc M always have a motive? This is gonna get harder. They don't care about Trey like I do—they don't know him like I do. It's on me to try to give him choices. Protect him.

CHAPTER 31
LAKE

On Friday, June 19, 1992, Rick zipped into the Fair Lakes parking lot at 1516 and only shrugged at Trey standing cross-armed on the curb in front of his office.

Trey hopped in and buckled up. "You said 1500."

Rick did not respond but pulled down his Ray-Bans and nodded to the back seat.

"What's in the packs?"

"A surprise."

"Where are we going?"

"Paris."

Trey's mouth gaped open and his eyes widened. "For real?"

"No. We're gonna go camping, Tiger."

Trey grinned wide. "Camping. Where?"

"You'll see. Fresh air. Hunt food. *Make fire!*"

"Ha, ha, caveman." Trey rolled his eyes but continued. "Seriously, where we going?"

"What part of *surprise* do you not get? Now, find us some tunes, DJ."

Trey turned on the radio.

Rick took a left instead of a right and headed east on Route 123 to 95-South.

"Mind if I sleep?" Trey yawned.

"No." Rick lowered the volume of the music.

For two hours, Rick drove as Trey slept.

He really is cute. Relaxing, listening to me, and hell, maybe he's finally trusting me. Tell me I don't know what I'm doing. If Doc M, Tibbins, and Claren just let me, I could modify the protocol—evolve it.

They're too old-school. Just getting them to let me take him off the grid was hard enough.

When Rick had pitched the idea to Claren earlier that week, he'd done it at her office on Campus, hoping his appeal would be stronger in person.

"Got a minute?"

"This is a surprise. Officer Morgan on campus instead of soaking up the rays by the pool. Isn't this your afternoon break? Is there a problem with our recruit?" She motioned for him to enter her office and to her opposing side chairs.

"No, he's at work. Everything's good." Rick walked in but stood behind one of the chairs. "I wanted to ask for something."

"Let me guess . . . more budget?"

"No, we're good." Rick took a deep breath.

Claren narrowed her eyes.

"Wait, hear me out."

She lowered her chin. "Fine. Let's hear it."

"We've been cooped up in that tiny one-bedroom apartment for nearly two weeks. He's doing great. I wanted to take him out this weekend."

"Where?"

"Camping. My cabin. Lost River."

"Are you kidding me, Rick?"

"Come on, Claren. Just consider it . . . fresh air . . . will get him out of his head—away from work, his world."

Claren crossed her arms. "Tell me. You okay?"

"Of course."

"What's this really about?"

Rick shook his head. "What it's about is getting him away. Outside. Fresh air. Away from his work, his gym, his routine."

"Introducing change and challenge."

"Yup, but in a different setting."

"Different, huh. Still holding the line?"

"What's that supposed to mean?" Rick shot back.

"It means exactly what it means." Claren stood up from her desk and walked to Rick. "You know every detail of this operation is being scrutinized. Hell, they're probably listening to us right now."

"Tibbins, Doc M?"

She pursed her lips and gave a single nod.

"It's just camping . . . two days."

"Just camping?"

Rick shook his head at her sarcasm.

"No, it's not just camping. I know you, Rick Morgan. You want some time alone, off the grid . . . no backup. The question is why?"

"Next phase of training. He'll never be out of my sight."

Claren shook her head and motioned to her windows. "What if he regresses? Out there?"

"He's not going to—"

"You don't know that—"

"I know him."

She again pursed her lips and folded her arms.

"Claren, you know that I've been by his side day-in and day-out since the intake."

"We have no backup. No safety net. It's too—"

"I know this kid inside and out."

She frowned.

"His favorite song, his laugh, his favorite food. The way his Southern accent gets stronger after a beer or telling stories about his family. What's this really about?"

"Ivan Dimitri," she stated flatly.

"Don't you think I know that? This will help me get him ready for Ivan."

"This isn't just my call." She nodded to her door.

"It's worth the ask."

"So, I'm suppose to march into Tibbins's office the way you marched into mine? You know shit rolls up and down the hill."

Rick lowered his voice. "I swear—never out of my sight."

She let out a deep breath and walked back to her desk. "So what is it?"

Rick frowned.

"His favorite dish?"

"Lasagna."

"Tibbins is gonna say no." Her lips parted ever so slightly. "But I'll ask."

Rick nodded.

"But Rick . . ."
"I know, I know. Hold the line."
"Now get out of my office."

"Dee?" Claren said as she knocked on the frame of Tibbins's open door.

"Hey. Come on in."

"Sorry to pop in on you."

"No worries—you're saving me from these stupid budgets." He pulled off his glasses and motioned her in. "I hate Excel. What's going on?"

"Our special project. Blue bird."

Dee nodded and got up from his desk. He closed his office door, then took the facing side chair opposite her. "How is our blue bird?"

"Good. He's besting our expectations."

"That's what Carlos said. And your team?"

"All good. Rick is really stepping up."

"Excellent."

"So, this weekend, Rick wants to take our civ-5 offsite."

"We're already offsite. Where?"

"Camping. His cabin in Lost River."

"Why? What's his objective?"

"He says change and challenge phase but . . ."

"Huh. Interesting idea, but not Lost River."

"We can't afford *interesting ideas*." She shook her head slowly. "No way. I only asked you to keep my word to Rick."

"His idea?"

"Yeah, but I felt sure you'd say no."

"Camping . . . the question is where."

She widened her eyes.

"The Farm."

"Our blue bird's an untrained civ." Claren frowned. "Aren't you worried there's too many eyes?"

"It's closed, controlled, and between training sessions. We can explain it to Hammonds—he's your buddy, right?"

Fuck you, Dee. Nothing happened between me and Sean Hammonds. She tightened her jaw. "I can speak to Sean. Minimal intel."

"Good, but one more thing. I want to have eyes on them."

"Why?"

"Especially Saturday when they train. Conceal it—even from Rick. I don't want them to know."

"I don't like to snoop on my team without reason."

"We're gonna make a propo."

You gotta be kidding me . . . use our boys in propaganda. "Why?"

"Things are changing, Claren. Several high-profile challenges to the ban on homosexuals serving. Decorated soldiers forced to come out or be outed—it's like a goddamn witch hunt. *The Post*, CNN."

"We're still dark."

"For now. Our protocol could offer a unique perspective. We selectively widen our circle."

"A top secret, dark ops unit on US soil—"

"Select brass. Trust me on this."

"Trust goes both ways. Why keep it from Rick?"

"We need him and his recruit training, unobserved. We need to capture Rick being Rick. If he knows, it'll get in his head. His instincts make him a damn good officer, but . . ."

"Make him self-conscious. Throw him off his game."

"Exactly. My gut tells me Rick and this civ-5 could enlighten some of these homophobic Pentagon pricks."

"So the Farm, minimal intel, and some random surveillance team."

"No, your team and only Hammonds."

"Okay," Claren conceded.

"Three cameras. Night vision. I'll get Carlos to update the training outline for Rick. This is a closed test. Confidential."

"What are we hoping to capture?"

Tibbins sighed. "Truth? I don't know exactly."

She sensed his conflict in his tone and eyes.

He stood and turned toward his large windows. "It's complicated, Claren. Things are changing. We've had some success with the protocol, but this little project—this bubble we have created for these agents could pop at any time."

"So, you want to blow up the notion a gay recruit can't cut it?"

"Precisely."

"But risk exposing Rick, our only recruit, and the protocol?"

"No, Claren." Tibbins turned to her. "Yes, it's risky, but we can show a tight circle, select group the inevitable future. A future staring us in the face, but the Pentagon has their head up their ass."

"Swinging wide for that fence, aren't we?"

Tibbins grinned slightly.

"When?"

"Maybe next week—"

"And Ivan Dimitri?" She narrowed her eyes. "Is this detour, this little movie worth the risk?"

"We don't need to decide that now. Let's see what we capture, edit a bit to protect Rick—then I'll make some calls. You think our hot-headed civ is ready? That was quite the temper tantrum at his intake."

Huh, so you have been reading my notes and watching the tapes. "Yes, that's partly why we selected him."

"Right, propensity to action," Tibbins said.

Claren nodded. "This select audience for your screening—if word lands on the wrong desk. This town is too small. Forget our protocol, we could ignite an interagency war. The risk seems bigger than only shutting us down. You really want to take a call like that from POTUS, from Tanner?"

"Step by step. We'll make that call later. Don't get ahead. For now, our boys are going camping."

"Has to be the Farm, Rick."

"You know I hate the Farm, Claren. Why?"

"Your cabin's too risky. Tibbins said the Farm or you stay put. Your call?"

"Fine."

Rick gritted his teeth even now thinking about her call. He turned to his sleeping recruit. *But you didn't say where on the Farm. I'm still gonna do this my way. We're nearly there. Better wake him up.*

"Hey, Trey?" Rick gently shook his leg.

"What?" Trey stretched and yawned as they approached the main gates. "Where are we?"

"Camp Perry."

"Military base?"

"Kind of. We're near Williamsburg. I'll explain later. Right now, we've gotta hustle, sun's getting low. Sit up and follow my lead."

Trey sat up as they entered the gate. Rick lowered his window and flashed his ID.

The guard studied his clipboard, then stared at Trey. He cocked his head and clicked his radio perched on his shoulder. "Sir, our special guests have arrived."

"Great. Thanks, Private," a squawking voice echoed through the speaker.

Fucking shit—she told Hammonds. Rick gripped the steering wheel but held his gaze on the guard.

The young guard glanced back at Trey and then motioned Rick through the gates.

Rick closed his window and drove in.

"Geez, tight security," Trey said glancing back at the gate.

"You have no idea. Trey, we call this the Farm. They think we're gonna camp by the practice fields, but I know a better place." Rick drove out beyond the buildings to the back of a parking lot and turned off the car. He glanced around. *Quiet. No one's tailing us. Huh, maybe she only gave Hammonds the bare minimum. There's no recruits hanging around—must be between sessions.*

"Come on, you'll want to change," Rick said, nodding to the back seat.

"You packed for me?"

"Yup, get dressed."

Trey stripped off his work clothes and pulled on the khaki shorts, T-shirt, and trainers that Rick had packed. "So these aren't duffels."

"Nope. Backpacks." Rick pulled out both. "We carry our gear from here."

"Wow, these are nice."

"Borrowed them along with the sleeping bags from Jeni and Kristin." Rick stood by the car in his shorts, T-shirt, and hiking boots and waited for Trey to finish changing.

"Ready?"

"Yeah. Where's our camp?"

Rick flashed his pocket compass. "'Bout two miles, that way." He pointed and then hoisted his backpack to his shoulders and buckled the straps. "Let's go, Trey. We've got maybe two hours of daylight. We need to make camp before dark."

A half mile into the hike, Rick looked around. *Nobody's trailing us. Time for our detour.* He led them off trail. Another few yards, the tops of the base buildings were gone. They were in thick Virginia pines now, and the sun was hanging low. An hour later, they rounded a knoll and came to a large clearing with a pristine lake and a field in the distance.

Rick looked at Trey. "We're here." He saw Trey grin wider than he'd ever seen. He sensed the young man let go of the frustrations of the past two weeks.

"Yeeeaaah!" Trey yelled like a kid as he ran ahead of Rick toward the lake.

He started stripping twenty yards out, leaving a trail of gear and clothing. Without hesitation, he charged into the water.

Rick smiled as he unpacked their gear.

Knew I was right. He's in his element—change and challenge. I can ease him into our next phase here. My way. This is perfect.

Trey splashed around naked in the water.

Ha! Look at him. Just a kid being a kid. Keep that innocence, Tiger. We'll get through this. Ivan. One and done.

"Come on. It's warm. Have some fun!" Trey hollered.

"You're such a redneck!" Rick dropped his pack and tugged off his shirt.

They splashed and swam before making camp. Rick finished setting their tent and digging a fire pit as Trey forged the nearby trees for kindling.

"Is this enough wood?" Trey asked as he brought the last pile to their now blazing campfire.

"Yeah, for tonight. Looks like we lucked out on weather. Not a cloud in that night sky. Stars will be amazing later." Rick continued to finish setting camp.

"What's for dinner?"

"Steak kabobs with onions and peppers and a little *off the record* surprise."

"Surprise?"

"Beer. Not supposed to have it on base. Keep it between us?"

"Of course, but beer's what got me into this mess."

"Ha! Good point," Rick said. "Fine, I'll drink yours too."

"Not-uh." Trey stoked the fire. "Sounds like a good dinner."

"Yup, we'll eat great tonight, but tomorrow . . . we'll have to find and catch our dinner."

"Here?"

"There's food all around us. I'll show you tomorrow." Rick handed him a raw kabob. "Six to eight minutes for medium. Nine to ten for dead and charred—but turn it slowly."

They cooked over the open fire as the sun disappeared.

Rick watched Trey sear his kabob and carefully slide the vegetables and steak cubes onto his camping plate. "Looks like you've done this before."

"My church youth group used to go camping on the AT every year."

"Appalachian Trail?"

Trey nodded and kept eating.

"How is it?"

"So good. Thanks."

Rick smiled.

After eating, Trey followed the routine, clearing Rick's camping plate and utensils along with the other dishes. Rick leaned back against a large rock, beer in hand, and stared up at the stars. He watched Trey head down to the lake shore to wash up and a few minutes later return.

"You know what? It looks the same from nearly every point on this earth. No matter how shitty your day, if you can see the sky at night . . . it's peaceful."

"You've been all around the world?"

"I've seen enough to know that a place like this—with nature all to ourselves—is heaven." Rick popped open a beer and tossed another to Trey.

"Were you raised religious, Rick?"

"Yeah, but not like you. We were sometimes Episcopalians." Rick studied Trey's expression through the dancing flames. *What's on your mind, Tiger? Come on, spit it out. Keep him talking.* "How's the beer?"

"It's actually good." Trey took another sip and gazed up at the night sky. "Rick, when did you know?"

Aha, the universal question every gay man is eventually asked. Deep. Okay, let's do this. "I don't know, maybe eighth or ninth grade. But I guess I always knew."

"Did you hide it?"

"Of course. Through ROTC and sports. Wrestling saved me in high school."

"How so?"

"In my school, you were either a jock or not. And it was always 'fag, faggot, or cocksucker.' I learned quickly that no one could know my secret."

"What 'bout college?"

"A little easier, I took some chances—had some fun." Rick took a swig. "But then the Corps. Parris Island was no joke."

"What you told me at Iwo Jima—that really happened?"

"Yeah."

Rick watched Trey grimace and stare intently at him.

"What did you think? That I made that up?"

Trey shrugged. "I don't know. Sorry that happened to you."

Rick tilted his head and sipped his beer. "Enough 'bout me—how 'bout you, Tiger?"

"What about me?"

"When did you know?"

"I guess eleven or twelve."

"How'd you know?"

"I guess I just knew, but this one time. Spencer's— You know that store in the mall?"

"Yeah."

"They used to have these posters. It was off-limits by my Church, but my friends and I would sneak back there. They'd gawk at Heather Locklear, but I'd sneak a peek at David Lee Roth."

Rick leaned forward a bit. "David Lee fucking Roth?"

"Yup. This dude from Van Halen—"

"I know who he is, geez. Why?"

"His muscles, those ripped jeans."

"Ha! You're serious?"

"Don't laugh—my options were limited."

"I'll say. Well, to David Lee—that's a first." Rick held up his beer.

"It was that or National Geographic."

"Naked explorers, right?"

Trey nodded.

"So who've you told? Who knows?"

"No one." Trey shook his head.

"Not even your best friend?"

"Mark? No."

"Why not?"

"You don't get it. He grew up like me—"

"And you think what? He'd ditch you if he knew?"

"Yeah, but worse."

"How so?"

"Beyond not ever speak to me again. He might let it slip out."

"Maybe, but you'll never know if you don't trust him. People can sometimes surprise you—if you let 'em."

"Maybe." Trey turned his attention to the stars overhead. "I haven't figured it out yet. That's why I'm kinda trapped."

"The closet is tricky. Can I ask you something?"

"Yeah."

"Tell me about that." Rick pointed to his own left temple.

"What? My scar?"

Rick nodded.

"It's nothing—just a scar."

"Every scar has a story, Trey. What happened?"

"I got hit."

"By who?"

"Just a guy."

"How old were you?"

"Eighteen."

Rick widened his eyes and lowered his chin.

"Come on, Rick. You already read the police report in my file."

"Yes, I did. But it doesn't tell what *really* happened. Something happened—there's a six-, seven-month gap in your file."

Trey sat motionless but Rick saw his eyes grow heavy.

"Look, you don't have to tell me, but I want to know you. The real you—not what some stupid intel file says."

"Like you care who I am." Trey tossed a stick into the fire.

"Why do you think we're out here tonight?"

"I don't know. It's your job?"

"Bullshit—I'm not on the clock tonight. In fact, I'm gonna catch hell for this. Not too many people know about this part of the Farm. This lake."

"So this isn't part of our training?"

"Not tonight. Tomorrow we'll train a bit, but out here . . . just us. OTR."

"OTR?"

"Off the record—but for the *record*—" Rick paused and waited until Trey's eyes connected with his. He softened his gaze. "I do care. Please?"

"You won't get it."

"Try me."

"It's a long story."

"We've got all night."

Trey let out a deep breathe.

Rick tossed another branch onto the fire. He turned back to Trey and nodded.

"All right, my parents, our church were so strict. Just like Mark's. They controlled everything. What music we could listen to, television, books we were allowed to read—even friends we could have. It was like a prison. My brother and my sister both rebelled the second they graduated from high school. That tripled the pressure on me. I never really pushed back."

"Sounds tough."

"It was suffocating—it was so much worse knowing that I was different . . . gay."

"So then you broke out?"

"Kinda, I'd just finished my freshman year at Pensacola Christian College—it makes Liberty look like a party school."

"Liberty? No shit?" Rick said, raising an eyebrow.

"Super strict. During summer break, back home in Atlanta, I snuck out a few times. Dropped off my girlfriend and . . . went to Midtown."

"Gay bars?"

"Yeah, the Armory, Backstreets, LaVitas."

"At eighteen? They'd already upped the drinking age to twenty-one. How'd you get in? Fake ID?"

"No. They looked at me and just let me in."

"I bet they did," Rick whispered. "Did you go back?"

"Yeah. They had these club cards that they would give you."

Rick nodded.

"I had one for the Armory, Backstreets, Pharr Library, and . . . anyway, I got caught."

"Police?"

"Worse."

"Worse?"

"My mom. She said she found the cards while cleaning my room." Trey shook his head. "She told my dad, then our pastor. Everybody freaked out and gave me an ultimatum. I called my brother, who was at Tyndall with his wife and daughter. I denied it and begged him to let me stay with him. He'd run away from home a few times. He hated our church and knew how ridiculously strict it all was—he totally got it."

"So, you moved in with your brother? On base at Tyndall?"

"Yeah. Decided not to go back to Pensacola . . . drop out for a semester till I figure things out. I got a job but was miserable. He, his wife, and kid went back to Atlanta for a long weekend. That's when I found the small gay bar in Panama City Beach. I walked in and met Kirk. He bought me a drink and seemed cool at first."

"How old was he?"

"Twenty-four. He drank too much—though I didn't know that then. A few weeks went by and he asked me to move in with him. I thought he loved me. I moved out. Told my brother we were just roommates."

Rick narrowed his eyes at the scar. "Did he do that?"

Trey nodded.

"What happened?"

"Kirk got transferred to Albany, Georgia. He asked me to go with him. I shouldn't've but—" Trey stopped.

"What did your brother say?"

"I think he suspected we were more than roommates. He tried to talk me out of leaving . . . I should've listened. I quit my job and jumped. So stupid."

"We've all done stupid things. What happened in Albany?"

"At first it was cool. I got a great job at the Delta commuter at the airport. I was a ramp rat but a college dropout. Freedom. Rock music. Being able to go to the movies. Sex." Trey paused and took a sip of beer. "His drinking got worse and I didn't let him . . . you know—so he started bringing other guys home. I moved into the other bedroom. That's when things got worse. He'd get drunk, beat on the door, and yell. I'd push my dresser in front of the door and sit in the dark as he screamed and screamed. Then he'd cry and beg for forgiveness—the next morning, things were good until they weren't. Over and over."

"When did he do that?" Rick said, pointing again to Trey's temple.

"One night, I forgot to move the dresser."

Shit, Trey. Don't interrupt him. Rick slowly nodded.

"He was strong—had played football at FSU. He broke down the door. He got me here, here, and here." Trey pointed to his lip, chin, and left eye. "He wore this stupid ring."

That sonofabitch. Don't react. Let him keep talking. "What'd you do?"

"I should've fought back, but I didn't . . . couldn't. I just took it." Trey turned away from Rick and looked at the dark lake. "I thought he loved me. He finally stopped swinging and started crying. Begging me to forgive him. Maybe 'cause I wasn't fighting back or 'cause of the blood."

"What'd you do?"

"I got up off the floor. Pulled on my jeans and T-shirt. Drove to my only friend in that town. He took one look at me and instantly knew what had happened."

"Who?"

"Bobby. Porsche. He was a drag queen at The Place."

"The Place?"

"The only gay bar in a sea full of rednecks. He told me later he knew Kirk was no good."

"Did he help you?"

Trey nodded. "He tried to clean me up, but it was too much blood. So, he dropped me off at the hospital. He couldn't go in."

"Why? Was he in drag?"

"No. His mom was the ER nurse there, and they hadn't spoken in years. She X-rayed me, stitched me up, but she called the police."

"Yeah, saw the report. You didn't press charges though?"

"No, I couldn't—" Trey voice trembled over the crackling fire between them.

Rick fought the overwhelming urge to go to Trey and hold him tightly. *What the fuck do I say? Don't make him feel badly. Say something.* "Tiger, I am so sorry that happened. You don't have to tell me any more, but I wonder why—not like you should've or shouldn't. No judgment, only why?"

"You'll think I'm stupid—"

"Never."

"I was . . . embarrassed. Abandoned my whole life . . . moved to the middle of nowhere 'cause I thought he loved me."

Kinda like Bari—Tel Aviv. I know that feeling, Trey. "I get it." Rick paused and allowed a moment to pass before pressing. "What'd the police do?"

"Not much. Treated me like I was toxic. Wore gloves. Scared to even touch me or my blood. Looked at me like I was . . . an abomination like my preacher used to yell from the pulpit. Pervert." Trey closed his eyes. "They wrote it up and wanted to call my parents in Atlanta, but I begged them not to. Technically they couldn't—I was eighteen." He tightened his jaw and whispered, "I couldn't let them see me like that."

Rick nodded. "Did you leave?"

"Bobby walked into that hospital. Confronted his mom and the police. He got me from that ER. He didn't want to, but I convinced him to take me back over to Kirk's."

"Why?"

"Drop off his car, get my stuff, and leave . . . for good."

"You went back?"

"I shouldn't have. Should've listened to Bobby, but I snuck in. Kirk was passed out on the couch. I grabbed up my things and quietly made it to the door. That's when I heard the click of the gun."

Jesus, Trey.

"He knew this was it. I was leaving. Started begging me not to go." Trey again closed his eyes. "It was kinda slow-motion. He's yelling louder, raising his arm, and aiming that gun at my face." Trey opened his eyes and stared at Rick. "It was weird but I wasn't scared. I should've been, but something changed."

"What were you feeling?"

"I don't know. Numb. Sorry for him. But then I focused on that gun and then his eyes filled with hate. He didn't care about me . . . this wasn't love."

"How'd you get away?"

"Two words. 'Bye, Kirk.' Turned my back and walked out."

Rick grimaced. "Where'd you go?"

"Couch-surfed for a few weeks with coworkers. Got my stitches out and my face healed. Got my transfer to Atlanta, but my parents insisted I move back home. I had nowhere else to go. We nearly had to get a restraining order as Kirk wouldn't stop calling or showing up."

"They took you back in?" Rick asked.

"Yeah, but on the condition not to tell anybody and do Exodus. It's this gay reparative—"

"I know what it is, Trey," Rick interrupted. "They didn't want anybody to know?"

Trey nodded.

"Jesus, they were more worried about their reputation?"

"I guess."

"What did they say about the scar?"

"Nothing. They never asked me about it. No one ever has till you." Trey paused.

"So that's the gap?"

"Yeah. I did Exodus, stayed in the closet, and transferred to Liberty to finish college. Now you know."

Trey tried to look away but Rick caught his eyes. Rick's face filled with his concern. *I knew it—Claren has no idea how deep this went. Exodus, religion, domestic abuse. Jesus, Trey.*

"You think I'm weak."

"No."

"That I should've fought back. I should've—"

"No, I don't, Trey." Rick waited to catch his eyes. "You were barely eighteen—a kid. One muscle reflex, intentional or not, and he'd have killed you. What I think is you're brave."

"I don't know."

"Why?"

"Every time I stare in a mirror and see it, I relive it. Him."

"We all have scars, Tiger. Some are more visible than others."

"I guess."

"You were right though."

"'Bout what?"

"That wasn't love."

Trey rubbed his face and tightened his shoulders.

Rick sensed Trey's emotions boiling from reliving the memory. "Trey, I just—"

"So now you know you weren't the first man to hit me."

"What—"

"Or put a gun in my face."

"The first was an accident." *Great, so our intake triggered him and now he thinks I'm like that asshole. Hell no.* "I'm not Kirk."

They sat in silence and watched the embers glow for a few minutes.

"Come here?" Rick asked.

Trey didn't move.

"Come here."

"What?"

"You really are stubborn. Please?"

Trey got up and flopped down next to him, leaning back against Rick's strong cradle.

"It happens more than you think. Not only to straight people. You're not alone." Rick squeezed him. "Let me see it." He kissed Trey's scar. "You tired?"

"Yeah."

"Come on. Let's get some sleep."

Whether it was the beer, moon on the lake, or the fire, once they'd crawled into the tent, Trey's breathing grew louder and in rhythm as he fell asleep instantly. Rick rolled over and felt Trey's body against his. *You better hope that I never meet you, Kirk. Never again. Not on my watch.*

Trey awoke to an empty tent and the sound of the zipper flapping in the wind. One of his favorite sounds: he heard splashing in the lake. He got up, stepped outside.

"'Bout time, sleepy head! Did ya sleep well?"

"Yeah."

"Come join me?"

Trey stripped down, walked down to the water, and waded in. Rick came up with a big smile and splashed him.

"Refreshing right?"

Trey grinned and splashed him back.

Ring, ring.

The two short bursts awoke Claren early on Saturday morning.

"Hello."

"Claren?" Chris asked.

"Yes."

"Your guys are up."

"What? Rick?"

"Yes. Sorry I woke you, but you asked me to call."

"No, it's okay." Claren glanced at her bedside clock and tried to clear her mind. *Jesus, Rick, 6:35.* "Where are they now? Did they leave base?"

"No, but they're way out on the perimeter. There's a lake. I didn't even know it was there."

"What are they doing?"

"Right now, skinny-dipping."

Ha! That sounds about right. "Do you have clear sight line?"

"Yeah, all three cameras. We're even getting audio when they're by the packs."

"Good."

"Should we keep recording?"

"Yes, Tibbins wants all the footage. We'll edit and review next week."

"Okay."

"Nice work. I'll log on later to see. Please keep me posted."

"Will do."

Claren hung up the phone and pictured Rick and Trey frolicking in the water. *Be careful, Rick. Keep your head. You're not totally alone in the woods.* She opened her laptop and logged into her secure network. *Nice work, Chris. All three cameras—every angle. Geez, put on some clothes.* She shut her laptop.

I hate snooping. Dee, you better have a point to all this.

CHAPTER 32
TARGET

As they dried themselves and dressed, Rick noticed Trey staring at him. *Time to distract him a bit.* "Today, we've got target practice. Now that you know the equipment, you'll need to know how to use it." Rick pulled on his shorts and then reached back into his pack. He removed the Glock 17. "We'll follow it up with cleaning it and oiling it. Then lunch."

Trey dressed in his shorts and a T-shirt.

"After lunch, we'll hunt for dinner followed by an hour more of training." Rick added, "See, I didn't lie. Only a couple hours of training today. Hungry?"

"Yeah, what's for breakfast?"

Rick tossed him a lighter. "Light the fire and I'll make us some coffee to go with our boiled eggs and beef jerky."

After breakfast, Rick returned their focus to training. In his nightly sessions, Rick had taught Trey every detail of the firearm. They had practiced disassembling and reassembling the Glock more than a hundred times over the past week. Trey could recite the details when Rick prodded, "How many parts to a Glock 17, Trey?"

"Thirty-four."

"Good, take it apart."

Trey disassembled it on the floor of the tent.

"Not bad. Two minutes. Reassemble it. Now tell me about it," Rick said.

"Not again—"

"Yes, again."

Trey huffed but relented. "It has integrated recoil spring assembly, which replaced the original two-piece recoil spring and tube design."

"Good. Let's go." Rick led them out to a clearing behind their campsite. "Today we fire it. I remember you saying you were used to shotguns. Have you ever fired a handgun?"

"Yeah, but never a Glock."

In their time together, Rick learned that Trey had spent most of his summers on his mother's family farm near Mobile, Alabama, which explained two things about this suburban kid from Atlanta. First, he had a deeper Southern drawl at times than most Atlantans. Second, he had been around shotguns and rifles most of his life but did not have much experience with handguns.

"Now we need some targets." Rick took the empty beer cans from the night before and placed them in a line on a fallen log about thirty yards away, toward the open field, before the tree line. He returned, took the Glock, and asked, "Odd or even?"

Trey shook his head. "I don't know. Odd?"

Rick's hands furiously loaded the magazine, re-clipped, and fired. *Pop! Pop! Pop!*

The first, third, and fifth cans blew off the log in a matter of seconds.

Rick removed the magazine, recoiled the clip, and handed the warm gun to his recruit.

"Whoa! How did you do that?"

"Practice. Lots of practice. That's what I'm gonna teach you."

"For real?"

"Yup. Your turn. Load it."

Rick observed him carefully. *He's too tense. Loosen him up.* "You can do this, pull it all the way back till it clicks."

"Like that?"

"Yup. Now do it again." Rick made Trey repeat the same process five or six times. He coached until Trey exhibited a fluidity in his movements to assemble and load the gun.

"How's that?"

"Good, good. Now let's see your stance."

Trey stood rigid and held up the gun with both hands. Rick came from behind and kicked his legs apart casually.

"Wider stance. Good. You want a solid footing, but loosen up." Rick tapped the backs of Trey's knees with his own. "Don't lock out your knees. Stay loose."

He reached around Trey and readjusted his outstretched arms as he spoke into his left ear. "You want to stay loose but firm. The recoil's not as bad as your PawPaw's shotgun, but it's got a kick that you'll need to get used to."

Rick felt a tingle in his chest as Trey eased into his arms.

"Now?"

"Hold up, you gotta call your shot. You fire only at what you intend to hit. Understood? What number?"

"Got it. Two."

Pop.

The bark below the second can split off, but the can remained.

"Not bad, not bad."

"But I didn't hit it."

"So? You came close. What—you thought you could pick this up that easy? Again," Rick barked.

Pop! Pop!

Trey loaded and fired again and again. Each time they would reset the cans, and also added pinecones. After a half hour, his aim was coming to him.

At this point, Rick pulled out his P22 and they began taking turns.

An hour later, Rick said, "All right, last one. Call your shot."

"Three and six."

"Two targets? Okay."

Pop! Pop! Pop!

Three shots rang out and both cans flew off the log. Trey turned to Rick, beaming.

"No shit, that's impressive, Tiger." Rick smiled. "Proud of you."

Trey grinned even wider.

The following week, Director Tibbins mirrored Trey's grin as the room full of Pentagon brass chuckled and nodded in agreement with Rick's statement as they watched the screening.

Lt. Colonel Bradley Smithers broke the silence. "Fag or not, the civ's got skills."

Tibbins nodded but glanced at Claren. *I know, Claren. I don't like the F-word any more than you or our civ—but we both can see he meant it as a compliment.*

Rick and Trey returned to the blackened, smoldering campfire. "Let's take it apart."

"Again?"

Rick nodded and held up his watch to time him. He made him assemble and disassemble the gun ten times in a row. "All right, done. Good job. Now we clean it."

"So I have to do this every time?" Trey asked.

"Yes." Rick explained using an unorthodox analogy. "It's like your cock, Trey. Keep it clean. Only point it at someone you want or intend to use it on. Aim it and shoot your load."

"Yeah, but mine only shoots blanks."

"So, you got a long barrel, and yours is easier to clean." Rick winked. "Besides, in the right circumstance, even a blank can scare the shit out of your enemy."

"Ha, ha—he's gotta point," the colonel said.

Tibbins breathed deeply and smiled at Claren. She rolled her eyes. He had intentionally left Rick's analogy in for his audience. The chuckles in the room confirmed his decision. *I knew it. Men are men. Straight men may not like another man's cock but we love our own.*

"Let me see it." Rick took the Glock and looked down the barrel. He engaged the empty chamber and released the trigger.

Click.

"Done, it's clean. Pack it up," Rick said, and nodded to the case. "You hungry?"

"Yeah. What's for lunch?" Trey asked as he packed up the Glock.

"PB and Js! The lunch. Of. Champions!" Rick shouted, his voice echoing across the lake.

"Rick Morgan, do your corny jokes ever get you laid?"

"Every time, Tiger, every time." Rick gyrated his hips.

Trey shook his head. "Ha-ha-ha."

They ate the sandwiches and watched an egret fishing near the shore on the opposite side of the lake.

Trey asked, "What's next?"

"Let's go shopping."

"Where?"

"I told you, there's food all around us. You have to know where to look. Come on."

Rick guided Trey to the meadow and then they made a wide circle toward the tree line. "Here. Taste this."

"Wow, it tastes like—"

"Carrots?"

"Yeah, kinda. What is it?

"Purslane, the Native Americans used to eat it. And this is chicory." Rick was walking around and pointing to the plants. "That's fireweed."

"You're like a walking encyclopedia. Where did you learn all this?"

"Boy Scouts, the Corps, and here on the Farm for re-occurrents and survival training."

"Here?"

"Yeah, that's how I know this lake. Most people don't leave the fields around base. Me, I need fresh air."

"Why do they call it the Farm?"

"'Cause it looks like a farm from the road. And it used to be one. Not everything is so secret."

Trey nodded.

"Now we need a protein," Rick said. "Come on."

They walked back to camp and Rick retrieved a ziplock bag of fishing line, hooks, weights, and a red and white bobber from his bag. "Our tackle."

"What else you got in that bag?" Trey asked.

"Couple of grenades—don't go snooping. Now, go get us a fishing pole, grunt."

"How long?" Trey asked.

"I don't care. You pick."

Rick observed Trey go into the woods and look around. *I knew I was right. He trusts me and he's even having fun.* Rick pulled off his T-shirt and shorts, leaving on only his boxers. He went down to the shallows of the lake and dug in the soft mud near the water's edge.

"Will this work?"

"Yup. Nice pole," Rick said, with his corny laugh.

"Yeah, that's what your dad said."

"Ha!" Rick laughed. "Go get our tackle."

Trey hurried back to the campsite. Rick watched him strip down to his boxers. *Damn you look good, Tiger. And now you get my humor too.*

Trey returned. Rick pulled up a worm and baited the hook. He grabbed the stick, tied the loose end of the line, and waded out into the water.

He looked at the pale white skin of his recruit. "I think your granny Carter would smack you right now and say 'Tigerboy, you bettah slather on sunscreen—or you gonna fry like an egg.'" Rick tried to imitate a Southern accent.

"Ha! Well she would smack somebody all right—you, for that pathetic Yankee attempt. Do you have some in your bag?"

"Sho 'nuff."

As Rick fished, Trey rummaged through the backpack and pulled out the sunscreen. He lathered it on thick and then shoved it back in the bag, but noticed a roll of gold, square thin packages. *Condoms? Oh my god, is he into me too?*

Trey did his best to erase the thought and waded out to the water wearing only his boxers and a UNH ball cap he'd also found in Rick's pack.

"What's up, Wildcat? And here I thought you were a Liberty Flame—or is it Flamer?"

"What?"

Rick pointed at the UNH hat.

"Ha!" Trey splashed Rick.

They took turns with the pole for the next hour trying both worms and crickets as bait. They said little between them and eased into a comfortable silence.

How can he be so damn patient? Then a slight movement on the line, and the pole jerked.

"Hold on, Tiger," Rick said softly, as the pole dipped once more, "Wait for it . . .wait for it . . . now."

Trey pulled up, and the stick bent but did not break. He gently guided the catch to the shallow waters, and Rick picked up the croaking catfish.

"Nice. Look at her. She's a beauty! Five or six pounds. Nicely done, Tiger."

"My granny taught me."

Rick smiled.

Trey restarted the fire, filled the small pot with water from the lake, and boiled it for several minutes as instructed.

Rick carefully dressed the fish and filleted chunks for a stew. He wiped his long knife and handed it to Trey, guiding him to prepare the veggies.

By 1500, the water had boiled and the stew was simmering over the fire.

"Now we're gonna cheat a little," Rick said with a wink as he dug around in his pack. Trey widened his eyes. *Holy crap. Is that what he meant by hand-to-hand this afternoon?*

"Here, use this." Rick handed Trey a small packet. *What? A condom? Try to be cool. Calm down.*

Rick blurted out, "Salt 'n' peppa here."

"What?" Trey didn't laugh but looked down in his hand to see the packet. "Oh my god, it's just salt and pepper. Ha, ha, ha!"

"After all my good material today, and *that* is what you find funny?" Again attempting a Southern accent, Rick added, "Ya ain't right, that boy ain't right."

Trey gathered more firewood as instructed and returned to find Rick wearing his T-shirt, but he had changed out of his damp boxers and into a new pair. Following his lead, Trey grabbed his T-shirt and then dug into his pack to find similar boxers. He stripped off the damp ones and laid them on the rock next to Rick's by the fire.

Trey saw Rick steal a glance. *He's checking me out. Yeah, you're trying to act like you're stoking the fire but I saw you look.*

Rick added more wood, and then took his UNH cap off Trey.

"Come on."

Rick motioned as they walked twenty feet to the flat, grassy edge of the field. "In our work, you have to observe every detail and be prepared to act." Rick's serious tone returned. The jokes were gone. "Defense is essential, but sometimes you have to initiate an offense. Strike first."

Shit, we're gonna fight?

CHAPTER 33
DEFENSE

"Have you heard of Krav Maga?" Rick asked.

"No, who is he?"

"Not who . . . what. It's an Israeli combat technique, like judo or aikido. It combines gymnastics, boxing, and wrestling. I've tried to make some of our training fun—but this part's serious. Got it?"

Trey nodded.

"Look, you're a civ and I want you to avoid conflict and combat at all times, but if you need to, I want you to know how to protect yourself."

"I used to box. I can throw a punch."

"That'll help, but this is *different*. They don't teach this on Campus or at the Farm. This stays between us."

"Okay. How do you say it? Crave Muga?"

"*Krav Maga*. It was started in Eastern Europe by this guy, Imi Lichtefeld. He was both a wrestler and a gymnast."

"Like us?" Trey said.

"Exactly. Imi brought KM to Israel in the late forties after World War II. It's about counterattacking, or attacking preemptively *after* you have assessed a situation. You want to target the body's most vulnerable points: eyes, neck, throat, face, ribs, knee, fingers, groin, or nose."

"The nose, huh?"

"That was an accident, Trey." Rick rolled his eyes. "Speaking of— let me take a look." He examined Trey's nose. The bruising was nearly gone, and it had healed nicely with only a slight curve to the right. Pressing down and side to side, Trey didn't flinch. "No tenderness?"

"Nope."

"Great," Rick said. "Now, it's essential that you maintain awareness of your surroundings while dealing with a threat. Know your escape routes, other attackers, or objects that you can use to defend or attack. It's really about situational awareness. You have to be able to relax in a tense situation and observe your surroundings."

"Will I be in tense situations?"

"Yeah, but you'll have your training, and me. Now listen to me, zone out everything. Focus and apply force."

Trey furrowed his brow and tightened his lips.

"Attack me," Rick barked.

The following week, Director Tibbins glanced at the audience of Pentagon brass in the room, who were staring at the large screen displaying the video of Rick and Trey.

"Did you learn KM in the Marines?" Trey asked.

"Fuck no. Long story, but I dated an Israeli special-forces interrogation officer. The Israeli training center in Eilat makes Parris Island look like Club Med."

A rumble and a few chuckles emanated from the men assembled. *Perfect! They got it but they don't see it. Ha! I was right. Claren thought it too risky. Thought that we should edit, but Rick did not use the pronoun "him" to give away the gender of his Israeli lover. They only registered the wisecrack over the comparison of Eilat versus Parris Island.*

As Rick and Trey sparred, several comments were elicited in the room.

"Jesus, he looks like a natural."

"Rewind that, Dee. There. See him. He recoils back to fighting stance."

"Yup. He's mimicking Rick's moves."

"You're telling me the kid's never had training?" Smithers interjected over the comments.

"No." Tibbins glanced at Claren.

"We selected our civ based upon criteria of our ops desk." Her tone was clinical. "Every tactic, pressure point—Dr. Martinez has spent the past decade refining our protocol."

Smithers turned to her. "How? What's the bottom line?"

"Propensity to action." She rewound the tape and stood. "He's outsized and outmatched, but again and again he doesn't back down."

On screen, Trey picked himself off the ground. He endured multiple punches, kicks, and shoves, landing dozens of times on his back.

"He's a tough lil sonnavabitch. But this is a mock simulation," Smithers countered.

Claren glanced at Dee. He nodded slightly.

"We've field-tested." She lowered her jaw but said nothing more.

"Shit. I always knew you Langley boys kept secrets but damn— fag spies?"

Claren clenched her jaw tighter.

"Training is training, Bradley. Don't miss the point here," Dee snapped. "This *gay* recruit went through a Ladder, and we have him in a field test in two weeks."

"And a critical assignment at the end of next month," Claren added.

"Why disclose? You show us this video. What do you want?" Smithers darted his eyes from Claren back to Dee.

"Show you a different perspective. A civilian recruit."

"Horseshit—" Smithers sat rigid. "Don't play me, Dee."

"He's a civilian recruit—"

"Service ban." Smithers's two words hung in the air.

Dee nodded.

"Yes, Bradley." Claren sat forward in her chair. "We've quietly recruited nearly forty candidates over the past decade to our ops desk."

"All military?"

"Yes. Except this one." She stared up at the screen.

"Where, then? Did he volunteer?"

"Not exactly." Dee stared at the colonel. "Should we continue?"

Smithers nodded slowly and turned to the screen. Dee pressed Play and glanced at Claren, who widened her eyes.

I know, I know, Claren. Not how I thought it would play out. Patience.

Rick used his full strength, slamming Trey to the ground and into a submission hold. After the final submission, Tibbins had edited out the next few minutes and subsequent dinner by the fire. This was intended to protect both Rick and the protocol. He chose to pick up the training Sunday morning after Rick and Trey awoke by the lake. The missing footage showed several minutes of struggle, followed by physical contact between the men. The KM lesson was over.

Only Tibbins, Doc M, and Claren had reviewed and analyzed the final footage.

"Well they are certainly into one another." Dee raised his eyebrows.

"I think our recruit's doing great, healthy bonding," Doc M said to assure Claren and Tibbins.

"Rick better hold the line," Claren said as she hit Rewind to watch the footage again.

By the lake in the final submission hold, Rick saw the panic return to Trey as his eyes widened and he struggled under Rick's weight.

"Takedown, takedown."

Rick immediately loosened his grip but remained straddling Trey's torso.

Trey's panting intensified.

"Relax, Tiger. Breathe."

Trey exhaled deeply and his rigid body melted beneath Rick.

"You're okay?" Rick smiled.

"Yeah." Trey broke his gaze and stared at the groin now inches from his face. Suddenly, Trey craned his neck, tucked his chin to chest, and buried his nose in Rick's boxers.

"Whoa, easy, Trey."

Trey leaned his head back but avoided Rick observing him. He squeezed his eyes shut. "Sorry, I—"

"Don't apologize. It's okay. Why did you do that?"

"I don't know . . . Took a chance."

"You like it, don't cha."

"Yeah." Trey bit his lip.

Rick saw his hesitation and observed Trey's left eye twitch as tension washed over his face. *Damn. He's gripped in fear.*

"Rick, please don't tell anyone I did that."

"Geez, you are too paranoid, Tiger. Who the hell am I gonna tell? Only us out here," Rick said, unaware of the cameras. "Trey, look at me. It's perfectly healthy—totally natural. I know you were taught a lot of garbage, but you gotta stop beating yourself up."

Trey's frown softened.

"Besides, beating you up is *my* job." Rick slid down and rolled over onto his back, lying next to him. They were both scratched up from the grasses and covered in dirt.

"Was that a beginner session?"

"No, my little overachiever. Come on."

As Rick rolled up to stand, his tip popped out of his boxers' flap. He readjusted, but Trey couldn't resist.

"Hello, Mr. Pecker."

Rick seemed to ignore the joke and helped up Trey, but then put him in a quick headlock.

"Hey—let go."

"What am I gonna do with my Tiger?" Rick said, rubbing his head playfully. He loosened his grip as they returned to camp.

"Can you hand me that spoon?" Rick said, and stirred their dinner. "So, what'cha think?"

"I think you'd probably kick my ass. You were holding back—weren't you?"

"Of course, but not toward the end. You're stronger than you look . . . and stronger than you think."

Trey grinned at the compliment.

"Dinner will be ready soon. Let's get washed up." Rick grabbed a bar of Ivory soap from his pack, a small towel, and stripped down.

They walked naked back to the lake and scrubbed up. The water stung their grass hives and abrasions from an hour of KM training. They toweled off and pulled on dry boxers. Rick then pulled out a small tube of Lubriderm.

"Ouch."

"Hold still," Rick said as he applied the lotion.

The lotion was soothing, but touching Trey was a bit sensual. *Hold the line—damn it, I only want to hold him.* Their familiar tension was back, but it lost to their mutual hunger.

Rick looked up to see the sun setting over the lake.

Nirvana.

For their last night, they splurged and burned a huge pile of wood to keep the mosquitoes at bay.

"The stew was awesome. Can I have seconds?"

"Of course." Rick smiled at the compliment. "But last bite means last dish."

"Worth it."

Trey cleaned all the dishes and returned to the fire as the night stars once again shined overhead.

"No beer tonight?"

"I always have a little contraband." Rick pulled out a metal flask, unscrewed the top, and took a swig. "Here, you need some hair on your chest."

Trey took a whiff of the whiskey. "PawPaw stopped drinking before us grandkids were born, but during a hurricane all bets were off. He drank whiskey. Granny would get so mad, but me and my cousins loved it. He would get lit and tell us stories."

Rick laughed. He was growing fond of his recruit's stories.

Trey took a swig, but coughed and choked.

"You get used to it." Rick chuckled.

"Tell me a story. About you?"

"What do you want to know?"

"I don't know. What was your training like?"

Rick thought a moment, as if finding a good one. He talked about his first time dropping from a chopper on a line with his Marine squadron. He skipped around but also told Trey about meeting Jeni for the first time. They passed the flask several times, taking sips.

"Do you ever go out?" Trey asked.

"You mean to gay bars?"

"Yeah."

"Time to time. Mostly when I'm overseas or on holidays. Not too often in DC, but I have gone dancing at Tracks a couple times with Jeni and Kristin."

"Dancing? This I have to see."

"Oh I can bust a move."

"I bet you can. If I pass all this—will you take me?"

"Sure."

"Seriously, promise me."

"I promise." Rick looked up at the night sky. "When I dance, I think of all those who can't."

"What do you mean?"

"I'm lucky, Trey. Before, we'd all go dancing. I don't know how but I'm HIV negative. You have no idea how many friends I've lost."

"AIDS?"

Rick nodded. "No one knew back then. So fucking unfair. Beautiful men. Dancing, laughing, loving life one moment—then withered, gaunt, hollow—gone." Rick closed his eyes tightly. "No one knows their names, their smiles, their bodies. Some of them only exist now in my mind." Rick opened his eyes and stared at Trey. "When I dance—I dance with them and for them."

They sat in silence and gazed up at the stars in a solemn moment, a prayer for those gone before. Trey said softly, "I've never known a time without AIDS. You can only imagine what they taught us at my Christian school. God's punishment. I think it's why I am so afraid of sex. That and what happened to me when I was thirteen . . ."

Rick nodded.

"Are you seeing anybody now?"

"Not at the moment."

"What happened to the Israeli?"

Rick darted his eyes and took a deep breath. "Complicated."

Trey nodded. Again, the comfort of silence returned. The fire crackled.

Rick studied Trey's face in the glow. "What's on your mind, Tiger?"

"I know we can't pretend that . . ." Trey stopped.

"What?"

"That this is all normal."

Rick sat forward and tilted his head.

"I get that we're here for training, but can I not be a 'job' to you tonight?"

Rick grabbed him by his arm and pulled him into his familiar cradle.

"Come here. You think too much. Let it go." Rick kissed his forehead. "Look at these stars. We've had perfect weather and we're at this beautiful lake."

"I know, and I'm grateful, really, thank you. It's just . . ."

"What? It's okay to say what you want, Trey."

"I want a redo."

"A what?" Rick frowned.

"A redo."

"What do you mean a 'redo'?"

"My first time wasn't my choice. The few other times weren't that good." Trey was literally starting to shake but tried to find his courage. "Rick, it's not my first time, but I wish it was . . . tonight. Here. With you."

Rick tightened his jaw. He put down the flask. "So how would this *redo* start?"

Trey shook his head slightly.

Rick pulled Trey tighter to his chest and kissed the young man deeply. *Oh man, he is candy.*

"Hold the line." Claren's voice echoed in his head.

Trey opened his mouth and reciprocated Rick's passionate kiss. Rick felt Trey's erection against his own.

Damn, he wants it. I want it. Fuck it.

Rick pulled back and grabbed the flask. "Last swig. You?"

Trey shook his head.

Rick emptied the flask and tossed it over at his pack.

"Sure about this?"

"Yeah," Trey said as he slipped his hand down to the edge of Rick's waist.

Rick met his hand and guided downward to his hard muscle. He kissed him again softly, pinching his bottom lip between his teeth lightly. The young man shifted under Rick's larger frame. Their bodies were entangled as their breathing deepened in unison. *Go slow, take your time. He's not ready. Keep your head.*

Rick stood and pulled Trey to his feet. "So, I'm a redo?"

"Totally."

Rick smiled and led Trey toward their tent. They stripped down, and then Trey grabbed at his cock.

"No, not yet. Let's go slow. Okay?"

Trey nodded.

Rick unzipped the tent and motioned for Trey to enter. "I'll be right there." He dug into his pack and found the lube and condoms.

He entered the tent to find Trey naked and sitting cross-legged in anticipation. The small camping lamp illuminated the green walls and glowed from Trey's pale skin. Rick crawled toward him slowly. He paused and kissed Trey's shins, knees, thighs, and stopped at his scrotum. He gently licked Trey but skipped his shaft and head, going right to his navel, which tightened at the touch of Rick's scruffy beard.

"Lights on or off?"

"Is on okay?"

Rick nodded, grabbed Trey's waist, and drew him down into his embrace. *God, you feel so good. He fits like a glove. Tight little muscle man. My tiger boy.* He explored Trey's body with his tongue from his navel to his neck, then over to his armpit before returning to his mouth. Trey's tongue met his own as they deepened their embrace. Trey opened his legs under Rick and tilted his hips. Rick could feel the heat of Trey's shaft against his navel as his own pressed against Trey's tight ass.

Trey clenched and his body went rigid.

Check in again—don't press this. Rick stared into Trey's eyes. "You sure?"

Trey nodded and pulled Rick downward into his embrace.

Rick moved his rough hands from Trey's neck to his chest, and traced his abs. He grabbed the bottle of liquid and squirted a dab on Trey's shaft and head. He then applied an ample amount to his own wrapped cock and lathered it with his right hand.

He probed Trey's groin with one finger and massaged in a circular motion.

"Relax. Breathe," Rick instructed and inserted his wet fingers.

Rick gently increased his pressure against the young man for several minutes before attempting to enter him. Using his experience, Rick postponed his own pleasure. "Easy, relax. Feel me pulsate. You feel it?"

"Yeah," Trey whispered as his warm, muscular body melted against Rick.

Slowly, Rick entered as he studied Trey's face. His eyes had widened. "That's it, relax. Does it feel good?"

"Yeah, so tight but I want you."

"You have me. Breathe."

Trey kissed Rick as he pressed deeper into the young man.

Oh my god, so warm. Fuck yeah. Electricity shot through Rick as he explored deeper into the tight void and pulsed.

"Ahh." Trey moaned and let out his breath.

Easy, let him relax. Deeper, deeper. Rick licked Trey's neck and moved toward his right ear. He nibbled his lobe and softly whispered, "You feel so amazing. So awesome. You okay?"

"Yeah."

"Feel good?"

"So good."

"You've never really done this before?"

"No, not like this . . ." Trey nibbled at Rick's neck and loosened his ab muscles before closing the gap between their hips. His abs pressed in and out. Rick could feel Trey's throbbing cock sandwiched between them.

Fuck yeah. Feel it. Give into me. Rick kissed him and energy pulsed through them as they moved in one motion. *That's right, hold on tight.* He closed his eyes and felt Trey wrap his legs around his torso.

What the fuck are you doing? Suddenly, Bari's voice echoed in his head.

Not now, Bari.

Rick, what the hell are you doing with this kid? What about us?

First, he's not a kid. Us? Are you fucking joking? There is no us—you walked out on me. Rick squeezed his eyes tight and built his rhythm. *Trey, fuck yeah. Trey.*

"Trey?"

"What?"

"Still good?"

Trey squeeze harder and pressed himself into Rick's pulsating motion.

Rick opened his eyes and stared into Trey's intense expression. Breathing as one, moving as one, Rick leaned down and kissed him passionately.

After several minutes, Trey found Rick's left ear. "I'm close. Are you?"

"Yeah, me too. Go for it."

Trey's body tightened intensely, and he arched his back. Rick watched as Trey pushed his chin up and grunted.

"Oh fuck, oh fuck."

Rick could feel his spasms, and for a moment the tent around them faded.

"YEAH. FUCK . . . ARRGH," Rick yelled as he released.

Rick kissed him passionately. He felt the cool beads of sweat from their passion. He pulled out and removed the condom. He kissed Trey on his neck, lips, and forehead.

Rick rolled onto his back.

Fucking your civ operative. Classic.

Shut up, Bari.

What the fuck? You're using that kid to get back at me?

It's not like that—it's not about you.

Not sure Claren would agree.

What's that supposed to mean?

You call this holding the line?

Rick shook his head.

"Rick?" Trey interrupted his thoughts.

"Yeah?"

"What's wrong? Where'd you go?"

"Nowhere. I'm right here."

Trey widened his eyes.

Busted. Fuck. Rick exhaled deeply. *What should I . . . Stop hiding. Be honest with him.* "It's fine—I'm fine."

Trey frowned.

"It's that . . . I've never done this with someone from work before."

"Work? So I am just a job?"

"No, you're not, Tiger." Rick kissed him again. "I have to be careful—this could get us in some trouble."

"I won't say anything."

Rick looked at Trey's eyes, which were now staring up at the tent. *He's in his head about this too. Talk to him. Talk it out.*

"What are you feeling?"

"A little bit of— I don't know, love. But a lot of guilt."

And that's why you don't fuck your civ.

Get out of here, Bari. Now!

Rick sat up on his elbow. "You wanted this, right?"

"Yeah."

"You okay?"

"You don't have to keep asking me that."

He leaned over and kissed Trey's forehead. "You said you'd done that before but I don't know—it felt like your first time."

"No, but—yeah." Trey turned his head and sat up. "I'd never done that before. Had someone inside me like that."

Fuck me. It was his first. Be cool, don't freak him out. "Was it good for you?"

"Yeah—it's weird but it was the first time it was fun. Raw. Kinda wild."

"No fear?"

"None."

Rick smiled. "Sounds like a great redo, then."

Trey nodded.

"Wanna go for a swim?"

"Right now?"

Rick took his hand and led him back to the lake, naked in the moonlight. Trey floated on his back as Rick sank below the water.

You think you dodged a bullet? Bari's voice returned.

He's fine. Let it go.

Always playing the edge, dodging bullets. He was innocent—but now.

Now what?

You'll be in his head.

Like you're in mind. Get out, Bari. We're done. I'm done overthinking all this.

Rick emerged from the water and again saw Trey floating peacefully beneath the stars.

Look at him, he's right. A redo is rare. Receive it, don't overthink it.

Rick stared up at the stars and again saw the flashes of former lovers.

He's lucky. Not all of us get a redo.

CHAPTER 34
SUNDAY

Where's Rick? What time is it? Trey awoke alone and glanced at his watch: *Sun - 9:22.*

Mom and Dad will be headed to church soon. I hate Sundays.

"Rick?" Trey called out, but there was no sound beyond the flapping of the unzipped tent door. He stepped into the morning air. The lake was as still as glass. No ripple. No Rick.

His pack's gone. Where'd he go? Was this about last night? The redo?

Trey scanned their campsite but only saw his own backpack and a bottle of water on a nearby rock. As he approached the rock, he saw a note pinned under the bottle.

Morning Tiger,

Today you need to find me. In your pack, there's a map, a compass, and the coordinates. Pack up the tent and your gear. Be here by 1100 or else.

RM

P.S. Thanks for the special night. ☺

9:33. Shit, I better hustle. Trey smiled and re-read the note. *"Special night"—last night was better than "special." At least for me it was.* His thoughts were foggy. *Rick Morgan, my redo. Well, at least there's a smiley face.*

He got dressed, packed up the tent, and grabbed the remaining gear. In his bag he found some beef jerky. *Sweet. That'll be breakfast.* Trey pulled out the map and clipped the compass to his shoulder strap. *Looks like east is that way.* He ate as he set off, orientating to the location on the map.

Thatta boy. You got this, Tiger. Rick was observing Trey from the tree line a few hundred feet away using his compact field binoculars. *You gotta hustle but you can make it. I better stay at least a clip ahead.* Rick hoisted his pack to his shoulders and continued to stay ahead of Trey for the next two hours.

He's gonna ace this. Damn, Tiger. Rick grinned as the young man patiently orientated ever closer to the drop spot. *I guess that church youth group was good for something.* Trey had talked about hiking the Appalachian Trail north of Atlanta with his youth group near Springer Mountain. He had hiked several miles of Georgia's AT over the years and it had clearly left him with skills and a love of being in the woods.

As Trey neared the drop and stepped out of the tree line, Rick was sitting on a bench by a large hangar-like building two hundred yards away.

"You're late," Rick barked. "Let's go, let's go, let's go!"

Trey sprinted to him and then dropped his pack. "I . . . I made it." He gasped and walked in a tight circle with hands on his head.

"You owe me thirty."

"For what?" Trey was about to argue when he saw Rick's raised eyebrows.

"Thirty." Rick repeated.

Trey dropped and banged out the thirty push-ups.

"Good job. You were late, but you made it. I've seen a ton of recruits get lost out there."

Trey stood up and tried to regain his breath. "Is it that important, orientating to drops?"

"Critical. I'll explain in the car. Let's get packed and head home."

They loaded the car and drove toward the main gate exit. "Keep your head down." Rick glanced at the MP at the gate. "Shit."

"What?"

"He's waving us over. Not a word, Trey. Hear me."

Trey nodded as the guard approached Rick on the driver's side.

"Officer Morgan, I need you and the civilian to come with me."

"Is there a problem?"

"Sir, please park and join me in my vehicle."

"What's the problem?"

"No problem, sir, but I was told to bring you to CI for a phone call. Langley."

"Fine." Rick rolled up his window and glanced at Trey. "Follow my lead, keep your mouth closed, and stay calm."

They parked and got into the back of the MP's Ford Explorer. The guard drove them to a set of buildings on the north side of the base.

Who wants to talk? This is exactly why I didn't want to use the Farm. Damn it, Claren. Rick kept his cool exterior but inside he was starting to boil. *Don't spook Trey. Damn this pencil dick—most of these clowns don't even know about our existence. Much less some Army grunt assigned to protect the Farm. I bet they were pissed that they couldn't find us out there on the outer edge of the southwest perimeter. Bet he's never even seen the lake. Look at these cars. Claren said the training center was in between sessions. Something's up.*

Upon stopping the car, the guard spoke up, "Sir, I'm supposed to escort you here. First floor."

"Thank you, Private," Rick said, glancing at his rank. The one-story brick façade building was simply marked *CI Training* as the three men entered.

"All civs need to wait here." The guard motioned to Trey to take a seat on the oak bench just inside the door along the hallway.

"It's cool. I'll be right back," Rick said and then followed the guard through a brown door marked *Operations* in white lettering. The room was quiet except for three officers at opposing desks.

"Oh, Officer Morgan. Here." Rick was directed to the young officer at the desk. "I have him now, ma'am," she said and then handed the phone to Rick. The guard stood by the door, silent and at attention.

"Rick?"

Rick clenched his jaw and turned from view of the officer. "Claren, what's up?"

"I wanted to check in. How'd the training go?"

"Fine."

"Your weather held. How'd he do?"

"Yeah, no rain. He did great. I will write it up when we get back tonight."

"That's why I asked them to grab you. We've had a special request come up."

"What?"

"Since you are already there, Doc M would like you guys to stay over and put Trey through a modified Ladder tomorrow."

"Stay over? A Ladder?"

"Yes, a *modified* one."

"What are we doing here? He's a civ."

"Yes. But we've authorized clearance for him. Is there a problem?"

"No, I've never heard of a civ popping into the Farm and taking a Ladder."

"Rick, his phase two scores and offsite training have all been outstanding, better than most of our recruits from the past two years. He can handle it, especially with your guidance."

"What about his job? Tomorrow's Monday."

"We're on it. There may be a problem with McGuire, but we can speed up the transition."

"Transition?"

"We've got him an interview for Global Airways."

"Global?" Rick paused. *Classic, Claren. Blaming Doc M or Tibbins but you're still fucking with Trey now the same way with me and Jeni. Death grip, by the balls, with our careers dangling. Next that bitchy tone about how this is coming from Tibbins or POTUS. Blaming everybody else as you do the bidding. Damn it—screwing me and Jeni is one thing but now Trey. His job. How is this still a one and done?*

"Rick?"

"Yeah."

"Thought I lost you for a second. Where'd you guys camp?"

"Outer perimeter."

"That explains the call I got. They thought you were AWOL. Glad all went well."

"Yeah, we did target practice, orienting to drop, endurance, and he picked up KM like he'd been doing it his whole life."

"How's his temper? Emotions in check?"

"He's fine."

"Good. And you?"

"He's a pain in the ass but he's picking everything up and growing on me."

Claren paused. "And the line?"

"Clear and intact."

"Good. Listen, you'll need to explain to our cub about the Ladder."

"I'll get him through it."

"Great. One more thing. Doc M would like the session filmed tomorrow. Are you okay with that?"

Like I have a fucking choice. No doubt you already ordered them. "Sure. Anything else?" Rick said.

"Doc M is faxing over the outline for tomorrow. The MP with you will get you guys some bunks, but tonight take our cub off campus and buy yourselves some steaks. Let's check in tomorrow before you guys head back."

"Sounds good. Thanks, Claren."

Wait, she called him "cub"? Something's up. Rick held the phone for a moment and darted his eyes to the three officers pretending to work and not scan his every movement. *A shift. They all know and she knows it or else she'd never let us off campus for dinner or call him "cub" instead of "tiger." She wants me off base for a secure call. The phones are bugged. Be cool.*

Rick handed the officer her phone receiver. "Thanks for grabbing us."

"Of course, Officer Morgan." She smiled. "Let me know if you need anything. The Ladder will be at 0730 and the mess is open at—"

"Six thirty. Thanks." Rick returned her fake smile. *You fucking amateur. I never confirmed the Ladder. You already knew.*

"Right, you know." She blushed a bit. "Well, I'm here till 1900 if you need *anything.*"

"Will do." Rick exited and walked to Trey. "Ready, Cub?"

"What?"

"Let's go." Rick gave Trey a *no more questions* glare.

"Yes, sir."

The three of them rode back to the guard station in silence. Rick glanced at the guard's name and stripes. *Time for me to take charge.*

"Private Cooper, thanks for catching us for my call. I'm expecting a fax now. Have you received it?"

"Let me check at my station desk, sir."

"Great, we'll wait here. Where are you bunking us tonight?"

"Blair East, rooms Alpha and Bravo, first floor, but I can drive you, sir,"

"No need. I know my way. I trained here in '81 and '88. We'll wait here and then head over in my car. Say, Cooper where's a good place for steaks tonight? Is Annie's still over near W & M?"

"Yes, sir. It's great. I'll check on your fax."

"Thank you, Private."

Rick and Trey exited the Explorer and hopped into his BMW.

"Now we wait."

"Okay," Trey said.

Five minutes passed when Private Cooper returned, he had a long strap with three keys, along with a brown envelope. "Here are your keys, sir— entry door and room. And here's a base map and your fax. Again, the mess opens at 0630. Have a good dinner."

"Thank you, Private."

Rick drove across the base to the dorm with the windows up and music blaring. He pulled out a piece of scrap paper and pen from the glove box and scribbled.

Good instincts. Ears listening. Keep casual. Explain @ dinner.

Trey nodded.

They unpacked only essentials in their adjoining rooms and showered with limited small talk.

Before leaving the base at 1630, Rick stood by his car and looked around. He placed his index finger to his lips.

Trey nodded.

Rick opened the trunk and retrieved a box-like device with two wire antennas. He flipped a switch and it beeped, flashed red and then green. Rick swept his car from hood to bumper for devices. The box suddenly beeped at the back bumper.

"Yup," Rick hissed. "Sonnavabitch."

Trey's eyes widened.

Rick circumvented the car twice before opening his driver's-side door.

Beep!

"Got ya." He reached under both seats, fished out the three small devices, and showed them to Trey as they got into the car.

"Wow—"

Rick immediately placed his index finger over his lips again, then shoved all three into the driver's-side door pocket of his BMW.

They drove to the base exit, where Rick stopped. "Private Cooper. I may show this civ Busch Gardens. How late are they open till tonight?"

"Till 2300, sir."

"Great, don't wait up."

Rick drove to US-64 east toward Williamsburg, glancing into the rearview mirror. *No taillights—now let's get rid of these.* He opened the window and tossed out the three tiny devices.

"Now we can talk."

"All this is for real?"

"What? Of course," Rick snapped.

Trey shook his head.

"What, you didn't believe me before, Tiger?"

"No, it's just—those were spy gadgets?"

"No shit, Sherlock."

"But why would they bug your car? Aren't you pissed?"

"Yes, but remember what I told you. We're dark ops. We move among them but none of those clowns know about us."

"Are we okay now?"

"Uh-huh. Hungry?"

"Yeah. Are we really going to Annie's for steaks?"

"Hell no. We're going back to Richmond for barbecue, but like last night—that stays between us." He held out his fist.

"Got it." Trey bumped his fist, top then bottom.

Rick doubled back along an old farming road past the base and onto US-64 west toward Richmond.

"The agents they send to Annie's will be pissed that we made them, but at least they'll get a good steak on the Agency's tab."

Trey rubbed the back of his neck. "Can I say something?"

"What?" Rick asked.

"About last night?"

Shit—knew this was coming. Be cool. Let him talk. "Okay."

"For me, it was incredible, but I'm not naïve. I know we're not in love, and this situation is crazy. I don't have a clue about my assignment but I wanted you to know that I'm glad it's you."

"Me?"

"Yeah, that you're my . . . coach."

"Coach, huh?" Rick glanced over at Trey and flashed a smile. "Look, we're only fifteen days into forty-five together. There's a lot of work ahead before your field test and the assignment."

"I get it, but I'm still glad it's you."

"You may not feel the same way in a few weeks."

"Yes, I will. Don't care how tough it gets, Rick Morgan, you were my redo."

Rick shook his head. *So, now I'm a redo. Give it to him. Let it go.*

"Yup. I enjoyed every second of it."

"Me too, Tiger." Rick grinned. "For the record, *some* sexual contact is permitted within the protocol, but I did push it this weekend. OTR, cool?"

"Yup. Always. Only wanted to talk it out—I know I'm just your job."

"Bullshit. I do care about you, and my . . . no . . . *our* first priority is getting you through training and this whole situation. I want you to find your footing. Until then, I got you, Trey. Understand?"

"Totally. One more question?"

"Let me guess: What's going on? Why are we staying over?"

"Yeah. What about my job? I got to be at work tomorrow."

"I'm sure we'll figure something out. Let me call it in when we reach Richmond." Rick shifted in his seat. "Speaking of calling in, when I was in the office with the guard, I got a call from my superior. They want us to stay over and put you through a Ladder. She told me what was going on but also subtly alerted me to a *shift* by calling you *Cub,* not *Tiger.*"

"Huh, I was wondering why you called me that."

"You see. It's essential to observe not only *what is* being said but what's *not.*"

"Got it and that's a *shift*? A problem in the plan?"

"Kinda. Remember, our team is dark ops. So not a lot of folks at the Agency even know we exist. The few that do, well . . . we have our skeptics. Some of them even don't want to see our team continue."

"Within the Agency?"

"Yup. That's why I didn't want us at the Farm this weekend. I wanted to take you to my cabin."

"Where's that?"

"West Virginia. Lost River."

"So these skeptics knew we were here?"

"Yeah, they insisted. Obviously, I complied, but I never told them *where* on the Farm—there are more than nine thousand acres—so they assumed we'd be at the camps by the evasive driving track. Out at the lake, we were safe. Most agents have never even heard of the lake, much less seen it. It's rarely used. The only person who knew our exact location was my boss."

"And she wouldn't tell 'em?"

"Nope, you can trust her, Trey."

"This spy shit is so complicated—"

"Yes, it is."

"I can't believe they bugged your car."

"Nah, part of the game. Point is we're free—no eyes or ears. Like at the lake."

"But back on base tonight and tomorrow?"

"Every fucking one of them will be watching us." His stern tone returned.

"Great so no pressure." Trey shook his head. "And, I'm guessing a Ladder isn't simply a ladder, then?"

"Nope."

"Geez, it's like y'all have your own language. What is it?"

"A series of operational exercises that you're gonna fucking ace," Rick said. "The most important thing is to clear your head, trust your judgment, and relax. Remember that temper, panic, tears—they won't help you. Let's talk about it over dinner, but try to remember that it's a game."

Rick pulled off and into a Hess station. "Fill 'er up with premium. I'll be right back."

Trey took his credit card and they both got out of the car.

Rick opened the trunk and retrieved a small black case with a mobile phone. He walked over to the back corner of the station and placed a call on the secure Comsat.

"Rick?"

"Claren, what the hell is going on—"

"Listen to me carefully, I wanted to tell you in advance, but . . . we had eyes on you guys at the lake—"

"What the fuck?"

"Calm down. Only the protocol."

Rick shook his head, squeezed the Comsat, and resisted the urge to smash it. "Okay, so what? You feel that I crossed the line?"

"That's not my area, and Doc M hasn't reviewed the tape yet," she said. "Besides, physical contact is a part of the protocol. I want to make sure that you *really* are good and holding the line."

"Yeah. We worked through a lot of his baggage . . . I went with my gut. We actually talked it out in the car. He called me his 'coach.'"

"Coach? That's good."

"I guess. Anyway, what are we gonna do about his job? He's worried."

"I may have some bad news, but why don't we talk about it when you guys get back?"

Bad news, shit. Focus on now. "Fine, what about this Ladder? Who's running it? And don't you dare say that prick of a base command Hammonds."

"I hear the feeling is mutual, Rick. Look, get our civ through the Ladder and then make your exit. I have a call with Tibbins first thing in the morning. Have you reviewed the exercises?"

"Yeah. He'll ace it. For CI, a drop, a placement, and a pick-up. For PA, the rope, obstacle course, and the pool. We should be done before 1500."

"Good. One more thing. They know our civ is gay. Only him."

Just full of good news, aren't you. "Why? Is this Hammonds's doings too or you?"

"Does it matter?"

"No, but—why, Claren? Don't we have enough pressure?"

"Look, get him through it. You know how all this interagency bullshit comes up, but we're on it. The point is they may press him a bit harder on the Ladder."

"He can handle himself if they take a cheap shot or two, but if one of Hammonds's good ol' boys yells 'fag'—it's too soon. I'm working on it, but you've seen his temper."

"Look, I get it—"

"Do you?"

Claren paused. "Protect our boy, and keep me posted."

"I will. You can count on that."

"Oh, and Rick?"

"Yeah?"

"If you want BBQ, check out Cimarron Rose in Richmond."

"Aha, you pinged my cell signal."

"You can't be surprised."

"Guess not. Yeah, I kinda went rogue."

"Where will Hammonds's team be tonight?"

"Back in Williamsburg at Annie's or Busch Gardens tonight."

"I figured as much. Fine, I will calm down Hammonds when he no doubt calls again to scream at me about my 'goddamn team.'"

"You're the boss."

"Enjoy dinner. Good luck tomorrow."

"Thanks."

Rick hung up the mobile and zipped the phone back into the case. *She's always a step ahead*, he thought as he returned to the car, but suddenly a worry entered his mind. *Where the hell is Trey?*

Rick scanned the car. *Where's Trey?* He walked into the station. *Where the hell is he?* He returned to the car and scanned the entire gas station. *Goddamn it, Trey.*

Suddenly, a figure emerged from behind the building.

Trey walked back to the car. "What's wrong now?"

"Where the hell were you?" Rick barked.

"What? You were on the phone. I had to pee."

Rick let out a breath and shook his head. "Get in."

They drove another thirty minutes and enjoyed great BBQ at a small dive, not the suggested Cimarron Rose. Rick used the restaurant as an exercise.

"Okay, pop quiz. Why did I pick this booth?"

Trey scanned the room. "It's thirty feet from the front door. No back access to ambush us from behind. *Booths over tables for leveraging the wall in an attack.*"

"Good, but is that it?"

"Oh, no. All the people in the room are in our sight line."

"Great. Now eyes closed."

Trey closed his eyes.

"How many people are at the bar right now?"

"Three—no, four if you count the bartender."

"Excellent."

Trey opened his eyes and smiled. "So tell me about this Ladder tomorrow. Why do y'all call it a Ladder?"

"Huh, good question—everyone calls it a Ladder. Probably just Slangley."

"Slangley?"

"Yeah, our team—well mostly me and Jeni—have our own terms. Agency jargon. Slang. Langley. Slangley."

"Ha! Got it. So what's it really?"

"Like I told you—a series of tests both psychological and physical. You need to trust me now, Trey. You can do this, but it will be difficult. My guess is that they'll try to ambush our protocol, press your buttons a bit," he said pointing to the papers.

"'Cause they don't like y'all?"

"They don't know us—and they don't do well with unknown. Look, remember, it's an exercise. Not real. Not yet. So don't let them get in here," Rick said, pointing to his temple. "Now let's walk through it." Rick opened the briefing document folder. "For CI—counter intel—you have a drop, placement, and pick-up—hold on." Rick stopped and closed the file as their waitress approached.

"Hey, handsome, you boys want another beer?" the waitress interrupted.

"Thanks, Katie. I think we will," Rick said with a wink.

Rick waited for her to leave, then reopened Doc M's outline for the Ladder.

Trey was grinning.

"What?" Rick narrowed his eyes.

"You're a good guy."

"Not really—"

"Yes, you are. Want to know how I know?"

Rick shook his head.

"I waited tables for two years at Red Lobster in college. People could be real assholes—especially church folks after Sunday service. The best tables always said my name. They gave the best tips."

"I'm really not—"

"Katie, Private Cooper. You play tough guy but . . ."

"But what?"

Trey shook his head. "So what else is on this Ladder?"

"Looks like CI and PA, physical assessment. You'll ace those—basic shit, physical exercises. Let's focus on the CI."

After reviewing the information twice, Rick finally closed the folder.

"What do you do for fun?" Trey asked.

"Watch movies, read books, watch football."

"Who's your team?"

"The Skins."

Trey nodded. "What else? Do you have friends beyond Jeni?"

Rick raised an eyebrow.

"I'm only trying to get to know you—can you at least throw me a bone here?"

"I threw you a bone last night."

"Ha, ha . . . seriously. Please."

Rick melted his scowl into a smile. "I work out, read Russian literature, cook, and I like art museums, music—"

"Music, me too. What kind?"

"Pop and classic rock."

"Like?"

"Eagles, Beatles, Journey."

"I know Journey." Trey relaxed back into the booth.

"How about you? What kind of music do you like?"

"I don't know. Pop, country, but I only started listening to secular music in 1990. Our church didn't allow us growing up."

"No shit? You missed the '70s and '80s?"

"Yup. I once got suspended for three days for listening to Madonna."

"Are you fucking serious?"

"Yeah. What song's this?" Trey pointed up, indicating the music playing in the background.

"'Hot Stuff.'"

Trey shook his head.

"Tiger, you really don't know this song?"

"No. The beat's awesome. Who sings it?"

"I can't believe how sheltered you grew up. You're like an alien."

"So now I'm E.T.?"

"Yup! Geez, you really don't know this song?"

"No, this whole past year since Liberty has been playing a massive game of catchup. Mark and I only discovered ABBA on a road trip to DC in 1990."

"ABBA is classic."

"I do like this song though. Who's singing?"

"Donna Summer."

"Who's Donna Summer?"

"*Who's Donna Summer?*" Rick widened his eyes. "Only the queen of disco. Are you fucking kidding me?"

Trey shrugged.

"Wait. You know Ma-Donna, but you don't know *the* Donna?"

"No."

Rick shook his head. He chugged his beer and signaled for the check.

"*Who's Donna Summer?*" he repeated. "Well, that ends tonight."

Rick revved his engine and turned to Trey. "You best buckle up, Tiger. You 'bout to get hit with some 'Hot Stuff.'" "Love to Love You Baby," "She Works Hard for the Money" and "MacArthur Park." They jammed to Donna Summer for the fifty minutes back to the Farm.

Back at base, as they cleaned up, Trey still had questions. "Where is MacArthur Park? New York?"

"I don't know. It's a song."

"Fine but I don't get it. Whose cake got left out in the rain?"

"No one does." Rick shook his head and turned off the lights. "Good night, Trey."

Trey spoke out in the dark, "I mean seriously, why can't she bake another one?"

"You really are an alien."

CHAPTER 35
LADDER

Trey awoke to his bunk being rattled. "It's 0600 . . . wakey, wakey, Cub," Rick mocked.

"Why so early?"

"Come on. Mess opens at 0630 and I want you to eat before the Ladder."

Trey got up, hit the shower, and dressed.

"Ready?" Rick was dressed and pacing a bit.

"What's up? Shouldn't I be the only one nervous about this?"

"I need coffee. Come on."

They were the first to enter the mess, ate breakfast, and kept to themselves before heading over to the CI training center. As they approached, Trey scanned the surroundings. *Training center? It mimics a town.*

"Not what you thought?" Rick studied Trey observing the setting.

"No, it's like a real street—a city block."

"Yup, we use it to simulate real-life scenarios."

"Huh, I thought when you said training center that it'd be like a gym."

"Nope, but you'll see the gym this afternoon."

Trey spun around slowly, taking in the full-sized buildings and cars. He turned back and saw a man walking toward them wearing khakis and a navy-blue polo.

"Rick."

"Sean."

Rick offered his hand. They shook.

"Claren was tight-lipped as usual—is this him?"

"Yeah. This is our civ-5 recruit, Trey Carter." Rick motioned. "Trey, this is our Director of Officer Training, Sean Hammonds."

"Nice to meet you, sir."

He nodded to Trey but did not offer his hand.

Trey nodded back.

"How old are you?" Hammonds narrowed his eyes.

"Twenty-one, sir."

Hammonds stared at him and then shot a look at Rick. "What kind of bullshit this time?"

Rick clenched his jaw. "Just a Ladder."

"Right?" Hammonds shook his head.

Trey could feel the icy void between the two men. *Geez, y'all can't stand each other.*

After a long minute of silence, Hammonds finally spoke. "Fine. Let's get on with it. My squad's down here." Hammonds motioned them down the street.

Trey followed the two men as they entered the landscape of empty buildings, cars, and streets. They turned the corner and he saw his training team waiting for them. Four total.

Trey froze thirty feet away. *Are you kidding me? Hammonds's squad looks like the offensive line of Alabama. All four of 'em is over six foot.*

Rick remained with Trey as Hammonds approached the muscular men dressed like Hammonds.

"This feels unfair," Trey whispered to Rick.

"What?"

"One versus four. And they're all twice my size."

"Stop. Remember our training. Don't let 'em get in your head."

"All right, huddle up." Hammonds motioned to the center of the street. The training squad jogged over and formed a semicircle to Hammonds's right. Each man in khaki shorts, black trainers, and the same polo as Hammonds.

Rick and Trey joined the group. "Morning, fellas," Rick said.

They all nodded and glanced at Trey.

Why are they looking at me like that? An odd sensation shot through his gut as Trey tried to clear his mind.

Hammonds stepped between them and began to recite instructions. "Gentlemen, today we'll go through a basic Ladder. As you know, it's a series of counter intel and physical assessment exercises intended to reflect real world, real life. The Field, not some desk at Langley. We're live, full-contact but it is a simulation." He turned to his team. "Keep it clean and not extreme."

They all nodded.

What the hell is that supposed to mean? Don't let 'em actually kill me?

"Civ, I'll explain each exercise. If you have any questions, please ask me or Special Officer Morgan. Any questions?" Hammonds stared at Trey.

Questions, huh. Yeah, how about why am I here? Why are you scowling at me like you're annoyed? "No, sir."

"First exercise is a Drop. Civ, you will take this package to the designated location marked here on the map. Understood?"

"Yes, sir."

Hammonds motioned to the squad. "Let's go. Get in position. We start on my whistle."

The men scattered into the city street and buildings.

"Hey." Rick leaned into Trey. "Don't over think it. You got this."

Trey nodded.

Got it. A simple drop 'n' go. Like we practiced.

Trey held the package in his left hand and studied the map in his right.

Two short blocks down and left at that fake stop sign.

Chirp!

Trey shot a look at Rick, who offered an encouraging nod.

I need a song. Trey liked to clear his mind using music. "Like a Virgin" and Madonna echoed in his head as he hummed along. After a few hundred feet, he slowed his pace. He continued to the stop sign and slipped down the shorter side street. He glanced around to see if he was being watched.

No one. That's odd. He approached the mailbox that was designated as the drop and again scanned the empty street around him. He slipped the package into the narrow slit on the red box as two agents rounded the corner now thirty yards from him.

Done. Let it go. Trey turned and walked away.

Turn and go—turn and go. Yes! Rick watched the images on the monitor.

Chirp!

Hammonds clicked his timer, made some notations, and glanced at Rick.

Yup, I trained him, asshole. Rick masked his pride. *Great job, Tiger. Cocky recruits usually take the bait—push forward and engage out of ego. I'll be damned—he must've actually listened to me.*

In their training, he had instructed again and again. *"In CI, it's essential to use the minimal energy in the situation for the goal of the assignment. Once completed, stop, turn, and disappear."*

Rick motioned Trey to his side.

"Was that okay?" Trey asked hopefully.

"You did great."

"Yeah." He lowered his voice. "Honestly, that was kinda easy."

Rick bit back his smile and kept his voice low. "Well, it's going to get harder as we go along today. Pace yourself."

"How much harder?"

"You can handle it all. You okay?"

"Yeah, a little nervous but—"

"Just breathe and stay calm."

Hammonds finished his notations on the clipboard and then barked, "Huddle up."

As the men gathered again around him, Hammonds motioned to the blue and gray building on his left. It was taller than the others and had large brown glass, smoky windows across the front. "To the office."

They all walked across the street and entered the building storefront.

Trey scanned the simulated office. *Kinda looks normal. Desks, chairs, monitors, and keyboards but no computers. The walls had scuff marks and empty sockets. Nothing's plugged in.* He inspected closer and saw scratches and a few gouges on the furniture. *This place has*

*taken a beating or two. Shit, this isn't an office—oh god—it's a fighting
arena.*

"Civ, this exercise is called a Placement—or tagging a target.
This is your tag." He held up a small, red plastic card. "It represents
a mock listening or tracking device. You have a target and a decoy."
Hammonds pointed to each designated agent playing the roles. Each
stepped forward. "Your objective is to place the tag on the target in
one of his pockets. Got it?"

"Yes, sir."

This is nuts. Trey turned to Rick and widened his eyes. *This ain't
how we trained for tagging—and not one but two agents. How am I
supposed to pull this off?*

"Can you give us a minute?" Rick asked Hammonds.

"One minute," Hammonds said.

Rick took Trey by the arm and walked away a few paces.

"Direct interaction? Two of 'em—"

"Lower your fucking voice," Rick hissed through clenched teeth.

"How am I supposed to tag him when they know that I'm doing
it?"

"Calm down—"

"They know I'm doing it."

"Listen to me. You have the advantage."

"How? They're bigger than me—"

"This is going to sound crazy, but pretend this is happening at a
gay club—Tracks. The target over there. Clock him from across the
room. Strut over like you're the shit."

"What?"

"They already know you're gay."

A shock reverberated through Trey. "What? You're serious?"

"Damn serious. Fucking flirt with him, Tiger."

"Really?"

"Take it as far as you want. It'll freak him out and give you the
edge. You only need a second to tag him."

Trey mind raced. *Listen to Rick—he's one of the best.* Chulpa's
voice echoed in his mind. *Rattle the cage.* Rick's training rang true.
"Kinda like that tactical stuff . . . 'rattle the cage'?"

"Bingo." Rick winked.

"Any day now, Rick," Hammonds barked from behind them.

Rick held up his right hand and laid his left hand on Trey's shoulder.

"You don't like him, do you?" Trey asked.

"Don't worry about me. Focus on you."

Trey took a deep breath. "Rattle his cage."

Rick narrowed his eyes and nodded.

They turned and walked back to Hammonds.

"Gentlemen, when I blow the whistle and until you hear the whistle to cease the exercise—we are live, full physical contact. Understood?"

"Yes, sir." Trey scanned the room. *I can use that phone. The angle of the handle. The cord. With some force, it's a decent weapon.*

"Civ, you start at the door. Decoy. Target. Get in position over there." Hammonds barked and motioned them to the far wall. "We're over here." He led Rick and the others to the far wall, thirty feet away from the exercise. "On my whistle."

Trey walked to the door and stepped outside into the quiet street. The door closed behind him.

Y'all know I'm gay and you think I'm scared—but I ain't. Time for a jam. Rattle his cage. This time he chose Paula Abdul's "Cold Hearted."

Chirp!

Trey took a deep breath and re-entered the now *gay club* as instructed. He pulsed the beats of Paula in his head. He pulled his shoulders back and locked eyes with the target across the room. The target grimaced and rubbed his black cropped hair. Trey glanced at the blond-haired decoy's eyes and saw them widen.

Showtime.

Trey ogled both of the agents as he strutted toward them. "Sup, sexy boys?"

"Huh?" The decoy balked as both men frowned.

"Party don't start till I get here. Who wants to dance?" Trey squeezed between them.

"What tha?" The decoy's eyes narrowed as Trey puckered and offered a kiss.

"No fucking thanks."

"That ain't what you said last night." Trey licked his lips.

"Are you shitting me?" The cropped-haired agent looked over to Hammonds, then back at Trey.

"Oh sorry, Hammonds doesn't know you're bi—"

"Fuck you—"

"Damn, daddy, slow down. Buy a boy a drink first." Trey stepped back, intentionally bumping into the target agent behind him. "Oops! Sorry," he said, turning and locking eyes. "Damn, Mr. Muscles—I like those shorts. What are you delivering?"

"What?" The target agent snarled and leaned into Trey. "I'm not delivering anything."

"Well, something's in that package." Trey looked him up and down, pausing at his crotch. He lightly thrust his tongue out and in.

The target's face turned red.

Damn, he's taking the bait.

The target widened his eyes and slowly shook his head.

Now.

Trey dropped to his knees, pressed his face into the target's groin, reached around him, and grabbed his ass cheeks.

"Whattha fuck!" the target exploded, shoving Trey back.

Trey stumbled but gained his footing. He stood right as the target clenched his fist.

"Your loss, sexy," Trey said, backing up.

"What? No, you lose, faggot." The target took his swing. Trey bobbed but still caught the fist on his right cheek. The decoy assumed a fighting stance.

Trey ignored the sting and scanned the nearby desk. He snatched the phone and hurled it with all his strength at the target.

Smack.

"Aargh!" The phone impacted his right ear and temple. Trey jumped up atop the opposing desk, grabbed the monitor, and slung it at the decoy, who jumped back and swatted it to the floor.

Crash.

Trey glanced to Rick, who had turned to Hammonds. Trey's eyes darted to Hammonds, who wore a mocking grin. *You ain't gonna blow that whistle.*

Trey shot back at the advancing agents and immediately assumed his Krav Maga stance.

He judged the distance and forced himself to wait a second longer before lunging feet-first at the decoy agent, aiming for his chest. The impact flattened the decoy, landing him on his back, gasping.

Trey recoiled, then sprang to his feet and bolted for the door. His hands touched the door as his collar tightened in the grip of the larger target agent, yanking him backward. Trey donkey kicked the body behind him.

"Aargh!"

As Trey's T-shirt ripped, the grip loosened. He shook free and ran out the door to the middle of the street.

Chirp!

The door burst open.

"What the fuck!" the decoy screamed, as the non-participating agents each pulled back the enraged target and decoy. Rick and Hammonds followed as the commotion spilled onto the street.

"Stand down!" Hammonds barked as he slammed the door behind them.

"But he—" the target yelled.

"Stand down!"

The decoy lunged again but was held by his fellow agents.

"I said break it up, now," Hammonds shouted and motioned to his agents.

Everyone separated. Rick walked to Trey. The four agents were behind Hammonds.

As they grumbled with one another, the target agent dabbed the blood from his ear with the tail of his shirt. The decoy rubbed his own chest and grimaced.

"You all right?" one of the agents asked the target.

"This is bullshit," he shot back. "Did you hear what that little fag said—"

Trey turned to the agent as Rick laid a hand on his shoulder.

"Let it go."

"But—"

"Now." Rick squeezed and turned back. "We need a minute. Sean?"

Hammonds nodded slowly, then walked to his team.

"I *hate* that word." Trey snorted.

"No shit, like I don't know that."

Trey shook his head.

"Your intake—faggot-maggot," Rick reminded him.

Trey pursed his lips.

"You okay?"

"Yeah, he got me though," Trey said, rubbing the side of his face.

"You're fine. That decoy on the other hand—perfect drop kick to the sternum, Tiger."

Trey looked over at the agents.

"He's gonna be hurting tomorrow." Rick nodded.

"Really?"

"Yup. Look, you did great, but you have to stay calm."

"Did you see how he let it go on?" Trey motioned to Hammonds.

"Yeah."

"He didn't even stop it."

"It's a game, Trey."

"Doesn't *feel* like a game."

"It's only simulation. Meant to feel real—full contact like your football scrimmage lines."

"Rick?" Hammonds motioned them back.

"Ready?" Rick asked. Trey breathed in deeply and they walked back to join the others.

"Civ, where's the device?" Hammonds asked.

"I don't have it."

"Well, where is it?"

"It's in his pocket." Trey pointed to the target.

"No, it's not, faggot," the target agent blurted.

"Check your right ass," Trey shot back as Rick laid a hand on his shoulder.

"Stay calm," Rick whispered.

The target reached into his right hip pocket and pulled out the tag.

Hammonds glared at his officer and then back to Trey.

"Supposed to put it in the front pocket—it doesn't count!" the target yelled.

"Y'all never said *which* pocket!"

Hammonds raised his eyebrows. "Stand down!"

The target approached Trey. "How the hell would it pick up any com or intel in the *real* world?"

"Perfectly, since you seem to talk out of your ass," Trey shot back.

"Fuck you, you little punk ass!"

"Fuck me?" Trey lunged but was held back by Rick. "You wish—I should've shoved that tag *up* your ass."

"Enough! Back off, both of you!" Hammonds yelled.

The other men pulled the target back as Rick loosened his grasp of Trey.

"Look at me." Rick held both his shoulders. "Stop letting them get in your head. Understood?"

"Yeah."

"Breathe a minute. I'll be back."

Rick walked over to Hammonds and they briefly chatted. Then he returned to Trey.

"What's next?" Trey asked.

"You calm?"

"Yeah."

"Okay, this is a Pick-up. It'll be harder—all four of them—"

"All four—"

"Stop, you can do this. There's a post office one street over where you'll meet an agent, your asset. You'll be trailed by the other three agents. Your goal is to go to the post office and meet the asset. He'll pass you the packet. You'll take it, conceal it, and make your way back over there to the bus stop," Rick said pointing to the mock bus stop. "Avoid the trailing agents. Get to the bus stop. Give Hammonds the packet."

"That's it?"

"That's it."

Trey scanned the fake streets, roof tops, facades, and parked cars. "Is everything in play?"

"What do you mean?" Rick asked.

"You keep saying this is a game. So, is all this area in bounds? Or is there an out-of-bounds?"

"You can use anything here, but keep in mind the objective is simple. Get to the post office, pick up the packet, return to the bus stop over there, and give it to Hammonds. Remember our training?"

"Yeah, 'minimal effort to achieve the goal.'"

Rick smile slightly and held out his fist. Trey bumped it top and bottom.

"Do they know the route?" Trey asked.

"Given the last two exercises—yeah, probably. Look, do your best and be safe."

"Ready, guys?" Hammonds shouted and motioned to them.

All right, musclehead—you want punk-ass? I got your punk-ass. Trey scanned the cityscape. As Hammonds recited the same instructions Rick had shared, Trey tuned him out. He closed his eyes and mentally joined Anthony Kiedis in a metallic jock and body paint in the desert.

Trey blocked out the men around him and only heard Flea's riff erupting on guitar. *"Give It Away."*

Chirp!

Hammonds's whistle shot through Trey as if it was electricity. His blood rushed as he darted between two cars, and down the street. He found the post office and walked in. *Empty.*

Where's the asset? "Hello, hello?"

The asset officer stepped out of the dark doorway behind the counter, toward the sunlight pouring in from the windows behind Trey. As the light reached his face, Trey registered it was the same hot-headed target from the previous exercise.

Shit—just my luck. This isn't good. Trey squeeze both hands into fists and stood still.

He narrowed his eyes on Trey as he held up the envelope. "You think you're cut out for this?"

"What do you mean?"

"I mean, what are you doing here?"

"Give me the packet, please."

The officer walked up to Trey. "Are you gay? For real?"

Trey froze and breathed deeply. "Yes."

"Are you really a civ?"

Trey nodded.

He shook his head and tossed the envelope at Trey.

Trey scooped up the letter and bolted to the door as he heard footsteps behind him. He stuffed it in his back waistband to conceal it with his shirt, freeing up his hands. Through the glass doors, he spotted two agents crossing the street, closing in on the post office. Trey exited and slammed the doors closed in the face of the advancing asset agent. Trey darted right and hopped on top of the hood, then the roof of the minivan. He looked up at the hanging sign over the adjoining store. The horizontal support bar was kind of like a high bar. *Focus and grab it. It'll hold.*

Trey leaped for the extended horizontal pole with all his might. The rough metal hit his hands. It was thicker than any high bar in his gym. It creaked and swayed slightly under his swinging weight. *Phew!* He kipped over using a high-bar release and grabbed the edge of the roof before pulling himself up to safety. *Yes!* Relief flooded through him.

Trey looked around. *Damn, it's all one big flat roof. From the street, it seems like multiple buildings, but it's one big building.* Trey heard the agents arguing and peered down at the street below.

"What the hell?"

"How do we get up there?"

"Look—there he is."

"Should we try to climb it?"

Trey backed away from the ledge. *That bar won't hold any of you. Wait, there was only three. Where's the asshole target?* He ran the length of the roof diagonally toward the bus stop and looked down to see the target agent join Rick and Hammonds. Suddenly, Hammonds looked up at him, pointed, and nudged Rick.

"Did you tell him to do that?" Hammonds pointed to the roof.

"Do what?"

Trey's head peeked above the rooftop and then disappeared. Rick shook his head but grinned faintly.

"You think this is funny?"

"Of course not."

"So what is it?"

"Sean, what's your beef?"

"You. Your secrets."

"As if you don't have secrets."

"I don't pretend."

"What's that supposed to mean?"

"What the hell?" Hammonds again motioned to the roof. Trey had swung his leg over as if to scale down the building. "I've been doing this for nearly sixteen years. And you're telling me *that's* a civilian, huh?"

"He is—"

"Bullshit." Hammonds turned to his fourth agent. "Get back in the game. Go."

Trey looked down from the roof. *Yikes, a twenty-foot drop is too far; I'll break my legs or worse. Gotta get a toehold, then climb down.* He scanned the side of the building and spotted the window casement. *That's at least five inches and solid concrete. I can use that.* He carefully hung down and found his toehold on the top of a window. He inched his way down using the drainpipe and window frame until he could safely drop the remaining eight feet to the street.

The second his feet touched the ground, someone struck him from behind. *Ouch! Damn it, it must be the asshole.* Trey fell to his knees, feigning unconsciousness, he grabbed a handful of dirt as the agent kicked his head. Trey threw the dirt up into his attacker's face and lunged upward aiming both fists at his groin.

"Aargh!" The agent writhed in pain as Trey stumbled back to the ground.

Shit. The pain from the kick clouded his thoughts, but one remained: *Get up and run!*

Trey leaped up and over the agent doubled over in pain. It took several steps and then he found his running stride. In the distance, three figures emerged in front of Rick and Hammonds, forming a wall.

Trey jumped on the old Crown Victoria parked in front of him to get his bearings and a higher vantage point. He glanced over at the fourth agent stumbling now to his feet. He turned back to the three agents blocking his path to Hammonds, his goal line.

It's at least fifty yards to Hammonds. Think. Improvise.

His eyes caught Rick's and saw Rick nod.

"They think we're weak—they don't know us. Show 'em, Tiger." Rick's mantra melded suddenly with a Bible verse from his past. *Show 'em. Philippians 4:13. I can do all things—*

A surge of energy ran through Trey—the same feeling before a Liberty football game when he would run out of the tunnel ahead of the team and tumble his way to the end zone with back handsprings. *Who cares how big they are—I can do all things!*

Trey jumped down, tucked, and rolled up to his feet in one movement. His run gave way to a full sprint toward the wall of men.

"Shit, this kid's crazy," the decoy agent yelled to his team. "Get ready."

As soon as Trey was ten feet away, he dropped both hands to the ground into a round-off and then executed four back handsprings. The agents' wall split as Trey exploded through them. A cloud of arms and legs writhed as Trey tried to struggle through. The agents tackled him and piled on. The final agent caught up, crouched low, and raised a Glock to Trey's temple in the pile of bodies.

"Got ya, you little—"

Oh no, you don't. I ain't heard a whistle. Keep digging. Trey swung his left arm, knocking the gun away. He wrestled to his stomach, arms and knees trying to muscle his way out from under their pummeling and pulling. *Keep digging. I can do all things.* Trey never stopped inching toward the bus stop. He closed his eyes and clenched his teeth as a fist punched his chest.

Chirp!

"Break it up!" Hammonds barked.

The fighting stopped. Trey gasped for air as one by one the weight lifted as they untangled themselves. Trey opened his eyes to see the target agent from the previous exercise extend a hand to him.

No way. Trey cautiously reached for it.

Halfway up, the agent's eyes narrowed. He let go and kicked the center of Trey's chest, sending him backward, where he fell at the feet of Rick and Hammonds.

The men looked down at him but said nothing. Trey reached into his back waistband and pulled out the torn but intact envelope. He stood up and delivered it to Hammonds.

Hammonds took the envelope.

Rick reached over, but Trey shrugged away. "Give me a minute." *I failed. I failed him.*

Rick remained with Hammonds as Trey walked to the bus stop.

Trey sat down on the bench and fought back tears. He squeezed his eyes shut. Suddenly he heard a voice in front of him.

"Hey."

Trey saw the target agent standing over him and simply shook his head. "I'm done—"

"Look, I was a douchebag just now. I'm sorry for kicking you like that."

"I'm sorry for grabbing your ass."

"Haha. You really are a civ—aren't you?"

"Yeah."

"Come on." He motioned Trey to follow. "Meet the guys."

Trey stood up and walked with him to the group. "You guys kicked my ass. I have a lot to learn."

"Yeah, but you fought hard." The target extended his hand to Trey. They shook, then the agent pulled him into a playful bear hug. "You're crazy, but you got guts. Seriously, though, what were you thinking?"

"Honestly, I was scared but I zoned out, put myself in the desert with the Red Hot Chili Peppers. 'Give It Away.'"

Without missing a beat, the ex-decoy agent mocked an air guitar, and the other three all started jumping around singing "Give It Away."

See, Tiger, people can surprise you if you let 'em.

"What the hell?" Hammonds's mouth was agape and his eyes bewildered. He motioned to Rick, then back at the five young men jumping around, singing and hugging. "I'll be damned. What the—"

Rick grinned. *Damn, I hope they got that on camera.*

Will they get it? Just a minute more. Tibbins sat quietly as his audience of Pentagon brass watched Trey digging and scraping toward the finish line. They saw the whistle, the late hit, and the hand with the letter. In the end, it was the exchange between the four rookie agents and the civ that clenched it. They were dancing at the end of the three rounds, and the obvious camaraderie seemed to provoke chuckles. No one said anything, but Tibbins sensed a stirring in the room of gray men who'd started the hour of footage deeply skeptical and now appeared impressed.

Did it move the needle? Probably not. But I'm proud of Rick and our civ-5 recruit. Tibbins kept his thoughts to himself and said, "Thank you for your time today. Dr. Martinez has an overview briefing, should you want to read further." The lights turned on as he finished.

There were no big conclusions, debates, or posturing. Claren spoke up, "Gentlemen, I don't need to remind you of the top secret classification and highly confidential nature of our protocol. We have targeted assets where bending is sometimes to our advantage." She looked around the room. "Should you require our unique service, please contact us."

"How long have you been at this?" Smithers asked.

"Over a decade," Tibbins shot back.

"Carter, Reagan, and 41?"

"Yup. Since that mess in Iran."

Smithers stood and the others followed. Tibbins reached for the door handle but stopped. He turned and lowered his tone. "The existence of this protocol is an extremely tight circle. If so much as a whisper of any part of what you saw today—this protocol— leaks, we'll know. He'll know." Tibbins nodded to the photo of George H. W. Bush on the wall above them. "Have a great day, fellas."

CHAPTER 36
POOL

Trey saw Rick walking toward him. *Is he pissed? Disappointed in me?*

"Proud of you," Rick said, and stuck out his fist.

"What?" Trey bumped his fist top and bottom though. "But I didn't win."

"Yes, you did, Tiger. I'll explain tonight when we get home. Now we have the easy part—the PA. You'll ace it. Do your best."

"Okay."

They walked back to Hammonds.

"Ready?" Rick asked.

"Yeah."

"All right, grunts, thanks for participating in the Ladder. You're done," Hammonds said.

"Sir, can we come and watch? The PA?" one of his team asked.

Hammonds turned to Rick, who nodded in agreement. "Sure, fine by me. But you'll have to hoof it. I've only got room for Rick and the civ. Let's go."

Hammonds drove them across the base to the field house where the team had set up the timed physical assessment in the large gym.

"Can I quickly use the restroom, sir?" Trey asked Hammonds.

"Over there—second door on the right."

Trey headed to the men's room.

"So we're gonna stand here and keep pretending that kid's a civ?" Rick shook his head. *Give it a fucking rest.*

"Rick, how long have I known you?"

"Nearly ten years but—"

"But nothing."

"Sean, how many times have I got to tell you? He's a civ."

"Right. Claren calls me out of the blue—after five months—says she needs a favor. You're here *camping*. Only you're nowhere to be found. I have to send those four agents out searching. Five hours. On a Saturday."

"We were out at the lake."

"I know that now—but." Hammonds breathed out deeply. "You're not gonna tell me, are you?"

"You know I can't."

"So what then . . . Dark ops? Covert? What is he?"

"He's my assignment." *Geez, he's a class-five civ operative, you fucking limp dick. Claren, Doc M, and Tibbins are calling the shots.* "I'm doing my job."

"I get it—"

"Here he comes," Rick interrupted. *Perfect timing, Trey.*

Trey walked to them and looked up at the long rope hanging from the center beam. Near the top, roughly twenty-five feet up, a flag had been Velcroed to the rope.

Hammonds spoke up. "This is straightforward. You have two minutes to climb up, take the flag, and get down. Be careful, young man."

Two whole minutes—are you kidding me? He won't even need a minute. Sean, you're about to get a show.

"Now, sir?" Trey asked.

"When you're ready."

"Cool." Trey grabbed the rope and went up hand over hand as if it were a ladder. He grabbed the flag and then wrapped the rope in his legs and descended quickly.

"Easy, Trey," Rick cautioned.

Trey complied until he reached the final five feet from the bottom, where he inverted, flipped, and landed on the mat.

"Stop showboating—save your energy," Rick barked.

"Yes, sir."

Hammonds clicked the timer. "Forty-eight seconds, wow." He shot a look at Rick.

Ask me again if he's a civ—I'll shove that timer up your ass. "What's next?" Rick asked.

"Obs." Hammonds led them outside to the large obstacle course. Trey's gymnast foundation was on full display as he sprinted and dug his way through easily, as Rick had predicted.

"Whatever he is—he's doing great. Nearly beat the course record. Missed it by only three seconds," Hammonds said to Rick.

"What's next?" Rick asked.

"The pool."

Hammonds led them back inside and over to the pool deck. "This is it—survival tactics and assessment, our last station. One of our tougher assessment skills to test or teach. Survival requires adaptation, mental strength, and often involves sensory deprivation. To simulate that, in this drill you'll be blindfolded and bound. Your equipment." Hammonds pulled out a long blade with a black handle.

Trey reached for the blade but Hammonds interjected, "Nope, not that easy."

He tossed it into the water in front of them.

Plop.

"You'll have to dive for it. Blindfolded and bound. The goal is to free yourself and exit the pool."

"How deep is the water, sir?" Trey asked.

"Twelve feet."

Trey shot a look of fear at Rick.

I get it. You hate blindfolds—you're tired. Don't panic, Tiger.

"Can you give us another minute, Sean?" Rick asked.

"Sure."

Hammonds walked a few paces away but Rick saw that he was watching them closely. Rick placed his hands on Trey's shoulders and pulled him in.

"This is it. We're almost done and you've been brave."

"I hate blindfolds. They freak me out."

"Stop. Clear your mind. Relax and use the environment around you. Listen for the whistle and follow your gut. I'm right here, and we'll be home tonight."

"We can go *home* after this?"

"Yes."

Trey shook his head. "How much time do I have?"

"Don't think about time. What song you gonna use?"

"'I Will Survive.'"

"Perfect." Rick grinned.

The young man began stripping off his clothes until he stood in only briefs. Rick took his clothes and placed them on the bench by the pool. The four rookie agents had entered the pool house now and were watching from the other side of the deck. Shouts from the team echoed across the water.

"You got this, Trey."

"Let's go, man."

"Get it!"

"You can do it."

Trey was grateful for the encouragement as he stared at the pool bottom to spot the knife.

"Ready?" Hammonds asked.

Trey nodded as Hammonds asked for his hands. Remembering the zip ties from his intake, Trey made two large fists and flexed his muscles as hard as he could to fight the tightening of the ties. Maybe when he hit the cold water, he could relax and make his hands small to create extra space.

"Feet together."

"My legs too?"

"Yup." Hammonds zip tied his legs tightly above the ankles on his shins.

Hammonds then took the blindfold. Trey glanced back at Rick.

He nodded reassuringly.

As Trey turned back toward Hammonds, he felt the blindfold tighten and total darkness enveloped him. *Breathe, just breathe.*

Warm hands grabbed him and carried him to the pool edge. He heard Hammonds voice echo as he counted down. "Five, four, three two, one."

Trey drowned out the rest of the sounds and tried to hear only Gloria Gaynor as she sang to him even as someone shoved him into the pool.

Splash!

In the blackout from the blindfold, the water felt even colder. Trey kicked his feet in unison to tread water. *Relax. One stroke kick, like a dolphin.*

Chirp!

After the whistle, Trey kicked a few more strokes, tried to relax his muscles, and took a deep, last breath. He surrendered to the water and sank below the surface.

Stay calm. Do this in steps. Blindfold. Blade. Cut legs free. Cut wrists free. I can do this. Blindfold first. Trey sank deeper as he tugged at the tight blindfold with his bound hands. The stretchy fabric seemed to now be glued to his head in the water. He tugged harder. *It's too tight.* His head started to pound as the rough pool bottom made contact with his feet. Trey planted both feet and jerked with all his might, and one side gave way. His right eye saw the blue water around him. *Go up. Get a breath.*

He surfaced and took in a deep gasp. As he treaded water, his bound hands found the tight knot at the base of his skull. *Don't fight it, stop pulling up, try pulling down.* The black fabric began to inch downward, first covering his freed eye, then both eyes were free. He left it around his neck like a bandana.

Now blade. Find the knife. Trey allowed his face below the water and spotted the metal object. *Got it. Breath.* He raised his head up and took another deep inhale. He dove, flipper kicking his way to the shiny blade with black handle in sharp contrast to the white bottom.

Got it. He gripped the handle and easily freed his legs with a simple pull of the blade. The black plastic ties snapped and fell to the sides. *Now your hands, but first another breath.* He pushed off the floor back to the light above him. *Geez, how do I cut this at this angle treading water?* He thrashed his legs and tried to twist the blade, which escaped his grip and sank back to the bottom.

Damn it.

The agents on both sides of the pool were watching him. He turned to see Rick staring intently at him.

Rick nodded.

I know, stay calm and focus. Use my surroundings—the bottom of the pool will give me leverage. Trey gasped another deep breath and dove, releasing only enough air to get him to the bottom. He retrieved the knife as his head again began to pound. Carefully, he shifted the blade and used the pool floor to press into the bindings. As the blade sliced, his hand slipped.

Stay calm Trey. You can do this. Rick glanced over at Hammonds, who was darting between his stopwatch and the pool's surface. Across the pool, the four agents paced back and forth. One had his hands now covering his mouth. All were staring at the pool's surface. The cheering had stopped. The silence was ominous.

Come on, Trey. Come on, Tiger. Rick looked at his watch. *Seventy-five seconds. Shit, he should have resurfaced already.* Rick had started to kick off his shoes, when Hammonds spoke.

"Wait, he's coming up."

Trey finally re-emerged, gasping and coughing.

Yes, you did it. You did it— Wait, what? A cloud? Red . . . Fuck. Rick's voice shattered the silence. "He's cut!"

Trey coughed and dropped the knife on the pool deck. Blood began to paint the white concrete.

"Call a medic, now!" Hammonds yelled across the pool to his agents.

"Hang on, Trey, let me see it," Rick said. *Oh my god, that's deep. Too deep.*

Trey turned his wrist and forearm, revealing the deep cut.

Hammonds kicked the knife toward the wall. "Shit, let's get him out. On three."

Rick nodded. *Easy, hang on, Trey. I got you.*

Hammonds grabbed Trey's shoulders and Rick grabbed his right leg.

"One, two, three, up!"

They hoisted Trey up and laid him the pool deck as the beads of water and blood puddled on the white concrete rim.

Shit, that's a lot of blood. Rick's medic training took over as he ripped off his own shirt. Wrapped it tight. "Sean, take his pulse."

Hammonds placed his fingers on Trey's neck.

"His pulse strong?" Rick asked.

"Yeah, but that's deep."

"I know."

Trey closed his eyes.

"Trey, stay alert. You're gonna be fine. We got to keep him alert." Rick saw Trey's eyes were heavy and he was starting to shiver. "No, Trey. Look at me. Trey Carter," Rick barked.

"What? Did I pass?"

"You did great, Trey," Hammonds said. "Now lie still and keep talking to us."

"Yes, sir." But Trey closed his eyes again.

"Trey, open your eyes," Rick snapped. *Shit, I knew this was a stupid idea. I should have been in the pool with him, or a diver.*

"I'm sleepy, Rick."

"I know, but keep your eyes open," Rick said, nodding at Hammonds. He squeezed the makeshift tourniquet with both hands, white knuckled as beads of sweat began to form on his brow. *Where are the fucking medics? Keep it together—keep him talking.* "Trey, tell Sean about coaching."

"What?"

"Your gym. Your boys."

"I coach gymnastics."

"That's where you learned to climb a rope like that?" Hammonds asked.

"Yeah. I was a gymnast."

"Really? Huh. That explains your acrobatics."

The medics arrived and within minutes had Trey at the base infirmary. Rick sat hunched over with his face in his hands in the waiting room, shirtless. *I should have been in that pool. This is on me. Please be okay. No muscle or ligament damage.*

Hammonds returned and handed Rick a white polo with the Camp Peary logo. "Here." He sat down next to him.

"Thanks." Rick pulled on the shirt.

The two men sat in silence for several minutes.

"I know what you're doing, Rick."

"What do you mean?"

"You're blaming yourself. I know that look—and I know that feeling."

"I should have been in the pool."

"It wouldn't matter."

"Maybe."

Hammonds breathed out deeply. Rick could sense there was some other concern.

"What, Sean?"

"Rick, I hate to ask this, but do we need to worry about his—"

"His blood? No, he's HIV negative," Rick said.

Hammonds nodded.

"Has that ever happened before?" Rick asked.

"No, but most recruits don't get it done on the first attempt."

Rick held his silence.

"And we usually have one or two divers in the pool."

"I thought so."

"And we should've today."

Damn right we shoulda. Rick glanced at the clock. *It's been over an hour. What is taking so long? We shoulda got an update by now. I hate all this helpless waiting.*

They sat in silence. Then Sean spoke up. "Rick, I don't know the nature of your unit, but I've heard the rumors. I want you to know that I'm sorry. Regardless how any of us *feel* about that kid being a homosexual, he did not deserve to be put in danger today."

Rick nodded. Sean was trying and using the only vocabulary he knew.

The base doctor swung open the door. "Gentlemen?"

"How is he?" Rick jumped to his feet.

"Well, he's a very lucky young man. Two millimeters to the right, and we'd have had to airlift him to VCU in Richmond. We're not equipped here for vascular surgery."

"He's okay then? No ligament damage?"

"No, I don't think so. He'll be fine, but he lost a bit of blood—he needed quite a few stitches. I gave him a sedative, so he's groggy. Are you Rick?"

"Yeah."

"He's asking for you. Come on back."

Rick entered the room, followed by Hammonds. He walked to the gurney, and Trey held up his bandaged wrist and forearm.

"Hey."

"Hey, Trey."

"I guess I lost my grip. How am I gonna explain this?"

"We'll think of something. What is it with you and pool parties, Tiger?" Rick said with a smile.

"Well, at least I didn't get nekkid or try to grope anyone this time."

Rick smirked as he stepped aside to show him Hammonds on the other side of the room.

"Oh sorry, sir."

"It's okay, Trey. You gave us quite a scare. You all right?"

"I think so—I'm tired though. Did I pass?"

"Yes. I wanted you to know . . ." Hammonds glanced at Rick and back at Trey.

He knows. Fuck it—I don't care. Rick laid his hand on Trey's shoulder.

Hammonds cleared his throat. He stepped forward, grabbed Trey's left hand, and gave it a squeeze. "I just wanted to say . . . you did great."

"Did I pass?" Trey's voice was hoarse and low.

"You passed. Not sure, but you may be the first and only civ to complete the Ladder."

"Really?"

Hammonds nodded and gave a slight smile. "Have a safe trip back. I'll tell my guys you're okay."

"Thank you, sir," Trey said groggily. "Rick, how'd we get here? Are we flying back?"

"No, Trey, we drove. We're driving home," Rick said with a chuckle.

"Can you drive? I don't think that I can drive like this," Trey said.

Rick and Hammonds both laughed.

"Goodbye, Trey."

"Bye, Officer Hammonds."

"Rest, Trey. I'll be right back." Rick followed Hammonds out of the room.

"Thanks for the shirt."

"No problem."

"I'll check in with the doc and then we'll be on our way. Thanks again for what you said earlier, but, Sean, can we keep this between us? Him and me?"

"Of course. Give Claren my best."

"Will do . . . And, Sean? He really is only a civ."

Hammonds turned to leave, then looked back. "Rick, I don't need to know what's next, but take care of that kid. Protect him."

"I will—no matter what."

CHAPTER 37
HOME

Rick eased Trey into the packed-up BMW. They drove off the Farm and headed north on 95. Trey slept off and on the whole way back, only rousing fully when they reached his apartment.

"Hold on, Trey. Let me help you."

"I think I can do it—"

"You're still foggy." Rick took hold of his arm as they climbed the stairs of the apartment, and opened the front door. *Wow, something smells great. Dinner. Jeni's chili.*

"Hey, handsome boys. Oh my god!" Jeni dropped the spatula and rushed to Trey. "What happened?"

"I'm okay," Trey said with a smile. "I got cut."

"Cut? How did you get cut camping?"

"He did a Ladder at the Farm," Rick said, helping Trey to the couch. "Aced it, in fact."

"Huh, I'll help *you* get your gear." She widened her eyes at Rick. *Shit, I know that look.* Rick walked to the car with Jeni in tow.

Once there, Jeni exploded. "What the hell were you thinking?"

"Me?"

"Yes, you, Rick. A civilian at the fucking Farm?"

"Claren insisted. I wanted to take him to Lost River."

"And the Ladder?"

"Hammonds set it up."

"Hammonds is an asshole!"

"He doesn't know the assignment, Jeni. Tibbins ordered it, Claren went along with it." Rick explained the exercises, assessments, and what happened at the pool. "Hammonds stayed for an hour to check up on him."

"He could have died."

"I get it."

"Do you? There should have been a diver, Rick, or a *really* modified Ladder. The kid is *not* trained after— What? Like two weeks, part-time. Then you guys throw him in the deep end . . . literally?"

"You know the drill, Jeni. We both do. All I can do is train him and try to protect him best I can," Rick said. "And I did."

"I'm sure you did and, knowing you, beat yourself up all the way home." She placed her hand on his shoulder.

"This feels different. He's not like our Army grunts. He didn't volunteer for this shit." Rick frowned.

"Stop it."

"What?"

"Beating yourself up." Jeni smiled.

I know but still, I shoulda done more. Rick held his thoughts. "Did I smell Jeni's chili?" Rick said and managed a slight smile.

"My *specialty*."

They stood in silence for a moment.

"Thanks."

"Anytime, asshole," Jeni said. "I'm on campus this week—Let me focus on why Tibbins and Claren insisted on the Farm. You just focus on protecting him."

"I will."

"Later, handsome." She punched his arm and then left.

Rick opened the apartment door quietly and glanced at the couch. *Dinner can wait, best to let him sleep.* Rick's Patriots throw blanket hung over a nearby chair, so he grabbed it and gently laid it on Trey. *I'm so sorry, Trey. I promise I'll get you through this.*

Twenty minutes later, Rick turned off the chili and set the bar for dinner. "Hey, Tiger, it's 2000 and you need to eat something."

Trey sat at the bar and ate two bowls of chili.

"How ya feeling?"

"Okay, aside from this." He held up the bandage on his forearm.

"I know."

"But I'll have a good story to tell about it if it scars." Trey raised his eyebrows.

"Yes, you will. That was pretty intense. Those guys were so freaked out—we all were."

"Yeah? After they kicked my ass in the CI stuff."

"No, you kicked some ass too—"

"I'm sorry, Rick."

"For what?"

"Not getting to the bus stop—letting you down."

"You didn't let me down." Rick leaned over and kissed his forehead.

"What was that for?"

"I'm proud of you, Tiger. Now go get ready for bed. I'll clean up tonight."

Trey went to the bathroom to wash up as Rick finished the dishes. Rick got in bed and began reviewing his messages on this laptop. He looked up to see Trey in the doorway.

"Rick? I don't want to sleep on the couch anymore."

"Then don't." Rick tapped the empty left side of the bed twice.

Trey smiled and crawled into bed. He exhaled deeply and fell asleep within minutes.

Rick listened to him breathe as he typed his report for Claren and the team. It had been a rough day, but Trey had made it.

Two days had passed since the Farm when Rick pulled something from his pocket. *He's earned it.*

"I have a surprise." Rick laid Trey's car keys on the counter.

"Seriously?" Trey grinned wide.

"Yeah, you've earned it, but don't forget our rules. If you're running late, you call home and tell me. Deal?"

"Deal."

"We're twenty days into this. You're doing great, but keep it up."

"I will."

"And I want you to call your parents and your brother. Check in with them—keep it casual but make sure they know you're okay."

Trey nodded.

Over the next few days, their routine fell into a rhythm with Trey's work, coaching, Rick's training, and the ever-present chores. Trey concealed his bandage with long-sleeve shirts at work and took it easy when coaching, and by the following week, the stitches had dissolved. The scar was healing well.

Trey drove to the office and felt different. He walked taller and felt more in control of himself. His training was easy at times, but then Rick would turn it up to an intense level.

"Morning, Trey." Cindy, his boss, said as he entered the sleek modern offices of American Seniors Initiative. "You seem different today. Everything okay?"

"Yeah, all is good. Finally got my car back."

"Wow, those repairs took forever."

"Tell me about it. Are we still on today?"

"Your annual review?"

Trey nodded.

"Sure, grab some coffee and meet me in my office."

A few minutes later, Trey entered her office. She motioned to her side chair.

"Relax, Trey. This will be an easy review. You're doing great."

"Phew. I wasn't sure."

"Nonsense. Don't be so hard on yourself."

They reviewed his first-year attendance, performance, and several additional projects he had taken on. "You excelled at pulling together the petition drop. That's why I've recommended you for a twelve percent increase in base pay."

"Wow, thank you."

"You earned it. Now, there is one area that I wanted to discuss with you. The election is going to heat up."

"President Bush's re-election. Will we be doing campaign work for him?"

"Actually, no. Robert leads the conservative wing of the party and we are no longer aligned with this Bush White House."

"Really, are you flipping support to the Dems?"

"God no." She sat back in her chair and narrowed her eyes. "You have a choice, Trey. Recently, I— Well, I've been assessing my life. In part, because I have breast cancer."

"I'm so sorry. I didn't know. What can I do to help?"

"Nothing. I'm getting great care and they caught it early. Stage one. I'll be fine. But it made me take a moment to think about things. Have you ever re-evaluated your life's choices?"

Trey shook his head.

"Trey, we need to know you're on board—fully on board. We're about to drop a grenade on the GOP and Bush. We're gonna back a new, conservative candidate: Ross Perot. Each of us has stuff—" She paused and leaned forward, staring at Trey with intense eyes. "We all think highly of you in your first year with us—but we do have some concerns."

"Concern? I don't understand."

"What are your hobbies? Interests outside of work?"

"Gymnastics."

"Coaching right?"

"Yes, ma'am. Is that a problem?"

"No, of course not. Are you making new friends?"

"Yeah, I've been coaching a lot and also meeting new friends in the city."

"Any girlfriends?" she asked.

Oh god. She suspects. "Not yet."

"I see."

Trey tilted his head. "Is that a problem?"

"Could be—Robert's *concerned* about you."

"Robert? Why?"

"You need to understand that you represent American Seniors, especially outside of work. You think it's been intense—just wait." She shook her head. "The media are always prying and things are about to explode."

"Like *60 Minutes*? I thought I did what I was supposed to. I was polite but firm. They left."

"You did fine, but it's going to intensify as soon as we make the announcement. You ready for that?"

He nodded.

"I'll process your pay increase and talk to Robert. Want my advice?"

Trey nodded again.

"Get a girlfriend."

Are you kidding me? Trey got up and left her office, still unnerved. *Glad I got the raise, but what was that all about? So odd.* He returned to his desk and immersed himself in work.

At three o'clock, his manager packed up and headed to the door. "Trey, can you lock up tonight?"

"Yes, ma'am."

"Great. Finish up the mailing and get out of here early. Celebrate your raise. Enjoy your weekend."

"Thanks. See ya Monday."

Trey finished his work over the next thirty minutes. He then locked up and got into his car. *What was she getting at? They must think I'm gay.*

He drove home and found Rick working on his laptop. Trey told him about the meeting.

"Do you think they suspect I'm gay?"

"Stop being paranoid. You got a raise, Trey."

"I know but—"

"No buts—be happy."

Trey shook his head. "I guess, but who's Ross Perot?"

Shit. Think of something. Rick closed his laptop and shrugged. "I don't know—I think he's from Texas."

"Huh, like Robert—he's from Texas. But isn't Bush from there too?"

"Yeah."

"Rick, it wasn't so much what she said but how she said it. Does she know about all this? Us?"

"Of course not. Not unless you said something."

"You know I didn't."

"I know. I'm busting your balls. Let it go, Tiger. Don't read too much into it. Go get changed and let's grab dinner."

Trey left the room and Rick opened his laptop.

His cursor paused and blinked. A reply message was waiting.

Claren: *Did he figure it out?*

Rick: *No. But he's started to ask tougher questions. His boss gave him an update. They're backing Perot.*

Claren: *Well, we suspected, but POTUS needs to know. It's started.*

Rick: *But what happens to Trey?*

Claren: *???*

Rick: *His job. Are we hiring him?*

Claren: *No. We'll get him an interview at Global. Step by step.*

Rick: *Fine. Enjoy dinner.*

Claren: *You too. Rick?*

Rick: *Yeah.*

Claren: *This is going to get messy. We may need to use his intel with WH DPB tomorrow for POTUS.*

Rick stopped typing and tightened his jaw. *Fuck—just ask her.*

Rick: *Why no job with us?*

Claren: *He's a civ, but we'll figure it out. He'll be fine. Good night.*

The screen went dark and a single pop-up window appeared with the CIA logo below it.

TRANSMISSION ENDED

CHAPTER 38
PARK

Wednesday, June 17, 1992
McLean, Virginia

Tamara observed Robert McGuire exit the offices of the noted psychologist Dr. Roland Begalla. *Damn, Robert, if you're nothing else, you are predictable. Every Wednesday. Marriage counseling.* She watched Estelle mouth something stern at him and then storm off to her Porsche, leaving Robert standing isolated in the parking lot with his back to his car.

Poor Estelle. I can't imagine being married to that asshole. Tamara lowered her chin as the silver Porsche crept past her Toyota Camry and out of the lot. She glanced back at Robert who stood still. *Feeling a bit lost, Robert? Showtime.* Tamara exited her car and rounded his blue Lincoln Town Car. Robert fumbled with his key and appeared to not see her approach. *Perfect surprise.*

"Hello, Robert."

"Whattha?" He turned to square off with her. "So what? Now you're stalking me?"

"How's Estelle? She left in a hurry."

"Leave her out of this," he hissed. "Coming here . . . is a new low, even for a spook like you."

"Why? Is marriage counseling not going well?"

"If you were a man, I'd—"

"Save it. This whole macho routine is tired. Besides, some of us girls are trained to snap your arm like a twig at first swing." Tamara scanned the parking lot. *Good, no witnesses. Get ready to blow your lid, prick.* "How's your book?"

Robert shook his head and tightened his jaw. She saw his cheeks turn even redder than usual. "What do you want, Tamara?"

"Never one for small talk, huh?" She pulled out an envelope. "You have a young recent graduate of Liberty working for you?"

"Who? Trey?"

"Yes. He doesn't share your views. We've profiled your team. You're slipping, Robert." She pulled out a photo of two naked young men at a rooftop pool and held it up to his eyes, then studied his reaction. A scowl slowly pulled his face tight. *Yup, it's Trey. Now you get it.*

"I'll fire him today."

"No, you won't."

"What? Why?" He reached for the photo.

"No." She quickly put it away. "Not if you don't want us to leak this to the *Washington Times* or *The Post*. Imagine the rumor of the great Robert McGuire and his gay male protégé."

"You wouldn't dare!"

"Try me." She narrowed her eyes.

"Nobody would believe that horseshit."

"Maybe not, but given your marital troubles and having this young man on your team." She shook her head. "Who knows—a leak and you'd have a week's worth of headaches . . . headlines, tabloids, and a couple of awkward rounds on beltway shows, *Meet the Press*—"

"What do you want?"

"Stop this Perot nonsense."

Robert pursed his lips. "You actually thought blackmailing me—"

"No, but consider this an initial shot across your bow. Unlike you, we've done our digging."

"You thought what, then? That'd I back down?"

Tamara shrugged. "A girl can dream."

"Never."

"Careful, you may regret that. This town is filled with failed ultimatums."

"So what game are we playing?"

She only offered a slight smile.

"Fine. Get me a meeting?"

"I'll see what I can do. But this kid?" She handed him the envelope. "What do you want me to do with him?"

"Keep Trey on till July, then cut him loose—quietly. I'll be in touch." She turned, started to walk away, but stopped after ten steps. "Oh, and give the kid six months' severance—up front."

"What do you want with him?"

"Six months, Robert. Don't get cheap on me or we'll know and then the media will. Understood?"

Robert shook his head.

Thatta boy. Done.

CHAPTER 39
FIRED

Thursday, July 9, 1992
American Seniors Initiative HQ / Fair Lakes - Fairfax, Virginia

"How was your Fourth, Trey?"

"Great. Yours?" Trey tried to listen as Cindy talked of BBQ, fireworks, and a neighborhood party. *Sounds better than running eight miles, a hundred push-ups and ten rounds at the firing range. And I'm still sore from the KM grappling with Rick.* Trey kept his thoughts and only said, "Sounds like fun."

"You feeling okay?"

"Yeah."

"Can you pick up Robert today? He's supposed to land at Dulles later this afternoon."

"Sure, what time?"

"I think 4 p.m. should be good—in his car."

"Got it: 4 p.m. in the boat."

Being the youngest employee by far, Trey had often picked up dry cleaning, run errands, and shuttled his boss in Robert's navy-blue Lincoln Town Car. When he'd asked Robert if he had to use a mooring line to park the behemoth, he'd quickly learned that his boss had a narrow sense of humor.

"Young man, drive" was all he'd gotten from the gruff Texan in the back seat.

At 1550, Trey packed up and got into the blue boat in the parking lot. By 1610 he was at the arrivals level of the massive, cathedral-like Dulles main terminal. Robert McGuire walked out, head down with his briefcase in his right hand and a black suit bag in the other. He was a Texan with a ruddy complexion and near constant frown.

Trey dutifully jumped out and greeted his boss. "How was your flight?"

"Take these. I need to get home." Robert shoved his garment bag at Trey.

Trey unlocked the trunk and placed the baggage inside. He came back around to the driver's door, but to his surprise, Robert was taking off his suit jacket and getting in to drive himself.

"Keys?" he snapped.

What's going on? He never drives himself home. Trey handed him the keys. "Can you drop me off at my car at the office?"

"No, this is where we part," Robert said, reaching into his pocket and handing him a twenty-dollar bill. He motioned to the adjacent taxi line. "Find your way home."

Trey tensed. *Calm down—you're only an employee to this asshole. Kill him with kindness.* "Have a great night, Robert." Trey held up the money. "Thanks—oh and say hello to Michelle."

Robert flinched at his daughter's name. He turned back to Trey. "You need to think about your *choices*—this town can eat you alive. You better know whose team you're on."

What the hell is that supposed to mean? Even for Robert, that's weird. The blue Town Car sped away, leaving him awkwardly standing in the traffic lanes. Trey walked to the cab line, a sinking feeling pitted deep in him.

The following morning, Friday, July 10, Trey was at his desk when Cindy, his supervisor, and a senior coworker called him to the conference room. They did not look him in the eye as he entered. His gut wrenched as he took a seat. Cindy closed the door before she started.

"Thanks for coming in; let's get to the point. Okay?"

He nodded.

Her tone was distant as she spoke in a flat, almost rehearsed voice. "Trey, we spoke to Robert—thought a lot about it and, well, you're not headed in the same direction as the organization . . . politically."

What? Is this about Ross Perot or that congressman you outed back in May? Trey's mind raced. "I don't understand—have I done something?"

"No, Trey. Which makes this—" She paused and glanced down at her notes. "Trey, this is gonna sting a bit, but in the long run it's best for you and us."

Trey did not break his focus on her.

"This isn't the place for you."

And there it is, you're letting me go. Trey's lungs emptied, and a heaviness landed on his shoulders like a thick blanket. *"This is where we part. Find your way home. Whose team are you on?"* Robert's last words haunted him.

So that's what he meant.

"Trey?"

Trey moved his gaze from his hands to again meet her eyes. *What did I do wrong? This isn't fair. Oh god, my rent—what am I gonna do?*

"We have termination papers here. I know this feels like bad news, but Robert has been most generous." She slid the one-page document from her folder to Trey across the table.

He stared blankly at them without looking at the letter. He swallowed hard. "So that's it? Today's my last day?"

"Yes, please pack up your things." She looked at her colleague and then back at Trey. "We think you should use this time to really think about your choices and . . . your lifestyle."

All my hard work, late nights meant nothing. You want nothing to do with me now. Rent, bills—you owe me money. Ask her about pay?

"Any severance? My vacation pay?"

"Again, Robert's been very generous—six months' salary." She pulled out a check. "Conditional on your signature. We don't want this discussed in the media." She pointed to the one-page letter in front of him.

Trey took the letter and scanned it. "So if I sign this?"

"You get $10,498.17." She pulled out a pen and slid it across the table.

Trey's pulse beat loudly in his head. *This isn't fair. What should I do? Go to CNN—then what? Out myself? Lose my family, friends, and Rick?* He closed his eyes and tried to calm his thoughts.

Rick's voice echoed in his mind. *Fuck them, Tiger. Take the cash. Sign it.*

Trey opened his eyes, took the pen, and signed the letter.

She immediately handed him the check. And twenty minutes later he was heading for the door with a box of his belongings. Cindy met him there with a copy of the letter. "Goodbye, Trey. For what it's worth—I'm sorry."

Trey nodded and walked out into the sunlight, stunned.

What now? I've got no job, no income.

Trey drove back and entered the apartment. *Where's Rick? I'm all alone.* For the first time in nearly a month he was by himself. He laid the letter and last check on the counter, changed into his running clothes, and ran the trail for the second time today. *Now what? Can't tell my parents or my brother. Can't tell Mark. What's next? First job outta college gone. I'm ruined.*

He wanted to call his brother, but couldn't. He wanted to call Mark, but felt he couldn't. He wanted to call Rick but couldn't— despite the fact that he had lived by this man's side day and night since the pool incident a month ago. *Rick? I don't even have his phone number.*

I've got no one. Trey opened the door to the apartment and saw Rick standing with the severance letter in his hand. Trey lowered his head and walked straight to the shower without speaking.

"Trey, wait. Talk to me."

He stripped and got in right as the tears started. The fear was choking him, the thought of having to call his parents tore apart his fragile, newfound confidence. But he was determined not to be broken. Not to let Rick see him cry.

The shower curtain opened. Rick stood there naked.

"Leave me alone."

"No." Rick's eyes narrowed. "Please?"

"I don't want to talk about it."

"You don't have to, Tiger."

Trey squeezed his eyes closed and let the water flow over his face. Suddenly Rick's warm body enveloped him. His tears concealed by the spray, they stood in silence together. He was broken.

"It's over, I've got no job, no—"

"Shh. I know it feels like a dead end but trust me. You and me, we're only at the beginning."

CHAPTER 40
CHANGE

"**A** flight attendant? Are you kidding me?" Trey said.

"Shut up and listen to me. Not like a regular, civilian carrier. It's a special friend to the Agency and DoD. Have you heard of Global Airways?"

"No."

"Most of their business is with defense contracts. They haven't had a new class of flight attendants in more than three years, not since the Gulf War. It's the perfect cover for you."

"I don't know—"

"There's an open house next week. We pulled some strings and got you a slot. We're going to prep you for the interviews, but there's no guarantees. There'll be hundreds of candidates. We can only get you to the door. You'll have to get selected on your own."

"Then what?"

"Then you'll head to Philly for three weeks of training after our assignment."

"When's that?"

"Still firming up but in a few weeks, but let's not get ahead of ourselves. We have your first field test next week."

"So all this will come to an end." Trey motioned between them.

"Don't go there. Step by step, okay?"

Trey nodded. "Field test, next week?"

"Yeah. Forty-five days, remember." Rick paused. "I really think if you take a step back and see this objectively . . . it's a win-win."

"How is it a win?" Trey asked. "Besides, I was thinking about grad school at UVA. My friends are all in grad school, but without a job— feels like I'm trapped in this holding pattern."

"I'm not trapped." Rick shot Trey a look. "And neither are you, Tiger."

"I lost my job today and it's not like you guys are offering me one."

"You didn't want to continue to support those assholes at American Seniors, did you?"

"No. I guess not, but I don't get it. Why promote me if they were gonna turn around a few weeks later and fire me? Why did they suspect? Did you guys tell them?"

"Stop. Think about it. You've been coming out more and more over the past three months. They saw you bulking up and getting the buzz cut—missing work here and there. Didn't you tell me you spoke out at their homophobic crap last month in that newsletter meeting?"

"Yeah, they were attacking Rep. Studds. You swear you didn't tell them?"

"No, I didn't tell them."

Trey held Rick's gaze for a second, then let out a breath and turned away. "I don't know what I'm gonna do."

"Trust me. This thing with Global could be a great experience for you. You'll literally travel around the world. Anyway, you don't need to decide right now." Rick stepped forward and placed both hands on Trey's shoulders. "What we need to do right now is turn this day around and put it behind you. It's 1700. Let's blast through surveillance training for an hour, then get changed and go out—dancing."

"Serious?" Trey's eyes widened with excitement.

"Yup. I always make good on my promises."

Rick guided Trey through several surveillance training tactics for the next hour, then they closed the books and hit the town.

Trey had gotten the shit kicked out of him several times over the past few weeks, both literally and figuratively. He had just lost his first job out of college. He needed to blow off some steam. They both did.

"Where are we going?"

"You'll see. Buckle up." Rick revved his BMW engine and gave Trey a quick wink. *Hunan #1, JR's, Tracks and Abe. Perfect date. I'm gonna blow his mind.* First, they grabbed Chinese food in Arlington and then stopped by JR's, a gay pub at Seventeenth and P, for a quick drink.

"Relax, Trey."

"Why are they staring?"

Rick smiled wide. "Enjoy it—trust me, one day they won't."

Trey seemed nervous, but the stares and drink offers boosted his ego. Rick sat back and watched, pleased. *Look at him. He has no idea how hot he is. This is good for him. If he was five years older, I'd— Stop. This is still work. Hold the line.*

"I've got more surprises," Rick said after they left and got back into his car. He turned down Mass Avenue and headed to Southwest DC.

"Tracks?"

"Do a little dancing? Beside I made you a promise—right?" Rick put out his fist. Trey bumped it top and bottom.

At 2310, they parked and entered the club as it was getting started. The warm summer night pulsated with electricity as the dance beats grew louder. The darkness was pierced by flashing colors as a growing crowd moved in unison under the large shiny disco ball.

"All right, let's see your moves. Come on." Rick guided them into the sea of bodies. "Rhythm Is a Dancer" blared as Rick and Trey began to gyrate to the beat.

"You're a great dancer, Tiger!" Rick shouted over the beats.

"You too."

"Don't look so surprised."

"Ha!"

After two songs, Rick leaned in. "I'll be right back!"

Trey nodded.

Rick made his way through the crowd to the bar. "Can I get two G&Ts?"

The bartender looked Rick up and down before nodding and pouring his drinks.

Rick pretended to not notice. *Well at least somebody here still thinks I've got it.* "Fifteen," the bartender shouted over the beats. "Can I get your number?"

Rick handed him a twenty. "No, I'm here with someone, but thanks."

"He's lucky, the guy you're with."

Rick smiled. "Do you know the DJ tonight?"

"Tiffany-Z, why?"

"Any chance she'd take an old school request?"

"Maybe. What song?"

Rick motioned and leaned in. He whispered into his ear.

"Ha! Fuck yeah, I think she'll do it."

"Thanks."

Rick found Trey and handed him his drink as the DJ transitioned into an old remix with a familiar piano opener. He grabbed Trey right as Gloria Gaynor erupted with "I Will Survive."

Trey shouted to Rick, "Oh, no, you didn't!"

"Come here, boy!" Rick exaggerated his best cocky nod.

The dance floor exploded into an unbridled, rave sing-along. The DJ intermittently turned down the music to the sound of hundreds of men and women screaming, "I will survive!" Then returned the volume for the next line seamlessly.

It was an anthem. Transcendent—in the swirl of disco lights and the mass of humanity connected in joyous rapture—everything slowed down into a singular moment for both Rick and Trey. As if out of their bodies, they looked around the room.

Young and old. Women and men. Black and white. Everyone united in a song of love, struggle, and determination to survive. Surviving the decade of death brought by HIV/AIDS. Surviving the twelve years of oppressive, anti-gay politics of Reagan and Bush fueled in part by Falwell's religious right. Surviving loss of family, friends, and jobs.

Many within the crowd wore Clinton-Gore '92 T-shirts. The night was fueled by hope that a new day was dawning. Nothing could stop this crowd, this night. They would survive.

Rick and Trey left the club at 0115, elated. He observed Trey walk a bit taller and more determined. He felt Trey looking at him as he drove.

"What?"

"Thank you." Trey placed his left hand on Rick's thigh.

"For what?"

"I'll never forget this feeling or this night."

"All right, all right—don't get all weepy on me. Stop the waterworks."

"I'm not. I'm happy."

"I can see that. That was my plan, Tiger." He grabbed Trey's hand, kissed it, and held it. "You up for one more surprise?"

"Sure."

"Let's go see Abe."

"Lincoln?"

"The one and only. On a clear, warm night—it's magical." Rick drove back toward Rock Creek Parkway and parked. "Have you ever snuck in at night?"

"No." Trey shrugged.

"It's one of the most impressive monuments in DC at any time of day, but check it out," Rick said, as they climbed the white stone steps up to the sitting giant.

"Look at the moon, Rick."

"What did I tell you? Moon glowing in the reflecting pool—it's magic."

"It's so massive, like these columns. Huge." Trey stared upward.

"Henry Bacon."

"Who?"

"The architect." Rick slid down the groove of the column and sat on the top step. "Took 'em fifty years to build it. He based it on a Greek temple."

"He had one of the toughest presidencies." Trey sat beside Rick. "The Civil War and all."

"Yup, the country ripped apart—it could have all ended, if not for him. He was a sage even after he died. His words live on. Somehow he saw beyond the deep divides of our struggling nation teetering on destruction." Rick put his arm around Trey. "And we're damn lucky he did."

They leaned back against the massive white columns, looking down at the wide dais.

Trey broke their silence. "There's a ton of history here."

"Yup, there's where Martin Luther King Jr. inspired the whole nation to dream."

"Freedom." Trey sighed. "Do you ever feel trapped?"

"You mean 'cause of being closeted at the Agency? Our ops desk?"

"Yeah."

"Sometimes, but everybody has secrets."

"You think it will ever change?"

"Maybe, look at you, a civ. That's never happened before."

"Really?"

Rick shook his head.

"So what happens next? For us?"

"Things are gonna start changing a bit. Our time together—"

"I know but not tonight." Trey squeezed Rick's thigh. "Can we go home now?"

In the darkness of the small suburban apartment, they coupled upright for the first time since the lake, Rick sitting up and supporting Trey, who sat on top. Their torsos were tight, their eyes fixed, and their legs in opposite Vs like roots extending from their joined tree. Breathing as one. Feeling as one. Trying to hold back change, which was impossible.

CHAPTER 41
MORNING

Rick got out of bed. *Wish I could cuddle more and let him sleep, but it's for his own good.* "No time off," Rick barked. "Let's go, let's go."

Saturday was filled with training, running, and exercise. He took Trey to a private shooting range in Sterling near Reston. They practiced with the Glock for two hours. Rick noticed that Trey had sharpened his skills over the month, and his aim was decent. Most importantly, in terms of safety, he could assemble, disassemble, load, and unload effortlessly.

At dinner Rick had a surprise. "Movie night!" He held up a tape. "*Monty Python and the Holy Grail.* It's a classic that I bet you've never seen."

"Seen it? I've never even heard of it."

"Oh my god . . . You're from a different planet, Tiger."

Not ten minutes into film, Trey was laughing so hard he was crying. The two cuddled on the couch. The tape ended and they gave in to their physical needs.

For a nearly an hour, they pushed beyond their experiences at the lake and pushed the boundaries of their pleasure. Edging and then releasing. Finally they exhausted themselves and fell asleep in each other's arms.

At 0700 the next morning, the phone rang twice in close succession and startled Rick awake.

"Rick Morgan," he answered in a groggy tone as Trey grunted and rolled over, still asleep.

"We have a shift," Claren said. "Our field test, the target will be at Worldgate this morning at 1100. The recruit's a member, and you'll have a guest pass at the front desk."

"I thought it was 1300."

"So did we, but Darius has been trailing the target and called it in."

"What about the uncle?"

"The target's uncle is booked on the 1230, United: Dulles to O'Hare. The aunt is still in Dubai."

"So our target will be alone."

"We think so."

"So, Trey's to set the bait and follow if engaged? Got it." Rick shook his head. *Shit, I thought we had more time.*

"Rick?"

"Yeah."

"Is he ready?"

"Not fully, but he will be." Rick grabbed his watch: *0708—we gotta hustle.* "How many plants?"

"Two DSPX 9-volts with caps."

"Got it. Where?"

"One in the office and one in the kitchen. I'll call you later."

"Okay. We'll be ready." Rick hung up the phone.

Trey stretched and yawned widely.

"Morning, sleepy head." Rick rolled over and on top of Trey, pretending to wrestle.

"Who called?"

"Well, my little overachiever, your final exam got moved up a bit."

"Was that your boss?"

"Yeah."

"Am I ready?"

"You will be. We need to go over a few more things this morning, though."

"So, we don't have time for . . ." Trey pressed upward, lifting their hips off the bed.

"No, we've got to get going." Rick rolled off Trey and onto his back.

"It's Sunday—"

"Well, there's been a shift; the timeline has been sped up yet again." Rick got out of bed. "I'll make coffee and we'll review the assignment in full." Rick tossed on a pair of boxers.

"What do I have to do?"

"Grab a shower—I'll explain over breakfast."

"Rick?"

"What?"

"Am I really ready?"

Rick kissed his forehead. "You'll be fine, Tiger. Let's go."

They showered in turns, then ate breakfast while Rick outlined Trey's assignment.

"His name is Professor Mahmoud Ahmed Hassan. He is a tenured professor of international studies at Cairo University and an adjunct professor at George Washington University. His wife is a journalist with *Arab News*."

Trey's eyes widened. "*Arab News*?"

"It's an English newspaper funded by Saudi Arabia. That's not important. Listen, they have a nephew who's arrived from Cairo to live with them for the next several months."

"Who's the target?" Trey asked. "The aunt, uncle—"

"No, the nephew."

"Why him?"

"He's an easy conduit to Professor Hassan."

"Why not the uncle, then?"

Rick bit back his instinct. *Don't get mad. Explain it to him. Take your time—get him on board.* "He's been tracked by both the NSA and Agency for more than five years. At first, he was simply an outspoken advocate for the PLO and several Arab organizations. But lately, he's danced on a thin line between friend and foe."

"To the US?"

"Razor thin. The Bureau, NSA, and others have tried several times to get closer, but the professor and his wife are well connected and savvy. Some think possibly trained in counter intel."

"Spies?"

Rick shrugged and retrieved a thick folder from his bag. He carefully laid out a set of photos onto the counter of an athletic, dark-haired Egyptian. "Your target: Samir Morsi Hassan."

Trey studied the photos. "What do I have to do?"

"Meet him at your gym, study him—get close to him." Rick thumbed through the dossier. "He goes by Sami. He's your first field test."

Trey took the photo and stared at it. "What do we know about him?"

"Great question. A lot of basics. He's twenty-three and a recent graduate of Cairo University. He lives with his older cousin back in Cairo, who's the general manager of a Marriott Hotel."

"What about his parents?"

"They were killed in a car accident in '86."

"How?"

"We don't know."

"Okay, but why me?"

"You're both recent grads. You both run, lift, and like to, uh . . ." Rick raised his eyebrows.

"Are you sure?"

"Based on intel from our Cairo desk, his English is strong. He's gay but very closeted."

"Does his family know?"

"Not entirely sure but his aunt and uncle are very conservative. They love their only nephew and may look the other way. This will be his first time on his own over the next three days."

Trey shook his head. "So . . ."

"So, we think he may have an itch to scratch."

"What exactly do you expect me to do? Flirt with him at my gym?"

"Cruise him at Worldgate and see where it goes. If he is open to it, invite him to the Reston Town Center—grab some frozen yogurt or a late movie. Build his trust. If he invites you over to their house, enjoy yourself but be safe."

Trey shook his head and tightened his lips.

"What?"

"Nothing. What else?"

"And you need to place these in the house." Rick pulled out two seemingly normal 9-volt batteries with two small black caps.

"What are those?"

"Listening devices that work by radio frequency up to two hundred yards away. The RF signals are so low they're nearly undetectable, and even with advanced scanners they show up as a radio or remote control stuck in the 'on' position."

Trey widened his eyes and held up one of the devices. "These are real?"

"Of course. What'd you think?"

"Nothing it's just— Till now they've all been fake."

"Careful." Rick took the device from Trey. "Yes, these are the real deal. Now, pay attention. This is how you assemble them. Here and here. Click it and bingo—see, the tiny red light turns on."

Rick watched Trey's eyes narrow and stare at the red glow. *Yup, shit's getting real now, Tiger.*

"Now you try." Rick clicked off the switch and flipped down the antennae.

Trey took the device and carefully repeated the steps.

"Easy. That's it—now, pop the cap in place."

The red light turned on and a wide smile came across Trey's face. "So that's it? Place these in the house?"

"Yup," Rick confirmed. "Let's do it again. You need to be able to feel the positive and negative poles on top without looking. Like this." He demonstrated again.

Trey nodded and took the device.

"Try to pop the caps in place silently and then raise them gently." Rick pointed to the two, half-inch antennae.

"Like this?"

"Perfect. Now do it again."

Trey practiced several times until Rick was satisfied.

"Now, here's how to conceal them." Rick placed them head down into his pocket using his pointer and middle fingers.

"Why like that?"

"So you don't catch the antennae on your seam and break them off. Then, they're useless."

Trey again repeated the motions several times.

"Excellent. Great job."

"What's next?"

"Now, it's 1000. Let's go over the layout of the house, change into our gym clothes, and then head out at 1040." Rick removed blueprints from the folder and unfolded the detailed schematics of the house along with surveillance photos of the interior.

"How did you get these?"

"Really?" Rick rolled his eyes.

Trey shrugged.

"Now study them like we practiced."

"Wide mental picture—try to take it all in an overview first."

"Exactly."

Trey opened and shut his eyes ten times and each time studied the image using the method for mental imagery that Rick had taught him.

"Now eyes closed." Rick waited. "Where's the kitchen?"

"Seven or eight steps left from the front door."

"How do you get downstairs?"

"Four steps from the front door dead ahead."

"How many steps down?"

"Uh . . . ten—no nine if you don't count the downstairs floor."

"Perfect. Now look here." Rick flipped the map around and pointed. "In the kitchen, place one here under the island on the lip of the support if it's wide enough."

Trey exhaled deeply. "One down. Where does the second go?"

"Head downstairs to the lower level."

"Why? The sliders outside?"

"Exactly. We're not one-hundred percent, but we believe Sami is bunking here."

"Opposite the office and with easy exit out the slider to the backyard if needed."

"So, you were listening these past few weeks."

"Tried to. Where in the office?"

"There are plenty of places in offices, but ideally near the phone. Like behind a photo frame, in a pencil holder, or under the desktop."

"Outside of the phone, okay, but why not use a phone bug?"

"Great question." *Tell him, no harm in giving him a bit more intel.* "We think the professor's using mobiles even inside the house."

"Why use me and the gay nephew? Why didn't the Agency break in and set the plants?"

"We did."

"What happened?"

"The first two lasted less than twenty-four hours. The devices were older technology, and their dogs went berserk. Professor and his wife came home, and within the hour both phone plants went dead. The next two never came online. These look simple." Rick held up the DSPX unit. "But they are virtually undetectable. Any other questions? You got it?"

"Yeah, I think so."

"You *think so*?"

Trey shrugged.

"That's not good enough, Trey. When you walk into that gym, you're not practicing anymore. This is a real assignment."

"I get it, but can I say something?"

"What?"

"I ain't gonna do more than mess around a bit if it comes to that. Spy shit or not, I'm not gonna prostitute myself. Till now, I've done everything that y'all've asked of me but—"

"Stop! We are *not* asking you to do that. Look at me. You control your body on any assignment. Got it? *You*." Rick laid his palm on Trey's chest as if sealing the statement in his heart. "Besides it won't even escalate. He's as conservative as you. Muslim, Baptist, gay, or not, at best you guys may have a sword fight."

"Okay, what if he doesn't invite me back to his place? Do I fail?"

"This isn't practice." Rick's tone deepened. "There is no fail. If he invites and you feel safe, then go. If he doesn't, set up a 'second date.'"

"Okay."

"Now, one more thing." Rick pulled out a small black pouch. "The earpiece."

"I hate those."

"Got to wear it—like we practiced in our *secret shopping*."

"Like at Fair Oaks Mall?" Trey smiled. "You hate malls."

"But I like smoothies—and it was the perfect crowded space to practice with me in your ear."

"Right, getting you a banana berry smoothie with protein whey."

"Yup—don't knock my training methods. That was only to get us ready for this."

"Got it."

"Your equipment." Rick took the small pouch, three DSPX with three modified 9-volts, and the earpiece. "I threw in a spare just in case," he said as he secured them into the inner pocket of Trey's gym bag.

Trey reached for the Glock 17.

"Whoa, easy cowboy, not this time." Rick took back the gun.

"Oh, I thought—" Trey laughed. "Wait, so after all the bruises, blood, and cuts, you want me to cruise a guy at *my* gym. Clock him and try to initiate a circle jerk? Hell, Rick, I could have done that day one without the last month. Why put me through all this?"

"Trey, this is your first test, not your first assignment. It's meant to be low value, low risk. Simple plants: one in the kitchen and one in their home office on the lower level near Sami's guest room. Got it?"

"Fine. So *if* he invites me over, I go. Set the plants and exit. If not today—how many days do we have?"

"The uncle's gone until Wednesday."

What Rick did not tell him was that Mr. and Mrs. Hassan had known ties to both Iranian and Palestinian extremist groups. Sami was a low target, but a crucial entry. Getting to Sami had the potential for a much larger value.

Trey repeated the assignment verbatim. *Why does he make me always say it over and over again?*

"Again, Trey."

Rick was a big believer in repetition and pressed Trey to repeat back training, concepts, and questions in his own words. If Rick did not like or could not answer a question—he would now simply give Trey a look and nod. Instinctively, Trey would either drop it, think it through on his own, or rephrase the question.

"I think you've got it." Rick held out his fist. Trey bumped it. "Now let's get dressed."

They got dressed and grabbed their gym bags. Rick stopped and grinned wide.

"What now?" Trey asked, fearing some new task.

"I got you something." He pulled out a set of car keys with a metal key ring.

"Oh my god, you got me a new car?"

"No. Jesus, you really go to extremes. Trey, I got you this." Rick flipped the keys and showed Trey that they were his same keys but with a new silver metal key ring in the shape of a Tiger's head. On the back of the key ring, two words were engraved.

"*Semper Protege*. What does it mean?"

"Always protect." Rick leaned over and kissed his forehead. "You got this, Tiger."

They drove separately and parked in adjacent spots in the downstairs garage at 1110, entering the gym separately. Trey felt at ease in his own gym. The same gym where Officer Ryder had spotted him. He would not be using an alias, nor handling a weapon. The whole assignment felt almost boring except for the planting of the devices.

He entered the locker room behind Rick and selected one of the pale oak lockers about twenty-five feet away, across the room. He had worn his workout clothes. He changed his shoes, threw his stuff into the locker, and took off to the weight room downstairs.

There, Trey ran into a trainer, Trish.

"Where have you been?" she said with a smile.

"Hey, Trish. How's it going? Wow, you look tan."

Trey had been a regular for the past year and knew most of the trainers. He and Trish chatted a bit about nothing, but really he was scanning the room.

There on the flat bench was the young man from the photo. The butterflies in his stomach fluttered. *That's him—he's cute. This is so weird.* Trey glanced over to see Rick enter the cardio level above them. *Showtime.*

"Great to see you, Trish, but I'd better get on with my workout. I'm jealous of that tan."

Trey grabbed a towel and walked over. Sami looked. They exchanged glances, and then Trey walked over to the flat bench as Sami lay back for a second set at 185.

"Hey."

"Hi."

"What set are you on?"

"Finished my first. You want to work in?" Sami offered. His English was perfect.

"Do you mind?" Trey asked.

"Hop in," Sami said. "Want me to put it back to 135? I can take off the twenty-five-pound plates for you."

"Thanks, man."

Incredible, he hooked him in like two seconds. Rick observed from his treadmill above them on the mezzanine. *Incline, decline, RDLs—damn, he usually hates those. Tiger, you are either focused or you like this guy.*

Nah, just focused.

The two appeared to quickly hit it off with a minimal amount of gym talk. They banged out four sets at five reps each: 135, 185, 225, and back to 185, matching each other rep for rep.

This actually might work.

After they finished their last sets on bench, Sami asked, "What's your routine today?"

"Chest, back, arms, a little cardio—jump rope—and maybe a quick soak," Trey said. "How about you?"

"About the same, but I wanted to run later today, so no cardio here."

"Cool." Trey smiled.

He observed Sami go over to the mats to roll and stretch. *He's looking my way.* Trey went into one of the two wooden floor studios partitioned by a wall of glass. He flipped on the lights and grabbed a jump rope. He executed a ten-minute set, carefully glancing out to observe his new friend.

Is he still watching me? Trey saw the stretching dark-haired Egyptian turn and smile. Trey smiled but lost his focus. The rope smacked his chest hard. *Ouch, fuck!* The sting of the missed skip burned his chest. He glanced up and saw Rick slowly shake his head. *I know, I know: Focus, Tiger.*

Trey walked back to the weight floor to grab a paper cone of water from the cooler and approached Sami. "It was awesome to work out with you. I'm going to steam and soak. Hopefully I'll see you around," he said, extending his right hand. "By the way, I'm Trey."

"Sami." He smiled and took Trey's hand. "Good to meet you."

Rick watched as Trey turned and went upstairs, observing the target's gaze follow him. Sami finished his last set quickly, then headed for the locker room. Rick smiled. *Geez, that didn't take long.*

Trey waited for a minute until his new friend entered the labyrinth of oak lockers and green plush carpeting. Then he pulled off his shorts and T-shirt. Sami was full-on cruising him. *Damn, this is real. What do I do? Be yourself.*

Trey took down his jock and grabbed a towel but did not wrap it. He confidently strode across to Sami and stopped at the scales at the end cap of the lockers.

"C'mon—please be 165," he said with a grin.

"Why?" Sami asked.

"Oh, I'm trying to get back to 170."

"What is 170 pounds? Like seventy-five or eighty kilos?"

"Gosh, I don't know, but I think this button will convert it. Hey, check this out, Sami," Trey said, as he stood naked on the scales. Sami modestly wrapped his towel but walked over. He tried to seem like he was looking at the red numbers, but Trey knew Sami was really staring at Trey's flaccid member.

Trey grinned and caught Sami's eyes staring downward.

"Sorry," Sami apologized and looked away.

"I'm gonna hit the Jacuzzi." Trey walked down the tiled corridor and hung his towel before stepping down into the spa.

"Ah, this feels great." Trey eased into the bubbling waters.

"Not as hot as that steam room, right?" Sami nodded to the steam room.

"No, it's perfect."

Sami dropped his towel and walked down the three steps into the bubbling cauldron. He waded toward Trey and plopped down a foot away.

Trey wiped his eyes.

Sami relaxed and spread his legs under the roiling currents, allowing his calf to connect with Trey's leg.

Trey smiled.

Sami nodded slightly.

"Good workout?" Trey asked.

"Yeah."

A hand grazed Trey's shaft and touched his scrotum.

Whattha? Trey recoiled in spite of himself, then threw Sami a reassuring smile. "Not here. Too risky."

"Want to go somewhere?" Sami offered.

"Yeah, but I can't. My roommates—they're straight. They don't know about me."

"I'm staying with my uncle, but he's supposed to be heading out today. He's leaving about now."

"I don't know. I want to, but . . ." Trey bit his lip.

"It's okay, Trey. Come over, we'll hang out and maybe go for a run later on the Reston bike path—it runs right by my uncle's house."

"Are you sure?"

"Yes."

Trey paused and looked around. "Okay."

The two young men showered, got dressed, and met at the top of the escalators.

"How do we do this?" Trey asked. "I'm parked on level two."

"Me too. You can follow me. It's like ten minutes, over in Reston."

"Okay."

Trey followed his new friend over Van Buren to Herndon Parkway, then onto Sunrise Valley. The house was in a golf community on Lake Anne.

"Nice place," Trey said as they walked in. *Don't break the antennae. Get this over with and get out.* He shoved his hand into his pocket and felt the listening devices.

As the front door opened, barking erupted instantly. Sami punched a code into the house alarm keypad as Trey leaned down and greeted three little dogs.

"Hello, hello."

The barking stopped as he dropped down to his knees and started playing with his new friends, especially with the reddish-brown, long-hair dachshund.

"I can't believe they like you . . . especially her," Sami said. "She's usually a total bitch to strangers."

"That's 'cause she knows that *I love doggie-dogs*," Trey said in a childish voice to her as she wagged her tail wildly. "They're great. What are their names?"

"Situ, BuonBuon, and Max."

"Arabic?"

"Yes."

"Cool. Come here, Situ."

Sami seemed relaxed as he walked into the kitchen of the open-floor plan. "Do you want some water, Trey?"

"Yes, please. Oh no, Sami!" Trey yelled as BuonBuon took a dump right on the tile floor of the entry hall.

Sami ran back. "You little shit. They won't do their business in the backyard. It drives my uncle crazy, but they're like my aunt's *kids*."

"Grab some paper towels. I'll clean this up so you can take them," Trey offered.

"Are you sure?"

"Yes, but hurry before the others drop one."

Sami smiled.

"Go." Trey widened his eyes.

Sami walked back to the kitchen and returned with a roll of paper towels.

"Here." Trey reached for towels. "I got this. Take 'em out."

"Be right back." Sami marched the three dogs down the stairs.

From studying the plans, Trey knew the house had walkout sliders to the backyard. *Now, I've got like three minutes.*

Trey quickly scooped up the little turds and walked into the kitchen to dispose of the waste. He pulled out the first DSPX and connected the battery and antenna. The tiny light glowed red. He felt along the edge of the island and found the perfect ledge, wide enough for the device.

Done. He took a deep breath. *Guess I'm a spy now. Sorry, Sami.* He grabbed his water and walked downstairs as Sami returned with the dogs.

"All good?" Trey asked.

"Yes, all set for now. They drive me crazy, but they are so cute," Sami said.

"They are. Is that your room?" Trey said, pointing to the adjacent room with the FIFA poster on the wall.

"Yeah. You want to see it? My room or . . ." he said, looking down at Trey's bulge.

"Sure," Trey said. *Lame pick-up line, Sami.*

Bark, bark, bark!

Sami and Trey froze as the front door opened, and the dogs ran back to the stairs.

"Is that your uncle?"

"Yeah, he was supposed to be flying out."

Trey saw the fear in Sami's eyes as a voice bellowed down the stairs.

"Sami, whose car is blocking the driveway?"

"Waa faqri!" Sami hissed and shook his head.

"Sami—"

"If he finds out—" Sami whispered.

God, what would Rick do? That's it . . . be Rick. Like how he talks to me. "Stop," Trey said calmly. "I am your friend from Worldgate. We met last week and bumped into each other. You invited me over to explain American football to you. The game starts in ten minutes. Got it? We're two buddies hanging out."

Sami nodded and took a deep breath. "Wait here." He followed the dogs upstairs to greet his uncle.

Trey heard Arabic and only made out *Redskins, Football,* and *Worldgate.*

Shit, get this done. Now. Trey's hand shook as he pulled out the second device. He frantically scanned the office before placing it next to the phone, under a photo frame on the desk, snapped the activator in place, and waited.

Red light! Done.

Trey turned and caught his image in a mirror. *What am I doing here? I barely know this guy and I'm betraying his trust.* He shook his head and walked back into the large den. *Stop, get through this, and get out.*

The voices were getting closer, so he clicked on the large TV, and sank casually into the leather sectional.

"Come here, Situ," Trey called his new "girlfriend" as she bounded down the stairs and joined him on the couch as the pregame show blared.

"Sami, the game is about to start!" he yelled right as a tall, Egyptian man with salt-and-pepper hair entered the room. He looked at Trey, then at the television. He looked back at Trey and narrowed his eyes.

Don't run out. Be calm. Be natural.

"Who are you?" the six-foot-two uncle asked.

"Sorry, sir. The Skins are kicking off . . ." He stood, walked over, and extended his right hand. "I'm Trey Carter."

Sami's uncle frowned but shook his hand. "Mahmoud Hassan. How do you and my nephew know one another?"

"We go to the same gym. Worldgate."

"Why are you here?" His tone sounded deeper.

Trey's nerves and instincts took over. "We've worked out a few times, and when he told Trish and me today that he didn't understand American football, I told him we could watch together, and I would explain it. But if—"

"Who's Trish?"

"Oh, Trisha Patterson. She's a trainer at our gym."

"Where are you from? I can't place your accent."

Trey's Southern drawl always was thicker when he was nervous, tipsy, or trying to persuade. "Georgia, but I graduated last year and moved up from Lynchburg."

"Lynchburg College?"

"Oh, no, sir. Liberty."

"Liberty University, Jerry Falwell's school," the uncle said. His scowl softened into a smile. "Falwell, huh?"

"Yes, sir."

Trey noticed the man's shoulders relax. *Ah, I get it—now you think Sami has a new Christian conservative friend to steer him from his evil homosexual tendencies. Your new ally to help steer him back toward women.*

"So the Skins are on?"

"Yes, sir. I'm sorry if I barged in on your Sunday. If this isn't a good time for me and Sami to watch the game, I can—"

"No, sit. It's not you. I'm irritated at United. Got bumped off my flight and didn't want to wait at Dulles for two hours."

Trey sat back down and Situ crawled into his lap.

"I have to head back over in an hour for my new flight— I can't believe she likes you." He pointed to Situ.

"She reminds me of my parents' schnauzer," Trey said.

Sami walked in with the other two dogs, holding a bag of chips in his teeth and two glasses of water.

Trey looked at Sami, then back to the professor. *Guess we're watching the game.*

Sami joined him on the couch. The two young men sat in the den for about an hour, eating the chips and watching the game. The uncle came in and out of his office several times to offer his perspective on Joe Gibbs, the Skins, and American football.

Finally, he said, "I'm off. Great to meet you, Trey."

"Great to meet you too, sir."

"Sami, I'll call you from Chicago. Enjoy the rest of the game, guys, and Trey, I hope we can have you over for a proper dinner soon."

He then spoke in Arabic to Sami, who nodded and smiled. The dogs followed him up the stairs and the door shut.

"Oh my god—finally. Thank you," Sami said to Trey, visibly relieved.

"No worries. Trust me, I understand. Do you think he suspected anything?"

"Not a thing, in fact, he liked you and said you would be a 'good influence' on me."

They laughed.

"Sami, it's getting late and I should go. Can I use the bathroom?"
"Sure."

He closed the lower-level guest bath door, which was no doubt a disappointment for his new friend. He peed, flushed, and turned on the water. He felt the third device in his pocket.

Ha! I should put this one in here so the Agency will have to listen— farts and all. Serves them right for making me do this.

Leaving the water running, he hopped up on the sink and planted it in the hidden top groove of the mirrored medicine cabinet just below the four bare vanity lights.

"Look, I'm sorry we got interrupted, but maybe we can hang out again soon . . . I mean, if you still want to?" Trey said as they walked upstairs to the front door.

"Of course," Sami said, but lowered his head.

Trey felt a tinge of guilt. He liked Sami. He was awkward but athletic and no doubt under much of the same stress Trey had with his family about being gay. The Bible and the Koran were both used as weapons and justification for intolerance.

Trey hugged him.

"Hey, you want to go running with me tomorrow?" Sami asked.

"Sure. What time? Where?"

"Let's meet at the Reston Town Center fountain at five?"

"Cool. Bye, Sami."

"Bye, Trey."

Trey got into his car and tuned out his training to check his surroundings. *Hope Sami is okay. Glad to get that over.*

Lost in his thoughts, Trey only vaguely noticed the white car behind him as he drove back to his apartment at Fair Oaks.

CHAPTER 42
MEMORY

Trey opened his apartment door and started to enter when Rick grabbed his right arm, shut the door, and punched the code on the beeping alarm.

"What?" Trey asked, shocked.

Rick didn't speak but took him by both shoulders and stared intently.

"Why are you so pissed?"

"Why didn't you respond?" His tone was emphatic yet calm, but there was anger in his eyes.

"What do you mean?" Trey asked, puzzled, but then sighed. "Oh . . . the earpiece."

Rick raised his eyebrows and nodded.

"Trey, I followed you and monitored you from outside for nearly two hours. Two fucking hours. I tried to warn you about the uncle. Tried to guide you. *Protect* you."

"I'm sorry—I forgot to put it in."

"You *forgot* to put it in. What the hell were you thinking?"

"I'm sorry, Rick."

Rick remained silent as Trey's eyes welled up.

"Does this mean I failed?"

Rick did not speak.

"I did what you said, but BuonBuon took a shit so I went for it. Placed the one in the kitchen. Then Sami's uncle comes home, and we both freaked out. He grills me for like ten minutes. We were scared—Sami's not out, and technically, neither am I. Nothing happened. We never messed around. I explained the Skins, the

Cowboys. The uncle went back to Dulles. I only hugged him good night. We didn't even kiss or anything . . . I swear, Rick."

Rick's intensity broke into a puzzled grin. "Wait, what the hell is a BuonBuon?"

"A badly behaved cockapoo."

"Cocka-what?"

"Cockapoo."

"Come here, Tiger . . ." Without warning Rick hugged him and said, "I'm not jealous, Trey. I was worried. No, you didn't fail, but you missed an important element. And you owe me a hundred push-ups."

"A *hundred*?"

"This is the real world now. Mistakes have bigger consequences. Thirty isn't going to cut it anymore."

Trey dropped and banged them out in sets of twenty-five. By the fourth set, his muscles were aching. Rick leaned over him and assisted on the last six to get him to the finish line. Trey was spent but stood.

"Now tell me what happened," Rick said. "But slowly this time."

Trey recounted the story in full detail. He then stopped.

"Rick, is it weird that I feel badly? I like Sami, but I don't trust the uncle. It was so clear the moment he heard Liberty and football—he switched from really mean to super nice."

"No, it's not weird, but similar to your faith, they don't want a gay kid in their family. Actually, it's far more dangerous than even your family, Trey. Back in Cairo, Sami could be killed or at the least imprisoned. Look, you have to learn to separate yourself from the assignment. That will come in time, but you've gotta split what's real from what's work. We call it holding the line."

The phone interrupted with the familiar two short rings.

"Rick Morgan."

"Is he back?" Claren asked.

"Yeah, he's here. He completed the assignment."

"Seriously? Both plants?"

"Yeah, kitchen, office, and a bonus one in the downstairs bath."

"Great. I'll let the Bureau's team know we are green to test the lines. Heard he went dark on you though."

"He fumbled but recovered. He even met the uncle and set up a run for tomorrow with the nephew at 1700. And get this, the uncle invited him back for a *proper meal*. Overall, he nailed it. And got us further access if we want it or need it."

"Wow, then we'll let the silence, the fumble go. Okay?"

"Yeah."

"Good work, Rick. Tell him that I'm pleased."

"Will do." Rick smiled at Trey. "Anything else?"

"Yeah, have him go on the run. No agenda. Spend an hour or so with his new friend."

"Got it," Rick said.

"Oh, and tell him good luck tomorrow night at the Global Airways interview."

"All right."

"I'll be in touch."

The phone clicked and Rick hung up. His mind raced.

Is she really gonna let it go? Three plants isn't enough. Now you want more contact—she's pushing this wider. One and fucking done. It was supposed to only be Ivan.

"Something wrong?" Trey asked.

"What? No, you did it. She's pleased."

Trey smiled wide.

"Now I'm gonna cook us a celebratory dinner."

"Morgan Meatloaf?"

"Yup. You ready for your interview tomorrow with Global?"

"Nah, I still need to go over the packet they sent."

Rick cooked as Trey reviewed the materials on Global Airways. After they'd eaten and Trey cleaned up, he joined Rick on the couch for another of Rick's favorite movies.

"*Cool Hand Luke*. Have you seen it?"

"No." Trey shook his head.

"It's a classic, and Paul Newman." Rick widened his eyes. "My first crush. Who was yours?"

"Elvis," Trey said without hesitation.

"What? You gotta be kidding me."

"Not side chops, jumpsuit Elvis . . . *Blue Hawaii, Girls! Girls! Girls!* Elvis."

"You really are warped." Rick pulled Trey in close and started the movie.

Trey kept his running date with Sami and showed up at 1700 at the main fountain at the Reston Town Center in his running clothes to find Sami stretching.

"Hey, Trey. Ready?"

"Let's do it."

They took off down the trail and settled into a mutual pace.

"What's Egypt like? Do you miss it?" Trey asked.

"Hot this time of year. Yeah, I miss my friends."

Trey glanced around them. No one in ear shot.

"When did you know you were attracted to guys?"

"I don't know, guess a couple of years ago. I didn't date in the summers and was at an all-boys boarding school during high school."

"In Cairo?"

"No, Geneva. Switzerland."

"How was that?"

"Lonely but all right."

"Did your folks send you away?"

"No, my cousin after they had their accident."

Trey stopped running and Sami joined him. "Accident?"

"Yeah, my parents died. Car crash when I was fourteen."

"Oh my god, I'm sorry."

"Thanks. That's why I moved in with my dad's cousin."

"Back in Cairo?"

"Yeah, but he worked all the time so the whole family thought I should go away to boarding school. Then I did undergrad at University of Cairo." Sami motioned for them to restart their run. They settled back into their pace but kept talking.

"How did you end up here in Reston?"

"Long story but my cousin walked in on me and a friend three months ago."

"A guy?"

Same nodded. "He freaked out—hit me."

"Whoa. Intense."

"Yeah, but he hid it for me. Didn't tell anyone there, and called my aunt and uncle here. He asked if I could come here. They immediately said yes as they feared for my life."

"It's dangerous back in Egypt?"

"You're joking right?"

"No."

"Trey, guys like us get thrown off of buildings or worse."

"What about the police?"

"They're in on it too. They raided a bar a year ago. Thirty men were arrested, but most of them never made it out of the jail."

"They killed them."

"The police say they *disappeared*. But yeah, I'm lucky to be here."

Geez, why is the Agency messing with Sami when he's been through so much? Does Rick know about this?

"We should get back." Sami turned from him. They ran back down the trail in silence. Suddenly, Trey reached out and caught Sami's shoulder.

"Hold up."

"What?"

Trey offered a sad smile. "I'm really sorry, Sami."

Sami nodded.

They finished the last half mile and were back at the fountains.

"Thanks for running with me." Sami smiled wide. "Let's hang out again soon?"

"Anytime."

"Can I get your phone number, Trey?"

Trey smiled and they exchanged phone numbers before parting. As Trey walked alone to his car, he felt choked by his secret. *This isn't right. I've got to make this right—under different circumstances we'd be friends.* Suddenly the weight and meaning of Rick's words hit his gut.

Hold the line.

When Rick returned, the shower was running. *Check in with him and be calm.*

"Hey, how was the run?" he said, through the shower curtain.

"Great, he's cool."

"You okay?"

"I guess."

"Talk to me, Tiger."

"It's kinda confusing, Rick. I'm holding the line, but . . ."

"But what?"

"I don't like lying to Sami."

"I understand."

"How do you do this? It feels wrong."

"You get used to it and you focus on the real objective."

"I don't know the objective and besides, I like him. He's cool."

"That's good."

"Wait. So, you're not jealous?"

"No, of course not."

"Why him, then? Why are we spying on his family?"

Rick took a slow breath, then said, measuring out each word carefully, "It's a job, Trey. We don't always get to know the specifics."

"Like classified?"

"Yes. Top secret. Even if I knew, I couldn't tell you."

Trey turned off the water and opened the curtain. "You really don't know."

"No." Rick handed him a towel.

"You didn't pick them?"

"Of course not, Tiger."

Trey took the towel. "He's been through a lot, back in Egypt."

Rick nodded, then walked back into the living room. He made his tone casual and called back, "So tonight, what's your game plan for the interview?"

"Like we rehearsed, I'll be friendly when I sign in and meet the panel, and be sure to sit up front." Trey walked into the living room with the towel wrapped around his waist.

"And?" Rick prodded.

"Be confident but not cocky when I talk about work—"

"I had a different thought. Instead of PR or politics, I think you should talk about your coaching."

"Coaching? Why?" Trey asked.

"'Cause you radiate joy and enthusiasm when you talk about gymnastics. Stuff you love doing, and you love coaching your kids."

"Okay, but what if—"

"Stop. No more what ifs." Rick reached over and pulled Trey into his embrace. "Just be you. You're more than enough."

CHAPTER 43
INTERVIEW

"*You're more than enough.*" Rick's statement calmed Trey as he drove to the Dulles Hilton Hotel off Route 28.

He parked and entered to find a sea of young, fit professionals milling about. *Geez, this place is mobbed—everyone is so good looking. Like some casting call for a soap opera. I'm outta my league here.*

"*Just be you, Tiger.*" Rick's words steadied his nerves. Trey took a deep breath and approached the check-in table.

"Hey, I'm Trey Carter."

"Hi, Trey. Welcome," said the woman in the navy suit and gold wings pinned to her lapel. "Let's see, here you are." She crossed his name off the list, smiled, and handed him a packet with an assigned number before motioning him to enter the ballroom.

Trey walked to the front row and took a seat next to a beautiful, long-haired girl in her early twenties.

"Hi, I'm Trey."

"Sydney." She shook his hand. "Are you nervous too?"

"No. Should I be?"

She motioned to the four hundred seats behind them.

"Not really."

"Well, I am a bundle of nerves," she said.

"Why? You look great."

"Thanks, Trey."

"Where are you from?"

"Kentucky. You?"

The crowd started to hush. "Georgia. Looks like we're getting started."

The crowd behind them quieted as the panel of interviewers, six in all, filed in and took their seats at the draped table. They all wore navy suits with white shirts. The two men wore matching ties and the four women all had the same patterned scarves.

A woman stood and went to the podium with the Global Airways logo. The room fell silent as she spoke.

"Good evening. I'm Margo Greene, Head of Recruiting, on behalf of Global Airways, I want to welcome you to the Washington, DC, open house. Thank you all for turning out tonight—this is quite a crowd," she said in a Germanic accent. She motioned to her team. "We have been in five other cities across the US and Europe these past two weeks and this is our final stop. Please take a moment now and turn your attention to your arrival packets. Each of you received a number this evening. We will be selecting a few of you one by one to stand and tell us a bit about yourselves. Be brief, thirty to ninety seconds only. Unfortunately, we only have twelve slots remaining, but I encourage each of you not selected tonight to continue to pursue your dreams. Ready?" She turned to her colleague who nodded. "Great. We will start with fifty-six."

One by one candidates were selected. They stood and spoke about family, friends, why they wanted to join Global Airways. Trey counted as they were called. *That's twenty-three total. How many will get called? Be you.* Trey reconfirmed his number. *One Zero Seven.*

"Thank you, and now number 107."

A bolt of energy shot through Trey as he stood. "Good evening, I'm Trey Carter. I live here in Fairfax, but I'm from Atlanta." His Southern drawl was unavoidable now with his nerves. "I graduated last May with a degree in communications and work in public relations, but my passion is coaching gymnastics here in Chantilly, Virginia."

"What do you like about coaching?" a panelist asked.

"I love empowering my team. Watching a young gymnast work through their fear, dream big, try a new trick."

As he was about to sit, Margo said, "A gymnast, huh? Well, can we see a trick?"

"Here?"

She nodded as the room clapped to encourage him. Trey blushed but quickly took off his blazer and tucked his tie into his shirt. He glanced around and took two steps forward, then did a standing back flip, arching with easy momentum to land dead in front of his seat. Applause erupted in the room as Trey sat down.

"Wow, thank you," Margo said as the panelists smiled at him. She called out another five numbers.

"And now our final candidate, number 127."

To Trey's left, Sydney stood. "Hello, I'm Sydney Bauman. I'm twenty-two and a recent graduate of University of Kentucky."

"Tri Delta?" A panelist asked.

"Yes, but also Phi Beta Kappa. I majored in International Business, which is why I'm excited to be here tonight, but I minored in psychology, which I hope will help me should there be difficult passengers."

"Ha! No doubt," a panelist blurted out. The panel chuckled.

"Good job," Trey whispered as she sat.

"Thanks," she whispered back.

"I'm sorry but that concludes our thirty candidate selection." Margo pursed her lips. "For those of you selected, please remain. All others, please take your exit but remember to keep chasing your dreams. On behalf of Global Airways, thank you for joining us this evening. Good night."

Hotel staff opened the back doors as the disappointed attendees stood and headed to the back. As the room emptied slowly, the noise dampened and the doors closed loudly as the last of the non-selected candidates exited.

"Well, round one is completed. Congratulations to each of you." Margo widened her eyes. "You have made it through our first round of selections, which is *very* thorough. Now, I would like to call on senior purser and head of training, Ted Perry. He'll offer you some additional insights on our past and future. Ted?"

Ted stood and went to the podium. "Thanks, Margo. Howdy y'all. Thank you for coming out tonight. I'm from Amarillo in the great state of Texas."

Trey relaxed at the sound of his drawl. He seemed to be in his midforties and quite tall.

"Some of you may've heard a little bit about us, but we aren't like most airlines. We have a rather *colorful* history." Ted nodded to the hotel employee standing at the far side of the stage, who wheeled in a large television, plugged it in, and awaited Ted's signal to start the video.

"Global Airways was launched in 1948 right after World War II but the real secret to our airline came two years later when the maverick Mac Purvis bought the airline. Over our next thirty years, Mac took us from a small commuter in San Francisco to a bona fide global commercial carrier. He was a bit of a John Wayne, Hugh Hefner, and Howard Hughes rolled into one." Ted turned to his colleagues who all laughed. "I think we all have a story or two that we could share over drinks if you're selected and we fly a line together."

"He was more of a cowboy than you, Ted," a panelist said.

Another panelist added, "He shot from the hip and chased a few of us back in the hot-pants days."

"No, he was not PC," Ted said. "But he had a heart of gold and for thirty years he was the face of Global Airways. Because of Mac the Maverick, we were able to save 328 lives in the last flight out of Da Nang near the end of the Vietnam War. Don't believe me? Here's a clip." Ted motioned to the hotel staffer and the television turned on.

Music played as black-and-white images of vintage aircraft and flight attendants in suits evolved to chromatic color images of wide lapels, big hair, and hot pants with go-go boots. The airline logo morphed from an old block lettering to the famous swoosh, then to the new blue "pumpkin." Suddenly footage emerged, with Purvis helping refugee children while fending off an onslaught of men from the back stairs of the Boeing 727 in the middle of taxiing. Apparently, Global's last flight from the airfield had rescued more than three hundred fleeing as the Communist regime had seized the nation. Dan Rather then appeared as a young reporter. Trey turned to Sydney.

"Wow, that was live on the news?"

"Yeah, look." She pointed to the video, where emblazoned onscreen: *CBS Evening News – Airdate: March 30, 1975.*

The new "blue globe" logo reappeared. The hotel staff member hit Pause as Ted continued.

"Interesting, right? Not your typical airline. We're not Delta, America, or United. It was during Vietnam that our special relationship with the US defense department started. We travel the world servicing many branches of our government. From the Pentagon to Congress and the State Department. This is why we must be discreet and selective in our process. Remember in your applications, we asked you about your willingness to serve in wartime missions? That's because we lend a hand when needed. You might have seen us on CNN during the recent Gulf War. So, we completely understand if this job is not for you. No harm, no foul. Please take this opportunity to leave if you would like."

Ted, Margo, and the other four panelists scanned the three rows of applicants. Trey held his breath and stared at the panel. No one stood or left.

Wow, I get it now. They are close with the DoD and I bet the Agency. This really could be cool. Hope Sydney and I both make it.

"Great, let's continue then. After Mac passed away, we went public for a brief period, then back to private. In the early eighties, we moved our operations from the Bay Area in California to the East Coast with operations here in Washington's Dulles and our training center in Philadelphia."

I bet they moved to DC to be closer to the Pentagon, NSA, and the Agency. I wonder if other people are embedded as operatives at Global?

"You may ask yourself what's next. If selected tonight after our interviews, you'll be invited to join our third and final class of trainees for three weeks in Philly." Ted took a sip of water before he continued. "So, we have a special relationship with DC, which is why it's our last stop. Our only rival is ATA. We enjoy many exclusive contracts for MAC flights, group movement, and special international envoys—which is also why we ask each of you about your personal backgrounds. If selected, you will have to undergo a clearance for the Department of Defense." He turned to Margo. She nodded.

"Now that you've heard about us and our unique past, let's circle back to that point about discretion." He took another sip of water. "It is essential to our operations. How many of you saw the Gulf War ignite on live television two years ago? C'mon, let me see hands."

Most every candidate raised their hands.

"That was thanks to a commercial airline flight attendant. Crazy, huh? Truth. She told one person—her neighbor. Supposedly so that they would feed her cat while she was away. Sounds reasonable, right? I mean the poor kitty needs his dinner."

Everyone chuckled.

"But her neighbor pressed her *why* and *where* she was headed out in the middle of the night for three weeks. So she told them. Innocent breach? No. Her neighbor in Atlanta was a reporter for CNN. The rest is—as the saying goes—history. So, if you are selected tonight after our individual interviews, we will expect absolute discretion."

Shit. That's what Rick said. Damn, I thought he was trying to sell me on the job but I get it now. Why do I feel like I'm not the only one in this room with a secret?

Trey looked up from his thoughts and to see Margo scanning him. *Oh my god, does she know?*

CHAPTER 44
SELECTION

"**C**an you believe this shit?" a guy with a thick Boston accent blurted out over his shoulder while at the urinal. "Hate to burst your bubbles, boys, but most of *yous guys* won't make it." He zipped up, flushed, and turned to Trey and four of the other male applicants who were waiting. "Such a shame too 'cause damn all the tail out there—whoever makes it is gonna clean up on those long, lonely layovers."

"I don't think you'll need to worry about that, pal." The booming familiar voice echoed from the adjacent stall. Ted walked out and over to the sink. "Was it Mr. Figermille?"

"Sigermelli. Pete Sigermelli."

"Mr. Sigermelli, you can leave now. We wish you well in your pursuits."

"But I was joking—"

Ted spun around and stared down at the crumbling young man. "Well, son, I'm not joking. We're done."

Pete exited without washing his hands.

Ted dried his hands and opened the door. "Discretion, gentlemen. Discretion."

Geez, they are watching our every move. Trey tightened his posture as he left the men's room. He scanned the lobby looking for his assigned group.

"You in group three, too?"

Trey turned to see a tall and muscular guy in a blue suit with a Semper Fi lapel pin.

"Yup. Trey Carter."

"Louis Jones, but I go by LJ." He presented his hand.

Trey shook it. "This is quite the process, huh?"

"Yeah. Did you see that shit go down just now in the bathroom?"

"Yeah, he didn't know Ted heard him, but couldn't have happened to a nicer prick. Right?" Trey said.

"Total douche."

"No doubt you saw worse in the Corps."

"Yeah, how did you know?"

"Your pin. How long did you serve?"

"Five years. Gulf War," LJ said.

"Thanks for your service."

"Thanks." LJ smiled. "I think that's us over there by the couches."

Trey spotted the sign on the easel. *Group Three.* As they walked, Trey wondered about the others. *Could LJ be Agency too? What is a former Marine doing here?* "How'd you know about Global?"

"My career placement officer told me. To be honest, if I'd known how tight this job market is—I would've re-upped. Stayed in."

"I hear ya."

"How'd you hear about this open house?"

"Uh, a friend told me." *Not a total lie.*

He and LJ approached the other candidates, and everyone introduced themselves.

The doors in front of them opened. Ted and Margo emerged and approached their group.

"All right, thanks for coming out tonight. We'll meet with each of you now one by one," Ted said.

"Please sit tight and either Ted or I will call your name for your interview," Margo added. "We'll start with Sydney Bauman."

Over the next hour, candidates were called into the room. Some emerged smiling. Some emerged frowning. The last woman emerged in tears, leaving only LJ and Trey as they watched intently. Margo appeared in the open doorway.

"Louis Jones."

"Good luck, LJ," Trey said.

"Thanks, man."

The door shut, and over the next ten minutes the whole lobby adjacent to Trey emptied out completely. A few of the other Global interviewers emerged from their respective rooms and headed toward the bar in the lobby. *What is taking so long? This must be intense.*

Suddenly, the door opened and LJ emerged. He gave a quick smile and thumbs-up to Trey, then departed, leaving him alone.

"Well, I guess you're next then, Trey," Margo said, with a smile from the doorway.

He entered and saw a table with three chairs.

Ted was standing and stretching. "Come on in Trey."

They all three shook hands and re-introduced themselves.

"That was some back flip," Margo started off.

"Yes, that was cool. Best candidate minute in all five cities, easy." Ted motioned to the chairs and they all sat.

"Thank you." Trey tried to relax at their compliment but his suspicion of Margo lingered. *Does she know? Is she Agency?*

Margo scanned his application. "Pensacola Christian High, honors student, athlete, football, basketball, gymnastics, Liberty University. 3.2 GPA. Communications. College cheerleader. American Seniors Initiative. Well, you certainly have a balanced and interesting past." She looked up from the papers and tilted her head slightly. "Did you like it at Pensacola?"

Trey cleared his throat. "Yes, the beaches were beautiful. I finished high school there."

"How old were you when you went away to boarding school?" Ted asked.

"Fifteen."

"I understand it's an Evangelical school and a bit strict," Ted added.

"Yes, sir. It was very strict, but I got into gymnastics and also did a little musical theater, *The Pirates of Penzance*."

"Huh, and basketball?"

"Yes, sir."

"What position did you play?" Ted asked.

"Point guard. Did you play, sir?"

"I did."

"Did you, ma'am?"

Margo glanced up quickly. She pursed her lips but answered, "No. Not basketball but I played football, or as you say *soccer*, while at university."

They asked him several more questions about his background. Finally, Ted wrote on a pad and showed it to Margo. She nodded.

"Well, partner, we'll see you in Philadelphia on Monday, August 3," Ted said.

"Wow, thank you." Trey exhaled and sat back in his chair.

"Any questions for us?"

"No, I guess not."

"All righty then. Take this slip out to the front desk. They'll give you an orientation packet with all the details." He and Margo stood as she began to pack up. "See you in Philly."

Trey stood. "Thank you. It was great to meet you both, and I look forward to the training."

Wow, I did it. Can't believe this process . . . so many people here for only so few slots. But one of them is mine.

Trey walked out of the room to an empty lobby. *Where is everyone?* All that remained was the signage for the open house. Hotel staff had dismantled the tables and were stacking all the chairs in the ballroom as Trey walked to through the lobby.

"Do you have your signed note?"

"Yes." Trey handed it to the woman at the front desk.

"Right, here's your packet. I'm supposed to tell you not to open it and not to talk to the others but everyone's gone. You're last."

Trey took the packet. "Thanks. Have a good night."

She nodded and stared back at her computer.

As Trey drove home and approached the turnoff for his gymnastics gym, he suddenly veered and took it. In the dark, empty parking lot, he switched off his car. Even in the darkness through the window he could see the large spring floor, pommel horse and rings hanging motionless. *This gym's all that remains of my former life. My routine.* He sat for several minutes in the darkness before opening the blue packet and scanning the instructions. He closed the packet and stared at the empty gym. *I can't give up coaching, even to travel the world. Who will I be then?*

He restarted his engine and drove back to his apartment. Even though he had driven this route a hundred times—it now felt different.

Trey pulled into his parking deck next to Rick's white BMW. *What am I doing? Does Rick really care about me? Should I take this job?* He grabbed the packet.

He entered and saw Rick sprawled on the couch in his T-shirt and boxers watching television.

"How did it go?" Rick clicked off the TV and sat up.

"I got in—three weeks in Philly for training."

"That's great. Congrats." Rick smiled wide, then narrowed his eyes. "So what's wrong then?"

"What do you mean?"

"That look. Talk to me?"

Trey shrugged. "I don't know. It was a little odd."

"How so?"

"There were like four hundred people there, and we were the fifth city, the last stop. They only picked thirty of us to interview."

"They're super selective."

"But the math is insane." Trey shook his head. "Five cities, two thousand candidates. The odds must have been ten to one in applicants."

"So?"

"That means they screened like twenty thousand people to fill sixty slots?"

"Maybe, but you got a slot. You're happy right?"

Trey nodded. "I am but . . . all that for flight attendants."

"It's not *just* any airline—"

"Believe, I get it now."

"Proud of you, Tiger. You did this on your own. We had no pull beyond the application."

"Really?"

"Really."

"I wondered that, 'cause there was this one woman there— I don't know. It felt like she knew. You swear?"

"Come here." He cuddled Trey to the couch. "We only got you to the door. I swear. You did this on your own."

"Thanks, I—" Trey searched for how to explain his feelings. He didn't know what else to say though, so he repeated the words from the key chain. "Semper protege, Rick."

Rick's eyes widened and mouth opened. "Why would you say that to me?"

"From the keychain you—"

"I know that. It's . . ."

"What? I didn't know what else to say."

"It's what we used to say to each other."

"Who? You and your Israeli?"

Rick nodded and kissed his forehead, then his lips. He pulled Trey to his chest and whispered, "Semper protege. I'm proud of you. What did you say when they called on you?"

"I talked about coaching, like you said. Then they were like 'show us a trick.' So I did a back flip."

"Show off! Bet they loved that."

Trey shrugged.

"What else?"

"They talked about their history. Vietnam, Gulf War, military support—even that stuff about Delta you hinted at."

"I tried to tell. After the leak, the Pentagon pumped millions into Global—five years of contracts. On paper, Global Corp. reports forty-eight percent in defense contracts, but in reality . . . north of ninety. You will be safe and see the world. It's the perfect cover and really we'll both have the same boss—Uncle Sam."

"I met a couple of the others who'll be in my class. The job could be cool."

"See, I'm not a total asshole." He kissed Trey softly. "I'm determined to leave you better than I found you."

Trey smiled.

"We only have a couple more weeks together."

Trey's smile faded. "Forty-five days?"

Rick nodded.

"Can I ask some questions?"

"Are they good questions?" Rick smiled.

Trey rolled his eyes. "I'm serious. It's about my assignment."

Goddamn it. How does Doc M always predict this shit—like clockwork?

"Your civ-5 is going to start asking tougher questions, Rick. About the assignment. It is essential you are clear and factual with him."

All right, here we go—shoot straight with him.

Rick sat up on the couch. "Go for it. What do you want to know?"

Trey sat up. "The assignment . . . will you be with me?"

"Yes, every step of the way. Jeni too."

"When is it?"

"Two weeks from tomorrow."

"Where?"

"Germany"

"Before my Global Airways training?"

"Yup."

"What am I going to be doing?"

Shit. Keep it brief, simple. Don't lie. "Meeting someone."

"Kinda like Sami."

Rick scanned Trey as he furrowed his brow and looked at the floor.

"So, the target is gay?"

"We think so."

"You're not sure—"

"I profiled him myself. I trailed him in Germany a couple months ago."

"What's he like?"

He's a sick fucker. "He likes young men. It's why we selected you."

"Yeah but—"

Rick placed his index finger over his mouth, tapped his ear, and then pointed around the room. "What?"

"Nothing." Trey nodded.

"Good. Now if this interrogation is over—I've got to pee, finish my movie, and shower before bed." Rick hit Play on the remote and Bruce Willis continued to wreak havoc in *Die Hard* loudly. He stood and motioned for Trey to follow.

In the bathroom, Rick turned on the sink and the shower fully. He leaned into Trey and whispered, "You know we still got ears here. Right?"

"I don't care—I only want the truth."

"Tiger, cut me some slack. I've never lied to you. There are things we know and things we don't about the target. It's *highly* classified."

"Okay, I want to know ahead of time."

"And you will. I promise. I'll talk you through it, but I want to do it my way. OTR. Not here, not like this. Got it?"

"Yeah. But then what?"

"What do you mean?"

"After Germany. Will there be other assignments?"

Fuck no! Rick took a deep breath. "Not if I have anything to do with it. One and done. But—"

"But what?"

"It's not totally my call."

Trey exhaled. "I'm glad you'll be with me in Germany."

"Never out of my sight. I promise. We good?"

Trey nodded and held out his fist. They bumped top and bottom.

"Wait, one more question?"

Rick frowned. "One more but then I get one."

Trey rubbed his hands together "Would you've dove in the pool? At the Farm, if I hadn't got it done?"

Rick's face saddened slightly. "What kind of question is that? Are you kidding me? Of course I would've. Hammonds too, and probably all four rookies. You spooked the shit out of us all, Houdini."

"Hammonds? Really?"

"Yeah. You want to know the last thing he said to me as we were leaving?"

Trey shrugged.

"He said you were special and that I was to watch out for you. Protect you. There is only so much I can control here, but I do care. This has been intense for me too, you know?"

Trey nodded.

"What would you say if my director asked you about our time at the lake?"

"Why? Am I going to meet her?"

"Not sure, but I learned that not only were they filming us, but portions of the video have been screened by brass at the Pentagon. I didn't know, Trey. So, what would you say?"

"I would say that the training was intense. The setting was pristine, and that I will never regret one minute from that weekend. Even my scar from the pool training. In a weird way, I'm grateful."

"Grateful? Why?"

"Every scar has a story. All this led me to you."

You've been used and abused, but you're grateful? This must be Doc M. The protocol. Fuck, the mind games. What do I do now? Rick let his instincts lead as he took Trey into his arms. "Me too. I'm grateful to know you, Trey." They stood for a moment in a tight embrace.

"Wait. What do you mean filmed us?" Trey pulled back and stared at him.

"They had hidden cameras. At first, I was pissed, but now that I've heard your answer—I agree with you."

"Do you regret anything from the lake?"

"No." Rick pulled Trey's foreman up and kissed his scar gently.

"Why do you do it? Stay with the Agency when they pull stuff like secretly filming you?"

"To serve my country used to be my answer, but lately—I don't know."

"Know what I think?"

Rick raised his eyebrows.

"You're trapped too."

Rick nodded slowly. "Maybe. It's complicated. I'm no victim. But, yes, they kinda have me by the balls too."

"What, these?" Trey slipped his hand down and groped him.

Rick grinned and tightened his hug. "Ha! Now you're starting to get my humor."

"Seriously, if they ask me, I'll say they saw a damn good coach training his recruit. Beyond our messing around, it was pretty SOP. Are you worried, Rick?"

"A little, but the protocol allows us to flex and blur the boundaries a bit."

Should I tell him anything else? The video? Ivan? No. It can wait. He's gonna be nervous about being on campus for our last ten days. He'll have a ton more questions. Not tonight—let's have one night before our cocoon rips open.

Trey kissed him.

"What was that for?" Rick asked.

"To bring you back here—with me." Trey stared intently at Rick.

"What do you mean? I'm right here." Rick kissed him passionately. "Let's go to bed?"

Trey's eyes widened and they stripped naked.

Rick led him to bed and allowed his memories from the lake to pull him to Trey and into one breath, one motion, and one intense release. They didn't care about neighbors or any Agency members listening to their most primal sounds. They were bound beyond the protocol in their passion. Connected in a bond had been forged over thirty-five days of sweat, blood, stress, and release.

The training was nearly complete. Rick and Trey would now be exposed to the full weight of the Agency.

CHAPTER 45
ESCALATION

Claren had called Rick at 1630, right as Trey had left to meet Sami for a run at the Reston Town Center.

Ring, ring.

"Rick Morgan."

"Hey, can you hear me?"

"Claren?"

"Rick? Damn, the connection's bad. Can you call me back?"

Shit. Something's up. She wants an OTR call. Damn it, Claren. This better not be another shift. Rick headed out to the parking deck and retrieved his burner, a hidden private mobile, from his trunk. He stayed outside and awaited her call. *Wonder what's going on? C'mon, call already.* Several minutes passed before the familiar vibration.

Buzz, buzz.

"Claren? What's up?"

"Our target has shifted. Intel now says Nuremberg. I have recommended that we escalate to July 23."

Fuck! That's only ten days away—we're not ready. "Okay, so what—now I have ten days to assemble a new team and plan? What about my civ?"

"He's on the team," Claren said.

"You can't be serious—after one field test? We've already sped this up. Normally, we'd have a full three months."

"I know that. I warned Tibbins and Doc M, but nothing about this is normal."

"No. We need more time . . . at least one more test here, stateside."

"The window is locked now: July 23-25. Given his progress, it does seem doable. Right?"

"Yeah, I guess."

"How is he?"

"Good. He's running with Samir Hassan as we speak."

"Excellent. Look, we're going off script a bit to make things easier for training. These next ten days will be here."

"On campus? And you agreed to this?"

"Doc M wants an in-person evaluation before Germany. And before you say it, so help me god, Rick, do you honestly think I had a choice here?"

Shit, stand up to them, Claren. You always go along with them. "No. But how're we going to explain his presence to the gawking Agency staffers and officers? Hell, this could expose our whole team."

"My concern exactly. Look, we'll give him a civ-5 operative training pass. You'll need to move around discreetly, but it could be good to allow eyes. It would also give you better access to training facilities for this final push."

"Huh. Campus would be easier. We've had to get pretty creative here offsite. His gymnastics gym has been great after-hours for KM, but the nearest firing range is over in Sterling."

"Understood. So, really, OTR, how's he doing?"

"He's getting there."

"What is it, Rick?"

"A rumor."

"Let me guess: a film screening?"

"Yup. Am I blown? Did you out me?"

"Of course not. We edited."

"Why have eyes on me, Claren?"

"Rick—"

"What the fuck? Why would you risk it?"

"Shut up and listen to me carefully. Tibbins believes that Clinton could win. Things will begin to change, quickly. That and the pressure on the Pentagon with higher and higher ranks coming out."

"Yeah, I've seen 'em, but they lose everything. Pensions, rank—"

"Rick, Tibbins and I will protect you. Do you hear me?"

"Yeah."

"Your record in the field is stellar. Twelve years. Nobody—nobody can take that away from you."

But if you're not successful, you damn well know that I could lose everything.

"Rick? Are you there?"

"Yeah. Can I see the tape?"

"Let me clear it with Tibbins, but I'm sure it'll be fine."

Rick squeezed the phone tight and shook his head. *Fine my ass.* "Can *we* see it? Trey's eyes need to be opened a bit wider before Germany. It'll also help me set boundaries for our time on-campus training."

"I like it. Good strategy. I'll get clearance. We can send it over on a one-and-done. No replay. We'll deliver the tape to you. He'll also need papers—at least two sets and an alias. Should we offer him a choice? On his names?"

"Yeah, that would be good. It'll help me explain all this new arrangement. He's still adjusting."

"Do you think we should brief him here on Ivan?"

Fuck no. I want to do this my way. He could freak out. "Campus, Doc M, you—it's a lot of new hurdles. Can you give me a few days to let you know?"

"Sure, let's wait and you take the lead. His final briefing needs to be tight—no redshirts, no backup."

Claren's nervous and overreaching. She knows this is too fast. I haven't heard that tone since Mexico City. Rick closed his eyes and saw flashes of faces, then blood. He shook his head.

Never again. Overestimation gets people killed.

CHAPTER 46
DISPARITY

Thursday, May 19, 1988
Ring, ring.

R*hattha.* Rick awoke to the sound of the incoming Agency call. He scrambled to find the receiver in the dark.

"Hello."

"Rick? So sorry to wake you?"

"Claren?" Rick strained to see the red glow of his bedside clock: *2:13 a.m. Why the hell are you calling in the middle of the night?*

"We have a situation. There's no easy way to say this—Terry's dead."

Rick jolted up in bed. "What did you say?"

"Terry is dead."

No! What the fuck? Rick rubbed his face. "How, Claren? Where?"

"Mexico City, tonight. Details are still coming in—"

"What happened?"

"I'll explain, but we've got less than forty-eight hours to reassess and get the target."

"Who did this?"

"One of Escobar's men, Fipé—I have a jet waiting. Can you engage?"

"Yeah, putting you on speaker. What do we know?" Rick clicked to speaker and got out of bed.

"Terry engaged the target at a bar in Mexico City tonight. When they were leaving the club, there was gunfire. He was shot."

Rick's head pounded. He grabbed his pre-packed emergency bag from the back of his closet. He tossed it on the bed and unlocked his equipment locker at the foot of his bed. "In Mexico City?"

"Yeah."

"What happened, exactly?"

"Still getting details, but there was some sort of ambush."

"Ambush?"

"Yeah, we haven't confirmed, but most likely the hit was for Fipé. We don't think that they even knew Terry was Agency, but . . ."

Rick stopped packing. "But what, Claren?"

"The press got pictures. The story's exploding. They're trying to tag him—as an American."

Shit! Rick shook his head. "Who's on the ground?"

"John Fernandez. Our station chief. He's guiding the media suppression, but Fipé has vanished. We have only a few hours to get you to Mexico City, along with Das."

Donald Allen Sullivan. Shit, he can't handle this. "Why Das?"

"He's one of us."

He's straight and a fucking Langley desk jockey. He's not field.

"Rick?"

"Where's he now?"

"Already en route."

"So that's it—Das?"

"You need backup and eyes that know *us*. Right now, I don't care how you feel about him. Fipé's men have poked holes in our desk—they've made several of John's team—it's like they can smell their credentials."

"When do I leave?"

"The transport's waiting at Andrews. Can you get there within the hour? We're filing the flight plan."

"I'll be there."

"Good. I'm faxing over the briefing report now. Read it on the plane. Das will explain further, but, Rick?"

"Yeah?"

"We must *contain* this situation."

He gripped the phone tightly and resisted smashing it against the wall. "Understood."

Rick stood naked under his shower as the warm water washed away his tears. He squeezed his eyes tighter to try to block the image of his blond friend with the wide smile. *Special Officer Terrance "Terry" Jackson. We're the same age. Height. This could have easily been me. Who would she have called then? Jeni? Das?*

He shook his head and turned off the shower. He grabbed his towel and tried to replay the details of her call. *Terry deserves better. Who the fuck is Fipé? If I get the chance, I'm gonna kill him. Painfully.*

He dressed quickly and grabbed his bags. The Agency car was waiting for him in front of his building in Silver Spring. As they sped up the BW Parkway, Rick looked out at the dark night—not another car in sight.

The Air Force base was a ghost town at this hour as the guard waved them through the security gate and directly onto the tarmac to the unmarked Learjet.

"Officer Morgan?" the pilot asked.

Rick nodded.

The pilot motioned up the short stairs. Rick entered the jet and the pilot followed, closing the door. "Welcome aboard. There's food and coffee in the galley here. The head's back there through the door. Let us know if you need anything, sir."

"Thanks, Captain."

"It's a long flight. Try to get some shut-eye."

Rick stowed his bags and took his seat as the pilot rejoined his co-pilot and closed the cockpit door. Alone in the cabin, Rick felt acid gnawing at his stomach. *This one's different—personal. Terry wasn't just some random agent—he was my friend.*

The engines roared to life and the plane lunged forward. Rick sank deeper into his leather seat.

We're not doing this by the book. We're doing this my way, for Terry. Stay outta my way, Das.

He glanced out at the dark skies and twinkling lights. The cabin lights turned off, and he switched on his reading light. He scanned the report.

Guide me, Terry. Show me what happened. What went wrong?

He studied the details of the incident. Terry had arrived in Mexico City on Delta Air Lines under his cover of Antonio Luis

Melendez on Monday night, May 16, 1988. He flipped the page and saw Terry's Agency headshot.

He closed his eyes and remembered the first time he'd met Terry at the Farm, during one of their required recurrent trainings.

"No way—you're a Pats fan too?"

Rick looked up to see a blond, muscular near-mirror image of himself pointing to Rick's New England Patriots blanket on his bunk.

"Yeah, why?" Rick frowned.

"No shit—me too. Most of these assholes are Skins fans. I'm Terry. From Situate, Mass."

"Rick, New Hampshire."

Rick shook Terry's hand. Terry flashed his smile. Wide, toothy, and warm—like his blanket.

During their prescribed recurrent assessments, under the leadership of "Das," Senior Operations Director Donald A. Sullivan, the protocol team had been sent to the Farm for training and evaluations. Darius Morris, Jeni Yoon, Rick Morgan, Terry Jackson, and three others.

I can't believe we all passed that first time.

Rick had deduced that he and Terry were both thirty, both from New England, not Ivy, Patriot fans, and both hated the unofficial Agency football team, the Washington Redskins. But although they were both gay, albeit closeted, Terry had politely declined Rick's offer to *"rub one out together"* when they'd found themselves alone in the showers. Rick closed his eyes and remembered Terry's wet, muscular body and their exchange.

"I can't— I'm tempted but I have a partner—"

"Oh shit, I'm sorry. I just—"

"Don't be, Rick. You're hot as fuck. If we were here longer, I might take you up on it, but we've recently decided to be exclusive." Terry shook his head.

"How's that going?"

"You tell me," Terry said, pointing to his own half-erect cock. "Told you I was tempted."

"So how does that work?" Rick asked. "Having a partner."

"Not easy. The time apart is tough, but we make it work. Under the radar."

"*Does Claren know?*"

"*Not at first. She kept calling him 'the roommate' but after two years she finally figured it out.*"

Rick grinned wide. "*Wow, congrats.*"

"*What about you? Ever had a partner?*"

"*No.*" Rick turned to the warm spray.

"*Hey, when we get back to DC, we'll have you over—you and Jeni. He's a teacher and a great cook. You'll like him. Cool?*"

"*That'd be great.*"

Jeni and Rick had enjoyed a few nights at their home in Old Town Alexandria over the few weeks after training. By July, their team had been redeployed throughout the world. Jeni was in Seoul. Darius in Beirut. Rick was back in Berlin.

Terry had been posted to Cartagena and assigned to engage an emerging target, a Colombian drug czar's right hand, Francisco Pablo Garzia-Torre. Fipé, as he was known, was a personal assistant to the Medellin cartel leader, Gonzalo Rodriguez Gacha, who was a general in Pablo Escobar's empire. Rodriguez Gacha managed the Escobar cocaine operations from a ranch near Cartagena.

The Agency had observed that Fipé would travel to Mexico City periodically for a bit of pleasure and business. The situation was directly linked to the death of a Mexican journalist, Manuel Buendía Tellezgirón, in 1984, four years earlier. Buendía had been murdered in Mexico City, as the famed reporter had been breaking a story on a connection between law enforcement, organized crime, and drug trafficking. Buendía had discovered the dark ops collaboration between the DFS and CIA to curb and control the Medellin in Mexico and the US.

The Mexican Center of Investigation and National Security, CISEN, had not yet been formed as it grew out of the impending debacle to be established a year later in 1989. Many in the intelligence community speculated later that the events of May 1988 led to the breakdown of the DFS, Dirección Federal de Seguridad. The events and Terry's death challenged the CIA operations desk in Mexico City.

The Agency had successfully suppressed the story for four years since the murder of Buendía had remained unsolved. By May 1988, the DFS had been under tremendous stress as reporters and local authorities were sniffing out new leads on the old case.

To make matters worse, Fipé not only knew the details of the Buendía murder—he was suspected to have provided a few interviews to the growing number of international reporters investigating the case. When Fipé emerged as a target and his frequent trips to gay discotheques and bathhouses in Mexico City became known, the DFS confirmed him as their primary target. The DFS did not have a protocol to bend and use sexual orientation as incentive in his capture. He'd eluded their straight agents at every sting and was accompanied by six armed bodyguards at all times.

The DFS had quietly taken the Fipé case to the head of the Agency's Mexico City ops desk, Senior Field Director John Fernandez. John was from Odessa, Texas, a second-generation Mexican-American. He'd graduated from the US Air Force Academy and joined the Agency after serving as an intelligence officer in the Air Force for five years.

John and Claren were close friends and colleagues due to his time on Campus, so in April 1988, he'd taken a chance and reached out to her on the Fipé situation. Claren, in turn, had brought it to Director Tibbins. By May, the plan had been organized, but as Terry had emerged from baggage claim, no one could have imagined the bloody two days that would follow.

Terry had been taken directly to the US Embassy on Paseo de la Reforma 305 in Cuauhtémoc. Twenty hours later, he was on a slab in the morgue of the Centro Médico ABC.

Who knew he was coming? It doesn't add up.

Rick unbuckled and made his way to the galley. He poured himself a cup of coffee.

By the time we land, this could be over or splashed across the news wires. Langley will no doubt disavow Terry—they'd never allow the Agency to be linked to this mess. Shit. What am I missing?

Rick returned to his seat and looked out at the dark skies. The moon shone brightly, even at only a sliver.

That's it! I bet they only gave Terry half the story—never told him about Buendía or the murder. He was probably given the basic intel, a gun, and instructions for an entrapment with incentive on Fipé.

They'd probably planned to have the target join Terry at his hotel room where cameras would have recorded a sexual encounter. They'd then have used the footage as incentive to recruit Fipé. Turn him and use him.

The DFS and Agency must've hoped that when recruited, Fipé could then deflect the pressure that the Medellín was placing on the Buendía murder. Shit! They overestimated. Now Terry's dead.

The intel seemed to confirm Rick's hunch. Several sources speculated the media leaks were within the drug cartel. *They're threatening to expose the Agency's link to the murder—that's why they sent Terry to meet him at that club.*

Terry and Fipé met at a gay nightclub and left the club together—but had encountered intense gunfire in the streets awaiting Fipé's car. Terry had been hit and then left bleeding profusely as Fipé sped away.

Rick reread the known intel.

It doesn't add up. What are they not telling me?

He glanced at his watch. *Only two hours till touchdown—I better try to sleep.*

Reluctantly, he closed his eyes.

Bam!

The jet landed hard in Mexico City two hours later at 0720 local. Rick shook his head and stretched before grabbing his bags and pulling out his German alias passport for immigrations. He was still a bit groggy as his cab drove the tree-lined streets of the Polanco neighborhood to his hotel. Rick dropped off his bags in his hotel room and met Das downstairs along with John for breakfast at 0830 in the hotel restaurant.

Rick ate quietly for thirty minutes as Das and John briefed him about the situation and the known details of Terry's death.

They're cherry-picking details. Don't react. Not yet.

"That's what we think happened," John concluded.

"So let me get this straight, John. You're saying that it was simply a case of the wrong place, wrong time?" Rick asked.

"Essentially, yes." John sipped his coffee.

"I don't buy it. Why would the local gang even know Fipé?"

"Cocaine." John glanced around the room. "He controls the supply to DF, Monterrey, LA, Houston, Dallas—he has *many* enemies here."

"When he and Terry came out of the club, they were ambushed, probably by a rival gang. Terry engaged. Gets shot. They left him in the street," Das recited the supposed details.

"No." Rick shook his head. "It doesn't add up."

"Why?" Das asked.

"Because you're overestimating one fact." Rick sipped his coffee. "Escobar and Gacha already knew Fipé was gay."

"Bullshit," John barked.

Rick shot him a look and then turned to Das.

"No fucking way." John shook his head. "You think you can step off a plane and into my operations—"

"Stop," Das snapped. "Let Rick tell us what he sees."

"My gut says this isn't only about drugs—"

"We don't have time for this. We have to get the target." John crossed his arms.

"Precisely. But what if Fipé suspects? Do you really think he'll go out again today?"

"We're not sure." John leaned forward and rested his elbows on the table. "But if he does, it will be quietly to his local bathhouse. He won't risk going to a bar again this trip."

"Even if he does—what makes you think that I can get him alone?" Rick asked.

Das looked at John, who nodded.

"What are you guys not telling me?" Rick pressed.

Das took a sip of his coffee. "Rick, there is another important angle here. Four years ago, a high-profile reporter was gunned down by the DFS." His tone suggested he would reveal exactly what he wanted, and no more; there would be no point in questions. "There are several international news organizations seeking to uncover the truth about the death of this journalist."

"Buendía." Rick held up his mug.

"You already knew?" Das stared at Rick.

"Yup. Look, if we're gonna do this—no more secrets. I want full intel."

Das turned to John.

"Fine." John nodded.

"And we're doing this my way." Rick set down his mug.

"What tha—" John blurted.

"Are we clear?" Rick gave him an icy stare.

"Yes," Das said.

John threw up his hands but nodded.

"Why does this Buendía matter?"

John leaned across the table. "The DFS took out Manuel Buendía with our . . . *help*."

Rick nodded. *Of course, there's the missing piece. And what? Terry was collateral. Fuck these games.* "It was four years ago; what's the connection?"

"If it leaks, there will be significant ramifications for the Agency, White House, and US relations with Mexico. This is about more than simply taking down a drug king. You're a German reporter sent here to dig into the Buendía murder."

Rick sat down his coffee. "Where am I meeting him?"

"The Sodome Bathhouse," John said, pulling out the file. "It's located on Mariano Escobedo in Miguel Hidalgo, a few kilometers from Polanco."

Rick assessed the layout of the club with its lockers, lobby, saunas, and private rooms.

"Surveillance has indicated that if Fipé goes, he will be there by 1400," John said.

"How much time do we have?"

"About two hours."

"All right. Then I'm gonna go for a run first. Clear my mind and shake off the jetlag."

"Can I join you?" Das asked.

"Yeah, if you can keep up."

As they ran past the Parque América, Rick decided to ask his ops leader the obvious question. He stopped and turned to Das.

Das stopped. "What's up?"

"An important question for you."

"Shoot."

"Have you ever even been in a bathhouse before?"

Das shook his head. "No. Have you?"

"Many times. Do you know what to expect?"

"Not really," Das said.

Shit, higher tone to his voice, rigid stance, balled fists—classic tells. He's nervous as fuck. Houston, we have a problem—he won't bend convincingly. He screams straight, uncomfortable agent on assignment. Talk it out with him.

"Look, I know it's been a while since you were in the field, but you got to loosen up."

Das frowned. "Rick—"

"Hear me out?"

He nodded.

"Look, I don't want you to freak out. Everyone will be naked and you'll have these towels. There will be lots of sex happening in alcoves, the saunas, and in the private rooms. Gay sex—sucking, fucking—"

"Okay, okay—I get it." Das shuffled his weight left and right. "Just tell me what to do or not to do."

"Eye contact is the key. Keep your eyes locked on me like you are *hunting* me. It will be obvious to Fipé, but don't give him or others any looks. Your look could send the wrong signal. Stay focused on me—like I'm the pretty girl at the high school dance."

Das exhaled and nodded.

"Relax your arms."

Das opened his fists and relaxed his shoulders.

"Good. I will try and get him into a private booth. Be on point for me—guard the door but casually. Knock three times if we're made or his guards approach."

"Got it."

"If our cover is blown, we'll have to get out quickly. There are two emergency exits on the backside of the building, but we won't have our clothes. It'll be a crazy run back to the hotel. Keep your towel tightly wrapped around you. There will be *admirers* trying to entice you."

"Shit, Rick. I'm not—"

"No, think of it as being picked up. Be polite but firm. No means no. But if anyone touches you, break their hand if you have to," Rick said with a wink.

Das nodded. "Thanks, Rick. This is not my area of expertise."

"Ha! No, I guess not."

I only need four minutes alone with this fucker Fipé to break his neck and get out. Das doesn't need to know.

At 1350 both Rick and Das exited the hotel within minutes of one another, in separate taxis for the Sodome Bathhouse. *In and out, get him.* Rick rolled his shoulders before exiting the cab. *Let's do this . . . for Terry.* He entered and registered in German using his alias. He purchased a 24-hour pass along with a private room. Rick entered the locker room and took his time removing his clothes.

Das entered the locker room as Rick removed his underwear. Rick smiled slightly and stood naked with his towel in his right hand.

Follow my lead, Das. Take off your clothes and just follow me.

Robotically, Das removed his clothes, slipped on the rubber sandals, and wrapped his white towel tightly around his waist.

For an hour, Das followed Rick like a puppy. They wandered throughout the maze of rooms, casually scanning the patrons. Methodically, Rick scanned their faces while assessing threats. *What the fuck? He's not here.* Men were naked as described with oral sex and masturbation on full display. Rick and Das entered the steam room briefly to find a group of four men taking turns with a willing bottom. One of them motioned for Das to join but he declined.

Look at me, Das. Too busy in here—let's go.

Rick led them to the dry sauna and sat opposite the door with his towel loose around his waist. Suddenly, the door swung open and a familiar face entered. Fipé strode in naked, carrying his towel. He glanced at Das and then turned to Rick. His stare intensified as he took a seat.

Rick glanced at Das, who complained of the heat and exited, leaving the two men alone.

"*¿Como está*, mi amigo?" Fipé asked.

"No hablo español. Alemán," Rick said, pointing to himself. "Sprechen Sie Deutsch?"

"No." Fipé shook his head.

"English?" Rick responded in a heavy German-accented English.

"Yes. Where in Germany are you from, my friend?"

"Dusseldorf. But I live in Frankfurt."

"What brings you to Mexico City?"

"Business."

"Mind a bit more heat?"

"No, it is good." Rick allowed his eyes to look below Fipé's navel as he ladled water on the hot rocks.

"Ah . . . better. No?"

Rick nodded.

A few moments passed as the two men began to sweat and dart glances at one another from opposing benches.

Fipé caught Rick's eyes and smiled slightly. "So, what is your business, my friend?"

"A story. I'm a journalist but not today."

"No?"

"Today, I need some pleasure. Tomorrow, I dig into story."

Fipé nodded and widened his legs, allowing his uncut muscle to touch the wooden slat.

"And you? Here too for da business?"

"Export and logistics. I am from Colombia."

Rick nodded and smiled. He closed his eyes and rubbed his temples.

"Can't relax?"

"No, too much work on my head—how do you say? Brain."

"What is the story that you're working on?"

Rick shook his head.

"Come on—maybe I can help."

"A dead journalist."

"Let me guess. Manuel Buendía??"

Rick widened his eyes. "How did you know dis?"

"Relax, my friend. Everyone is asking about him these days."

"So, you're familiar with him?"

The Colombian nodded. "So what's your angle on him? His death?"

Rick nodded and lowered his voice. "Like everyone, the Mexican government killed him, but—" Rick leaned closer "—I believe the Americans assisted."

Fipé did not immediately respond. They sat quietly for several minutes, as beads of sweat trickled down Rick's neck and chest.

Let him simmer, but let's tease him a bit.

Rick used the corner of his towel to wipe his brow, allowing Fipé a full view of his thick uncut cock.

Fipé shifted as his cock began to lengthen.

Rick returned his towel but did not cover his groin. He arched his back, stretched his muscles fully, and yawned.

"What would you say," Fipé asked suddenly, "if I told you I know that your theory is a *fact*?"

"Then I think you would be my new friend. But what would you like in return?"

"Perhaps we could go somewhere more private and help each other?"

Gotcha. Rick's heart raced as he slowly rose and motioned for the Colombian to join him. Rick walked past Das as Fipé followed. He walked past the emergency exit to the farthest room at the end of the hall. Rick entered the blue-walled cubicle with a vinyl-covered platform that served as a bed. He waited for Fipé to enter and close the door before he removed his towel, showing that he also was at half-mast.

You like it, don't you? You want my fucking cock. Let him get a bit more excited before I attack.

Rick allowed him to grope and touch his body in the dimly lit room.

"You are so beautiful my friend," Fipé moaned as he ran his hands over Rick's sweaty muscles.

Rick grabbed Fipé's fully engorged cock. "You like?"

"Yes."

Methodically, Rick slowly turned Fipé around in his grasp while positioning in the center of the small space. Rick reached around and slowly stroked the Colombian's cock from behind. He glanced at the distance to the platform, then squeezed the warm muscle harder.

"Wait." Fipé tried to turn back. "Don't you want to talk about the journalist first?"

"No, let's have fun first." Rick leaned in and kissed his left ear.

"Ah, of course." Fipé softened in Rick's powerful arms.

Now you pay.

In one fluid motion, Rick rounded Fipé and placed him in a chokehold. Cutting off his blood flow and oxygen, Rick's vise grip rendered him unconscious within seconds.

Rick laid his limp body on the platform and stripped off Fipé's towel. He ripped it in several long strips to bind Fipé's arms, then his legs. As Rick took the final remnant to gag his mouth, the limp body began to flail.

Shit.

"Aahh!" Fipé shrieked. "¡Ayúdame, ayúdame!"

Rick shoved the rag into his mouth with all his might.

Suddenly, two of Fipé's bodyguards ripped open the back exit. Light poured into the dark hallway. The darkness thickened as the door slammed shut.

Beep, beep!

Shit, Rick. Das banged on the door three times, then took position outside it. With only his towel, he scanned the hallway. *I need a weapon. Fire extinguisher.* He yanked the heavy silver cylinder from the wall mount and returned to the cubicle door.

Beep, beep!

"¡Fipé!" the two body guards methodically called out and began smashing open each cubicle door, to the screams of other patrons.

Smash.

"Ahhh!"

Beep, beep!

"¡Fipé!"

Smash.

C'mon, Rick. Das gripped the extinguisher as the sounds grew louder, and in the dim light, two figures rounded the corner.

Beep, beep!

"¡Fipé!"

The chaos echoed outside the thin door. Rick tightened his grip as Fipé struggled.

Bang, bang, bang.

That's Das. This is it. End this shit now.

Rick heaved up the bound, flailing body with all his might, then slammed it to the concrete floor. He quickly straddled Fipé and grabbed his head by both ears.

Dazed eyes wild with fear stared back at Rick.

This. Is. For. Terry.

With each word Rick pounded the skull to the floor.

Crack!

The body beneath him was lifeless. Wet, sticky fluid coated Rick's hands.

"¡Fipé!"

Das scanned the two bodyguards as they came into view at the end of the hall. One had a knife and the other held a gun drawn. They began to sprint toward Das.

Wait for them to get closer, closer. Go for the one on the right—the one with the gun. Now!

Das swung the extinguisher with his full strength at the guard, catching him fully in the face.

Crack!

The guard fell backward and dropped his gun. Das ripped his towel from his waist and wrapped it tightly around his left forearm.

Swoosh. Swoosh.

The other guard stabbed wildly at Das, who deflected the stabs, then pivoted into a roundhouse kick into the sternum of the guard, sending him against the brick wall of the hallway. Naked now, Das took two quick steps back and resumed his fighting stance. Suddenly, a searing pain stung his neck and then his back. He grabbed his neck and felt warm liquid gushing. He stumbled back to the cubicle door and lost his footing. He slid down the door and tapped three more times before everything faded into darkness.

Rick heard the second set of taps. He bolted to his feet and shoved the body to the corner of the room. *Need a weapon. Make a rope. Now.* He ripped off both strips and tied them together at the ends.

Slipknot. Choke him from behind. Ambush. He prepped the knot and waited.

A moment later, the door burst open and a man entered. Rick attacked him from behind and brought him to his knees, tightening the knot around his neck as he swung the knife. *Close the door.* Rick kicked it, crashing it into the second guard. *Use his body.* He pivoted and slammed the man in his grip against the door, causing him to drop his knife. Rick scanned the edge of platform and gauged the distance. *Gravity.* He fell to his knees and pulled his attacker backward with both their weight.

Crack.

The man's shoulders slumped as his head was forced in the opposite direction, snapping his neck.

Rick picked up the knife and waited as rapid fire pierced the door.

Pop, pop, pop.

The second guard entered fast and tripped over the body of the first. Rick delivered two cuts to his right shoulder and a third cut his forearm to the bone. The man dropped the gun and tried to stand. He didn't seem formally trained and no match for an Agency officer.

Within seconds, Rick rounded him, pulled back his head, and slashed his throat.

Rick picked up his towel and re-wrapped his waist. He took Fipé's second towel from the platform and cleaned his arms and the blade. He picked up the gun and tucked it into his towel.

In the hallway, Rick saw several patrons emerge and scream.

Rick knelt down but then stepped back. Das was dead. He opened the emergency exit and disappeared into the alley.

Now Rick was naked and alone.

His only clothing were the rubber slippers and a towel around his waist. Rick tossed the bloody towel and knife into the dumpster.

Keep the gun and run. Now.

His jog gave way to a sprint as he scanned each fire escape in the long alley. Selecting one, Rick jumped and pulled himself up. He climbed to an empty balcony with laundry drying in the afternoon sun. He grabbed a T-shirt and a pair of shorts, yanking them on as a woman began yelling.

Get to the roof. He scaled the building, ran along the roof, and jumped to the adjacent building. He descended the fire escape on the other side and dropped to the street. *Walk, don't run.*

Rick made his way several blocks from the sirens now in the distance. At the hotel, he phoned Claren. "I am all done here, but my coach is going to be late. He won't be able to make it to the meeting."

"I see. John's waiting. Get there," Claren said.

Rick had only minutes to get to the US Embassy before the Mexican authorities descended on the bathhouse. He washed the blood from his face and hands. He yanked on his own pants and a clean shirt. He took the stairs to the street, hopped into a cab, and arrived at the embassy. Televisions in the lobby of the embassy were breaking the story on local news media.

Rick flashed his badge and saw John waiting for him at the elevators. They went into the secure conference room. They phoned Claren and Director Tibbins on an encrypted line.

"Fipé's dead and two of his guards—it's a mess but the situation is contained," Rick said.

"My clean-up team is already there," John said.

"Das didn't make—"

"We've recovered both him and Terry," John added.

"It's done, then." Claren paused. "All right, lay low tonight. I want wheels up 0600. Rick, I'll meet you at Dulles."

Rick watched the news at an airport bar the next morning as he took a whiskey and soda instead of a morning coffee. The media reported that a lone assassin killed the drug lord along with two of his bodyguards. There was no mention of Das since John's team had successfully bribed and recovered both his and Terry's bodies.

"Ready, Rick?" John asked.

Rick chugged his drink.

They walked across the tarmac to the stairs of the unmarked jet as both coffins were being positioned to load in the rear cargo. Rick ignored the stairs and walked to the tail. He laid a hand on each box and stood. The Agency detail stopped and waited in silence.

"I don't know what to say, Rick," John said from behind him. "I'm sorry for all this—"

Rick turned to face him.

"I'm truly sorry."

Rick walked back to the stairs. He climbed up and took a seat alone in the cabin.

The pilot pulled the door shut and turned to him.

"You good? You know the drill?"

Rick nodded.

The pilot closed the cockpit door. Rick waited for the engines and the movement forward before he reached into his pocket. He pulled out Terry's head shot from his file and closed his eyes.

The jet touched down at Dulles at 1040 and taxied to the private terminal on the edge of the western runway opposite the grand sloping terminal and gates.

Rick was shocked but relieved to see Claren as he emerged from the jet. *She actually came herself.*

She met him at the bottom of the stairs.

"You came," Rick said.

"I said I would." She squeezed his arm.

They got into her car and drove off the tarmac and through the gates. As she drove to Langley, she broke the silence. "There's a debrief with the team, but give me a nod. I'll stop it—I mean it."

The meeting centered only on the facts and his actions. Rick answered all the questions, only stopping once for water.

"Well, I think that's enough. You guys got all your answers." Dee Tibbins stood. "Rick's actions were well within the range of conduct and use of force. I think we're done here."

The oversight team stood and exited as the meeting adjourned. Dee turned back to Rick. "Thank you. On behalf of the entire Agency."

Rick stood. "Thank you, sir."

Dee left and Claren walked to Rick. "You okay?"

"Did anyone call Janet?"

"I called her myself."

"How is she?"

"Devastated. She and Das have three kids."

Rick nodded. "Has anyone called David?"

"No, not yet."

Of course you didn't. He should have the same right to mourn as Janet. Rick let out a deep breath. "I'll tell him."

"Are you sure?"

"Yeah. I know him and I'll head over there now."

"Want me to go with you?"

"No, it'd be better with only me."

Claren nodded grimly and gave his left shoulder a squeeze.

Rick drove to Terry and David's restored Federal townhouse right off Prince Street in Old Town. He tried to think of what to say but no words came to him. On the porch Rick hesitated, took a breath, then finally lifted a hand and rang the doorbell.

David opened the door. "Rick?"

Rick slowly shook his head as tears welled in his eyes.

David's mouth fell open as his legs buckled—Rick reached forward and caught him. A guttural moan came from deep in his soul. "Nooo!"

Rick carried him back into the townhouse and shut the door. He held David and guided him to the couch as he sobbed.

"What happened?"

"It's classified."

"I need to know. Please . . . where? How?"

"He was shot. Mexico City. That is all I can say."

David nodded.

"He loved you so much."

David covered his eyes and again nodded.

"I hope you know that. I want to tell you something else, but it has to stay between us."

"I promise," David whispered.

"The men who caused this—they're gone." Tears welled in Rick's eyes. "Do you understand me?"

David slowly shook his head.

"You don't need to worry—it's done. I did it myself—for Terry."

"Thank you." David hugged Rick tightly. "I have to call his parents now. Can I tell them some of what you told me?"

"Yes. I'm truly sorry."

"I know."

"Do you want me to stay?"

"No, but thank you for telling me."

They got up and walked to the door. "Do you think they might be allowed to go to the service on Campus?"

"I don't know. I will ask and see if I get permission. I will call you later. I'm so sorry, David."

"Thank you, Rick."

Rick drove back to his apartment in Silver Spring with tears flowing down his face.

Terry, we both know they're not gonna let David attend the memorial. He won't get a folded flag. Janet will be there. She'll get it and a mold of the anonymous star that will forever acknowledge Das on Langley's memorial wall. We'll all hug her and offer condolences. But David will mourn alone.

You and I will never get a star.

CHAPTER 47
SHIFT

Tuesday, July 14, 1992
Fair Oaks - Fairfax, Virginia

Rick awoke at 0545 and rolled to his side. He resisted the urge to kiss Trey. *Don't wake him.* He got up and stretched.

"Rick?"

"Sleep, Trey."

"Where are you going? It's 0550?"

"I'm meeting Darius. I'll be back." Rick leaned over and kissed Trey's forehead as he fell asleep.

Rick dressed quickly into his running gear and ran out to the trail to their drop as Darius pulled up. He motioned from his idling car and Rick jogged over. He pretended to offer the driver directions and pointed toward the Mall, then Route 28.

"Here you go," Darius said, handing Rick the tape. "Sure you want to watch this?"

"Yeah, why?"

"Sometimes it can be better not to know."

"I need to see what I'm up against."

"Whatever it is, I got your back."

"I know. Thank you," Rick said.

"How's our boy?"

"Good. He's sleeping. He got the gig at Global."

"Jeni told me. That's great. I also heard about the Farm. Shit, four agents."

"Yeah."

"The kid's got balls."

"A handful, but he listens. Did you hear about the plants in Reston at the professor's?"

"Yup, the Bureau ops team says all three are live. Could be great intel."

"How's Nicole and the girls?" Rick asked.

"Great. Daddy's bringing home Krispy Kremes," Darius said with a wink, nodding to the box of doughnuts sitting next to him. "Still warm."

"Gimme one?"

"You know I can't, Mr. Six-Pack Abs."

"Just one—"

Darius pulled out one and held it up. "Nope, it's for your own good." He shoved it into his mouth.

"Ah, you are fucking killing me."

"Bye, Rick. Yum! Still warm." Darius waved and slowly drove away.

"Rub it in, old man," Rick shot back.

He jogged around the pond, then returned to the apartment by six thirty with the package secure in the pocket of his hooded sweatshirt.

"Rise and shine, rise and shine. The day is on and looking fine!" Rick loved waking up Trey with little corny tunes. After a month, he sensed Trey might actually like them too. "Forget your running gear this morning. Come in here."

Trey appeared in the doorway in a pair of shorts. "What's up? What's wrong?"

"Nothing, but I need to show you something. Want some coffee?"

"Yeah."

Rick poured two mugs and handed one to Trey.

"Thanks."

"Have a seat." Rick motioned to the couch and he took the armchair. "We've been cleared to step up your training for these last ten days together. On Campus."

"Campus?"

"Langley," Rick said.

"But I'm a civ—you said I'd never step foot there."

"I know, but things change. You're on my team now and our director wants to meet you. She got special clearance."

"When?"

"Today. We have to get you papers. You'll meet with our team doc, and there's debrief with our protocol team at 1000."

"Wow."

"Before we go, I need to talk about a few things with you. Trey, you know we're dark ops."

"Yeah."

"Which means same as at the Farm: no one on Campus knows about us. We're extremely classified."

"Right. Top secret."

"Technically, yes, but it's even tighter than that—a small circle."

Trey nodded.

"We move in and among the Agency, blending in, but we're not known. Do you understand?"

"Yes, sir."

"Sir?" Rick widened his eyes.

"It slipped—you're being so serious."

"Well, it is serious. You're a civ at only class five, so there are rules in place meant to protect you and the Agency. Got it? If you have questions, if you get pissed, or if you get scared—you wait. Save that for us, here," Rick said, motioning at the apartment.

"I will." Trey paused. "Rick, can I ask about something?"

"Depends." Rick pointed to his ear and around the room.

Trey nodded but asked anyway. "Will people know about me on campus? That I'm gay, like at the Farm?"

"No. They won't know, Trey. So don't worry. And those four rookies from the Farm are already deployed. Hammonds and our team. That's it. But there is one *more* thing."

Rick pulled out the VHS tape and set it on the coffee table.

"What's that?"

Shit, he's gonna freak. Don't be dramatic—just tell him. Explain it in words he gets. Rick took a sip of his coffee.

"Our senior director decided to have eyes on us at the lake and during your Ladder—some of your CI and PA tests."

"Eyes?"

"Cameras. They filmed us and edited the footage a bit for a special screening to Pentagon brass."

"They filmed us? Did you know?"

"No. But when I found out, I asked if we could see it before we head to Campus this morning."

"We're gonna watch it now?" Trey sipped his coffee.

"Yeah, but there's one more thing. Everything is classified. Got it?"

Trey nodded.

"We only see it once—it's called a 'one-and-done.'" Rick pointed to the tape.

"Like my assignment?"

"No, well, kinda. Look, there's no rewind. We get one shot to see it."

"Then what?"

"It self-destructs."

"Are you serious? Like *Mission: Impossible*?"

"No, it doesn't blow up. The Agency developed the technology a few years ago."

"What happens?"

"The tape has locking gears that only allow forward play, and a special coating. The heat from the VCR head activates the coating."

"So no explosion?"

"No, it melts, minutes after viewing. We have to pop it out immediately. Make sure you remind me. Okay?"

"All right," Trey said.

"We can't forget. I ruined my VCR the last time I used one of these. Fucking field ops still owes me—they never replaced it even though I filled out all the goddamn forms," Rick said out loud, looking around the room, then winking at Trey.

Trey shook his head.

Rick stood up, closed the vertical blinds, and turned on the TV. He popped the tape into the VCR player, grabbed the remote, and turned to Trey.

"Ready?"

Trey sank back into the couch as the first images of the lake came into focus. *What the hell? Why would they video us without us knowing? This is so messed up.* Trey tried to mask his anger.

Thirty minutes later, the tape ended with the image of Trey dancing with the four rookies pretending to play air guitar. They sat for a moment, then Rick jumped up.

"Oh shit, gotcha." He ejected the now-melting tape.

The faint, rancid smell of the melting tape seemed to confirm Trey's concerns.

Well, if they didn't have enough on me from the night at the pool—they do now. I am completely outed in this.

"Well, she didn't exactly lie."

"Who? Jeni?"

"No, our boss—I'm not necessarily outed in the film."

"But I am," Trey said with panic.

"It's okay, Trey. You're classified. All of this is extremely classified."

"Us touching, being naked, skinny-dipping, and glancing at each other—how's that classified?"

"I swear to you it is."

Aha, you shouldn't have taught me about tells. Your voice went up a whole octave. You're worried and we're exposed. You're trying to act tough right now.

"Talk to me, Tiger. What are you thinking?"

"I don't get it. I've done everything that y'all asked me to do—but you still did this?"

"Come on—don't go there."

Trey shook his head, stood, and walked to the bathroom. He turned on the shower and sink fully. Rick followed him.

"Calm down, Trey. Look on the bright side—"

Trey turned and narrowed his eyes. "What possible *bright side* is there?"

"At least they couldn't see us in the tent." Rick raised his eyebrows.

"You're unbelievable—"

"Although, we missed our shot, damn it. If they had filmed us in the tent, we could've sold it to Falcon Video and made a fortune. I could take early retirement."

"What? As porn? That's not funny—"

"It's kind of funny—ooh, think of the titles. *The Spy Who Plugged Me.* Or . . . *Asshole Royale.*"

Trey shook his head and hissed. "It's not funny—my parents—"

Rick clapped his hands. "Oh my god, I've got it. *MoonAssRacker* featuring me as Mr. Jaws—I could get metal caps for my teeth." He darted his tongue in and out.

"It's not funny." *Don't laugh—it'll egg him on.*

Rick stuck out his bottom lip and tried to hug him.

"Stop." *Why am I so mad? It's not his fault. They already have footage of me from the pool and the intake.*

Rick deepened his pout.

Suddenly, Trey rolled his eyes and allowed his frown to give way to a slight grin. "If we called it anything, it's *For Your Ass Only.*"

"Perfect." Rick kissed him.

"What was that for?"

"You get it—you get me."

Trey nodded.

"What's done is done—out of our control." Rick took him into his embrace. "I didn't know."

"I know. I hate being manipulated like this."

"I get it, but all we can control is our attitude about it—"

"Don't you ever get mad at them?"

"All the fucking time. Ask Jeni."

"I should be mad at you."

"Me? You think I asked for this?"

"No."

"Damn right I didn't. Does it suck? Yes. Could I get pissed about it? Yup. But in the end, what good would that do?"

Trey shrugged.

"So, I laugh about it." Rick threw his head back and sang, *"For Your Ass Only."*

"Shh—I do have neighbors."

Rick grinned. "Besides—I don't regret one second of the lake. Do you?"

"No." Trey kissed him. "Seriously though, do you know who's seen this?"

"Beyond our team? Officials from the Pentagon."

"Who else?"

"That's all I was told, but I'm digging in."

"You don't know." *Oh my god, Rick—you guys don't get it.*

"Come on, trust me here."

"You promised me, Rick. You said if I did all this that my parents would never—"

"Stop. Don't go there—you know I keep my promises. They're never going to see it."

"You swear?"

"Good god, help me. How is it possible that you're more paranoid than the Agency?"

"You don't understand how I was raised."

"Oh, I think after a month now that I do." Rick winked. "Think about it. Even if they were going to out you—they'd use your charging session from your intake—not this one. Rarely does a civilian ever see the Farm—much less a training center. Besides, we're top secret—dark ops."

Trey nodded.

"Now, OTR?"

"What?"

"Jeni's trying to find out who attended the screening. It happened on Campus. She has strong eyes and ears at Langley. If anyone can find out—she can."

"Why can't you simply ask your boss?"

"It's not like that, Tiger. Questions as well as answers require the appropriate timing and wording. Patience, observation, and time nearly always reveal the truth."

They stood in silence with only the sound of the running water.

"I saw something else in the video."

"What?" Rick asked.

"You."

Rick furrowed his brow.

"You were watching me."

"What do you mean?"

"You pretend like you don't like me, but I think you do."

"First, I don't pretend." Rick leaned over and kissed him. "Second, you know I care. You don't need some stupid video to tell you that. Semper protege."

CHAPTER 48
WAITING

Friday, July 10, 1992
Dimitri Apartment - Prague, Czech Republic

Ivan inserted the key into his mailbox in the lobby of their apartment building. A neighbor passed by and nodded. *Nosy bitch.* Ivan paused and nodded before opening the box. *Can't be too careful with the building's gossip.* She passed him and headed up the stairs.

He pulled out the mail and briefly scanned the envelopes. *Come on, please be there—aha!* He stopped at the sight of a colorful postcard.

Havana. Uri.

Quickly, he flipped over the card and saw the familiar handwriting.

Beautiful beaches await, I saw this and could not resist. Hope you and Hana are well.

There was no signature but he did not need one. Ivan immediately spotted in the bottom right two script notations upside down. *Yes.* He inverted the card and read through the 14 alphanumerics. He inverted the card and saw the two letters written as one.

UP

Clever, Uri.

The door opened behind him, and instinctively he tucked the mail under his arm and headed to the stairwell. As he turned the corner, he casually glanced down over the banister to see an elderly neighbor retrieving her mail. For a split second, he envisioned the beach. *One day, I'll have toes in that sand with you, Uri. Not trudging upstairs and constantly looking over my shoulder. Havana.* He sighed and continued to his apartment.

"Tea?" Hana asked as he entered.

"Huh?" Ivan said, lost in his thoughts.

"Do you want some tea?"

"Sure." He walked the eight steps through the small kitchen to the living room.

He re-examined the rest of the mail but concealed the postcard in his pocket. *Tell her about the agent—the American, but not about the postcard. Not yet.*

Ivan went to his desk and scribbled a note: *I was followed again today. Not KGB. Definitely Americans. CIA. Did you hear from Serbia?* Then he returned to the kitchen.

He placed a finger to his lips and handed it to her as he asked, "Did you see that Mrs. Propoff is moving out?"

"No." She shook his head. "But that makes sense. I saw her daughter last week—she was thinking of moving her in with her family."

"That's nice." Ivan widened his eyes.

"Any word from the Science Foundation?"

"Not yet."

"What is taking so long? I can't live like this forever." Hana handed back his note.

Ivan scribbled. *Got a signal from the contact. Serbia is interested.* He held it up. "Patience, my love."

Hana smiled.

CHAPTER 49
CAMPUS

Tuesday, July 14, 1992
Langley - McLean, Virginia

Rick flashed his badge at the gate and drove down the tree-lined road toward the imposing glass building in Langley. *Shit—this is it. Remind him again but don't scare him.*

"Trey, remember what I said—if you have any questions or get upset, please come to me. Okay?"

"I will. Wow, that's it?" Trey pointed to the CIA headquarters looming in front of them. "It's bigger than I thought."

Rick parked, then held out his fist and bumped it top and bottom with Trey. "You got this, Tiger. Come on."

As they entered the massive sun-filled atrium with thirty-foot walls of glass, Rick watched Trey stop before stepping over the polished granite seal of the CIA. "Whoa."

Rick grinned. "Come on, it's only a building."

They passed through entry security, where Rick left a small bag containing his Sig Sauer and the training Glock 17 at the checkpoint desk. The ID office was to the left of the checkpoint, and they entered to find Jeni waiting for them.

"Hey, Trey! Congrats on Global Airways. Welcome to Campus."

"Thanks, Jeni."

She glanced at Rick and then back to Trey. "You nervous?"

"A little bit."

"Don't be. We don't bite," she said with a wink.

"Hold tight here with Jeni. I'll be right back."

Rick entered the ID office and greeted the admin. He handed her his badge. "Rick Morgan. I have my class-5 civ here."

"Good morning, Officer Morgan. Let me check. Trey Carter?"

"Yes. He'll need his ID and two alias. One Canadian and one—" *Huh, what should I pick? It needs to be Spanish but not too obvious. Costa Rica—tons of expats there.* "Costa Rica? Would that work?"

"Let me check—we don't get that very often." She clicked her keyboard. "Yes, looks like we can do that. One Canadian and one Costa Rican. Anything else?"

"No. I'll wait outside for him. Thank you, Nikki."

She smiled.

Rick exited and approached Trey. "All set. Go check in with Nikki, have a seat, and wait for her to call you. She's pulling your records now to make your IDs: a government ID and two passports with aliases."

"Cool."

"Don't get too attached—you won't get to keep them, but you can pick out your names."

"Bit of advice," Jeni said. "Make it something easy to remember. Trust me, I once had to be Lilliana Gilderschitzen." She shook her head. "Couldn't even say it without laughing."

"Ha! Countess Lilliana *Glider-shitting*. I remember her." Rick grinned.

Jeni rolled her eyes and turned to Trey. "Something simple."

"Got it." Trey headed for the glass doors.

"Trey?" Rick called. "We'll wait out here. Do exactly what she says."

Trey nodded and entered the office.

"Wow, you've got him trained," Jeni said.

"It wasn't too bad. He's a good kid."

"He's cute too." Jeni widened her eyes.

"Stop it."

"Just saying."

"Did you find out any more about who attended the screening?" Rick asked.

"No, only that it was nine or ten total. Doc M, Tibbins, Claren, and like six suits and uniformed brass." Jeni stopped. "It's so odd. This is airtight—no leaks. Are you going to try to ask Claren?"

"Maybe. Doubt it'll do any good."

"You watched it this morning? Darius said you guys had an early drop."

"Yeah, *we* watched it."

"No shit—did he freak?"

"A bit but we talked it out."

They're talking about me? Trey watched Jeni and Rick from outside the ID office glass doors.

"Trey? I'm ready for you. I need to ink you on both hands," Nikki said.

She pressed his fingers and thumbs on several forms and then the back of the ID card stock.

"Okay, now sign here and here."

"Yes ma'am—what are these?"

"Consent forms."

Geez, looks like the Agency locks you down. What's next? Are they gonna tattoo their logo on my butt? He signed each form, and then the smaller card was placed into a thin plastic sheath.

"Picture time." She brought him behind the desk to a blue-lighted backdrop and took several pictures, facing both front and side profile.

"Okay, you're getting Canadian and Costa Rican aliases. Thought about your names?"

"Yes, how about Marcus Williams for Canada and Raul Rodriguez for Costa Rica?"

"Sounds good." She typed the names into her computer.

Finally, she pulled out a set of latex gloves along with two dental trays and smiled as she explained the next process.

"This will seem odd, but we need bite impressions. Try to relax and chomp down when I tell you. We'll do top and then bottom. It's sticky and doesn't taste too great."

"Yes, ma'am." *Why do they need impressions? Definitely gonna ask Rick later.*

"Great, you have a seat as it'll take me a bit to have this laminated and printed in your passports. Here, for your fingers," she said, handing him a packaged wet wipe. "I'll be right back." She disappeared through the door to the left of her desk.

Trey wiped the ink from his fingers and resisted the urge to stare at Rick outside the glass doors. Instead he picked up the tattered *People* magazine on the chair next to him and flipped through the photos. He glanced again at Jeni then Rick. *Whatever the topic, he's pissed. Look at his jaw, so tight it could snap. Is he mad about the video?*

Trey remembered Rick's advice.

"Not everything is about you, Trey."

"Why does Claren always go along with it? Why have eyes on us at the fucking Farm of all places?"

"I get it, but you know she always does." Jeni darted her eyes to Trey in the office. "He's watching us. How did he take the video?"

"It's odd. He's more worried about being outed to his parents and family." Rick paused and glanced at Trey. "I talked him down and reinforced that we're dark ops. Besides, they already have his intake and charging session. I can't explain it. We've done this before but this whole thing feels . . ."

"Fucked up?"

Rick nodded.

She added, "I agree. He'll be taking all the risks, and he's not technically Agency."

"Yup—trying not to get ahead of myself. We've gotta get through Germany."

"Ivan," she said. "Then what?"

"Then get him back to his normal life."

"And what's a *normal* life?"

"You know what I mean."

"Geez, lighten up, handsome." She smiled. "So what's on deck today for you guys?"

"Doc M this afternoon and then some training. This morning his papers here and then Claren's called a meeting at 1000."

"Yeah, that's why I'm here. She invited Darius and me as well. *Team* meeting," she said sarcastically.

"I got him a gift. Put all our names on the card."

"That's sweet, but . . ."

"But what?"

"Completely out of character—oh my fucking god, you're crushing on him."

"Stop. I only wanted to ease him into this place. Besides, he faces the mighty Doc M alone at 1500."

"First assessment." She shook her head. "No gift can ease you into that."

"Trey?" Nikki returned and presented him with his new documents. "Here's your State Department ID, a class-5 DoD card, and your passports—Rick will explain but these are only to be used in your time of service. Do you understand?"

"Yes, ma'am." Trey frowned and took the newly printed document. *Wow, warm. Looks totally official.*

"Is this your first time on campus?" Nikki asked.

Trey nodded.

"Here." She handed him a mint. "It'll get the dental-tray taste out of your mouth."

"Thank you, ma'am."

"So what do you think? Are we as scary as you thought?"

"No, ma'am. Everyone's so normal."

She chuckled. "You take care, Trey."

He inspected his new cards and passports as he exited the office. *Huh? The DoD card's kinda like my brother's USAF card but blue background instead of green.*

Rick approached him. "Can I see?"

Trey handed him the cards and passports.

"Damn, you're legit, Trey. Now, let's get to work."

Jeni glanced at her watch. "We should head up to Claren's."

Trey, Rick, and Jeni walked through the massive lobby and out across the back granite plaza along a path to a large gray building with a glass front. They entered the right-side doors and took the stairs to the second floor. Each showed their IDs. *Which do I use? I guess the*

State Department one? Trey flashed his card and the guard nodded. *Damn, this is real now.* The buzzer sounded and they entered the office. *Offices of Senior Field Director Claren E. Johnson, so this is Rick's boss.*

"What's up, Trey?" Darius gave him his hand.

Geez, night and day from my intake. I don't want to meet that side of you again. "Good to see you again, Officer Morris."

"Congratulations, civ-5." Darius grinned wide.

"Yup, it's official." Jeni motioned to the wall. *Welcome to the team, Trey!* The greeting was splashed across a whiteboard in multiple colors.

"Thanks, y'all." Trey nodded.

"We all got you a little something." Rick handed him a small gift bag with blue tissue paper. "Open it."

Trey opened the bag and saw a black leather ID card holder with detachable lanyard like the three of them had. He smiled at Rick. "Looks official."

"It is. You earned it." Rick nodded.

"Thank you." Trey took out the badge holder and inserted both ID cards. "Guess I made the team."

"Precisely, welcome, Trey. I'm Claren Johnson."

Trey turned to see Claren appear in the doorway. He took her hand. "Trey Carter."

She shook his hand firmly, and motioned to the conference table. Darius erased the board and they all took seats.

Claren is nothing like I thought. She oozes authority, but she's warm.

"We don't normally have a team meeting like this, but given our new civ-5, I thought it would be good. I have a few updates to go over but first let me start by saying thank you."

Rick, Jeni, and Darius all nodded slightly.

"No doubt, Rick has told you that you're being here with us is not only unusual but a testament to this team's work. We have reviewed your training notes and CI assessments from the Farm. Impressive. Congratulations."

"Thank you." Trey sat up and pulled his shoulders back.

Claren poured herself and Trey a glass of water from a pitcher on the table. "I also understand your field assignment on Sunday went well."

"All three plants are live and operational," Darius said.

"Excellent." She took a sip. "Rick has explained to you the necessity of discretion here within the Agency's facilities, correct?"

"Yes, ma'am."

"Good. If you have any questions, only those in this room are your resource. Curious eyes might follow you around campus. If someone approaches you, be polite, but no one needs to know more than the fact that you are a civ-5 recruit here with Officer Morgan to finalize your training. That will be all you need this week."

"Got it."

She explained that the remaining ten days would be a new routine. "Rick will review with you. Jeni and Darius will also participate as needed." She then informed him of the role of Dr. Carlos Martinez.

"Doc M is one of our team doctors. You need to be a hundred percent candid and open with him. Your first session is this afternoon at 1500. Rick will drop you off and pick you up. Your assignment with us is slated for Germany at the end of the month. The details are firming up, but Jennifer, my assistant, will work with you on travel arrangements. Any questions?"

Wow, so that's it. Germany. Trey darted his eyes at Rick and then back to Claren. "No, ma'am."

"Okay then. We are excited to have you on board. Now, if you wouldn't mind."

She motioned for Jennifer.

Oh, so now I need to leave the room. Guess I'm not fully on the team. Trey stood and met Jennifer at the door. She escorted him out of the conference room's glass doors and to some armchairs near the front of the office and her desk.

"Can I get you some water or coffee, Trey?"

"No, I'm good. Thanks." He wanted to use the bathroom but decided to wait for Rick.

Claren glanced around the room. "It's good to see you all here, together. No doubt this one has not been easy." She turned to Rick.

"He seems confident. Great work. What's on your training agenda for today?"

"This morning target practice at the range, then lunch. This afternoon, he has German lessons, Doc M, and then a couple hours at the gym with KM and conditioning."

"Good. Keep a low profile."

"I always do," Rick said.

"Jeni, any updates from the Frankfurt or Prague desks?"

"None yet, but I suspect we'll receive a revised briefing by Friday."

"What's our status?"

"Right now, we're still green for next Thursday the twenty-third."

"Good. There are a lot of eyes on this, so keep me posted if you hear any updates."

"Will do."

Claren turned to Darius on her left. "Any word from ops on the audio plants at Professor Hassan's?"

"Fully functional, nothing to report yet. The professor returns tomorrow night from Chicago." He paused.

"What?"

"It's probably nothing, but the nephew mentioned Trey as his *new American friend*. The Bureau told me."

Claren pursed her lips. "Interesting. Attachment. Probably nothing to worry about. Any other hunches?"

"No."

"Rick, have Trey call Sami and set up another workout or run," Claren said and stood. "That's it for now. Let's keep our heads down this week, people."

Jeni shot Rick a look and raised her brow.

"Claren, what about the screening?" Rick's pitch increased slightly.

"Standard review. Did you watch the tape?"

"Yeah."

"Then you know you're fine."

"Right, but, uh—wondered who attended. The screening?"

Claren turned and headed toward her office.

Rick looked back at Jeni and shook his head.

Claren turned in the doorway. "Let's catch up after your workout tonight. Say 1830? The benches by the outdoor circuit?"

Rick nodded, and that was it. *Guess the meeting's done. Good to see you too—geez.*

Crossing the short lobby and down a flight of stairs, Rick and Trey passed through a set of thick glass doors marked *Firing Range—Use Caution.* Rick checked in with the attendant and opened his firearms bag for inspection. They were assigned lanes two and three. Each station had a small counter and dividers with buttons marked *Up* and *Back* on the right side. Straight ahead was a hundred-foot shooting gallery with fresh new targets on each. The targets were paper with a six-ring bull's-eye imprinted over a human outline.

Rick explained the basics of the range and then asked Trey to assemble and load his weapon. They practiced his stance, loading and reloading using additional clips of 9mm bullets. They placed on the ear protectors and safety goggles required at the Agency firing range. Trey was no longer a beginner and had developed his aim, but he was no Officer Morgan. Watching Rick in his element was amazing. He could assemble his Sig Sauer in less than thirty seconds and fire off five rounds. His aim was deadly, his every movement efficient and lethal.

They grabbed lunch and sat by themselves in the large food court downstairs in the central hall main building. From across the tables, Trey spotted Nikki, the ID clerk, with her colleagues. She smiled, and he nodded.

"It all seems so normal, like a business park," he said to Rick.

"What did you expect? Nearly one thousand eight hundred people work here on campus and they've got to eat, right?"

"I guess. Didn't expect it to be so office-like."

"Ha! Well, look, we have four days of training here, and I am going to turn it up a notch. You ready?"

"I guess so. Rick, I've taken everything you've dished out so far," Trey said.

Rick laughed out loud. "Yes, you have. You've got to keep it up though. Now we get to train without your job interrupting us. We can train all day: CI, assessment, Krav Maga, lifting, running, and language classes. Your Spanish is a good start but not helpful on our assignment. You have a German class today right before Doc M."

"Awesome, I've never taken German. May I ask about Claren?"

"Sure."

"She seemed to be watching us all and sizing me up."

"No, more like testing the team as we add a new member. Like any team, Trey, a new player can enhance or throw off the dynamics. You focus on today for now. Let me worry about tomorrow. Deal?"

Trey nodded and took a bite.

"How's the burger?" Rick asked.

"Great. How's your *salad*?" Trey smirked.

"Smartass. Enjoy it while you can, Tiger. You'll see—thirty-five hits and your metabolism shifts."

"Well until then—*moo*." Trey bellowed and held up his burger.

Rick stabbed his salad and shook his head. "I hope I'm around to see you at forty with a muffin top, thinning hair, and puffy eyes."

"Me too."

CHAPTER 50
PERSPECTIVE

"Do I have to do this?" Trey asked.

"Yes. We all do." Rick led him down the long gray hallway.

"Why?"

"I don't want him inside my head analyzing me."

"You worried what he'll find in your noggin?"

Trey rolled his eyes.

"Look, don't be nervous. It's only a conversation." Rick continued walking down the hallway to Doc M's office.

"What's he like?"

"He's a little odd but you can trust him." Rick stopped at the closed door. "Ready?"

"I guess."

Rick knocked and then opened the door.

"Doc M? I've got our civ-5 recruit for you."

"Trey, come in. Come in." Doc M stood from his desk. "Thank you, Rick. We'll need an hour."

"See you then." Rick tapped Trey's shoulder, then disappeared down the long hall, back toward Claren's office.

"Hi, Dr. Martinez. I'm Trey Carter."

"Yes, I know. Please call me Doc M. Welcome to Campus. First day, right?"

"Yes, sir. Open or closed?" Trey held the door handle.

"Closed." Doc M motioned for him to enter. "I realize this is all new and a bit disorientating, but there is no need to be nervous."

Trey closed the door and scanned Doc M's office. *It's smaller than Claren's conference room but nice. Doesn't really feel like an office in the CIA except for that large cherry desk. I like the way he hides that dull gray carpet with the area rugs.* Trey scanned his ladened desk. *Whoa, he's a pack rat. Look at the piles of papers and reports. You can barely see the surface. So weird—all the rest of this office is spotless.* Trey glanced at the keyboard and saw coffee stains. Across from the desk was a beige couch on the second Tibetan tribal rug that was green and red.

On the couch were three pillows. *Those are beautiful—I bet Native American or tribal Mexican. Definitely an academic judging from that massive wall of books. Wow, it runs the entire width of the office.*

The opposing wall held a large watercolor of a singular man in a wooden dory seeming to emerge from the fog. Trey stepped closer and studied the lone figure.

"You like it?" Doc M asked.

"I do, very much. Is there a story?"

"There is. A dear friend painted it."

"She's an artist?"

"Was."

Trey frowned.

"We lost her to cancer two summers ago."

"I'm sorry for your loss."

"Thank you, Trey."

Trey walked to the lateral wall, which was entirely glass. He gazed out at the dense wooded area. "That's a peaceful view."

"I agree. If it weren't for these trees I'd suffocate spending so many hours here. I try to make it as cozy as possible."

Trey smiled and looked around the room. "It's like a doctor's office, but it's nice."

"Guilty." Doc M smiled. "Have a seat."

Trey sank deep into the couch and felt the warmth of the two lamps glowing as the overhead fluorescents were off. "In here, it doesn't seem like we're at the Agency."

"Then I succeeded." Doc M took a black wooden armchair with an academic crest in the center panel.

"Can I get you some water?"

"No, gracias. ¿Pardon, es posible practicar mi Español?"

"Sí, claro. Muy bien," Doc M said. "*¿Cómo aprendiste a hablar español?*"

"My roommate at Pensacola Christian College was from Puerto Rico. I studied three years in school, but I learned more speaking with him in our dorm room."

"Excellent. Yes, practice is essential. How did you enjoy your German class today?"

"Great, but we only spoke in German—it was my first time."

"Yes, we use an immersive method. Pedagogy can be tricky, but language is best learned by immersion like when we acquire our native tongues as toddlers. You grew up in Atlanta, correct?"

"Yes."

"Is your family there?"

"No, my parents now live in South Carolina—Greenville. My sister's in Atlanta."

"And your brother?"

"He's in Wichita Falls, Texas, at Shepherd Air Force Base."

Doc M nodded and jotted down a note.

You know all this stuff. Why ask me again?

He continued to ask Trey basic questions, then landed on a sensitive area.

"I hear your family is quite religious."

"That's an understatement."

"How so?"

"You wouldn't understand."

"Why not?"

"Can I speak freely?"

"That's all I hope you will do." Doc M peered over his glasses.

"You're Catholic, right?"

"Was, sometimes still, but I consider myself more of a *recovering* Catholic."

"My parents—and our church—taught us that all Catholics were going to hell."

"Must have been hard to grow up in such a rigid, narrow viewpoint."

"Suffocating."

"Not a lot of room for difference?"

"No. I knew by the time I was like ten or eleven that I had to hide. Couldn't tell anyone."

"About being gay?"

Trey nodded.

"Is that why you fear your family really knowing you? Finding out that you're homosexual?"

"It's not that I fear them. I don't."

"No?"

"No. I'm not ready to lose them."

"Maybe you won't."

"Now you sound like Rick." Trey shook his head. "Y'all don't get it. In our faith—Baptist—we're taught that it's not only a sin. In their eyes, I'm an abomination."

"Do you believe that?"

"That's just it—I don't know. And until I do know, I'm not ready to tell them. They'll turn their backs and I'll be alone."

Doc M breathed deeply and stared at Trey in silence.

"I kinda think that's why y'all picked me."

"We selected you and asked you to serve your country. Some would say that's a noble cause. What do you think we do here?"

"What do you mean?"

"At the Agency."

"Keep secrets, gather intel—"

"Those are simply tactics, tools of our trade."

"You study people."

"Yes, we study behavior, gather intel, recruit operatives, listen, analyze—all tactics." He again looked over his glasses. "We do all this to serve and protect one singular important thing. Care to guess?"

Trey shrugged. "National security?"

"Freedom. The same freedom that allows your parents to sit in their pew at their Baptist church each Sunday in Greenville and hate gays."

Trey shook his head. "But we have freedom as Americans."

"Yes, but it comes under threat more than you know. Why do you think we picked you?"

"I don't know."

"I think you do. Take a guess."

"'Cause I'm gay and fit some sort of 'profile' but . . ."

"But what?"

"You don't know me."

"What do we not know?"

"You have no idea who I am. You know a bunch of facts. You made a judgment about me based on data. What if I did the same about you?"

"Please do."

Trey raised his eyebrows and scanned the room. "Well, I know you're catholic. Latino. Probably the first in your family to go to college. That chair says Harvard, but you don't hang any of your degrees on the wall—probably 'cause you have more than most folks around here."

Doc M motioned for him to continue.

"You're straight and single. Judging by your worn, stained keyboard, you're chained to that desk and this job. I don't see any hobbies or sports in your photos."

"Anything else?"

"Judging by all those books, you love studying. So, no doubt you're studying me right now."

"Yes, I am."

"But like me—I don't know you, Doc M. Those are only details of your life."

"Ah, but details inform us. Details caught can save your life, but if missed. Well . . ."

"Did I get any of that right?"

"Yes. I attended Harvard. I am heterosexual. I'm Mexican-American, first in my family to attend college. And yes, me and the Blessed Virgin were once quite close—actually I almost became a priest." Doc M widened his eyes and smiled. "I'm single now, but not by choice." He removed his glasses. "Might I say, great observation skills, but you missed one important thing." He grabbed something from his desk. "And you still did not answer my question."

"Why me?"

Doc M nodded and tossed an object at him.

Trey's instincts fired and he caught it.

"Baseball. My passion I've had my whole life."

Trey looked at the worn leather ball in his hand.

"Propensity to action."

"What?"

"Beyond being a closeted homosexual—it's why we selected you for our program."

"Propensity? What'd ya mean?"

"You have a unique set of experiences that could cripple some, but not you."

Trey shook his head.

"Trey, your *propensity* urges you to question, to ask, to act."

Trey handed back the baseball.

"So may I ask you a tough question?"

Geez, we haven't even had the tough questions yet. "Yeah."

"How do you feel about all this? Our methods?"

"Confused."

"How so?"

"Y'all trapped me. You used fear to intimidate me."

"Are you still afraid?"

"Yeah."

Doc M narrowed his eyes. "Do you not want to serve your country?"

"No, I do. Why set me up? Threaten me?"

"Fair. Our methods on the surface can seem coercive. We've developed our protocol over many years of study."

"I'm not some lab rat. I know this is your job, but this is also my life."

Doc M made a notation.

"It's a lot to take in."

"That's why you have Officer Morgan. Rick is one of our best."

"Yeah, but Rick's really tough. I still don't know my assignment. Germany."

"You will soon. What about Rick?"

"What about him?"

"Do you resent him for your first few days with us during your intake?"

"At first, yeah, but not now."

"No?"

"No, he was doing his job. Like I said, I was confused and scared at first, but now . . ."

"Now?" Doc M probed.

"I don't know. You didn't give me much choice, but maybe if you had simply asked or had Rick ask me."

"Like he did at Iwo Jima?"

"Yeah."

"And what if we had?"

"I would've said yes—being gay, I couldn't follow my brother into the military."

"But now you see there are other ways to serve your country."

"Yeah, like Rick."

"Excellent." Doc M wrote additional notes on his pad. "How has your time been with him? Have you enjoyed getting to know him? You two seem quite close now, right?"

"Yes, I feel like at times he gets pissed with me, but I really have tried to do my best and pass my assessments."

"What is he to you?"

"I don't know. Kinda like my coach, trainer, boss, and big brother."

"Hmm." Doc M looked at his notes. "Well, your progress has been nothing short of extraordinary. But my question about Rick is more basic." He looked up at Trey from his pad and over his reading glasses.

"Do you find Rick attractive, Trey?"

Why are you asking me this? Screw it. "Yes, sir."

"Do you find yourself having sexual fantasies about Officer Morgan?"

Oh god, this feels like that night in the Hole when they drugged me. I bet he was the one on the other side of the mirror. I wanna get out of here. Suddenly Trey remembered Rick's advice.

"Just be you, Trey. No right or wrong."

"Trey? Are you okay?"

"Yes, sir. Doc M, I know that this is not love per se, but I care for him. A lot. And no, I don't regret being attracted to him. He's hot."

"And how is the sex between you?"

Trey shook his head. "The rule was: you can ask me anything but you couldn't see inside the tent at the lake—and you're not allowed inside our tent."

"Bravo. Boundaries are essential. Sounds like things are good with Rick."

"Yeah. This'd be so much worse if not for him."

"How so?"

"He makes me laugh. He's patient, when he can be. He pushes me but protects me."

"You trust him?"

"To my soul."

"Truly?"

"I've never felt so safe in my life."

"But you realize that he's training you for an assignment. Germany. For us."

"I get it, but I also know his secret."

Doc M tilted his head. "That he's also gay?"

"No."

Doc M leaned forward.

"He believes in me. For real. He wants me to succeed but beyond Germany."

Doc nodded.

"He wants to leave me better than he found me." Trey exhaled deeply.

"Extraordinary," Doc M whispered and wrote an additional note. *Geez, what's he writing down?*

"Your intimacy with Rick—this may be uncomfortable but allow me to approach it from another way." Doc M pressed a bit further, "How do *you feel* about the physical moments in your time together?"

He already knows everything from snooping at the lake and my apartment. He's gonna keep asking—tell him how you really feel. Trey took a deep breath. "Doc M, is all this confidential?"

"Absolutely."

"This may not make sense to you."

"Try me."

"I grew up fearing sex. At my church, we were taught that we could not have it outside of marriage. Being gay, I couldn't get married. And in my situation, I had a triple threat."

"What were the threats?"

"People finding out that I was gay, my surgery leaving me different—"

"Different? Your bladder surgery—the retrograde?"

Trey nodded.

"And the third?"

"AIDS."

"I see. Fascinating, I mean we knew, but didn't connect that so—"

Trey stared at him. *Are you fucking kidding me? I'm a person, you asshole, and those are some of my darkest fears.*

"My apologies, Trey. I realize this is deeply personal, and I intend no judgment. So, these three fears are connected? In sex?"

"Yeah."

"Do you have these fears with Rick?"

"No. With him, I don't worry. We just connect. He doesn't judge me. He makes it fun. Easy. Safe." Trey exhaled deeply and stretched. "Now the only thing I fear is afterward."

"After sex?"

"After my assignment—what happens then?"

"What do you mean?"

"Will I ever see him again?"

Doc M stared at Trey. "Do you *love* him?"

Trey shrugged. "I don't know. Maybe. Does that make me stupid?"

"No, it makes you human. And if I may say so, a remarkable one at that."

"Does that mean I pass?"

"Yes. Thank you for your candor." Doc M smiled slightly. "Now do you have any questions for me?"

For you? I thought this was a one-way street. "Could I maybe join the Agency after Germany?"

"Is that what you want? Be an officer?"

"Yes."

"Because by joining you think it would keep you close to him?"

Trey nodded.

"Hmm. I'm sorry, Trey. That's not possible—not right now."

"Why? Would I not make a good officer?"

"On the contrary, from everything we've seen, you'd rival Rick. Though don't tell him I said that." Doc M gave a slight smile. "No, there's a service ban similar to the military."

"So? Rick did."

"I'm afraid that's classified. Things were a bit different then. Now . . ." Doc M paused. "Officially no."

"I can't join officially but . . ."

"Not now, but who knows after the elections. Does Rick know that you might want to join us?"

"No."

"Does he know how you feel about him?"

"I don't think so—I don't know. But it wouldn't matter."

"Why not?"

"He doesn't love me in the way that maybe I wish he did, but I do know he cares about me. It's crazy, this situation we're in, but I think we've found our path."

"What's your path?"

"A healthy bond."

"Healthy bond," Doc M repeated. "Excellent. Any other questions for me?"

Wow, ask about the video. Trey cleared his throat. "This morning, we saw a video of us training at the Farm. I understand that observing me was part of the training, but was it shown to others? Outside the team?"

"Yes, indeed it has been. And you would like to find out who was invited to the screening. Correct?"

"Yes, sir."

"Forgive me, but that question does not strike me as yours, but rather you want to know the answer for Officer Morgan." Doc M sat, presumably allowing this statement to settle in the room.

"Yeah, I'm sorry. I—"

"You not only want to *please* him, but you also want to *protect* him too?"

"Yes."

"Extraordinary." Again, he wrote several notes, then looked up at Trey. "Thank you for your honesty and sharing your feelings. Unfortunately, I am not at liberty to discuss the circulation of the footage. Suffice to say beyond us it was limited to six individuals from the Agency, NSA, and Pentagon. You should know that your sexual orientation and that of Officer Morgan have not been declassified.

You are safe and should operate from the perspective that your private life is exactly that. Private."

Trey nodded.

"Any other questions?"

"Do you believe in me? You think I can do this assignment?"

"Absolutely, without one doubt."

Trey smiled.

"Good session, Trey. I would like us to meet again next Thursday. I will arrange with Rick. ¿Todo bien?"

"Gracias. Todo bien." Trey headed for the door.

"Cuidado, la pròxima sesion sera en español."

"Ha! Don't think my Spanish is good enough for a whole session." Trey opened the door and saw Rick standing outside.

"Ready?" Rick asked.

"Yeah. Bye, Doc M."

"Have a good week, Trey—you can leave the door open."

Our civ-5 is exceeding expectations. Doc M typed his last sentence and paused. He stared at the blinking curser, then hit the backspace several times—*all expectations. We're in new territory.*

"Well?" The voice jostled him from his thoughts.

He looked up to find Claren in the doorway.

"Well, what?"

"Don't make me beg, Carlos."

"Don't make *me* break client privilege."

"Client? What?"

He grinned.

"Damn you." She entered and closed the door. "You'd think after fifteen years I could spot your jokes."

"Ha!"

She rolled her eyes and took a seat. "Did it go okay?"

"Okay? No."

"No?"

"No, it went great."

"Really?"

"Like I was watching a birth. This experiment is beyond our expectations."

"Got it. Take your victory lap, but is he okay? He's not an experiment. He's—"

"He's fine." Doc M shuffled through his notepad. "He was so open and candid about Rick, their bond, his feelings—the intensity of all this—yet he hasn't crossed over into a disassociated state with the intimacy or the training. It's remarkable. We even talked about his intake."

"Was he angry?"

"No. Isn't that incredible? And before you say it. No, he does *not* appear delusional."

"Are you sure?"

"He willingly admitted his attraction, crush, and deep need to please Rick, but he seemed to understand what it all ultimately means—and what it doesn't."

"That's good, but . . ."

"But what?"

"This has to work. We have no backup. Germany is now in ten days. Ten days."

"It will. We've executed the protocol with a civ."

"We've been here before—initial infatuation, increased intensity, and then instability."

"Yes, but not like this." Doc M got up from his desk and joined her in the empty side chair. "Listen to me, the TB is working. He trusts Rick, even wants to protect him."

She shook her head.

"This time is different, Claren. We're—"

"I want to believe."

"Do you?"

"Yes, I do. But I have sat in this chair more than once and heard those exact words. Many times, we get close, then crash, then I have to pick up the pieces."

"Not every time. Jeni, Rick, Terry . . ."

"Not again." Her tone lowered. "We will *not* have another Mexico City on my watch—especially with a civ."

"Okay, okay." Doc M put both hands up. "Yes, we've had setbacks, but we have to think of the implications beyond the protocol. Beyond sexual orientation. Officers and operatives. New incentive and interrogation tactics. Real trust."

"I am."

"Untold benefits."

She shook her head. "I can't have my head in the clouds. We have a job to do."

"We are blazing uncharted neuropsychological behaviors."

"Yes, but I also have to make tougher choices."

"My choices aren't tough? What's your point?" His tone deepened.

"My *point* is that you *always* see it from a scientific lens. I get it. Your perspective is brilliant. But my perspective is rooted in the real world. I have to worry about nuclear proliferation. Ivan. The election."

"Our goal is the same and our perspectives make our partnership stronger."

"Hope so." She stood and walked to the windows.

"I know so. This time we're going to succeed."

"Sounds compelling here, on Campus, where theories drive training and fill up manuals. But what about out there?" Claren pointed to the trees. "In the field we don't get second chances. Ivan Dimitri won't give two shits about our theories."

Where's his head? What the hell did Doc M say to him? Give him space and ask him. Don't bark at him. An hour later in the field house, Rick knew that Trey was distracted as they grappled. Rick flipped him over his head, and he took him down to the mat hard.

Thud!

"Tiger, you're not thinking. Where the hell are you?" Rick pinned Trey fully by sitting on his torso and using his legs and arms to lock down the young man's legs and wrists in a full-body takedown.

"Sorry. Just thinking."

"About?"

"My session with Doc M."

"And?"

"I may have screwed up."

"How so?" Rick said, relaxing his grip and sliding to the right. Trey sat up across from him.

"We talked about a lot of stuff and then he asked me if I had any questions. I asked about our film, the screening. I'm sorry, Rick. I—"

"Stop. What did I tell you about Doc M?"

"That I could trust him and be myself."

"Exactly. So am I mad right now?"

"No?"

"Not one bit. There is no daylight between us, Claren, or Doc M."

"Got it."

"But I bet he was curious about your question."

"Yeah, he said that I was trying to protect you?"

"Perspective, Tiger." Rick grinned. "You have to trust me. It is all in the perspective. Did he answer your question?"

"No, he only said it was six officials from here, Pentagon and NSI or NS…"

"NSA." Rick nodded.

"But that we were still classified. He also told me not to be paranoid."

"Ha! Well you flunked that part, Tiger!" He playfully pushed Trey backward. "Come on. Let's get cleaned up and get out of here."

They showered, changed, and packed their gear.

"I need to meet Claren for a minute. Here," Rick said, tossing Trey his keys. "Wait for me in the car?"

Right on time, Claren. Rick spotted her on the secluded bench adjacent the running trail. "Hey. How are you?"

"Good. How'd his first day go?"

"Great."

"Doc M told me that he asked about the screening."

Rick nodded.

"There were six screeners besides us: two other senior field directors, two Army intelligence officers, an NSA liaison, and a Pentagon joint chiefs communication deputy officer."

"That's a lotta brass and a wide circle."

"You don't have to tell me." She shook her head.

"Why? What's the play here?"

"Tibbins is convinced that we need to widen the knowledge of the protocol. Says he knows them all and trusts their discretion."

"Do you?"

"Cautiously optimistic."

"I wish you'd told me about the cameras at the lake."

"You know I couldn't and you know I didn't like it."

"It rattled him, Claren. And me."

"You're safe. You saw the footage. Everything was edited."

"What'd they think?"

"A bit shocked, but they saw a recruit. Highly trained and ready."

"See *that* makes me nervous. One and done. Germany, but now you've—"

"Me?" She faced him. "You too."

"What're you implying?"

"Over reach."

Rick shook his head.

"How many times have I said it?"

"*Actions have consequences.*"

"What were you thinking? KM? A Glock?"

"I was trying to protect him."

"I know, but *they* don't."

"He's only a civ."

"Uh-huh, firing a Glock better than most of our officers and going toe-to-toe with not one, not two, but four rookies. No, they didn't see a *civ*. They saw a highly trained *potential* operative about to be embedded in Global Airways. A new way to *expand* the program with zero risk to them and their DoD witch hunts."

"So now what? Trey and I get pimped out—"

"I *hate* street talk."

"Sorry. More assignments?"

Claren took a deep breath. "Maybe. Look, we've enjoyed near untouchable status in dark cover for a decade. Sometimes we were essential."

"The Soviet fall."

"Exactly. But now things are . . . shifting. Budgets scrutinized. A new administration could be on the way—and you know what that means."

"Even if we slam dunk Dimitri, they'll have a tough road to get 41 four more years."

"You got it. I've lived in this town my whole life. Never seen anything like what McGuire is pulling with Perot. Against his own party. Trey's intel was helpful, but JJ's House investigation won't stop this. The train's going too fast—which brings me to my final point." She glanced around them. "Tibbins may have another point to make with the screening." She raised her eyebrow.

"Service-ban?" Rick said.

She nodded.

"How?"

"Think about it. How many groups can offer our *unique* insights?"

"None." Rick instinctively knew but hearing it made it all the more real. *Shit, of course she's right. They have us serve in the shadows but if daylight comes—they won't even admit we exist.* "What happens if any of them talk?"

"My worry too, but it's been more than two weeks. Nothing. A few rumors, but we're intact—still dark. Then I got a call today about our engineer, Ivan. NSA made the connection and didn't even know we were already working it."

"No way."

"Tibbins was right—it's starting to work."

"So essentially, it may uncover new opportunities for inter-agency support."

"Yes."

"Well, that could increase our budgets; maybe we get raises."

"Always on the bright side. Ha! Unbelievable, Rick Morgan, but yes. It could increase our chances for more budget. But that's for tomorrow. How did today really go?"

"Good. We kept a low profile. He did great."

Claren stood. "This conversation."

Rick lowered his tone. "Never happened."

"Anything else?"

"I was hoping for another outing this weekend with him—off grid this time."

"Where? Camping again?"

"No. I need to walk him through Germany and Ivan. A neutral setting would be better. So I thought Vieques. More training, but a little sun and fun."

"Hmm. Gets him out but not too far. The naval base is secluded. You guys could hop a ride on a transport. It's a great idea to test him in another environment. Keep a low profile—train on base but bunk off base."

"My thought too. I know a great little inn, but, Claren, no eyes this time. Please? I'll check in and record the training."

"I'll have to clear it with Tibbins, but for *now* no eyes."

Rick waited till Claren was out of sight before standing and walking to meet Trey. With each step, the weight of his next conversation with Trey grew. Vieques. Ivan. No more training. Now they would engage.

PART THREE:
ENGAGING

Third Law of Reciprocal Actions: For every force, there is an equal and opposite force.
— Sir Isaac Newton

CHAPTER 51
GATE

Monday, September 12, 1955
Bauman Moscow State Technical University - Moscow, USSR

"Ivan Dimitri?"

Finally. Ivan perked up at the sound of his name. "Yes, Good afternoon, Professor Jorgen."

"Good afternoon. Please." The admissions officer motioned to the heavy wooden chair opposite his desk. "How was your trip?"

"Good, sir, thank you. Long train ride, but fine. I hardly slept as it is my first time in Moscow," Ivan said.

Jorgen smiled. "Yes, I see you were born in Leningrad and joined the Navy at age seventeen?"

"Yes, sir."

"Ivan, why do you choose Bauman? What is it that draws you to apply to our university?"

"Engineering, sir." *Wait for his questions. Be calm.*

Professor Jorgen nodded. He reviewed the transcript and presumably allowed the silence in the room to test the twenty-year-old candidate before him.

"Submarines. Commendations from several commanding officers. Your scores on the aptitude exams are outstanding, but we have many young men like you applying to our program. What do you feel that you can contribute?"

Contribution? What does he mean? Ivan had rehearsed several key questions in preparation for this moment, but he had not thought about his contribution. He scanned his surroundings and studied the office. Jorgen's degrees, four in total, hung on the wall along with several abstract paintings. To the far right hung a replica of a Greek nude portrait of a young man. Ivan glanced beyond the blond professor who was in his early forties and saw only a few personal photos. He sensed the admission officer was studying his reactions and something felt familiar to Ivan. *Attraction? Test him. Use it.*

"I was born in a small town outside Leningrad. My father was a geologist. He was not home much and when he was home—well, my mother stayed out of his way. We all did. He loved vodka and his rocks. I learned to ask him questions—unlike my sister and brother—I watched him. Studied him."

"And what did you learn?"

Ivan opened his legs and adjusted himself brazenly. "I learned to please him."

Professor Jorgen swallowed hard and stared at him. "Were you good at 'pleasing' him?"

"I think so."

"You must have also pleased your commander, Officer Makar." Jorgen looked at the papers in front of him.

Makar. What?

"He wrote us a letter."

Ivan crossed his right leg over his left and pursed his lips.

"He said you stood out among your peers."

He nodded.

"Ivan, if you were to join our program, are you prepared for the long hours, study, and practicum labs?"

"Yes, sir. I have no distractions. No relationships to compete for my attention."

Jorgen nodded. "Your family struggled? Financially?"

"Yes, sir."

"How did your mother fare with three mouths to feed?"

"Not well. I would be the first of my family to attend university."

"Where is your father?"

"He died three years ago."

"Your mother?"

"Leningrad, along with my brother and sister."

"What does she do for work?"

"Factory. Glass. She packs glass, has done so for twenty years. My brother also works there."

"Your sister?"

"She's committed. An institution."

Jorgen narrowed his eyes and returned to the folder in front of him. He flipped through the papers for several long minutes as Ivan sat nervously awaiting his questions.

"How will you afford tuition?"

"Unlike my father, I don't love vodka. Saved my money while in the Navy."

"What is it that you *love*?"

"Learning new things, meeting new people, and science," Ivan said with a hint of excitement in his tone. "I love understanding how people think, how machines hum, and what drives us all forward."

"Forward?"

"Yes, I've noticed on land and at sea that the one thing all creatures have in common is the absolute resolve to move forward or die."

The professor nodded. "And you're resolved to also 'move forward'?"

"More than you will ever know." Ivan allowed his tone to deepen.

"If you don't get in this year, what will you do? The glass factory too?"

"No, sir. I'm not going back. I bought a one-way ticket to Moscow. There's nothing for me to go home to."

"What area of scientific research or engineering do you wish to study?"

"Atomic energy," Ivan said without hesitation.

"Why?"

"Because it's the future, sir."

"The future?"

"Yes, sir. The power within one fusion of an atom is infinite. Khrushchev says it's our destiny."

"Does he now? With great energy comes great power."

Ivan nodded.

"Ivan, if I open this door for you, there will be programs, tests, and special . . . agreements. You will serve the state. Mother Russia."

"Always, sir."

"Our atomic program is closely guarded. Secretive. It has come under scrutiny by the media."

"Totskoye?"

Professor Jorgen stared at Ivan. "You've done your homework."

"Whatever it takes, sir." Ivan uncrossed his legs and cocked his hips forward. He felt the professor's eyes move down his body. *I knew it.*

"Stand up, turn around."

Ivan stood and slowly turned 360 until his gaze once again met the professor's.

"You're fit."

"Navy, sir."

"I see that . . . Four years of service?"

"Yes, sir."

"What did you learn in the Navy?"

Ivan thought about his answer. "Hard work as a unit, sir. We moved as a team. Together. A ship must have all hands on deck."

Professor Jorgen closed the folder of Ivan's transcript and stared at him. He then reached into his top drawer and pulled out a two-foot section of cotton rope.

"Tie me a bowline," he said, tossing the rope to Ivan.

Ivan smiled and effortlessly tied the knot, then tossed the rope back to the professor.

"Welcome to Bauman, comrade."

Ivan walked out of the admissions building and down the white stone steps. The air was crisp, and he took a moment to watch a barge moving up the curved Yauza River before him. He had pushed upriver his whole life to this moment. Through this gate, he would now realize his dream to be an engineer.

CHAPTER 52
PLAYA DURA

Thursday, July 16, 1992
Casa Cielo – Vieques PR

For four days, Trey maintained a tight routine and low profile with Rick, moving around Langley utilizing facilities. Trey kept his running date with Sami, and coached Tuesday night. Things seemed to be going well, but Trey's college friends were leaving more intense messages and asking him what was going on, where he was, and why he hadn't returned their calls.

"It's about time, Trey. What took you so long to get back to me?" Mark questioned on their call together.

"I know—sorry. Work's been crazy." Trey glanced at Rick, who was listening in on the remote Agency phone.

"Whatever. What are you doing this weekend? I was thinking that I could come up?"

He widened his eyes at Rick, who shook his head. Trey shrugged and tightened his jaw.

No, Rick mouthed silently.

"Sorry, man. This weekend isn't good. I have to go to a gymnastic coaching clinic in Philly," Trey lied.

"All right, well, take care, Trey."

"Bye, Mark." Trey hung up the phone. "Shit, I hate this."

"What's wrong?" Rick asked.

"What's wrong—you heard me."

Rick cocked his head.

"I lied to my best friend."

"And that's a big deal?"

"Yeah, it's a big deal. Unlike the Agency, most people don't lie to their friends."

"Bullshit. Everybody lies, Tiger."

"I've never lied to him before—"

"That's not entirely true."

Trey shook his head.

"Doesn't he still think you're straight?"

"That's not the same—"

"Isn't it?"

"Rick, you know what I mean."

Rick held up his hands in balance of a mock scale.

"I'm serious."

"It'll be fine."

"I've got to get to the gym. I coach tonight."

"Come on—I'll take you."

Rick dropped him off at his gymnastics gym and pretended to leave, but snuck back in to watch Trey coaching his boys from the parents' observation deck.

"Which one is yours?" one of the moms asked Rick.

"Excuse me?"

"Mine is TJ in the blue shorts. Which boy is yours?" she said with a smile.

"No, I am a friend of Trey's. Giving him a ride tonight."

"Oh, Trey is so great with our kids. We love him. He is so patient."

Over the next hour, several parents talked to Rick about Trey as they stood in the viewing area looking out across the sprawling gym. At closing, Rick helped Trey lock up after the last parents picked up their little gymnasts.

Trey was vacuuming the floor and glanced up at Rick. "What?"

"Nothing." Rick tried to avert his attention but again turned back to Trey. *Can't wait to tell you.*

"What? You're kinda freaking me out."

"I'm proud of you."

"Why?"

"I snuck back in and watched you tonight."

"Spying on me now?"

"You're great with your boys. Patient, fun. The parents all love you."

"Really?"

"You're a great coach."

"So are you."

Damn, tell him already. "Let me help you with that." Rick coiled the vacuum. "Let's get out of here. I have a surprise for us. I wanted to tell you all week but waited."

"Is it a good surprise or bad surprise?" Trey asked.

"A *great* surprise, but we have to hustle and pack. Our flight leaves at 0500 tomorrow."

"Where?"

"Nope—it's a surprise."

"How will I know what to pack?"

"It'll be hot and humid."

"Hot?"

"A beach. That's all you're getting. Let's go home and pack. Three days' worth."

Buzz, buzz.

Geez, 0330 already. Did we even sleep?

Rick allowed Trey another few moments of sleep, going to the kitchen to start the coffee. *He's gonna love Vieques! This is gonna be fun.*

"Trey, good morning—come on. Get up."

"What time is it?"

"0335. We gotta shake a leg."

"No song for me this morning?" Trey rolled out of bed.

"Nope, this is early even for me. Our flight leaves at 0500. We're wearing these." Rick had laid out navy work pants and US Navy Seabees T-shirts.

"So we're going to be in the Navy now? Where are we going?"

"You'll see."

They threw on their clothes, grabbed their duffels, and headed to Andrews Air Force Base. The black tarmac bled into the equally black sky overhead. There was no hint of the coming sun.

"Is that our ride?" Trey motioned at the large green plane.

"Yup, a US Navy C-130 transport. Ever been on one?"

"No. It's massive."

"Wait till you see the tail section open up."

At 0500, the behemoth military cargo transport rattled awake as all four engines roared to life.

"Whoa!" Trey's eyes widened as the back tail section opened and bright lights shone down to the tarmac.

"Told ya."

Trey shouted over the engines, "Have you been on one of these before?"

"Yeah, many times—even jumped out of the back of them at ten thousand feet."

"You're nuts."

Rick motioned that it was time to board. They took low-hung seats on the right sidewall.

"Come on. Where are we going?"

"Guess."

"Pensacola?"

"Nope, but that's a good one. Strap in." As they buckled their harnesses, Rick leaned over. "Rank?"

Trey glanced at the stripes of the ground crew member. "Navy, E3 seaman. Easy one."

"Good. Vieques."

"What?"

"We're headed to the island of Vieques off Puerto Rico."

Trey grinned wide.

Rick had made a game of his training to identify all ranks by stripes and bars. The Navy logistics E3 motioned to double-check their safety harnesses and then handed them headsets to block the roar of the four prop engines. The air blew into the cargo hold as the seaman saluted them and then exited as the doors began to close.

"What do you think?"

"This is wild."

As the C-130 lumbered to Vieques, Rick turned to see Trey asleep and suspended in his harness. *Damn, you're lucky, Tiger. I can't ever sleep on these bouncing tin cans. Too damn loud. I guess I better review the assignment again and get ready to brief him.* Rick checked his watch. *Three hours to go—damn, and eight days till Germany.*

Rick opened his briefing folder and thumbed through the pages. He stopped at the photo of Ivan. *I've got to ease him into this and not spook him. Tibbins and Doc M better not get any ideas. One and done. That was the deal, Claren.*

Now, who is this Ivan Henryk Dimitri? Nuke engineer. Born in Leningrad. Soviet Navy—subs. Bauman—Moscow. GKAE—the once great State Committee for the Utilization of Atomic. You're too low-ranking for a golden parachute during perestroika so you're playing your hand openly. What makes you tick? You leave your wife and hop over to Germany for some man-on-man action. Bet she doesn't know. Still, why didn't you show up in '88 or '89 when all your nuke comrades were jumping ship?

Rick took a deep breath. *All right, we send Trey into a New Man bookstore in Munich and dangle him as bait.* He glanced at Trey. *Swear to god, you look sixteen, especially asleep. Trey's gonna be so nervous. No doubt Doc M is counting on that—it will only add more chum to the water for this shark.* Rick flipped back to Ivan's headshot. *He'll bite and invite Trey back to the inn in Nuremberg, then we're green. The team waits in the parking lot. Trey uses the inhalant, faking the asphyxiation. Jeni and I monitor from the next room. We capture the footage, get our incentive, and turn him over to the Prague ops desk. They'll take it from there, and we disappear. Trey returns to his normal life.*

He reviewed the layout of the inn and the bookstore, then the profile on Ivan. *Target has the expertise, contacts, and intelligence to increase his value on the global market. They're worried about hard targets. Reanimation.* Rick underlined that last word. *Trey doesn't need to know that. Focus on the incentive, hard proof: footage, graphic photos, and video of a gay tryst turned accidental homicide. Ivan will freak the fuck out. Threaten his career, his marriage—shit, we'll own him.*

From an adjoining room at the inn, Jeni and Rick would capture the incentive via photo and video, then allow Ivan to panic and leave Trey to make the drive back to Prague. The field desk in Prague would handle the intake by intercepting him at the border. If all went as planned, Rick and Trey would be on a return flight by Sunday afternoon. Rick reviewed the timeline, made notes, and tried to think about Trey's anticipated reactions. *Ease him into it, explain things—especially the safety of the inhalant. Let him ask his questions and try to be patient.*

Bam, bam!

The huge cargo plane touched down hard and immediately began braking.

Excellent—no diversion to the mainland. We're on Vieques. The shorter runway required immediate braking.

Trey awoke at the abrupt landing. "Are we there?"

Rick nodded and winked as they rattled to a full stop in the cargo hold strapped to the wall.

"You good?" Rick shouted above the engines.

"Yeah, I slept the whole way, but it's not quite Delta."

"No, not quite Delta." Rick laughed as the large rear transport doors opened. The humidity and intense heat licked their faces as the winds blew into the cargo hold. "Welcome to paradise, Trey."

They grabbed their gear and thanked the crew. On the hot tarmac, two young Seabees met them with a truck and an old Willys Jeep. The Seabees tossed the keys to Rick, explained the tricky clutch, and then hopped into their pick-up and drove back toward the low buildings and work crew in the distance. Rick and Trey looked at the old 1943 Willys Jeep glistening in the bright sun.

"Isn't she great!" Rick grinned.

"Yeah."

They hopped into the bucket seats and tossed their gear in the back. The Willys was well-maintained, light blue with Navy insignia and call letters.

"Full tank—let's see how she runs." Rick revved the engine. "Listen to that purr!"

They exited the pavement at the base entrance with a small one-man guardhouse. Right outside the gates sat a pair of brightly painted concrete structures: a bodega and a bar. The sunshine was intense and the temperature was already a balmy eighty-seven degrees at 1148, which only confirmed the tropical feel of the rough island.

"This place is incredible!" Trey shouted over the engine.

Rick nodded through his Ray-Ban aviators. They drove down the gravel road for more than two miles, then saw a small wooden sign that read, *Casa Cielo*.

Rick stopped and pointed at the sign. "That's us."

Trey gripped the dashboard as they rumbled up the rugged, one-lane dirt path into the hills.

They arrived at noon and were greeted by the old inn keeper, two dogs, and a gaggle of chickens that were roaming the yard.

"Hola, mi amigo. Tenemos una reservacìon a noche. Mi nombre es Gilbertson. David Gilbertson." Rick gave his usual alias.

"Bienvendio, señors. Entra, entra. Soy Joaquìn. Dos noches. ¿Verdad?"

"Sì."

The man shrugged and shook his head. "Pardon, pero querìas una habitaciòn en lo alto pero numero tres solo tiene una cama. ¿Es posible tener otro?"

Rick stumbled to reply, and Trey spoke up.

"No hay problema, mi tío y yo tuvimos que compartir una cama en mi casa abuela. Vamos a estar bien con una cama. El numero tres es perfecto."

Joaquìn smiled and handed them the key for room three, then pointed to the stairs.

They walked up two flights and found their room on the top floor. It was primitive but clean. A large mosquito netting hung over the queen-size bed, and beyond that a balcony held a view above the trees and stretched out into the blue sea.

"Nice Spanish," Rick conceded as he stripped off his pants. "But now I'm your uncle?"

"Sí, Tío Ricardo." Trey laughed.

"Whatever. We'll train a bit, debrief but we do it in paradise." He opened the balcony doors. "Check out this view."

"Glad we got the top floor— Whoa, you can see the ocean."

"Yup. Two nights and then we're back on Sunday." Rick stripped off his pants. "Honestly, I think that I needed this more than you, Tiger. It feels good to get outta DC and the constant surveillance of Langley."

"I hear ya. What's on the agenda today—the beach?"

"Not yet. First, we train."

They changed into the government-issued khaki shorts and opted for a quick lunch at the inn. They drove back to base for a long afternoon of training in the blistering heat. They stopped only to reapply sunscreen and hydrate.

"You gotta drink—it's essential. Hydration in the field is everything."

Trey took the water and chugged it. He then splashed his face.

Rick pushed Trey through ninety minutes of intense training, conditioning, and grappling on the beach. Finally, he set up sprints between two markers. The suffocating humidity was now slowing Trey's pace.

"Pick it up, pick it up." *This is it—I knew between the travel and heat—it'd get him, but damn, he's doing great. He made it longer than I thought he would.*

Trey stopped and hurled his lunch into the hot sand.

Yuck, argh.

As he heaved, Rick urged, "Push through. You hear me, Tiger? There are no breaks in a real assignment. Push through!"

Trey wiped the puke from his mouth and finished the sprint.

Rick clicked the stopwatch and tossed Trey another bottle of water. "Good job."

"Are we . . . done?" Trey gasped.

Rick glanced at his watch: *1545.* "Beat me on this last one and we're done."

Trey narrowed his eyes.

They were sweaty, gritty with sand, and exhausted. Rick blew his coaching whistle. Trey pulled ahead of Rick and passed the marker.

"Done!" Rick shouted as Trey collapsed on the sand heaving.

Rick recorded the times, then clicked his pen shut.

"That last one nearly killed me."

"Nah, you're tougher than you know. Proud of you." He held out his fist to Trey, and they bumped.

As they drove back to the inn, Rick could sense Trey was lost in his thoughts. *Give him space but check in.* "You okay?"

"Yeah, but I don't get why all the physical training? I mean, is my assignment going to be like that?"

"No, but I've learned that it's better to prep and train for all scenarios. I don't want you caught off guard. Underestimating a situation can be bad."

"Is this all part of what you do? Why you push so hard?"

"Yes. I meant my promise to you. Semper protege."

They arrived at the inn and trudged up the stairs.

"Grab your trunks, I have another surprise."

"Rick, please, I only want to shower and crash."

"Totally, but I know a better place to crash. One last surprise, Trey. Come on, get your stuff."

They grabbed towels, swim trunks, and large bottles of water. They drove out to a remote area and parked the Willys on a dune by several royal palms. It was late afternoon and the beach was deserted.

"See now? Wasn't it worth it?"

"Wow, yes." Trey grinned for the first time since they arrived. "How did you know about this place? Have you been here before?"

"Yeah, most grunts on base know about it, but today we've got it to ourselves." Rick hopped out of the Willys and spread his arms wide. "Playa Dura."

Trey hopped out and stripped off his dirty shorts and shirt. Rick stripped as well. They tossed their towels and trunks under a low hung palm and walked naked into the warm ocean.

Knew I was right. Rick watched Trey floating on his back and splashing. *He needed this weekend too. Push and pull. Train hard but play harder.*

Trey broke their silence. "Thank you."

"For what? Kicking your ass today?"

"No, for this—all this." Trey swam up. "Can I kiss you?"

"You never need to ask that." Rick pulled him close and tasted the salty sea as their tongues met before he pulled back. "I have one more surprise—hold that thought." Rick reached below the water and gave his cock a gentle squeeze.

Damn, why does he end things right as they start? I know I'm not simply a job to him. Right? Trey watched Rick jog up the beach naked. *Geez, he's so hot.* He followed and saw Rick grab his trunks and pull something out of the Jeep. *What is he doing? This better not be more training.*

Trey walked to the palm tree and tugged on his red trunks. Rick returned with a chilled six-pack of Medalla Light.

"Beer and skinny-dipping—your favorite. Right, Tiger?"

"You're nothing but trouble." Trey took a beer and spread out his towel under the shade of the palm fronds.

They cracked open the beers and crashed.

"To you. Trey Alan Carter. My civ-5."

"To my coach, Special Officer Rick Morgan."

They clinked beers.

"I never thought I'd say this, but I'm glad I know you." Trey swung his legs around and laid his head on Rick's chest. "I want to soak all this in and bottle it."

"Me too." Rick wrapped an arm over Trey. "Soak it in—you earned it."

They could have talked about the impending assignment, their training, or the future. Instead, they didn't talk at all as they watched the sun glow on the horizon. Words were not needed.

He's right. I wish we could stay here like this, peaceful. He's calm here. A week ago, he'd have been chatty and nervous, filling the silence. Shit, maybe I will leave him better than I found him—calmer, stronger, and a bit wiser. Rick suddenly felt a twinge as Trey rolled out of his embrace. *Damn, I don't want to let him go.*

"Sun will be gone soon and the skeeters will be ready to eat us alive." Trey got up and returned with a pile of driftwood, then dug out a fire pit with a palm frond and rimmed it with rocks. He created layers with the wood so it could breathe. Rick lay back, watching proudly as his recruit built the fire pit.

Geez, he's put on at least ten pounds of muscle. He's more confident in his skin and that temper has a longer fuse. He might not be a Marine, but he's damn near close.

Trey finished his fire pit and jogged back to the water to rinse off. "Hey, old man?"

"Who you calling old?"

"You." Trey ginned wide. He took off and tumbled across the packed sand with four back handsprings and finished his pass with a back tuck.

"Hang on, Trey!" Rick jumped up and ran to the Jeep. He pulled out a camera. "Do it again. Ready—go."

Trey repeated a second tumbling pass as Rick snapped a series of shots. He put away his camera and watched Trey floating in the waves.

"Don't get too close, candy's hard to resist"—fuck it, Claren.

Rick chugged his beer then, and went out to join him.

"So what do you think?" Rick asked as they floated.

"About what, this beach? Amazing."

"Yeah, it's incredible, but I meant about all this—our training, the team, your time with me so far."

"I don't know how to answer that . . . I'm glad it was you."

Rick nodded. "You know, Germany, we'll have to—"

"Let's not talk about Germany. Let's just be here."

Rick nodded. *You're right, Tiger. I'm not good at taking my own advice. Be in the moment. Always thinking ahead instead of—*

"Ha!" Trey chuckled aloud.

"What's so funny?"

"Does this count as my first gay beach?"

"What?"

"I always thought that my first would've been Rehoboth or Fire Island, but no—I didn't leave that pool party, didn't listen to my gut. Now, I'm here on this wild, rugged beach with a freaking CIA officer who kicks my ass but—"

"But what?"

"Knowing you, you probably have some crazy training planned tomorrow so I'm gonna enjoy this moment." He swam over to Rick, then wrapped his legs around his torso and floated on his back. "All of it."

Rick grinned and took hold of Trey. He smiled, pretended to kiss him, but then dunked him, laughing. Trey emerged and flipped Rick by his legs under the water.

Rick surfaced behind him and enveloped him in a bear hug. "You trust me?"

"I shouldn't but I do."

He turned Trey slowly in his arms. Their bodies in full contact now, feet to heads.

"I'm supposed to let go of you."

"After Germany?" Trey asked.

"Yeah." Rick squeezed him tighter.

"Aren't you tired of being alone?"

Fucking yes, but this never works. Remember Terry and David.

"Fuck that, handsome," Jeni's voice rang in his head. *"Yes, it can work. He's right there in your arms—literally and figuratively."*

Rick shook his head softly.

"What is it, then?" Trey asked. "Work stuff? My assignment?"

"No. I don't want to let go."

"Then don't." Trey kissed him.

Rick let go.

Trey stepped back and shook his head. "I'll never understand you."

"Let's light your fire?"

They returned to the last beers and lit the fire. The sun was now a glowing sliver on the horizon, and not even the smoke from the fire could keep the invading bugs at bay. They retreated to the Willys and returned to the inn. After a quick shower, they dressed and drove back to the small bodega that served as a restaurant.

"Wow, this grilled chicken is incredible." Trey dug into his meal.

"I told you. It doesn't look like much but the chicken, rice, and beans can't be beat." Rick looked around. It was Friday night so there were a few of the Navy seamen and Seabees also out at both the bodega and the adjoining bar.

After dinner, they returned to the inn for an early bedtime at 2200.

They were exhausted but Rick felt Trey reach for him in the dark and he did not resist as a warm, wet mouth engulfed him. He was about to release when he pulled Trey back. "Wait, I'm close."

"Rick, can I? You're safe, and I really want to."

"Go for it." Rick grabbed the back of his head.

Trey drank Rick's warm nectar.

"Ah, fuck. Yes." *Goddamn, Trey. That was incredible.* They lay quietly for a moment. *Don't be selfish —reciprocate. Do him.*

Rick pushed Trey to his back and disappeared under the covers. Using his mouth, hands, and experience, Rick brought him to the brink quickly. He felt Trey spasm three times. He moved upward to his mouth and tasted himself and Trey's tongue—mixed into an exotic blend of the island and the night.

As Trey fell asleep in his arms, Rick held him and thought about their time together.

Why do I feel so intensely about him? It's like I've known him forever but it's only been a month. How the hell did we condense ninety-plus days of training into only thirty? I'm exhausted but look at him. He's ready. We did it. He didn't quit and I didn't kill him, not yet at least. Ha! It's crazy but it worked. He trusts me. This isn't just Doc M's protocol. Trey really trusts me and I think that I trust him. I know him inside and out.

"See I told you, handsome—you could do worse," Jeni's voice echoed in his mind.

He's too young for me, Jeni.

"I'm calling bullshit. Remember that college freshman from Berlin."

That was one time. Rick shook his head. *Good night, Jeni.* He gently kissed Trey and released him. Trey rolled over. Rick quietly got up and went to their balcony.

Tomorrow's d-day. I've put this off as long as I could. Is he ready? He glanced at his watch. *2348—it's too late to call Jeni. Stop second-guessing. Why am I treating him different than other recruits? We've run more than one hundred miles. Done nearly a thousand push-ups, and hours of Krav Maga.*

Rick glanced at his watch. *What time is it in Tel Aviv? Nearly 0700—don't call him. It's been two years and too many arguments.* He crawled back into bed.

Stick to the protocol. This is what we trained for. Rick knew in his gut that things felt different with Trey. All their training was precisely that—training.

The real test was now in front of them. The real test was Ivan.

CHAPTER 53
RAIN

Rick awoke at 0700 to a heavy tropical storm. He walked over to the shutters and saw the gray morning. *Well definitely not a training day. Yes, I get your not-so-subtle hint, Mother Nature. I've put this off as long as I could. Time to brief him—time for Ivan.*

He stretched and opened the wooden doors. He took three steps out on the balcony and allowed his naked body to be doused in the cooling rain. Turning back, he saw Trey sleeping. *What am I doing? After this, there's no going back. He'll either hate me or not.* He closed his eyes and tried to let the rain wash away his guilt.

"Rick?" Trey said groggily. "What are you doing?"

Rick turned to him. "Just thinking."

"You're soaking wet."

He hopped back into bed on top of Trey. "Morning."

"Yuck! You're soggy—get off."

"Thought you liked me on top."

"Why are you up so early?"

"Thinking about our day and couldn't sleep."

"Do we have to train?"

"No, but we gotta do your briefing."

Trey nodded.

"But not yet—" Rick widened his eyes and kissed Trey while pressing against him.

"Well good morning to you too, Mr. Pecker." Trey suddenly rolled them both. "Now, I'm on top."

Rick pressed upward into Trey. "Sorry, but you do that to me."

"Nothing to be sorry for. Isn't that what you always say?"

Trey kissed him. Rick grabbed Trey and allowed their tongues to entwine. Their breathing increased and found a synchronous rhythm. They stayed in bed for another half hour, edging and retreating until finally reaching their climax together.

Rick washed up as the rain continued. He slipped out to get coffee and muffins down in the inn's office as Trey showered. They dressed and sat at the edge of the open balcony doors, eating and watching the rain. Rick retrieved a folder from his bag as they drank their coffee.

"Is that it?" Trey asked.

"Yeah. You ready?"

Trey nodded.

The folder was thick and outlined in alternating red and black hash marks around the perimeter. Across the top, above the CIA seal, Rick pointed to the header.

Confidential Classification: Top Secret.

"I'm supposed to tell you that once we review this, there's no going back. This really is the last chance. Up till now your exposure has been minimal but after we—

"I get it."

"You sure?"

"Yes."

Rick opened the folder and pulled out a photo. "This is him. The reason we recruited you." He handed the headshot to Trey. "Ivan Henrik Dimitri."

"He's the reason you guys snatched me, put me through all this?" Trey studied the photo.

"Yeah." *Don't say another word. Let's see if Doc M is right—he'll transfer his angst, his anger to Ivan.*

"Who is this douchebag?"

Perfect, now state the facts. "He's fifty-four years of age. Russian, but he and his wife, Hana, now live in Prague. Prior to the fall of the Soviet Union, they lived in Leningrad—what's now Saint Petersburg. He's an engineer and was in the nuclear fusion center of the former Soviet energy society. He's our target, Trey."

"So how does this work? Can I ask questions?"

"Of course."

"Why's he a target? What's he done?"

"He's tried to publish a theory, but it's not so much what he's *done* but what we fear he may do." Rick stared at his coffee mug and thought about his next words. "He has both contacts and knowledge that a lot of people want."

"Nukes?"

"Yeah, but not just the basics." Rick hesitated. *Don't say anymore— don't spook him.*

"Rick, you know my dad's an engineer. I literally grew up on job sites for fossil, hydro, and nuclear power stations."

"What's your point?"

"My point is you can tell me more—I want to know."

Rick took a deep breath. "Fine. His specialty is a theory, or what we all thought was a theory. Reanimation."

"What's reanimation?"

"Taking nuclear waste and reenergizing till you have low grade and higher grade levels of activity or animation."

"Bombs?"

"Exactly. We knew the Russians were close, but after the fall of their union, we spent most of '89 and '90 securing many of their scientists. We positioned them into intelligence and academic positions all around the world."

"But not him?" Trey handed the photo back to Rick.

"Nope, he popped up on our radar several months ago when he tried to publish."

"So his *theory* is potentially dangerous, but is he?"

"Not per se but yes, his knowledge is extremely dangerous if the wrong people get their hands on it."

Trey sipped his coffee. "Like who?"

Geez, you're not gonna let me get away with level-one intel are you? "Shoot straight with him." Rick thought about Claren's instructions. *"Get him on board—I don't need to know how. No backups." Well, here goes nothing.*

"Several Middle Eastern and African states are vying to capture exactly his type of expertise. The PLO, Iran, Syria, Libya, Iraq—take your pick. They've all made attempts to nab or kidnap similar nuclear scientists from the former Soviet system."

"This reanimation—what makes it so important? And why him?"

"Ivan's more appealing because of his theory and his last position. Waste. He was in charge of the dump sites all over Eastern Europe."

"So he knows how and where to get it."

"Yup. His scientific paper detailed accurately the reuse and reactivation. He tried to pass it off as reclamation or clean up, as if it was an environmental science paper."

"What if it was?"

"It wasn't, and we have to weigh out both sides."

"But what if?"

"Best-case scenario is that he's a hippie tree-hugger and clueless that he riled the global intelligence community."

"And the worst case?"

"He knows exactly what he's doing. Using the paper as a billboard to sell his intel to the highest bidder."

"But there's a chance he's a tree-hugger?"

"He's not."

"And his knowledge *really* is dangerous?"

"Extremely," Rick confirmed. "I asked to bring you here so we'd be off the grid. So we could take our time with *this* part—it can be confusing. You're asking great questions and I want you to keep asking, okay?"

Trey nodded.

"But you need to realize that everything changes a bit today. You're stepping through the looking glass."

"What do you mean?"

"Before you and I met, you thought the world was one way. You'd watch the news, read about events, and—well, sometimes what you saw was exactly what *we* wanted you to see."

"The Agency?"

Rick nodded and sipped of his coffee.

"What are you saying—that y'all plant stories?"

"All the time. We have an entire team in Langley dedicated to just that."

"Y'all control the media?"

"No. We don't control it, but we *massage* it from time to time."

"When?"

"When a situation requires us to provide cover or hide operations, that usually means keeping important people or things safe."

Trey narrowed his eyes.

"I know how that sounds but hear me out. On this side of the looking glass, we don't get the luxury of giving people like Ivan the benefit of the doubt." Rick held up the photo. "In our world, we have to consider that this guy is up to no good. We have to anticipate the worst of the worst even if it breaks rules."

"To keep the world safe."

"Exactly."

"Sounds a whole lot like the 'ends justify the means' argument."

"It's not easy. We have to make tough choices. Counter intel isn't black-and-white. It's mostly gray. His intelligence is a commodity that people will fight over, kill for with no remorse. So yeah, we sometimes bend the rules to protect—"

"And you're okay with that?"

"Yes."

"You justify that because in the wrong hands his intel is really bad."

"That's an understatement."

"How bad are we talking?"

Tell him exactly how serious this is—stop sugar-coating it. "We intercepted his research paper—but Ivan doesn't know that. He's still waiting on a decision from the Czech Science Foundation to publish it or not. Our scientists have analyzed his core theory, his data— it's real, totally solid. But worse, it fills in critical gaps to transform nuclear waste from toxic dumps that nobody wants into something more valuable than gold or platinum."

"Like Chernobyl?"

Rick shook his head. "Worse. Any rogue, extremist state that got their hands on him and his intel could leapfrog from conventional to nukes. Become a serious threat to us, Europe, Israel . . . if we don't contain this, we could be looking at anything from small-scale dirty bombs to World War III scenarios."

"Oh my god."

"This isn't a game, Trey. Look, I know our initial tactics— your recruitment—felt involuntary and like we kidnapped you or something. I went through it myself. But I've done my best to bring you along this journey with choices. Choices not even afforded to me. The path ahead is more narrow. I have to know whether you're on board or not. People could get hurt."

Trey stood and walked to the open balcony. "All you had to do was ask me—you know that."

"I know, that's why we're here. Why I'm asking."

Trey nodded.

"Should I keep going?"

"Yeah." Trey turned to him. "But I don't know how I'm supposed to help?"

"Let me explain."

Trey returned to his chair as Rick opened the file and pulled out Ivan's dossier with the former USSR seal and Cyrillic text.

"We outlined a plan to get to him. In order to do that, we had to study him and get inside his head. It's all here."

"You read Russian?"

"Of course, most of us at the Agency speak several languages."

"That's why the German lessons."

"Yup. You saw our language department."

"Is your Russian why they recruited you?"

"Maybe, but also 'cause I got outed in '80 just like I told you. My training and activation was during the Cold War. I'm fluent in Russian and German. I personally tracked Ivan in Berlin and Hana in Prague. We've tracked him now for six months."

"I don't speak Russian. So why me? Is he gay?"

"We know for sure he's bi."

Trey nodded.

That's it, Tiger, put the pieces together. Go at his pace. Don't hold back but make him ask.

"How do you *know* he's bi?"

"He leaves Hana once a month and drives over into Germany for some action—blowjobs mostly. Secret adventures in the back rooms of porn shops, though he's getting braver. We've followed him and other agents have tried several times to *entice* him. He's never once engaged."

"Let me guess, they were all straight?"

"Bingo. Not only us—the Brits and Mossad have him on their radars. He doesn't take the bait."

"So why not nab him and Hana and take them in?"

"We could but ..." *Don't scare him. Talk it out. Plain language.* "It's complicated. We've learned over the years that negative incentive only works when absolute fear is applied, and it doesn't hold. Ultimately, you have to bring someone to your side, and that takes time and patience. Yeah, we could show up in a blacked-out van and take them both. Then what?"

Trey shrugged.

"Or we can dissect what makes him tick, target his fear, and bring him to us."

"Sounds complicated."

"It is. Doc M is an expert in it, but it starts with small steps. In studying Ivan, we know now that he has particular tastes. Younger men."

"Like chicken?"

"Yeah, but *really* young and closeted."

"So he cheats on his wife, likes young closeted guys, and you want to entrap him? Threaten to out him? Is that enough incentive for him?"

Damn, you get it. Don't blurt it out. Walk him through it. "Not exactly. Your instincts and questions are good, Trey. His appetite is only satiated with role-play. Intense role-play."

"How intense?"

"He likes to dominate and inflict pain." Rick stopped. *Let him think it through. Let him absorb what you're saying.*

"How do you know this?"

"I watched him do it."

"When?"

"A few months ago, right before we recruited you."

"What happened?"

"Ivan escalated things and had an incident. The situation turned rougher than his *new friend* wanted."

"Where?"

"Berlin, in the back room of an adult bookstore."

"Did they call the cops?"

"No."

"Why not?"

"I'm guessing the young man wasn't out to his family. He'd never have pressed charges."

"Ivan hurt him?"

"Yes."

"And you saw it?"

"Nearly strangled him."

"And what—you just watched?"

Rick nodded.

"Why didn't you help him?"

"I was there only to observe."

"You let him hurt him—"

"The kid was okay, Tiger."

"How do you know?"

"I watched him run out. Look, that's not the point."

"What is the point?" Trey raised his voice.

"Please let me explain. We have a plan." Adrenaline heightened in Rick's veins. *Shit, calm down. You've got a lot to get through. Pause and take a minute. You have to get him there. Geez, this isn't even the tough stuff.* Rick picked up his mug.

"So, what's the plan?" Trey asked.

"Our assignment is to lure Ivan. His appetite is growing, and we know he'll head to Munich next weekend. He's going to meet a young blond American man." Rick turned to Trey. "A USAF Airman on leave."

Trey slowly nodded.

Don't say anything. Let him take it in.

"And then what?" Trey asked softly.

"We get him."

"You gonna let him hurt me?"

"Never." Rick took Trey's hands into his own. "I swear to you."

"What then?"

"We're gonna let him *think* he's hurt you."

"How?"

Here goes. Be patient. Rick pulled out room schematics. "We're gonna fake an asphyxiation. You'll be in this room with him. Jeni and

I will be over in the next room. We'll have cameras hidden here, here, and here." Rick pointed to each location on the diagrams. "You'll never be out of my sight. I'll be nine feet away through this adjoining door."

"I'm the incentive."

Rick nodded.

"And you'll capture it all on pictures and video?"

"Yeah."

"And Ivan'll think what?"

"He'll think he's accidentally killed you."

"Seriously—then what?"

"Then he'll most likely leave you there and run. Our teams will be out here in the parking lot. They'll follow him at close range and intercept him at the border, here."

"But what if he doesn't run? What if he tries to—"

"I'll bust through that door and take him down."

Trey breathed deeply. "Will the incentive be enough?"

"BDSM, gay sex, murder—more than enough. He'll be facing extradition and life in prison."

"For a fake murder?"

"He won't know that. Which is why it has to look and feel *real* to him and—"

"Me."

"Yeah."

"How?"

"We'll use an inhaler loaded with a special medicine, a small dosage—totally safe."

"What does it do?"

"It lowers your pulse to an undetectable level."

"But it's safe?"

"One hundred percent. This is what we do, Tiger. We have teams of people that test and plan every detail. I swear to you it's safe. I've taken it. Jeni's taken it. You won't know anything—you'll be out cold for a bit."

"Why aren't you acting as the bait?"

"I would have, but he likes 'em young, really young. And lucky for us, you look a lot younger than you are."

"You think he'll be attracted to me?"

"Without a doubt."

"You said the British and Israeli both are tracking him. Why aren't they doing this? Do they not have a team like us?"

"Not sure about the Brits, but I know that Israel doesn't. Like I told you at the lake, I had an Israeli lover. He was Mossad."

For two hours, they reviewed the travel logistics, city maps of Munich and Nuremberg, and the room layouts of the inn. Rick took his time and tried to answer all Trey's questions.

"What if he takes it too far?" Trey finally asked.

Let him voice his concerns. "What do you mean?"

"I mean, I'm tied up—unconscious from the inhalant—what if he—"

"Stop. Don't go there. I will *never* let him hurt you. You hear me?" Rick said in a serious tone. "Semper protege."

Trey nodded.

Rick glanced at his watch: 1145. *Geez we've been at this for nearly three hours. He needs a break. Shit, we both do.* "Look, it's almost noon. Rain's stopped. Wanna grab some lunch and take a drive?"

"Yes."

They wiped down the seats of the Willys. Rick drove them to the far eastern side of the island, where they found a small bluff looking out to the ocean. They sat quietly in the Jeep and ate their bologna sandwiches and chips that Joaquìn's wife had given them.

Check in with him—don't let him stew. Rick sensed from the silence that Trey was processing the information. "Hey, you okay?"

"Yeah."

"Do you have more questions?"

Trey nodded.

"Shoot. It's only us out here, Tiger. Ask me anything."

"Anything?"

"Anything."

"Does the whole team know what I may have to do with Ivan?"

"Yeah. Why?"

"I don't know."

"You ashamed?" Rick asked.

"Kind of."

"Why?"

"It's not how I thought that this would be—this spy shit."

"Trey, look at me." Rick waited until the young man turned to him. "This is a specific assignment that you are being groomed to execute. Ivan is an assignment. A target. You're not alone in this—I'm here for every step."

Trey nodded.

"If we're successful, then we could turn him—contain him."

"Then what?"

"Then he works for us."

"Doing what?"

"I don't know what the plans are exactly, but we've used these types of assets before."

"How?"

"We'd allow a foreign regime to recruit him. We would then have eyes and ears inside Iran, Syria, or Iraq."

"Wow, really?"

"Yeah, it may seem crazy, but we have perfected this type of incentive for more than a decade. Doc M, the team—a lot of work goes into these plans."

"So Ivan is why you picked me?"

"Yeah."

Trey shook his head.

"It's totally natural to be nervous, Trey. God knows I was on my first assignment."

"Where was it?"

"Turkey, outside Ankara in '81. I was nervous as hell."

"How did you calm your head down?"

"You gotta forget the bigger issues. Focus on one simple first step."

"What's that?"

"Attraction. We take advantage of his natural desire for you."

Trey nodded. "Did y'all look at other candidates?"

"Yeah, I think like three or four."

"So why me?"

"Honestly, you looked sixteen and fit the profile. That was it at first but now—you've done great so far. You've met every challenge. I'm proud of you, Tiger." Rick held out his fist. They bumped top and bottom.

"So you've done this too?"

"Many, many times, but not only me. Jeni, others—we didn't invent this type of CI recruitment. The Russians do it all the time. Mostly women, they call them sparrows, but they didn't invent it either—it goes back decades. Hell, even the Nazis in World War II used trained female agents to lure and coerce. What Doc M did was adapt it to us. We simply tap into what is natural to you and me—lend it to our country in specific situations."

"Being gay? Being bait?"

"Yeah, but it's not all sexual. And at times it can be dangerous. We're creating relationships and connections with an ulterior motive. Using emotions, desire, and attraction can be volatile, which is why you have to keep your emotions in check. That's why I've harped on it so much with you. Keeping your cool, your head, can save your life."

"So it's dangerous?"

Be honest with him. "It can be, but that's why I've trained you. I'll be there. Claren thinks I over-reached, but I want you to be ready to defend yourself if needed."

"Have you ever . . ."

"Taken a life?"

Trey nodded.

"Yeah. But only when the lives of those I was protecting or my own were in jeopardy."

"A lot?"

"I'd rather not talk about it, okay? One day, but . . ."

Trey mustered a smile and squeezed Rick's knee.

"It's beautiful here, isn't it?" Rick stared out at the blue water.

"Yeah."

"It's why I asked if I could bring you to Vieques. Talk this out, only between us. OTR."

Trey leaned over and kissed him.

"What was that for?"

Trey shrugged. "Okay, I'll do this. Germany. Ivan. But not for the Agency." He faced Rick. "I'm doing it for you."

Rick smiled.

No more words were needed.

They returned to the inn and reviewed the intel a second time. Then they grabbed dinner and crashed. The rain had given them a day off of sorts.

Sunday morning, they left the Willys on the tarmac and boarded the awaiting C-130. Neither man slept on the return flight. Several times, Rick observed Trey staring intently at the stark exposed structure of their lumbering transport.

He's stewing about Ivan, Hana, and that BDSM shit that I tried to explain. He's on board—don't know if I should be happy or kick myself. Either way, there's no going back now. Check in with him.

"You okay?" Rick asked over the roar of the engines.

Trey only nodded but stared ahead.

"You sure? I know it's loud but you wanna talk?"

"No. What are you reading?"

"Anne Rice." He held up the book. "*Interview with the Vampire.* 'Bout a bunch of vampires in New Orleans."

A few minutes later, he turned back to Trey. *Fuck, I know that look—the dreaded what-ifs. Don't let him get lost in his head.* Rick reached over, grabbed Trey's right thigh, and winked. Trey gave a half smile but closed his eyes.

Rick sensed that his touch was little comfort. *He's on the other side of the glass now. I bet he sees Ivan's face. We all do. Our targets haunt us. Damn it, like Ankara, Mexico City, Pusan, Berlin. What have I done? Fuck, it's already happening for him, and I can't do a damn thing about it now. This kid's haunted by a man he's never even met—that part never goes away.*

I'm sorry, Trey.

CHAPTER 54
DOUBLEDOWN

Trey saw the red message light was blinking when he and Rick arrived back at the apartment late Sunday afternoon. *Bet that's Mom and Dad.* Trey glanced around the room and the island faded. Vieques now seemed a world away. He hit Play.

Beep.

Instantly he knew his mom's Southern voice.

"Dave, I know that—I'm waiting for the beep. Son, it's Mom."

Yup and she's pissed at Dad.

"I need to talk to you—you said you'd call me back last Thursday. It's now Saturday. Remember that God loves you, son, no matter what you're up to. Call me back. Did it hang up? Dave, I know how this works. I'm not stupid. Stop—I'm not going to say that on his answering—"

Trey rolled his eyes.

"Dave's your Dad?" Rick asked.

"Yeah."

"She sounds mad—you should call her back now. Geez, you weren't kidding about the religious passive-aggressive stuff."

"You have no idea."

Rick raised his eyebrows.

"I'll call her back tonight."

"Why not now?"

"Can't—they're in between church services now."

"They go to more than one on Sunday?"

"Yup, at least two but sometimes three or four. It's pretty much all day."

Rick shook his head.

Beep.

A second message began to play. "Hi, Trey, this is Sami. I wanted to see if we could hang out tonight—maybe go for a run or work out? Let me know."

Rick looked up from a notepad. "You should schedule a run with him. Meet up again before Germany."

Trey nodded.

Beep.

A third message played. "Trey, where are you? I have been trying you all week. Don't forget that I'm coming up tomorrow. U2. The concert. Call me."

Shit! The concert is this week. "That's Mark."

"What's he talking about? A concert?"

"U2. We bought tickets like six months ago. I forgot. It's Tuesday night at RFK."

Rick frowned.

"Please, Rick. I have to go. We planned this. All my friends from Liberty—please, Rick?"

"Calm down—I'm sure it'll be fine, but we need to figure out the apartment. We can clear out and put things back."

"You don't need to go. Stay. What if he meets you?" Trey asked.

"Too complicated." Rick shook his head.

"He's my best friend. You gonna have to meet him at some point. Look, I know my poker face isn't that strong, but—"

"I can't—not yet. And how's he your best friend when he doesn't even know you're gay? When are you gonna come out to him?"

"I can't. He wouldn't understand."

"So, you do have a poker face then," Rick said.

"I guess so."

"You never know, Tiger. Sometimes people will surprise you—if you let them."

"You don't get it, Rick. If I tell him, he might say something to other friends, then they'll say something. Before you know it, my mom will be screaming on my answering machine, 'Son, you're turning your back on God. I did not raise my son to be like this—an abomination. Dave, talk to him.'"

"That's a pretty good impression."

"I can hear it now. No, thanks."

"Well, at least call Sami and set up a run again."

"I will."

Trey met up with Sami late in the evening on the Reston trails. *Something feels different. He's smiling more—I don't think I ever noticed his legs before. Damn, he's really cute.*

They ran down the trail and did five miles.

"My uncle wants to cook for you. Would you want to come over later this week for dinner?" Sami asked.

Shit, Germany. "Sorry, but I can't this week. I am slammed at work, and I've got the U2 concert plus coaching."

"No worries—we can connect next week maybe."

"Sounds good. Maybe next Sunday, same time, but I'll call." Trey hugged him and they parted in the parking lot. It would be tight and he might be jet-lagged. Still, he wanted to see Sami again after Germany and wanted to try and turn the relationship more toward a friendship.

Monday's on-campus briefing was exhaustive as Jeni, Darius, Rick, and Claren questioned Trey on the plan, the drops, the bookstore layout, and the small inn in Nuremberg. Trey knew the assignment forwards and backwards.

"Impressive. You're ready," Claren said.

"Thank you, ma'am." Trey glanced at Rick. *I did it—she seems pleased with me.*

Rick nodded. "Claren, I'm gonna to move out of the apartment and stay at my place in Silver Spring. Trey has a college friend coming up tonight and well, he's ready."

She glanced at Trey. "Okay."

"Thank you." *Wow, she agreed.*

"But, Trey, remember—this is all classified and the team is counting on you," Claren said.

"Of course."

"Have fun tomorrow night at the concert, but not too much fun. Rick, when do you head over?"

"Wednesday to prep, then I'll meet Trey and Jeni at the Munich airport Friday morning," Rick said.

"Jennifer has confirmed our flights. Trey and I will fly on Thursday night. I'll support our boys and provide communications to both Frankfurt ops and Darius here at Campus," Jeni added.

"Good. We're keeping a tight circle, but we may need to bring in the Czech ops desk too—along with the Frankfurt," Claren said. "I know the senior field ops at both desks. Rick, keep me in the loop as you prep. Say the word, and we'll increase the support to lean in on the interagency logistics."

"Will do."

"Forty-five days—I wasn't sure at first, but you all have done great. We have our civ-5." She turned again to Trey. "They all know that I don't hand out compliments often, but you've done well. Now, we all stay on plan and regroup here next Monday, after Germany. Are we good?"

"I think we're good," Darius said. "Trey, I have to say we've never had a civ-5 be so prepped and ready. She ain't gonna say it, but I will. Good job."

"Thanks," Trey said.

"You don't seem nervous. Are you?" Darius asked.

"I've been working on my poker face, 'cause I am."

"No need, Trey. Don't worry about the overall plan. You keep your focus on Ivan," Claren said. "We are your team. We're here to support you. I know you'll do great. Rick and Jeni will have eyes on you the entire time."

"Yes ma'am." *Geez, was that a compliment or a warning? Or some sort of double meaning.*

The meeting adjourned. Darius and Jeni left together. Claren and Jennifer went to another meeting.

Rick and Trey left Campus and returned to the apartment.

Trey helped Rick pack up his things and load them into his BMW. They returned to the apartment and double-checked each room. *He's really leaving. I guess this is it.*

"Looks like it did before," Rick said.

"No, it's cleaner and a bit—"

"Better?" Rick smiled. "Stop with the waterworks."

"I'm not." Trey stiffened his jaw.

"Come here." Rick pulled him into an embrace. "This isn't goodbye. I will see you in four days. You'll like Munich. We'll get through Ivan and try to hang out a bit before we bring you back here."

"Can I ask you something?" Trey asked.

"What?"

"Claren's last statement to me at the meeting seemed to mean two different things. It was like she—"

"Ah, you picked up on that, huh?" Rick interrupted. "Yeah, we call it a 'doubledown.' She's always a step ahead."

"So what, am I being watched?"

"Yeah, there's a lot of eyes on us, Trey. Both of us."

Trey nodded.

Rick released his embrace and picked up his last bag before turning to the door.

"Rick, wait." Trey pulled out a small box and handed it to him.

"What's this?"

"I got you a little something to remember me by."

"I don't need anything to remember you, but thank you." Rick opened the box and pulled out a white pukka shell necklace.

"It's not much, but I—"

"Where did you—"

"Vieques. At the island bodega."

"It's awesome, Tiger. I used to wear one of these when I was your age." Rick hugged him and kissed his forehead.

Trey's eyes were starting to water as he fought his emotions.

"Hey, look at me. This isn't good-bye. There are still ears here. You're not alone. It's only a few days, and then I will pick you up in Munich." He leaned in and kissed Trey on his lips and then again on his forehead. "See you Friday."

"Bye," Trey said and closed the door.

He was alone in his apartment. Everything looked as it had before June, before all that had happened, but it did not feel the same. He stripped and stared into the mirror as his shower warmed up. He saw the scar on his left temple from Kirk. He saw the now slight crook in his nose from Rick. He saw the scar on his right wrist and forearm from the pool at the Farm.

"Every scar has a story, Tiger."

These scars told his past, and he held a secret now that could not be shared. Nothing felt the same as he stared at his body.

Nothing would ever be the same.

CHAPTER 55
ACCIDENT

Trey swung open the door. "Mark! You made good time."

"Hey, Trey, yeah I guess." Mark entered with two duffels and dropped them on the living room floor. "What's up?"

"Nothing—great to see you. It's been a while. What's with all the books? Doesn't UVA Law give you the summer off?"

"Nope. Nobody told me there would be this much reading. You can't imagine how much."

"Whoa all that for second year?"

"Yup, and Law Review." Mark grinned widely.

"Are you serious? Congrats! That's huge."

"Yeah, well, be careful what you wish for, right?"

"How was your clerking in New York?"

"Amazing."

"Did you see much of the city?"

"Not a lot. Mostly I saw my computer, books, and eyelids. But they did take us to a Yankees game. The partners. Hold up, you look different?"

"What?" *Be cool. He doesn't know.*

"You okay?"

"Yeah, fine."

"What's with the haircut? I thought you were growing it out now that we were out of Liberty, free of Falwell."

"Nah, I got sick of it and buzzed it off."

"I hear ya. I tried to grow mine out after Liberty and couldn't stand it once it started touching my ears. Seriously though, how've you been?"

"Good."

"That's it—good? Since when does Trey Carter have a one-word answer?"

"No man, I'm good. I've been working and coaching a ton, but I'm stoked for the concert."

"Me too. It's gonna be epic. What have you been doing for a routine?" Mark asked.

"What do you mean?"

"Trey, you've bulked up by at least fifteen or twenty pounds. You're quiet all of sudden, which is kinda nice but totally not you. What's going on?"

"Nothing. Pretty much the same routine work: Worldgate and coaching."

"All right, high schooler. Spill it?"

Let it go, Mark. I can't say anything about any of it. He's not gonna give this a rest. We've known each other for what? Seven years—since Pensacola in the fall semester of 1985.

Mark had been a year older and a freshman in college. Trey had been a senior in the high school still but as a boarding student he'd lived in the college dorms with an RA, one of the upperclassmen who monitored each floor.

From Pensacola Christian to Liberty University, they'd been through a lot since they were seventeen and sixteen. Now, Trey feared that if his friend ever found out about any of his secrets, their bond would be broken.

"Trey Carter, I've known you for seven years. What is up?"

"Nothing." *Geez, let it go, Mark.*

Mark headed to the fridge. "Whoa, since when do you have beer?"

"Oh sorry, I had my neighbor over for the Skins game and he must have left that there."

Mark stared at Trey.

"It's not mine—I swear."

"Ha! I'm yanking your chain, dude. But can you imagine if your mom or dad saw that? They'd freak. Right?"

"You're not kidding."

Mark closed the fridge and plopped down on the couch.

"I got a new job, but it's different."

"Wait. What? Where?"

"It's for an airline. I start my training in Philly next month," Trey said. "Global Airways: they're a defense contractor. Starting in August, I will be in Europe for a while, at least that's what they tell me."

"That's great. Didn't you work for Delta back when you were 'off the radar'?"

"Yeah." *Off the radar. Here we go again—those dark eight months when I dropped out, moved in with Kirk, and then came home busted with my tail between my legs.*

He and Mark never spoke about it. After completing his required Exodus ministry, Trey had transferred to Liberty, and they'd picked up where they left off. His parents also never spoke about it or their insistence on conversion therapy. None of his friends knew. And now he was adding more secrets to his life with the protocol and Rick.

Damn it—I want to tell him. Blurt it out. So the CIA kidnapped me for five days, I'm training for a secret mission in Germany to let a psycho tie me up, drool over me, and then we're gonna fake my death on camera so that they can nab the bastard to stop a nuclear war. Oh and you should see my hot-as-hell assigned CIA officer—I think I'm in love with him. Cool, right? Oh shit, and I almost forgot the best part—I'm gay.

"Trey?"

"What?"

"Do you want to order a pizza?"

"Oh yeah, sorry." Trey picked up the phone and ordered.

"Do you need some cash?"

"No, I got it."

"You seemed checked out a minute ago. What were you thinking about?"

"Butch."

Mark nodded.

"Remember when he was delivering pizzas?" Trey asked.

"Pensacola—right, and that night you had to sneak him back on campus."

"Yup. We had to call Stephanie's sister to come get his rock tapes—"

"Oh my god, yes. Rachel was like, 'If this is drugs I'm not taking them—'"

"And we were like *'Drugs*? No, rock tapes!' She was livid. 'Wait, you got me outta bed—made me drive all the way over here 'cause y'all think he'll get kicked out over rock music!'"

"She was so pissed." Mark grinned. "So crazy."

"Yup. But they would've absolutely kicked him out. That place was so strict."

"No doubt." Mark laughed. "Expelled for rock music—can you even imagine it now?"

"Look at us—finally gonna see U2 in concert. We've come a long way."

"You're not kidding."

Trey held up his fist.

"Since when do we fist bump?"

Oh shit, right.

The pizza arrived and they sat up late laughing, remembering stories from their friends from Liberty and Pensacola. The urge to tell Mark everything didn't diminish, but he tamped it down. Luckily, Mark didn't question him further.

The next day they drove into DC and picked up another Liberty grad, Mike Butler. The plan was to meet at the apartment of Mike's girlfriend in Adams Morgan for an impromptu afternoon BBQ, then to head to see U2 at RFK Stadium on the Metro. They were all playing hooky. Ordinarily, before Rick and the protocol, this would have all felt so secretive and taboo for Christian college grads. Now it seemed innocent to Trey, and he was excited to spend the day together with his friends.

Trey was driving with Mark in the front passenger seat, and Mike in the back right seat. They had started up New Hampshire Avenue toward DuPont Circle when out of nowhere a black sedan slammed into their left side at a high speed.

Crash!

Without thinking, Trey's new training took over as they came to a stop.

"Are you guys okay?"

"Yeah."

"Stay here," Trey barked. He put on the flashers and put the car in park. *Black Mercedes—two o'clock. Go get him.* Trey's adrenaline surged as he jumped out of his car.

He sprinted toward the Mercedes and scanned the plates. *Diplomatic tags, what's that? Was this guy targeting me? Why is he weaving in traffic?*

Trey caught up to the sedan at the stoplight and pounded the hood. The car swerved around him, into the oncoming lane down O Street to Twentieth, then turned right on Q Street.

Bullshit, he's gonna head down Q to try and beat the light—avoid the traffic circle. I'll run through to the other side of Q—intercept them. He won't see me coming.

Trey's instincts were dead-on. The Mercedes stopped midway down Q and turned on its flashers. Trey ran down the sidewalk and approached on the opposite side of the street. He stood for a moment and watched. The driver and his passenger got out of the car.

"Stop!" Trey yelled and sprinted across the two-lane street. Four feet away, he dove at the startled driver with his full body weight and slammed him back into the car. Trey pulled back and assumed his new combat stance. The driver was stunned and reached for his waist band. Trey saw the barrel of the gun rise in the man's grip right as the DCPD descended.

"Freeze!"

After twenty minutes of questioning, the diplomat's car was impounded pending an investigation. Trey was pissed but sat on the curb as instructed with his hands on his head. Both the DCPD and US Secret Service had responded to this most unusual traffic accident, due not only to the proximity to the White House, but also the involvement of a diplomat. Trey scanned the street and saw more lights flashing as police arrived. Two familiar figures stepped between the DCPD and headed toward him. Jeni and Rick walked down the closed-off street.

As they approached, Trey tried to stand. "It's not my fault—"

"Sit down and shut the fuck up." Rick glared at Trey.

Trey returned to the curb.

Rick ignored him, flashing his badge to the two Secret Service agents and now six DCPD officers on the scene. "Can we talk, please?"

The officers nodded and they stepped away. Trey watched as Rick talked with the agents and police. They shook hands and suddenly both the diplomat and his driver were released. They were allowed to leave on foot. A tow truck arrived, and the black sedan was driven away on the flat bed.

After fifteen minutes, Jeni and Rick walked back to Trey. They did not speak but only motioned for him to join them in the white BMW. Jeni opened the passenger door. She tilted her head for Trey to get in.

"I'm going to give you guys a moment," Jeni said. "Rick, pick me up at Starbucks after you drop him off."

Jeni headed toward DuPont Circle.

Trey got in and buckled his seatbelt. The silence was deafening, and he could see from Rick's stiff jaw that he was pissed.

Rick started the ignition, but remained in park. He gripped the wheel, turned, and stared at Trey.

"I have one question. What the *fuck* were you thinking?"

"Me? That asshole hit *my* car. It was their fault. I was *defending* myself."

"Defending yourself?"

"Yeah," Trey said defiantly.

"Defending yourself. Interesting. Let's break this down." Rick's tone deepened. "So you were defending yourself when you left your freaked-out friends and ran five blocks? Defending yourself when you punched the hood of that sedan and caused a police alert for the 'crazy young man chasing a car through DuPont Circle'? Or defending yourself when you nearly broke the collarbone of the Syrian cultural attaché's driver?" Rick paused. "So, in light of this *new* information, Trey, please answer my question. What were you thinking?"

"Fine! I wasn't thinking. I got pissed and was scared for my friends. He totally intentionally side-swiped us!" Trey saw Rick's raised eyebrows. "But I should have reacted more like *normal* and stayed with my friends. And I guess let the police handle it," he said calmly, feeling a bit defeated. "I'm sorry."

"Oh yeah, you're sorry? Wow, that makes it all better," Rick hissed. "Trey Allen Carter, this is *not* a game. Germany is two days from now. You'd better be glad that Jeni and I had eyes on you. This is contained for now," he said, motioning to the scene in front of them. "You know what they asked me?"

Trey shook his head.

"What was I going to do with you—give you a lecture or an application?"

Rick popped the car into drive and drove Trey back to his own car in silence, where his friends were talking to a female uniformed DCPD.

"Look, um—I'm sorry," Trey said softly as he unbuckled to get out and join his friends.

Rick grabbed his arm. "Not one word to them. Are we green?"

"Yes."

"You go to that BBQ and concert tonight like all is good. You're damn lucky, Trey, that you're only getting a lecture from me. Now I get to have *my* lecture from Claren about *your* temper."

"I'm sorry. I get it."

"Do you? I hope so. I'll see you in Munich. Stay out of trouble."

"I will."

"You better. Darius isn't near as nice as me."

Trey got out of the car.

As the white BMW sped away, Trey's friends immediately laid into him.

"What were you thinking?"

"Are you stupid, dude? You could've gotten killed!"

"You are such a redneck sometimes."

Mark and Mike took turns grilling Trey.

The DCPD officer stood by and watched. "You should listen to your friends. The car's fine, but you need to get that mirror fixed."

"Yes, ma'am."

"You're lucky as shit that I ain't hauling your ass to jail." She tore off a written warning and handed it to him.

"Yes, ma'am. Thank you."

"You boys get outta here before I change my mind."

They went to the BBQ with the story of the accident and Trey's crazy attempt to catch the guys that had gotten away. He wanted to tell them the truth, but knew that he couldn't.

The burden of his secrets compounded in that moment. Trey feared that he was slipping from his past into an uncertain future. He looked around the small gathering and wondered when they would all be together again. A strange new feeling washed over him. Even in the midst of his college friends, he suddenly felt alone.

CHAPTER 56
CONCERT

They poured into RFK and found their section. The video monitors flickered and suddenly the lights went dark except for a singular spotlight. The guitar riff echoed and the crowd erupted under the dark summer sky. A second spotlight widened as Bono took the stage with the band and opened with "Where the Streets Have No Name." The lyrics spoke to Trey on a deep level. It was exactly how he felt.

The whole night was an incredible concert. He blocked out the accident, Rick, and all the shit from the past month for two solid hours of once-forbidden rock music with his college friends— clinging to an innocence that was now fading.

After the concert, they dropped off Mike and drove back on 66 to Virginia. On the ride, Trey's loneliness finally got the best of him, and he cleared his throat. *You have to tell him. If he walks away—he walks. Trust him.*

"Mark, I need to tell you something. There's no good way to do this."

"Yeah?"

"Listen, I've been wanting to tell you for a while now, but . . ."

"But what?"

"I, uh . . . I don't know. Today, the accident, then the concert tonight. I need to tell somebody."

"Okay—"

"I . . . I don't like girls." Trey exhaled deeply and gripped the steering wheel.

"What do you mean, you don't like girls?"

"I think that I'm— No, I know that I'm . . . gay."

"Gay?"

"Yeah." Trey never took his eyes off the road. *Oh god, there, I said it. Here it comes—brace yourself.*

"Are you joking me?"

"No," Trey said softly.

"Why are you telling me this? Why tonight? Why now?"

"I don't know. I've been afraid and then at the concert—I thought about the accident. What if I had gotten shot today? You're supposed to be my best friend, and I should've told you before, when I was off the radar."

"Wait, this isn't new news?"

"No. It's why I was off the radar."

"You knew before Liberty? Dude, that was like five or six years ago!"

"Yeah," Trey admitted. *Well, that's it—now you know. That's my truth and this might be our last conversation. Geez, say something, Mark.* "Well?"

"Well, what?" Mark barked. "Am I supposed to say, 'Oh, good for you'? You lied to me."

"No, I didn't." Trey pulled into his parking garage and Mark opened his door. "Wait?"

"I gotta piss, but we're not done talking about this." Mark headed to his apartment.

Trey had wanted to have the conversation in the car for privacy, and not in the apartment where Agency ears were listening.

For two hours, they sat in the apartment with Mark questioning Trey. Mark pulled out Trey's Bible and quoted four or five verses that supported his belief.

"Trey, you're living in sin. Turning your back on your faith, your family, and God."

"What? I tried everything. I went through Exodus ministries. It didn't work."

"Why? Did you really try?" Mark probed.

"Yes! Don't you get it?" Trey asked in desperation. "I have begged God to change me, but it hasn't changed. I tried everything—even slept with a few girls at school to change. Be straight. Be normal."

Still Mark, the litigator from UVA, came at him with more verses and arguments. Trey had known that his friend was a top-tier debate champion but now felt the full force of his skills.

Finally, at 2 a.m., they were exhausted.

"God doesn't make mistakes, Trey. He did not make you gay. You have to change or fight it," Mark said emphatically.

"I have tried—for fifteen years."

"Not hard enough, obviously."

"We'll have to agree to disagree," Trey said.

Mark left the next morning without much talk. It was Wednesday. Trey did not have a job. Rick was gone. His best friend was gone. He wanted to crawl back into bed and pull the shades, but instead he went for a run and then to Worldgate. During his workout, he ran into Sami.

The two young men cruised each other from across the gym and met up in the steam room where they teased each other a bit, uncovering themselves through the steam. Trey wanted to slide over the white-tiled bench and sit next to Sami.

We could touch each other and . . . feel— Shit! What am I doing?

Trey suddenly realized the stupidity of this moment. He was leaving tomorrow for his first assignment with the protocol. This was not a random guy. This was an Egyptian target in whose home he had planted listening devices for his first field test.

Hold the line.

Rick's voice echoed in Trey's head. He abruptly left the steam room, got dressed, and drove home.

An hour later, Trey was watching TV when he heard the double fast chime of his phone. "Hello?"

"Hi, Trey," Rick said.

"Hey, how's Germany?"

"I'm a little jet-lagged, but it's all good. You staying out of trouble?"

"Yeah, I'm fine."

"Talk to me. You're not fine. I can hear it in your voice. What's wrong?"

"You wouldn't understand."

"Will you let me try?"

"I came out to Mark last night after the concert. He grilled me hard, then left this morning. I don't think he's ever going to speak to me again." Trey's voice cracked.

"I know. Jeni called me. I'm so sorry. I heard it was a rather lengthy lecture."

"Damn it. Did everyone listen to the feed?"

"No, only Jeni."

"He's my best friend. What if he never speaks to me again?"

"Look, you have to give him time. People can surprise you if you let them."

"I guess."

"You should work out. It'll make you feel better."

"I ran this morning and then went to Worldgate. I wanted to work out, but I ran into Sami. We kind of flashed each other in the steam room, but I kept my head. I wanted to do more, but I didn't."

"You okay? Do you need to talk about it?"

"No. I miss you though."

"You leave tomorrow with Jeni out of Dulles. She'll pick you up at 1500. Review your papers and intel again tonight. Tomorrow, go resign with your gymnastics gym and get on that plane. I will be here when you arrive Friday morning."

"Got it. I will. Bye, Rick."

"Bye, Trey—Trey?"

"Yeah?"

"Semper protege," Rick said.

"Semper protege."

Trey hung up the call and dialed his parents. He chatted briefly about not much at all. He'd been worried that Mark had outed him, so he was relieved when his mother blathered on about his niece and nephew and then some other women in her church.

"Can you believe that she said that?"

Not interested in her gossip, he simply said, "No, that's crazy."

"Exactly. I told her as much."

"Listen, I have to go—early morning tomorrow. Love you guys."

"Love you, son. Take care of yourself."

"I will."

Jeni picked Trey up and drove them to Dulles airport. They parked and separated at the car. She would be traveling several aisles away but within sight. They passed through security and on to the gate. Seeing Jeni from a distance while traveling alone was comforting. At a newsstand, Trey picked up the book that Rick had been reading, *Interview with the Vampire*.

They boarded, and Trey looked back to see Jeni take her seat, three rows behind him. As the wheels pulled up and the Lufthansa 747 took off, he was relieved. His manager at the gymnastic gym had understood that with his new job, his schedule was too hectic, but they'd left the door open to sub and return to coach one day. Trey went through his checklist and reviewed the assignment four times over. He had spoken to his parents, but had not heard from Mark.

Hopefully, he'll reach out in a week or so. He can't stay mad at me forever. That's it—everything is in order.

As the plane lifted, Trey closed his eyes. *When we land in Germany. Game on. No more training, no more lectures. What'll happen after all this? Global Airways? Will I ever see Rick again?*

Rick's words echoed in his thoughts. *"Step by step, Tiger—focus on the next step."*

Guess the next step is Ivan.

CHAPTER 57
PREP

Wednesday, July 22, 1992
Munich, Germany

"Ich bin geschäftlich hier. Textilien. 3 Tage," Rick said to the German customs agent who nodded and quickly stamped his Canadian alias passport. "Wow, the airport is beautiful. When did you open?"

"In May—but we're still getting used to it. I miss Munich-Riem," she said.

"Ja, Veränderungen können schwierig sein."

"Ja. Nice German, Mr. Stuart, for a Canadian."

Rick smiled.

"Have a good day."

Rick exited customs and stepped into the arrival hall of the new Munich Airport. *Whoa! I've been away too long. Hope they still have my favorite rental.* He exited with his rental agreement and looked for spot thirty-seven. *Sweet!* The red Volkswagen GTI hatchback was a welcome sight. He got in and revved the engine. *Purrs like a kitten. Perfect.* He pulled over to a pay phone near a fuel station and checked in with the Frankfurt station desk.

The ops team gave Rick a drop location and the name of a field agent to meet at a local café.

He arrived and ordered a coffee. An attractive redheaded woman named Catherine met him within ten minutes.

"Rick, how are you? How was your flight?" Catherine greeted him and casually set a small black bag at his feet.

"Good, thanks for taking care of my equipment. Customs gets too snoopy these days to bring it over." He nodded to the bag.

"Yeah, reunification is pushing us all. Sorry, but I could only get you a couple of Gs though—no double Ss."

Huh, Glocks versus Sig Sauers. "No worries. Thanks."

"You look tan and fit. Have you been on assignment in Greece?"

"No, been stateside for the past two months prepping for our engineer."

"Huh, well we should be good to go. Here are the new surveillance photos." She slid a manila envelope across the table. "I've also confirmed that he's holding a reservation at the inn we discussed. We secured the adjoining suite."

"Perfect."

"Do you need anything else?"

"No, I'm good. I'll check out things here in the city and then prep the rooms at the inn."

"Sounds good. Let me know if you need anything else."

"Will do."

"When do Jeni and the civ-5 get here?"

"Tomorrow."

"Still can't believe you found and trained a civ so quickly. Was it weird?"

"No, what do you mean?"

"I heard he's *gay*. Was he squeamish or soft on the training?"

Real subtle, you homophobic bitch—answer her and get this done. "No, in fact—the kid's a beast."

"Really? Did he try to hit on you?"

Are you fucking kidding me? Rick never broke his gaze. "What?"

"I know I would have." She smiled.

"No, great to see you, Catherine. I'll check back in if I need anything."

"Just call me—there's a Comsat in there as well."

"Will do." He stood.

Catherine stood and hugged him. She planted two kisses, one on each cheek, and she was gone.

Rick chugged his espresso, grabbed the bag, and headed for his car. *Well, she's clearly never heard any rumors about me or our team.*

She thinks I'm straight—well, at least now I know. I've got your number, Catherine. Cunt, I don't want you anywhere near Trey.

In the GTI, he inventoried the contents of the bag: two Glock 17s, four clips, and an encrypted Comsat phone. Rick opened the envelope and found a series of new surveillance photos of Ivan. *Huh, good shots.*

Rick grabbed a quick bite and was heading north on the A9 when the Comsat rang.

"How's Germany?"

"Good, Claren. What's up?"

"I'm still putting out fires here, but everyone's calmed down since Trey's DuPont Circle incident."

"Did Jeni get things squared away with DCPD?"

"Yes. But there are still issues with the Syrians."

"It's strange. Did we find out any more on the diplomats?"

"Not really, not yet—but Trey was telling the truth, Rick," she said. "They hit him. Intentional or not, but they claim he wasn't a target."

"What does that mean?"

"They admit to speeding—seems they were in a hurry to leave a place that, if their ambassador found out, might have them on the next flight home to Damascus."

"Where were they?"

"The Camelot."

"No shit—that dive is still open? So what? They sped away from a strip bar. Why?"

"They were spotted apparently on the street—at least that's their story."

Bullshit—there's no fucking way these guys were only running from a titty bar, then bam—hit Trey. "It doesn't add up. So we're supposed to believe that?"

"OTR—my thoughts exactly, but the attaché says it was an accident. Trey and his friends were in the wrong place at the wrong time."

"Bullshit. Unbelievable. And we can't touch him cause of international law."

"You know as well as I do." She sighed and added, "That is the *official* word for now."

"Well, I don't buy it—"

"You don't have to, Rick."

"So what? We let it go?"

"For *now*, yes."

"Fine, but what about Sami or the professor?"

"Already have a team reviewing their phone transcripts with the Bureau. Yes, there may be more to it but not now." Claren paused. "Now we only focus on Ivan. How's Trey?"

"Fine."

"Jeni said you were pretty hard on him."

"Yeah, I was, but we talked it out."

"Is he solid?"

"Yes."

"You feel he's ready?"

Do we have a choice? Hell, does he even have a choice? "Yeah."

"You okay, Rick?"

"I'm fine, Claren." He clenched his jaw. "Holding the line."

"Great."

"Quick question?"

"Sure."

"What happens after Ivan? We let him go right?"

"Let's get through the next forty-eight hours and then have this conversation. Okay?"

Bullshit—I know that tone. "Fine."

"Good. Keep me posted."

Rick arrived at the Hotel Hellman in Nuremberg, 170 kilometers north of Munich, and checked into his room. After unpacking, Rick fought the urge to call the apartment again to check on Trey. *Check out the adjoining room.*

Knock, knock.

There was no response. Rick picked the lock and opened the door. *So, this is it. Ivan has this room for two nights. Huh, nice. I love these old, family-run Bavarian inns.* Rick scanned the room carefully, then closed his eyes. He pictured every detail: writing desk opposite the queen-size bed, two chairs—one at the desk and the other in the far corner of the room. Two nightstands flanked the bed, and each held heavy ceramic jar lamps. A picture of an old castle hung on the wall opposing the only window. He opened his eyes and confirmed the details. Using his training, Rick then counted the steps from the adjoining door to the bed. *Three strides and I got you.*

He returned to his room and shut the door.

The afternoon sun was low, and he needed to monitor the three drop spots. Tonight, he would drive back to Munich and review both bookstores to double-check layouts, back rooms, video booths, exits, and security. They were now twenty-four hours away from green light on the assignment. Rick knew that reviewing the mechanics of Ivan's BDSM would be frightening to Trey, so he'd opted to tell him in Vieques. *Talked him through it but used the clinical tone Doc M recommends. Reviewed the basics of role-play, domination, bondage, and various toys. No judgments, none of my corny jokes. Dry and tactical.*

In preparation, Rick had tried to anticipate all possibilities—but more than a decade had taught him that with any assignment, there was always the potential of a wrinkle or unexpected shift.

At 2300, Rick drove back to Munich and carefully scanned both adult bookstores over the course of two hours, disappointing several patrons who tried to engage with him in the back rooms. He made notes of walls, exits, and general layouts. At 0145, he called it a night and drove the 170 kilometers back to Nuremberg in a little over an hour.

Exhausted, Rick crawled into bed.

Buzz, buzz.

Rick slammed the alarm clock off. *Geez, Dad would say "Bet my pants are still swinging on the bed post from last night." No rest till this is done.* He showered and again drove the route back to Munich airport early Friday morning. As he exited the car, he grabbed his fake name badge and hotel arrival prop.

Jeni and Trey were under aliases and using Canadian passports. Rick met them outside customs with a small sign. *Hellman Hotel— Sarah and Marcus.*

Jeni waved. "Mr. Stuart?"

"Yes," Rick said. "Ms. Gilbert?"

"Uh-huh, and my brother, Marcus."

Rick smiled. "Hey, Marcus."

"Hey," Trey said and rolled his eyes as they greeted one another casually with their aliases. They exited and packed into the awaiting GTI.

"How was the flight?"

"Long but not too bad," Jeni said. "I slept mostly—how about you, Trey?"

"Yeah, I tried to sleep but ended up reading."

"What are you reading?" Rick asked.

"*Interview with the Vampire.*"

"What do you think?"

"So far so good. What's with all the alias names at the airport?"

"SOP—you never know who's watching," Jeni said. "Be glad there's no facial disguise or wigs. So hot and itchy. Right?"

"Yup," Rick said. "Besides—you got to pick your name."

"I guess." He sat in the back seat and stare out at the German countryside.

"Is this your first time in Europe?" Jeni asked.

"No, my brother was stationed in England for a few years. I visited him a couple of times. It's so green here."

"Yeah, this is known as Bavaria."

"Whoa, I didn't think there'd be cows here."

"Ha! There's a lot of farms here, Trey. Maybe you and Rick can sightsee a bit after the assignment." Jeni smiled at Rick.

"Cool. How long is the ride to the hotel?"

"About an hour," Rick said.

"Y'all mind if I sleep?"

"Go for it." Rick glanced up in the rearview mirror as Trey closed his eyes.

"Can I use the Comsat?" Jeni asked.

"Sure." Rick dug it out of the side-door pocket and handed it to her.

"Need to confirm our arrival with Darius for Claren." She dialed the number and paused. "Darius, what's up? We're green. Our bird is in the nest." She paused and then added, "Excellent, I'll check back in later. Uh-huh, will do." She hung up and turned to Rick and nodded. "Any news from Catherine?"

"Yeah, Ivan's confirmed at the inn for two nights. The rooms are exactly as we outlined."

"Good."

Trey awoke as they arrived at the hotel. They grabbed their bags and went up to their room. Jeni unpacked her equipment and they reviewed the basics of the assignment.

"Did Catherine have new surveillance?" Jeni asked.

"Yeah, here's the new pics," Rick said and laid them out on the bed.

"Nice. These are from Prague?" she asked.

"Yup. Four days ago."

Trey picked up one of the photos and studied the face of Ivan Dimitri. "Why is he looking at the camera in this one?"

"He's not. It only seems like that," Rick explained. "We use high-speed photography and capture nearly a hundred shots. These were selected for the clarity of his face."

Trey drop the photo.

"So, like we discussed—he's going to be instantly attracted to you, but he also needs to see you as willing," Rick said.

"And a submissive," Jeni added.

Trey narrowed his eyes and frowned slightly. "What kinds of things should I say or do? You know, to make it seem like I'm willing?"

"So, keep it short at first. I would say something like 'Have you seen my dad? I've been bad,'" Rick said.

"Exactly," Jeni said. "If he bites, then he'll extend an offer to discipline you or be your 'dad.'"

Trey frowned and shook his head.

"Hey, remember what I said in Vieques?"

"*It's not real. Hold the line,*" Trey said.

"Exactly."

"But it's so weird and sorta bogus."

Jeni smiled. "I know, Trey, but believe me, even in the real world, you should hear some of the shit guys have said as pickup lines."

Trey relaxed his shoulders.

"Look, it's no big deal," she said. "Some people, like our engineer, like to play games and take on roles. Think of it as part of your persona within this assignment."

"Okay, I guess."

"You can do this—remember you're pretending," Jeni said.

"That's it, though. What if he sees through me—I kinda feel like I have to really feel it."

Rick nodded but did not interrupt Jeni.

"Look, your body position is also important. I brought over some of Doc M's notes for us. He suggests that you kneel and present your wrists for binding," Jeni said.

"Kneel? Why?"

Rick noticed Trey's shoulders go rigid again and his left cheek twitch slightly. *Shit! He's getting spooked.* "Trey, don't stress. Remember when we met?"

"Yeah."

"Hold up your hands."

"Like when you zip-tied me during my intake?"

"Exactly," Rick said.

"Look, it'll feel weird, but if you need to believe—then go with it. Be submissive," Jeni said.

"How?"

"Think of your Christian school. You told me you used to get paddled by your male teachers. Right?" Rick said.

"Yeah."

"Well, in that moment, they held the power, but you had to yield to that power. Make sense?"

"I didn't have much choice, but I get what you're saying."

"You got paddled in high school?" Jeni asked.

"You have no idea. It hurt like hell," Trey answered.

"Wow, well, this will be a bit easier then." She shrugged. "Remember, though, you need to be committed but also thinking ahead. Ivan is more than likely going to be excited and want to take things a bit further than he did in Berlin. You need to allow him to think that's cool with you. The goal is to come back here."

"How?"

"Tell him you are staying at the hostel here in Nuremberg but that it's not safe to play there," Rick coached. "Too many guests. He'll then decide to bring you here."

"Okay, but what if he ties me up? In Munich instead?"

"Do not let him do that at the bookstore. Got it?"

"Yeah."

"If he offers to bring you back here—go with him. We'll be tracking you with this." Jeni held up a small tag. "We'll be tracking your every move."

"Even here?"

"Especially, here. You aren't alone," Rick interrupted. "We'll be right here. Nine feet away and watching every move." He motioned to the monitors and computers that Jeni had unpacked. "We'll see everything."

"Okay." Trey again relaxed his body as Jeni clipped their tracking tag to his shirt tail.

She then repeated the dialogue in both English and German. They took a break for lunch. Trey studied the dialogue written in corresponding sentences, English and German. It was now 1400.

"Guys, I'm gonna lay down for a bit. Okay?"

"Of course," Jeni said. "I'll wake you up in an hour."

Trey fell asleep.

Jeni and Rick opened the adjoining room. They wheeled in a small case.

"How many cameras do we have?" Rick asked.

"They only spec'd three, but I knew you'd want five, handsome." Jeni opened the case.

"You so get me. I'd marry you tomorrow."

"You wish. Besides you're packing the wrong equipment for me." She made a V with her right hand and stuck out her tongue.

"How is it possible you're worse than me?"

She winked.

He shook his head.

They positioned all five of the micro cameras in the room at various angles using the furniture, blinds, artwork and desk lamp to conceal them. Rick scanned the room several times as Jeni returned to her monitors to test each one.

"We're good," she said. "Even in low light—if he turns off some lights."

"Good, but hang on." Rick pointed to one remaining camera. "I can still see this one. What if we put it in the bathroom?"

"Huh, yeah why not." Jeni helped him place it above the casement lights below the drop ceiling. "Can you see it?"

"Nope. We're good."

Jeni glanced at her watch. "All set. Both the Prague and Frankfurt ops desks are here in the area and on standby." She glanced at the young man sleeping and whispered to Rick. "He's jet-lagged."

"Yeah, it's good he's resting up for tonight."

Jeni nodded. "You know—I think he is going to nail it, but I'm a little worried."

"About what?"

"I don't know. I got my twinge."

"You're not a sha-mannequin and neither was your grandma—"

"It's Shamanka." Jeni narrowed her eyes. "And yes she was. Now, did we miss something in the setup?"

"No." Rick brought his finger to his lips and motioned. They walked back into the adjoining room. "So, what's your *twinge* telling you?"

"If Ivan invites him back here and he has his *toys*, then he may push things. We have to be ready . . . especially if it escalates as quickly as it did in Berlin."

"We'll be on go. Nine feet."

"I know, but . . ." She paused.

"What?"

"Ivan's getting braver and taking more risks."

"I'm counting on that," Rick said. "Trey can handle himself, Jeni. After a month of KM, he's getting lethal. My only worry is his ability to stay calm when the inhalant kicks in. If he's bound or blindfolded—"

"What?"

"He may freak out before the sedation renders him unconscious. How long does it take?"

"Usually five to seven minutes from inhale."

"Then he's out for twenty or thirty minutes?"

"Yeah, but really until we jab him with adrenaline."

"We monitor and capture. Should be plenty of time to get the pics we need."

"And video," she added.

"The real question is what will Ivan do when Trey goes unresponsive and blue?" Rick widened his eyes. "The clock will be ticking. He better freak out and bolt so we can get in here and revive him."

"He will. I've seen it a few times . . . it's fucking freaky how real it seems. Trust me, Ivan will freak and believe he's killed Trey," Jeni whispered.

Rick nodded. "Then he bolts and the teams take him in. Either in the parking lot or at the border. Right?"

"That's really for them—they just have to nab him." She shrugged.

Rick shook his head slightly. "It'd be better at the border."

The Comsat rang. Jeni ran back to retrieve it.

"Yes? How much time? Okay, thanks. Yeah, we're green." She hung up. "That was the support team. Ivan's five minutes out. Ready?"

"Yeah." Rick suddenly saw Trey in the doorway.

"So, this is the altar where I'll be offered up, like Isaac bound by Abraham?"

"Okay, I grew up barely a Catholic so I don't know that story too well, Trey, but yeah, sounds about right." Jeni grinned.

Rick shook his head slightly. "I'll never fully understand you, Tiger. Come here." He motioned to Trey to enter the room. "The most important thing in this room is right here. See it?" Rick pointed to the flash of the metal handle of the knife that was barely visible between the mattress and bed frame at the foot. "If you panic, remember that this blade is here."

"And we're only nine steps over there." Jeni pointed. "We've got tiny cameras and audio plants all around this room."

"Five of 'em," Rick interjected.

"Eyes and ears. You're *not* alone, Trey." Jeni smiled and returned to the adjoining room.

"Ready?" Rick asked.

"Yeah."

"You're going to be okay, Tiger." Rick leaned in and whispered, "Semper protege."

Trey nodded.

"Hey, guys, Ivan's here," Jeni called out from the next room.

Rick and Trey exited Ivan's room and shut the adjoining door. They joined Jeni at the window and watched as their target exited his blue Peugeot with Czech plates carrying two bags into the inn.

"Excellent. Looks like he brought his toys," Jeni said.

Trey shook his head and stood rigid.

Rick sensed his tension and placed his hand on his shoulder.

The three stood in silence as they heard the turning of the lock and the door open in the adjoining room. Jeni turned on the monitors via her laptop and they saw Ivan shuffle around the room before heading to the toilet.

Ivan stood rigid as his flow hit the water for more than a minute.

"Guess it was a long drive from Prague," Rick whispered and widened his eyes. Trey rolled his eyes as Jeni shook her head. "Just say'n."

Ivan changed his clothes and stowed his things. He left the inn and a moment later the Comsat rang.

"Yeah?" Jeni answered. "You're tailing him. Uh-huh, train station. Munich. Okay." She hung up and nodded to Rick.

"Ready."

Trey nodded but his hands gripped the arms of the chair. His heart pounded as Rick and Jeni stood. *I guess this is it.* He stood slowly. "Let's get this over with."

They walked down the stairs and out the back door of the inn to the small parking lot. They got in the car and sat in silence as Rick sped the 170 kilometers back to Munich. Rick glanced at Trey in the rearview mirror and caught his eyes.

"You good?"

"Yeah. I'm nervous, but like you always say, 'Use your nerves, don't let 'em use you.' Right?"

"You got it."

"Here's your earpiece, Trey." Jeni handed him this device.

He plugged his ear and she tested the signal.

"Testing 1, 2, 3 . . . you copy?"

"Yeah, loud and clear."

Rick parked the car and they waited.

On time, Ivan emerged from the station and entered a café.

"Showtime?" Trey asked.

"You got this, Tiger." Rick held out his fist. They bumped. "Relax. We're here."

Trey crossed the street away from their parked car and headed toward the café.

I need to calm down. Trey's heart threatened to beat out of his chest. *I need a song. "99 Luftballons."* In his head, Trey sang with Nena as he walked the two blocks toward the blackened door and neon entrance of the New Man adult bookstore.

CHAPTER 58
DESIRE

*F*ear not for I am with thee, fear not for I am with thee. Over and over, Trey repeated Isaiah 41:10 as he watched Ivan Dimitri enter, pause, and then scan the dark back room of the bookstore arcade. *I knew he saw me. Geez, I wish that I had kept the earpiece now. "Relax, Tiger."* Rick's voice echoed in his mind. *That's what he'd say right now. He's right—relax your shoulders. Lean back in a submissive stance like Jeni said with your arms crossed behind your back.* Trey assumed the position and waited. Ivan did not move. *What's he doing? I know I'm not supposed to make direct eye contact but that doesn't feel right.*

Trey's heart pounded as the seconds ticked. Still, his target did not move.

Screw it.

Instantly, Ivan locked eyes with his. Trey looked away but could sense that Ivan was crossing the room.

Oh god, help me.

"Wonach suchen Sie?" Ivan asked.

What does that mean? Looking for?

Trey looked up into Ivan's eyes. He softened his face and tried to express desire through his eyes as Doc M's notes had suggested.

Say your first phrase. "Ich war schlecht und ich bin für meinen Vater," Trey said.

Ivan narrowed his eyes. "You bad, look for father?" Ivan said in accented English.

Trey only nodded.

"What is nice boy do in dis place?"

"You speak English?"

"Ja, All-American boy?"

"Yes, sir. I'm American."

"Ja, Air Force?"

Trey again nodded. "I took the train down from Frankfurt—from my base."

"Why you come here? Secret?"

"Yes."

"You want d' pleasure?"

"Yes. Can you teach me, sir?" Trey extended his wrists and crossed them.

"Ja." Ivan scanned the room. "No here."

"Too many eyes watching us?" Trey asked.

"Ja."

"Could we go somewhere private? I have to be so careful."

Ivan shifted his weight and pivoted. He leaned against the wall beside Trey. "Ja, I too careful. Where you stay? Munich?"

"No. Nuremberg."

Ivan narrowed his eyes.

Oh god, he's studying me. Be real, don't lie. I am *staying in Nuremberg.* Trey inhaled slowly.

"Where?" Ivan's stare deepened.

"A hostel, but it is not very private. There's a lot of people staying there." Trey bit his lip. "I don't have the money to get a hotel room."

"I do." Ivan leaned in closer and whispered, "Me stay Nuremberg too."

"Really?"

"You want? Come wh'd me?"

"Yes, sir."

Ivan put his arm around Trey and gently pulled him off the wall. "Now?"

"Yeah."

Just like that? He doesn't seem mean or dangerous as they'd said. He even looks younger. More fit. Oh god, I can't believe I'm doing this.

As they walked through the bookstore and to the exit, Trey's heart pulsed deeper in his chest.

They exited the blackened door and walked toward the train station. Trey did not need to pretend. Goose bumps now covered his arms despite the warm night air.

"You cold?" Ivan asked.

"Yes."

Ivan removed his leather jacket and wrapped it around Trey.

The smell of his cologne and the leather startled Trey. *He's nicer than I thought. What if they're wrong? What if he's innocent?*

They put their tickets into kiosks and entered the awaiting platform. The train arrived in minutes.

Trey reached into his pocket and felt both the indentation of the tracking tag and the inhaler. As the train left the station, they sat opposite one another in the warm rail car as it rattled its way to Nuremberg.

Trey removed Ivan's jacket and handed it to him. "Thank you?"

Ivan smiled slightly.

"Whattha fuck!" Rick blurted out as he looked up from the dashboard.

"What?" Jeni asked. "Oh my god—"

"Is he wearing Ivan's jacket?" Rick cranked the car.

"Holy shit! Are you kidding me? Eighteen minutes flat! Forty-five days, and he nabbed him in less than twenty minutes?"

"I know. This is crazy. Buckle up." Rick revved the engine. "Better call the support teams now."

"On it. Damn, I knew Trey had it, but—" Jeni shook her head.

"Right? Me too."

"Seriously, how many failed attempts were there to get to Ivan?"

"Like five or six. And that's only us—nearly a dozen if you count the Brits and Mossad."

"How the hell does he walk in and walk out—wrapped in his *jacket* no less." She dialed the team. "News flash—our civ-5 and the target are on the train. Yes, right now. I know—we'll be there in forty minutes. Right. Standing by."

"Are they all set?" Rick weaved through traffic.

"Yeah, they were grabbing a bite—they couldn't believe it either." Jeni turned. "We should probably call Claren but—"

"Doc M."

"Yup." Jeni shook her head. "I can picture him looking over his glasses with that smug expression. 'Of course, our civ-5 has followed the protocol.'" She mimicked his tone.

"I hate when he's right."

"Me too. Did he tell you that it could go so fast?"

"Kind of. Remember all that bullshit in his notes about *desire*."

"Oh, right. 'Desire is a powerful drug. The hope of quenching a secret lust has made men lose their minds throughout history.'" She mimicked the good doctor. "Seriously, who talks like that?"

"No, it's more like, 'Control or the façade of control will over time lead a man to higher and *higher* risks,'" Rick mocked.

"Speaking of risks." Jeni nodded. "Can you really beat the train back to Nuremberg?"

Rick grinned and gunned the engine of the GTI.

Should I try to speak with him more? What's he thinking? Trey tried not to stare. He glanced and observed Ivan looking out the window. *He's lost in thoughts. Wonder if he's nervous too?*

An hour passed between them with only a few sentences. Ivan picked up his jacket from the empty adjacent seat. "Dis station. Ready?" Ivan stood.

"Oh, this is us." Trey grabbed the overhead handle as the train arrived at Nuremberg. They exited.

Is Rick, Jeni, or the support teams here? Trey scanned the train station but did not see any familiar faces.

"Walk behind. Wait in da pub. I get you ready. Ja?"

"Yes, sir."

Trey walked twenty feet behind Ivan all the way to the inn. Ivan would turn and glance back to see if Trey was following. He nodded to the pub entrance and disappeared into the stairwell entrance. Trey sat at the bar and ordered a beer. *Nobody's here—or at least none of them look like our team. Where's Rick?*

Trey thought about Ivan as he waited. *What's he prepping? What if I walked out right now. Then what? Would they still out me? Damn, Mark may have already done that.* He felt the inhalant in his pocket.

I don't even know what this drug is or how it's gonna feel—can't believe I'm doing this! He sipped his beer and heard Rick's words in his mind. *Hold the line. One and done—then you're free to go.*

Trey patiently waited in the pub nursing his beer. *Rick? Jeni? Where are you? Upstairs monitoring Ivan? That's Rick—'bout time.* Rick came into the pub and ordered a beer. He all but ignored Trey as he took a seat in the far corner of the room. *He's scanning the patrons.*

Rick never made eye contact with Trey but he could feel his eyes on him.

I'm glad you're here. Don't leave me, Rick. Trey sipped his beer and tried to calm his thoughts. *No matter what happens in that room—get through it. Then move on. Global Airways—I have my training in Philly next month.* Trey looked up and saw in the back mirror the image of Ivan entering the bar. *This is it. What am I doing here? Geez, it's bad enough I have to let this stranger touch me. But Rick and Jeni will be watching and recording it!*

"Ready," Ivan said behind him.

Trey nodded and took one last chug of his beer. They walked up the narrow stairs of the inn and down the hall. As rehearsed, Trey pulled out his inhaler and took a hit in full view of Ivan.

"Asthmatic?"

"Yes, I have to use it when I get nervous or excited."

Ivan nodded and opened his room door.

As they entered, Trey nearly froze at the items on the bed. *Oh god, a towel, rope, duct tape, and a leather harness—what?*

"Clothes off," Ivan said sternly.

"What?" *I gotta get out of here. My head feels foggy—how can the drug hit this quickly?* Trey suddenly felt the first tinge of the drug moving in his system. He took a deep breath and steadied himself.

"Clothes off, bad boy!" Ivan barked.

"Wait, please stop. I can't do this." Trey again took a deep breath. "I've never done this before."

"Never?" Ivan's tone softened.

Trey shook his head. He felt his eyes welling up.

Ivan reached for him. "You want pleasure, no?"

"Yes, but—"

"Me help." Ivan unbuttoned Trey's shirt and motioned to the bed. Trey sat down as his head continued to swirl.

Ivan removed Trey's shirt, shoes, and socks. He gently pushed Trey back and removed his pants and underwear. He took both of Trey's hands and pulled him to stand.

Ivan stood back and stared at Trey's naked body. "Good."

He kicked off his shoes and his shirt. Trey saw a scar on his left pectoral along with a small tattoo on his left shoulder of two Russian letters. Trey's head was foggy and he reached for Ivan, who allowed him to hug him.

"Please go slow."

"Ja. Ja. We have night."

Trey knelt and unbuckled Ivan's black leather belt and jeans. *He's commando—no underwear—and smooth.* Ivan palmed the top of Trey's head and stared down at him. *Give him your wrists.* Trey sat back and leaned against the foot of the bed. He felt the cold blunt blade handle against his back. *You can do this—he's nicer than you thought, better looking. Give in and get this done.* Trey extended his arms submissively to Ivan.

A cold expression washed over Ivan as he took both wrists in his hands. He scooped up the rope and tied a tight knot around Trey's right wrist. Ivan pulled him to his feet.

Head rush. Stay alert. Stay calm. Ouch, what is he doing?

Ivan's grip tightened. "Ready?"

"Yeah." Trey felt his body lift and fall onto the bed. Suddenly, Ivan grabbed him and flipped him over to his stomach. He felt his arms bend back as the rope tightened. Ivan bound his arms behind him.

Ouch! This is not how we trained. It was supposed to be in front. Argh—stop tightening the knot.

Ivan finished the knot, leaving Trey on his stomach with arms bound. The pain in his shoulders pulled Trey from the fog of the drug working through his veins.

Rick? This is not what you said. What is he doing? Trey glanced around the room in panic. *I can't get to the blade handle like this. Rick, please be there.*

"Whoa! That is not like we thought, Rick," Jeni said.

"No." Rick stared intently at the monitor.

"Look how he's tying the knot. He's no amateur," Jeni said.

"This feels off. Are you getting this all?"

"Yes, all the cameras are live," she confirmed.

Rick stared at the screen but picked up the Comsat. "We are green. Rolling. Be ready. This could go down quickly. Great—copy that. Standing by."

Jeni shook her head as she monitored the equipment.

"Stay calm, Trey."

Trey tried to relax his arms as any tension on the knots sent pain shooting down his shoulders, back and arms. He began to feel the chaffing of the rough rope on the skin of his wrists and forearms.

"Sir, please don't hurt me too badly. I have to be back on base Sunday."

"Ruhiger Junge! Quiet!" Ivan straddled him and leaned down to his ear. "Must be quiet. Pain, pleasure."

Ivan showed Trey a washcloth from the bath. He covered Trey's eyes with the cloth. In the darkness, Trey heard the screeching of the duct tape as the blindfold tightened. Total darkness enveloped him. Ivan's weight left the bed. Trey listened intently, and the heavy belt buckle hit the ground. *He's naked now. Rick please don't leave here with him. Rick?*

"Stay calm, Trey. Stay calm," Rick said softly to the monitors as if Trey could hear him in the next room.

"Well, we knew that this wasn't his first time playing, but—what's he doing now?"

"Shit. He's hog-tying him." Rick reached for one of the Glocks and inspected the weapon, then repeated, "Stay calm, Tiger."

Jeni landed her hand on his and the Glock. "You need to stay calm too."

For a moment, Trey did not hear other sounds after the rattle of Ivan's pants dropping to the floor. Ivan's weight returned to the bed. He roughly pushed Trey face down. With fear spiking through him, Trey couldn't stay docile anymore, and he tried to yank his arms from his bindings. *Nothing.* He then felt the rough rope on his ankle, twisting and pulling. *Oh god, he's tying up my legs.* Trey struggled against Ivan and the ropes, but the more he struggled—the tighter the bindings gripped his feet, wrists, and forearms. He was helpless. His mind raced.

Rick? Don't you leave me in here with this freak. Protect me, Rick.

I'm sorry, Trey. Only a few more minutes. Hang on. Don't fight it. Rick stared at the monitors.

"Now what's he doing?" They watched as Ivan stepped off the bed and over to his bag. "What is that?" Jeni asked.

"Looks like a riding crop." Rick shook his head. "How much longer on the inhalant?"

Jeni looked at her timer. "Any minute now—he should be really foggy at this point."

"Hang in there, Trey," Rick whispered.

Rick watched Ivan on the monitor as he seemed to pace around the bed and stare at Trey. *That's definitely a leather riding crop. No.*

Suddenly Ivan's arm pulled back and he struck Trey.

Smack!

"Ouch! What are you doing?"

"Klappe halten!" Ivan hissed.

Trey heard him rustling in a bag. He again felt Ivan on the bed over him. Ivan grabbed his head.

"What? Argh—" A rubbery object was shoved into his mouth. *What the hell? Is he gagging me? Rick! Help me.* "Argh!" Trey screamed, but his voice was muffled by the object and pillow. His arms now ached from his struggle but wave after wave, the drug continued to wash over him. He felt light. Drifting into the darkness.

Protect me, Rick—you swore. Wow, it's . . . so . . . warm . . . now. Trey breathed deeper as his body melted into the warmth.

Again, Ivan smacked the sides of Trey's ass hard.

"Argh," Trey said in low tone. *So tired. Let go. Sleep.*

Through the monitor, Rick and Jeni observed as Ivan stood naked at the foot of the bed. He laid down the crop and put on the black leather harness. He then pulled out of his bag a pair of black chaps and a mask. Ivan took his time getting into the chaps with his groin and ass still exposed. He put on and adjusted the mask with two eye openings and exposed nose and mouth.

"A bound, ball-gagged submissive under his leather-clad persona—well, I guess this is his fantasy," Jeni said. "Doc M can write all the analysis he wants—this guy's a misogynist trying to get his rocks off."

"Maybe, but it's way more elaborate than anything we saw in Berlin," Rick said.

Ivan then slipped on a ring around his genitals.

"No, what? What the hell?" Jeni said.

"It's just a cock ring," Rick said.

"Just?" She shook her head.

Rick ignored her and stared intently at the screen as Ivan again climbed onto the bed. He pushed Trey's knees apart while prying open his thighs.

"Look, he's getting hard." Rick gripped the Glock. "Do we have enough yet?"

"Almost—wait."

"I'm not letting him—"

"Of course not," Jeni interrupted.

Ivan picked up the crop with his right hand while he stroked himself with his left.

Smack, smack!

Ivan hit again and again with the crop.

Oh god, Trey. I'm sorry. Rick turned and saw Jeni wince at the sound of the crop against Trey's sides, buttocks, and back.

"Argh!" The searing pain pulled Trey from the darkness back to the room. He felt Ivan further spread his thighs and searing pain on his exposed scrotum.

"Arghhh!" Fire lanced through Trey, and he cried out in pain. His muffled voice seemed to fall on deaf ears. *Rick? Oh god, can he not hear me?*

"Shh," Ivan whispered.

Trey felt him stroke his head. Ivan's weight shifted and seemed to be lying next to him. For the next several minutes, Ivan's touch alternated between light strokes and searing slashes. *Pleasure and punishment—oh god this is what he enjoys.*

Ivan hit harder and harder.

Ivan suddenly intensified his force—Trey felt searing pain with each slash on his back, legs, arms, and buttocks. Trey dug deep into the darkness and pulled his mind back to the room with all his strength.

"Arghhh!" Trey screamed with all the air in his lungs.

He felt Ivan grab a pillow and cover his head. His thighs were forced apart against the ropes. Trey struggled but could not move. Even as he felt something against his anus—the darkness was closing in. *I can't stay here—can't feel anything.* The searing slashes on his body no longer burned. He drifted deeper into the darkness. His last thoughts flickered in his mind. *Rick, please help me.*

Rick and Jeni sat motionless and watched Ivan hit Trey several times with the crop, harder and harder.

I gotta stop this. "He's cutting him. Look, those aren't welts now. He's bleeding." Rick pointed to weeping slashes visible even in black-and-white on the monitors.

"I know, Rick, but Trey has to stop fighting the inhalant. He has to let go and cross over so Ivan 'kills' him," Jeni said.

"What's taking the drug so long?" Rick shook his head. *I'm so sorry, Trey. It wasn't supposed to go this far. Let go, let go.*

Ivan stopped again and stroked Trey's back. They heard him ask, "You like? Ja?"

There was no response from Trey.

Ivan tilted his head. He removed the pillow from Trey and leaned down. Ivan got off the bed and hit Trey again with the crop.

Trey did not move or flinch.

"It's finally working," Rick whispered.

"'Bout time," Jeni said.

Ivan reached over and felt Trey's bound wrist—then he moved his fingers to Trey's neck.

"Surprise asshole—there's no pulse," Jeni said in a hushed tone.

Ivan pulled back his hand. He removed his mask and returned two fingers to Trey's neck for several seconds. Suddenly, he recoiled.

"That's right, motherfucker—you pushed this too far," Jeni whispered.

Ivan began to pace back and forth.

"Now whatcha gonna do?" Rick said.

They watched Ivan pace by the bed for several minutes.

"What's he waiting for? Come on, pack up and get out." Jeni turned to Rick. "What do you think?"

"We need the team." Rick shook his head and grabbed the Comsat. "Guys, are you there? Our bird is sleeping but the target isn't running. Repeat, target isn't running. Get ready. We'll monitor but if we need to intercept—can you intake here?" Rick nodded to Jeni. "Good, standing by."

Jeni grabbed the other Glock and inspected it. They remained fixated on the monitors. Rick motioned as Ivan finally moved. He scooped up his mask and put it back on.

"That is not a good sign." Jeni shook her head.

Ivan crawled back onto the bed and started to masturbate.

He moved closer to Trey and pulled his knees apart. He reached down.

"Is he fingering him? No fucking way," Rick hissed and bolted to the door, when Jeni stopped him.

"Wait, Rick. Look, look, I think he stopped." She motioned back at the monitor.

Rick glanced back as Ivan again began inching closer to Trey.

"Oh shit." Jeni grabbed the Comsat. "Taking target down now." She tossed the Comsat and grabbed the gun. "Wait, Rick. The hallway door."

"What?"

"We need to enter from the hall to keep our cover."

"Oh, right." They quietly exited and stood at the room door in the empty hallway. Jeni counted them down as Rick stood back to get full leverage. "Five, four, three . . ."

Crash!

Rick smashed in the door, ran into the room, and lunged at Ivan in one fluid motion. Using his body, he slammed Ivan against the wall, knocking off his mask.

"Nicht fucking bewegen!" Jeni barked.

Ivan's eyes widened at the sight of her barrel inches from his face. His eyes darted from the Glock to Rick.

"Hände hoch jetzt, Mutterficker!"

Ivan slowly held up his hands as Rick immediately zip-cuffed his right wrist. He shoved Ivan forward and pulled his hands to cuff his left wrist. Rick stood up.

He quickly nodded to Jeni.

She nodded and held her aim on Ivan's temple. "Bewegen Sie sich nicht!"

Rick turned to Trey and pretended to check for a pulse. When he turned back to Ivan, he pulled out the hood from his back pocket but allowed Ivan one last glimpse of Trey's lifeless body before jamming the hood over his head. Inches from Ivan's face, Rick screamed, "Er ist tot, du Ficker! Du hast ihn getötet!"

He's dead, you fucker! You killed him!

CHAPTER 59
CAPTURE

Two of the support team burst through the door with guns raised. Jeni shook her head and covered her mouth with her index finger. Each agent took a side as Jeni followed with her gun pressed against Ivan's neck. She turned to Rick and widened her eyes.

He motioned to her that he'd stay and she nodded. They disappeared into the hallway.

Rick turned back to Trey. *I'm so sorry, Trey—but it's done. It's over.* He grabbed his blade from between the mattress and went to cut Trey free. *No, she'll need to get a few more photos.*

Jeni returned to the room and pulled the door closed. "Lock's busted," Rick said and handed the camera to her. "Let's hurry—I want to bring him out."

"Of course." She snapped a few photos of the seemingly lifeless young man. Rick checked on Trey several times. He was still unconscious from the inhaler.

"Done?" Rick asked.

"Yeah."

Rick immediately removed the ball gag from Trey's mouth and tossed it in the pile of Ivan's clothes. They quickly packed up all Ivan's belongings and stuffed them into his two duffels.

Rick scanned the room. "I think that's it."

"Yeah, we're good—you ready to bring him back?" Jeni asked.

"Do you mind if I do this alone? He might—"

"No, I get it. This was *intense*, and he'll need help coming down from all this." She motioned around the room. "Let me get Ivan's stuff outta of here so he doesn't see it. Be gentle with him."

"I know, I will."

"Here's the adrenaline. Be ready, you know how fast it works."

Rick nodded and took the syringe. She lifted the duffels and headed to the door. She turned back.

"I mean it. Be gentle."

Jeni returned to the dark parking lot and gave the support team Ivan's duffels.

"Where's he?"

The agent motioned to the black Mercedes idling. She saw three officers standing guard by the trunk where they had placed Ivan.

"Let's finish this—you ready?" Jeni asked.

"Yeah, only in German right?"

"Yeah, follow my lead."

He nodded and they approached the trunk of the car. As instructed, they spoke in German to maintain cover.

"Is he in there," she said aloud in German.

"Yeah. Who called this in?"

"Some of the hotel guests heard shouting—glad we were downstairs at the pub," Jeni said.

"Right. How's the victim?'

"He's dead. We tried to revive him, but he didn't make it."

"Oh my god," the agent responded. "Well, we'll take him in—but we may need to consult with the Czech authorities."

"Why? Is he Czech?" Jeni said, playing along with their dialogue.

"Yeah."

"Why not drive this *trash* back to Prague? Save yourself the headache."

"That's not a bad idea. Let them handle it. They'll most like extradite him anyway."

"Exactly."

"Thanks, I think we might just do that tonight."

They nodded to one another and walked away from earshot of the car. Prague desk Senior Officer Parker Holmes approached Jeni.

"Great work, but we need to get out of here before the locals get wind of this."

"Yeah, we should be good." Jeni looked around.

"How's your civ?"

"Rick'll bring him out of it shortly—he should be okay." She paused. "Hopefully, he won't have too many memories of this night."

"I hear ya—such a sick fucker," Holmes said, pointing to Ivan entombed in the trunk.

"Yeah, but a valuable sick fucker," Jeni added.

"That's what we hear. Who do you suspect was approaching him? Iran or Syria?"

"I don't know. Whoever will pay the most?" Jeni shrugged. "I don't think he has much loyalty."

Holmes nodded. "You good? We're gonna hit the road. It's a long drive back to Prague."

"All good, thanks. Be safe."

He nodded and motioned for his team to exit. One of his agents got in to drive the black Mercedes with him while the other loaded the engineer's things into Ivan's blue Peugeot and followed them as they drove away.

As Jeni watched the Prague team exit, Officer Catherine Marks of the Frankfurt desk flicked her cigarette and stepped over to her.

"Quite a night."

"I'll say," Jeni said.

"You okay?"

"Yeah."

"Need anything else?"

"No, I'll get the footage edited and uploaded for you guys tomorrow," Jeni said. "You think we have enough—the incentive?"

"Hell yes, I mean bondage, gay sex, and murder? I think we have all the incentive we need. We'll take it from here. Thanks."

"Have a safe drive back."

"Oh, tell Rick goodbye for me?"

"Of course." *Geez, you are clueless Catherine. You're not his type.*

Catherine and her team loaded up and drove out, leaving Jeni alone in the dark parking lot. She glanced around and then back at the inn.

Hope Trey's okay.

Oh god, I'm so sorry, Trey. Rick winced as he inspected the deep welts and cuts on Trey's body more closely. *These are deeper than I thought. I need to clean these. It'd be better to irrigate them while he's still under.* Rick grabbed the empty ice bucket from the desk and went to the bathroom. He filled the bucket with warm soapy water and grabbed a washcloth, then returned to Trey. He sat the bucket and washcloth on the nightstand and pulled out his blade. Rick carefully cut each of the knots that had bound Trey.

How to do this on the bed? I don't want to move him yet. He settled for crawling onto the bed alongside him and gently wiping the cuts on his back, buttocks, thighs, and arms. Wringing out the cloth several times in the warm water, Rick cleaned all the cuts he could see before carefully removing the duct tape and blindfold.

"I'm so sorry, Trey," Rick whispered. He rolled Trey over to his back and removed the cap on the syringe of adrenaline. He gently lowered the tip to Trey's sternum to get his aim. He raised his hand up before jabbing the needle into Trey.

He quickly depressed the dosage and removed the needle. Within seconds, Trey jerked and then moaned.

"Aahh."

"Trey, Trey? Can you hear me? I'm right here."

Suddenly, Tray sprang to life and bolted upright. He balled his fists as panic was visible on his face.

"Whoa, Trey, it's me. It's okay."

"Argh! What?"

"Relax, relax. It's me, Tiger." Rick watched the panic in the young man's face turn into confusion and then tears. Rick wrapped his arms around him. "Shh, it's okay. I got you."

Trey shook as he quietly wept in Rick's strong embrace.

"We got him. You did it—you did great."

After a few minutes, Trey regained his composure. "Please don't tell anyone that I broke down."

"Never. You okay?"

"I think so. That stuff hit my head hard."

"What do you remember?"

"He was different than I thought. He was nice to me on the train—then in here, he flipped. Tied me up, so tight I couldn't move. I was scared he was going to—"

"He didn't. I swear to you."

"But he tried to?"

"Yeah."

Trey buried his head into Rick.

"You did everything right. It's hard, to allow yourself to be vulnerable like that. Awkward, right?"

"Yeah, did you see it?"

"Yes. You were never out of my sight. Jeni and I were right over there. He escalated things—so we had to take him down here."

"Where's he now?"

"The support team has him—they're driving him back to Prague. He's gone. You'll never have to face him again."

"My back is killing me." Trey leaned forward. "What happen? Did he cut me?"

"Yeah, he whipped you pretty good. I've cleaned them all. Do you remember any of that?"

"Not really, I was blindfolded and my head was so foggy—still is. I don't remember all of it," Trey said. "So, he beat me?"

"Yeah. I'm sorry, Trey." Rick grabbed a tube of ointment and applied a bit to each cut. *He's quiet—that isn't good. Check in with him.*

Rick put down the salve. "Hey, you okay?"

"I feel dirty."

I remember that feeling. Hold him. Talk this out. Rick embraced him gently. "I know that feeling too, but you're not. You hear me?"

"You don't think bad of me?" Trey whispered.

Rick pulled back from Trey and looked him deep in the eyes.

"Listen to me. This was not real." Rick motioned around the room. "You did not come here to this room with that piece of shit because you wanted to. You did it to save other people—you did it because it was your job. Your assignment. All this—" Rick again motioned around the room "—was so that our country could recruit that asshole. You did it to keep weapons-grade nukes out of the wrong hands. You hearing me?"

"I know, but—"

"No buts—this is important. Remember how I've always said 'hold the line'?"

Trey nodded.

"This is what it means—this is the line. Hold on to what is real and let go of the job. Separate it."

"But I still feel dirty. He was so repulsive."

"I know. My first assignment in Ankara—must have taken a dozen showers afterward."

"You really get it?"

"I do, but it's not real. I hope that makes sense."

"It does."

Rick kissed his forehead. "Wanna grab a shower?"

"Yeah, I want his smell off me."

"Of course. Let me help you."

CHAPTER 60
CLEANSE

R ick helped Trey get up and walk through the adjoining door. Jeni met Trey with a warm smile and a gentle hug. She held him closely for a minute and said, "You did it. Trey, you did great. I mean it."

Trey nodded and went into the bathroom where Jeni had already turned on the shower. Rick helped him into it, pulled the glass doors together, and left.

"Is he okay?"

"I hope so. He's pretty rattled."

"We got all the footage—it's beyond graphic."

"Is it enough to spook Ivan?"

"Catherine says more than enough. Now seeing it—they will *own* him now," Jeni said. "Does he remember any of it?"

"Some of it." Rick motioned that the shower had stopped. When Trey emerged, Rick handed him a towel before setting his clothes on the vanity. "Here you go." As Trey dried off, Rick saw red smears on the white towel. *Tell him but don't spook him.* "I need to dress those cuts, okay? Let me grab my kit."

"What? Oh shit, sorry—"

"Don't worry about the towel. Be right back."

Trey nodded.

Rick dressed the cuts and applied ointment to each one. "There. I got 'em all—a few days and you'll never even see them."

"Thanks."

"Trey, I'm sorry—"

"It's not your fault," Trey said.

"I helped drag you into this mess."

"No, I ain't going there. You were doing your job. Now who's not 'holding the line'?"

Rick smiled slightly. "Touché, but how can I make this better—easier for you right now?"

"You could start with dinner. I'm starving. You guys hungry?"

Rick nodded.

Jeni shouted from the room, "I'm starving too."

"You want to eat here—room service?" Rick asked. "Or are you up for going downstairs to the pub? Your call."

Trey pulled on his underwear and jeans. "Honestly, I want to get out of here, so the pub would be good."

"Pub it is then."

"But one condition."

Rick raised his eyebrows.

"We can talk about all this tomorrow, but I don't want to talk about Ivan or any of this crap tonight. Deal?"

"No problem. What do you want to talk about?" Rick asked as Trey pulled on his shirt.

"Y'all."

"Us?"

"Yeah, you and Jeni both been through stuff like this? I want to hear stories—fun stories."

"Okay," Rick agreed.

"Well, stories are my specialty." Jeni appeared in the doorway. "You have come to the right source, my beautiful boy."

"Easy, Jeni," Rick said.

"Back off, handsome." She playfully pushed Rick aside and stepped into the bathroom. "I've been waiting for this moment." She gently put her arm around Trey. "You see, my lovely, I know all the dirt on Richard Patrick Morgan. Every ex-boyfriend. Every assignment. Nearly every trick."

Trey mustered a slight smile.

Jeni's magic—of course. She's been the only one to lift me outta my funk so many times. Look at him—how does she do it? Even if it's at my expense—who cares. Totally worth it to see him smile.

CHAPTER 61
BLOOD

Senior Officer Parker Holmes blew out a breath. *What a fucking night. Well, at least we didn't have to fake an arrest at the border. The inn was quiet—hopefully Catherine can smooth things over if the locals get wind of it.* He was seated in the front passenger seat of a black Mercedes Benz as he and David, his ops leader, passed through the border at Grenzübergang Waidhaus and into the Czech Republic at Rozvadov.

"Border traffic's not too bad. Mostly trucks—not bad for a Friday night," Holmes said.

"No, not too bad—we should get through quick," David replied as he drove them toward the crossing station.

The road narrowed to two lanes as they approached the booth. David flashed their alias credentials and seamlessly the guard waved them through at right before midnight.

"Think he's okay back there?" David motioned to Ivan in the trunk.

"Yeah, he's fine. I called the team and told them to be ready. We'll take him to the safe house back in the city."

David nodded.

"Did Paul make it through okay?" Holmes asked.

"Yeah." David glanced at their other officer following in Ivan's Peugeot. "Wanna take the E50? It's longer but less traffic this time of night."

They turned onto the E50 and within twenty minutes the two cars were alone on the dark ribbon cutting through the blackness.

"Yeah, this is better—through Bor, right?"

"Yeah— Wait, did you hear that?"

"What?" David immediately turned down the radio.
Thud!

What the fuck? Paul clicked on the high beams on the dark two-lane road in the thick forest. *What the hell are you doing, David? Trying to miss a deer? I didn't see anything. What?*

The black sedan swerved again violently, crossing both lanes then back to the right.

Shit! Stop the car, David.

The sedan sped up and jerked to the right, leaving the road.

Crash!

"Oh my god, what the hell?" Paul slowed the Peugeot and angled his beams to the dark forest. The mangled car was partially wrapped around a large tree. "What happened?" Paul scanned the road for any sign of animals or other vehicles. *Nothing.* He got out to inspect the accident, using the headlights and his small flashlight. As he approached the wreckage, he smelled fuel. The trunk was intact and closed.

Paul walked to the driver's side. "David?" He shined the light through the shattered glass. *Oh god, David.* Clearly his friend was dead. David's head was flipped backward in an unnatural state and nearly severed from his body. Paul drew his weapon as he walked back around the tree to the passenger door to check on his senior officer, who was bleeding profusely. "Parker?" There was no answer. "What the hell?"

As his flashlight illuminated the back interior, Paul froze. The back seat was blown out. The trunk was empty. He opened the back passenger door to look closer when he heard a low voice behind him in Czech.

"Dobrý večer." *Good evening.*

He turned in shock to see the engineer nearly naked, bloody, wearing only black leather chaps and boots with his arm raised over his head, holding the small crowbar from the spare tire well in the trunk. Paul had raised his gun when it all went dark.

Crack!

Ivan again swung downward at the young agent, splitting his skull with the second blow. His last breath exhaled with a strange gurgle. *You left me no choice—but I will take your clothes.* Ivan quickly stripped and then removed the shirt and pants from the body of the agent. He ripped his T-shirt and used it to wipe the blood from his hands and face.

"Argh."

Hmm. Who's still alive? Ivan picked up the small flashlight from the ground and walked to the front passenger door.

"Dobrý večer," he said and inspected both David and Parker more closely.

"Argh," Holmes moaned while bleeding profusely.

"Oh, dis bad—you want me end you. Suffer. Huh? No." Ivan reached into his pocket and pulled out his ID and then took his Glock from his shoulder holster.

USA—Parker Holmes. State Department—bullshit. Fucking CIA. Ivan tossed his ID back at him and leaned into his right ear.

"V Mnichově musím najít pár velmi zlobivých kluků," Ivan said, then licked Parker's ear. *Leave him—let him die here.* He walked back to his running Peugeot. He pulled a U-turn and drove away in the night.

I'm gonna find these naughty boys and kill them.

"What the hell?" The Aldi supermarket trucker said aloud as he slowed his truck. *How did they veer that far off the road to the trees?* He was stumped when he saw the smashed Mercedes Benz on the side of the E50 near Bor. *0355. It's late—bet they fell asleep.* He pulled over on the deserted road, turned on his flasher, and grabbed a flashlight from his cab. As he approached, he could see glass and the outline of a driver and passenger. *Please be alive.* He stepped toward the driver side and flashed his light. *Oh fuck—he's dead. How in the hell did his head rip from his body—was it on impact?* He flashed his light and saw both of the passenger doors on the opposite side ajar. *Dear god—are they all dead?* He rounded the trunk and saw a man nearly naked laying on the ground. *Doesn't make sense. How the hell did his skull crack like that in the back seat? How was he thrown from the car out here?* He illuminated the dense trees and turned the beam back to the car. *No way—something is not right.* He stepped over the dead man on the ground and peered at the front passenger. The bloody face suddenly twitched and its eyes opened.

"Oh my god. You're alive. Be still, be still—I'll get help!"

CHAPTER 62
PUB

I can do this—I'm starving. Trey steadied himself as he, Jeni, and Rick entered the pub. He watched as they requested a table in the corner. Trey followed after them. They sat and reviewed the menus. Jeni and Rick ordered quickly.

I don't speak German—can't read this. What am I doing here?

"Trey?" Rick asked.

"I don't understand. It's only German."

"It's okay. It's only dinner—how about a burger, fries, and a beer?"

"Perfect."

Rick winked and ordered for him.

"Still want to hear a story?" Jeni asked.

Trey nodded.

"All right, Korea," she said.

"Jeni—"

"Hush, handsome. So there we were. Korea. Pusan. '87."

"It was '88," Rick interrupted.

"As if, it was '87, asshole. I met Kristin in '88."

"Oh yeah, right," Rick conceded.

"It was cold, Trey. We were there supporting the Navy in a one-off."

"Cold? It was fucking freezing," Rick added. "Wait, don't forget that piece of shit outboard you showed up in."

"If you'd shut up, I'm getting to that," Jeni said, snapping her fingers.

"So where was I? Pusan. Navy. '87," she repeated. "Yes, it was cold, and no, it was not the best boat. But I didn't have a lot of time to go shopping—"

"And by 'shop' she means hotwire and steal a boat in the marina."

"Yes, I *borrowed* the boat."

You guys are like a sitcom. Trey chuckled.

"Couldn't steal a yacht?" Rick laughed.

"Yes, I stole the oldest, piece of shit outboard."

"And you were late to our pick-up," Rick added.

"Yes, I was delayed, but you— Handsome here was on a yacht with a rather unscrupulous *business man* from China, trying to sell weapons to a North Korean spook."

"Spook?" Trey asked.

"Spy," Rick said. "I was standing on the deck staring at my watch waiting in the cold for her to cross the bay—late."

"It wouldn't start, asshole. Besides, I got there didn't I?"

"Yes.

"I cross the entire bay to rescue old green eyes here in an old john boat with a crappy outboard motor—then I get there. Instead of gently getting into the boat, Sir Handsome decides to jump down— like fifteen feet. Bam! He hits the boat and nearly swamps us and the engine dies—I mean like R-I-P dead."

"So what happened?" Trey asked.

"We start arguing over the engine—image that—and trying to start it," Rick said.

"That's when we heard *pop*! Rick's *friends* woke up from their *naps* and started firing at us. They shot up the boat. Somehow that engine cranked. I gunned it and we got out."

"It was insane, Tiger. We had to take that beat-up jalopy a mile out into the Sea of Japan—we're talking past the barrier islands to rendezvous with a Navy frigate."

"With a hole in the hull, thanks to you."

"Me?"

"Yes, you," she added. "Can you picture it, Trey? Three-foot rolling seas, practically a broke-down dinghy, and a spitting, sputtering engine barely making headway."

Trey grinned and shook his head.

"And all the while, I'm yelling at him to *plug the hole*."

"Meanwhile, I'm dumping water and holding a rag in the hole— trying to keep us from getting swamped."

"Yes, but we made it." Jeni grinned.

"Barely," Rick said.

"The point is we made it. The engine was smoking, freezing rain was pelting us in the face, and we're arguing like an old married couple."

"You should have seen the captain and his crew looking down at us. They nearly swamped us as we tried to board." Rick laughed as Jeni rolled her eyes. "Then once they realized we were Agency, all the men tried to ask Jeni up to the bridge. They treated her like a queen and I barely got a blanket. You would have thought Julia Roberts had boarded their vessel and they had not seen a woman in five years."

"I shared my dinner and cabin with you, Rick."

"Only after I begged."

"As you should daily," she said, holding up her hand with the ring extended.

Rick stood and kissed her ring. "I'm gonna get us another beer okay?"

Jeni turned to Trey after Rick. "How did I do, Trey?"

"Good, I nearly forgot about—"

"Nuh-uh—don't break your own rule." She squeezed his hand. "Thank you."

"My pleasure. Can I tell you a secret?"

Trey nodded.

"I haven't seen him smile like this—with you—since a certain someone broke his heart—"

"The Israeli?"

"He told you?"

"A little bit—but he doesn't feel that way about me."

"Bullshit," she snapped.

"He thinks I'm too young for him—"

"Well, he's an idiot. A beautiful one but—be patient, Trey. He cares about you more than you know."

"What'd I miss?" Rick said and sat down the three mugs of beer.

Who was the Israeli? Shit, I should have asked her.

"Looks like we have company." Jeni nodded to the three obvious officers entering the pub. "BND?"

"B and what?" Trey asked.

"Bundesnachrichtendienst," Rick said.

"Benderichard—what?" Trey asked again.

"Bundesnachrichtendienst—kinda our German counterpart." Jeni checked her watch. "Midnight. Guess they heard from the locals."

Rick shrugged. "We'll play it cool—besides Ivan's not here and they're past the border by now."

"Are they gonna hassle us?" Trey asked as they took seats at the bar.

"Nah—for what? Breaking a door, making some noise?" Rick held up his mug. "To Germany, the motherland."

They clinked mugs.

"And to Trey—best damn civ-5," Jeni said in a low tone.

Again they clinked.

Trey smiled.

CHAPTER 63
REMEMBRANCE

0800 *and he's still sleeping—that's good. We'll get out of here today and stay in Munich tonight.* Rick watched Trey breathing in and out. Jeni lightly knocked on the adjoining door. She opened the door carefully and motioned to Rick to join here in Ivan's room.

"It's good that he's still sleeping," she said as Rick closed the door behind him.

"Yeah, did you get the footage uploaded?"

"Tried to a few times but this damn encrypted line keeps crashing."

"Files are too heavy?"

She nodded. "You don't think the BND is hacking us? Blocking the signal?"

"I don't think so."

"Well, either way—I called Catherine and she's gonna meet me at the Frankfurt desk. We'll upload them there."

Rick nodded. "Good. I was gonna take him to Munich, but we can drive you to Frankfurt."

"No—that's silly. You guys go into town—show him some sights. After last night, he's more than earned a break. I'll catch the train."

"I don't mind—"

"It's all good, handsome."

Rick nodded. "You sure?"

"Yes—let's grab some breakfast, then head out?"

"Sounds good. We'll get ready and meet you downstairs at 0830?"

"Yup—I'll get us a table and some coffee."

Rick returned to the room and closed the door.

"Trey?"

"Huh? What time is it?"

"A little after eight—wanna get out of here? Grab some breakfast."

"Yes." He sat up and stretched.

They showered and packed up.

Over breakfast in the pub, they discussed their plan. Jeni insisted that she would take the train to Frankfurt alone and process the data, photos, and footage from the secure lines at the station desk. She would send the files to both Darius in Langley and Parker in Prague, then check in with some German friends and fly back early to get home to Kristin.

"Rick, you should take our new team member back to Munich and sightsee a bit. You guys don't leave until Sunday," she said.

"I don't mind going to Frankfurt," Trey said.

"I've already booked my train. I'll be fine," she said, cupping Trey's face and chin. "I am so glad that Ivan the Terrible did not touch this face."

Trey mustered a smile at her compliment.

"All jokes aside, that was not easy. You did great. Rick, get him out of here and go have some fun. I'll see you both Tuesday in Langley."

Fools, you stayed. Ivan looked down from the adjacent rooftop with direct sight line to the parking lot of the inn. In his scope, he centered the crosshairs on the Asian woman as she spoke to the man and his young man. *My naughty boy alive and well.* He watched them both hug the woman. They loaded several duffels into her black BMW. Then he saw the man pass two Glocks to her. *Huh, unarmed.* He watched them say their goodbyes. The woman walked away from the inn. The two men got into a red VW GTI and pulled out.

Munich. Bet they don't know I'm free. Time to hunt.

Rick drove out of the parking lot and onto the A9 south toward Munich. He glanced in his rearview mirror. *Nothing—don't*

be paranoid. Try to enjoy the day. He turned to Trey. *Don't force conversation—he'll talk when he's ready.*

After twenty minutes of silence, Rick spoke up. "Trey, you don't have to talk right now, but will you promise me one thing?"

"What?"

"When you're ready, will you talk to me?"

"Yeah," Trey said, staring out the window at the German pastures.

At 1005 they stopped for fuel, Rick asked the attendant about a nearby landmark in German.

"You mind if we stop?" Rick asked. "We're nearby."

"Sure, whatever." Trey shrugged. He continued to stare out the window.

He's not giving me eye contact—he's kept his arms crossed the whole time. He's not okay about last night—he's trying to act like he is. Rick pulled out of the station and reached over to place his hand on Trey's left thigh.

Trey jumped and grabbed his hand. He shoved it away with a panicked look.

"What tha? Easy Trey."

"Sorry, I'm jumpy."

"Last night?"

Trey nodded and turned back to the window.

Rick continued to drive. *Geez, is this a good idea? Visiting a camp like Dachau—could either freak him out or, I hope, show him what many others had to endure. His actions last night will help others.* Rick breathed deeply. *Either way, I should talk it out first.*

"Trey? Were really close by a sacred site from World War II—a camp and now a memorial, Dachau."

Trey turned to face him.

"If this was a stupid idea on my part—just tell me. I thought that, you know—last night was so intense. Seeing it might be interesting and also help put things in perspective a bit, but—"

"A concentration camp? From the Holocaust?"

"Yeah, but listen if it's too intense—"

"No, I want to see it. Are we close?"

"Yeah, but I mean it, Tiger. If it's too intense—we'll leave. Okay?"

"Okay."

At 1030, they walked into the small museum and visitor center at the entry of Dachau north of Munich off the A9. Rick purchased two tickets and asked if they could join a small group of Dutch tourists about to enter.

Rick and Trey followed the group but held back a bit as Rick quietly interpreted the tour and horrors that took place on these now-hallowed grounds.

Trey could not believe the artifacts on display. *Oh my god, it's all so real. These shoes, suitcases—people ripped from their homes to await death.* Trey shook his head as he listened to Rick interpret softly. *Makes the stinging from my cuts seem small. Millions of innocent people herded into these pens, barracks, and gas chambers, tortured and killed for their faith.* They walked the bunker, barracks, and through the international monument erected.

But it wasn't only Jews who had suffered at Nazi hands. Trey froze when he heard the German guide clearly say *Homosexuelle* and point to the grainy photos of the triangle visible on the emaciated men with hollow eyes staring across nearly fifty years.

"Gay men?" Trey asked Rick.

"Yeah. Alongside the nearly six million Jewish people killed in the holocaust, gay men were also targeted."

"Are you serious?"

"Yes, Trey. Men like us."

§175. Trey pointed to a panel with a pink triangle and paragraph symbol. "What's this say?"

"It's paragraph 175. Basically, all known homosexuals were arrested in Germany, nearly 100,000. They forced them to wear pink triangles."

"Like how the Jews had to wear the gold stars?" Trey asked.

"Exactly. They estimate that 15,000 gay women and men died in the camps." Rick looked around. "Like this one."

"I had no idea." Trey stepped up to the panel and stared into the gaunt faces and hollow eyes. "They could be you or me?"

"Yeah. You didn't know?"

"No, my school never taught us that—only about the Jews. You know and Anne Frank."

Trey's Christian-based education had only spoken about the Holocaust from the Jewish experience. He was stunned to see himself in something that until now had felt like a tragedy that had befallen others. Seeing the men's faces, the triangles, and ashes was nearly overwhelming.

"You ready to go?" Rick asked.

"Yeah—thanks though."

They exited and continued their drive to Munich.

"I think I get it now, Rick," Trey broke the silence.

"What do you mean?"

"Dachau makes last night feel insignificant compared to what they had to endure. Was that why you took me?"

"No, Trey. Last night was *not* insignificant. What you did last night—secured a dangerous asset. If his knowledge fell into the hands of Iran or Libya—geez." Rick shook his head. "I took you there to show you the horrible consequences of war—of deranged leaders left unchecked and empowered to force their ideology on others. There were many people who did step up and help—hid people. Resisted. They had to endure ugly things and put themselves in situations—"

"To help other people?"

"Exactly."

Trey took Rick's hand.

"Please don't try to compare last night to Dachau. That wasn't my intention. I only wanted you to see why we do what we do."

"To prevent things like that from happening again."

"Exactly—it's tough but it's so important to see it and know their stories. We must remember."

"I get it, Rick," Trey said. "But no one will know what we did last night. Will they?"

"No." Rick brought his hand to his lips and kissed Trey's hand. "No one will know our story, Tiger."

As they arrived in Munich, Rick zipped through traffic.

"You know your way around here."

"I have another surprise." Rick grinned and continued on until turning right into a parking lot adjacent a large museum.

"A museum?"

"The Alte Pinakothek."

"Art?"

"Yeah, one of my favorites, but look at the façade. See it?"

"The pockmarks? Bullet holes?"

"Visible wounds from World War II."

"How old is it?"

"Older than anything in the US—sixteenth century."

"They didn't cover them over when they renovated?"

"Nope—they left 'em. Guess why?"

Trey stood back and looked up at the building. "Remembrance."

"Bingo. Come on—I want to show you a few works."

They entered and Rick purchased tickets.

Look at him—he loves this place. I've never seen this side of him. He's always super cool but look at him—he's an art geek.

Rick absorbed museums with a ferocity and excitement that Trey had never experienced. He guided them around the museum and would call out the masters—making Trey confirm if his guesses were accurate.

"Van Gogh?"

"Yup—but that's kind of easy right?"

"You try it. Who's that one by?"

"I don't know, Rick."

"Come on, guess."

"Monet?"

"What?! No, it's too dark for Monet."

Trey shrugged.

"It's Rembrandt. Come on." He guided Trey into a large galley and paused in front of a battle scene.

Rick pointed out the warriors, fighting and passionate love depicted. He explained the use of animals and church symbols.

Geez, I've never seen all this before—I used to dread museums. He makes this actually fun—but don't tell him that. We'll be here another two hours.

"What?"

"Nothing." Trey said.

"Hungry? Want to get out of here and grab a late lunch?"

"Yes!"

They settled on an outdoor café near Marienplatz, close to the hotel that Rick had selected.

"So what'd you think of the museum?"

"It's great."

"Did you not study the masters or art in college?"

"Kinda—at least at Pensacola Christian College."

"What do you mean?"

"They would paint 'clothes' on 'em in the art books in the library and our teachers would block out nudity in the class."

"Are you shitting me?"

"No—they were super strict."

"You are *not* serious?"

"Totally serious."

"You're telling me that in 1992, I could walk onto that campus and see shorts painted on a photo book of the *David*?"

"Yup."

"All to cover his wee willy?"

"It was insane to us too. Mark and I still laugh about it—or did before I came out to him."

"You know it's a miracle, Trey?"

"What?"

"That you're even here and remotely normal." Rick shook his head. "You've been through far worse than Ivan."

"Well, I don't know about your typical Friday night—but that was insane. I don't ever want to see that guy again."

"Deal." Rick smiled and held out his fist. They bumped top and bottom.

"What's going to happen to him though? To Ivan?" Trey asked.

Rick took a deep breath. "He's probably in phase one of his intake right now near Prague."

"Using my 'death' as incentive?"

"He thinks he killed you. They have photos, film, and complete data on his activities in Germany. My guess is that he'll comply out of fear of losing his job. Losing Hana. Losing his freedom and going to jail for thirty years to life. That's a hell of a lot of incentive."

"But I'm not dead."

"Ivan doesn't know that. Now when our Iraqi or Iranian friends show up at his door—he'll work for us."

"It's crazy."

"What?"

"This—it's all so tricky."

"I know."

"Wanna know the crazy thing?"

Rick nodded.

"He was nice. In the bookstore, on the train—I didn't even see it coming before he flipped."

"I know. What were you thinking—in that moment?"

"I wanted to fight back, smash his face in, but I also kind of felt conflicted."

"How so?"

"I don't know, maybe kinda like you must've felt a bit when y'all trapped me—I tricked him. He trusted me."

"I know—I get it."

"It's confusing."

"Welcome to the world of counter intel, Trey." Rick held up his glass.

"Nothing like the movies."

"You sayin' I'm not as cool as Bond?"

Trey rolled his eyes. "I wished it was easier to tell the good guys from the bad . . . it's so complex."

"Ah . . . Grasshopper is finally seeing the gray." Rick clinked Trey's glass. "It's not all black-and-white like your church taught you. Is it, Tiger?"

"No."

"Now that we have twenty-four hours free in Munich, what do you want to do tonight?"

"I don't know," Trey said.

"Well, let's check into the hotel and rest up. There's a great club here if you're up for it—and I did promise you after all this that I'd take you dancing."

Trey grinned. "Yes, you did."

"And I keep my promises."

CHAPTER 64
AGENT

Rick checked into the Hotel Königshof near the Marienplatz after 1400. "Ist Club NYC heute Abend geöffnet?"

"Ja." The front desk representative smiled as she handed him two keys for their room.

"Danke." Rick smiled. *Trey's gonna flip when he sees Club NYC.*

"Ready?" Rick motioned Trey to the elevators. The elevator opened and they found their room. Once inside, Rick asked, "You tired?"

"Yeah. You?"

"Not too bad but if we're going to go out tonight, we should take a disco nap."

"A what?"

"Ha! A disco nap—it's what we used to call them."

"Disco, huh? I would love to see you in bellbottoms and gold chains." Trey shook his head and stripped off his shirt and pants.

"Oh, I was cool back in the day— Whoa. Hold on. Trey, turn around again. Come here."

"What?"

Rick inspected Ivan's handiwork. "Wow, these two are deeper than I thought last night. Does it hurt much?"

"Yeah. It's been a dull ache all day."

"Why didn't you tell me?"

"I don't know—you always say to 'push through, finish the assignment. No breaks in the field—'"

"*During* the assignment, not when it's over. I'll clean these and get you some aspirin."

"I'm fine."

"You know you could have told me, right?"

"I'm fine," Trey repeated. "Can I ask you a question though?"

"Anything," Rick said as he pulled out his first aid kit and began redressing the cuts.

"What was your first assignment like? Was it similar?"

"No—not like this. It was in Turkey. Ankara. I had to do a drop and pick-up."

"Are they all like this?"

"Hell no. Last night was way more intense than either Jeni or I anticipated." Rick reapplied the ointment to the large red cuts on the sides of Trey's back, thighs, and buttocks.

"Will they heal before my Global Airways training?"

"Absolutely." Trey was staring at the wall with his fists clenched. Rick frowned. "Hey, look at me." Trey turned to him. "I'm sorry—I didn't know that it would escalate like that. I'm truly sorry you had to go through that last night."

"It's done—I don't want to think about *it* or *him* anymore." Trey lay down on the bed. Rick gathered the wrappers from the bandages and went to the bathroom to find the aspirin.

Trey was asleep by the time he returned with a glass of water and aspirin. *Geez, he was tired. Asleep in a flash. I'll leave it here for him when he wakes up. I'm tempted to crawl into bed but I really need to run.*

Trey slept for nearly an hour, awaking at 1510 to an empty room. He walked to the desk and saw Rick's note.

Hey, sleepy. Hope you rested well. Here's some aspirin. I'm out for a quick run. Back by 1515. RM

P.S. I'm proud of you, Tiger!

Trey was about to turn on the television when he heard the muffled ringing of Rick's mobile phone. He debated whether to answer but picked it up.

"Hello, Trey Carter."

"Hi, Trey," Claren said. "Great job last night. I heard from Jeni how intense it was, but you did it. Thank you. We got him because of you."

"Thanks, ma'am. Yeah, it was intense."

"Yes, I'm sorry to hear that. Are you okay?"

"Yes, ma'am, only a couple of cuts. I hope you didn't mind me picking up. Rick went for a run but should be back any minute."

"No, I'm glad you did. Are you excited to begin your training at Global Airways?"

"Yes, ma'am. Can I ask you something?"

"Sure."

"What if I wanted to apply to the Agency? Officer training?"

She paused. "I'm sorry, but that isn't possible at this time."

"Am I not good enough?"

"No, Trey, you're more than good enough. It's not possible at this time. Besides, you're a part of our special team and as things progress, we can talk about additional compensation if that is your concern."

"No, ma'am, sorry, but thank you for paying my rent. I didn't realize that you guys were gonna do that along with my utilities."

"It's the least we can do. We're happy to work this out and make sure that you have what you need. If you don't mind, what makes you want to join us?"

"I don't know—serve my country and help Rick."

"I see. I'll talk it over with Doc M. Is there anything else?"

"No ma'am. But if things change, will you let me know?"

"I will. Tell Rick—"

"Hold on." Trey heard the door unlock and open. "Rick's back from his run."

"Who is it, Trey?" Rick asked.

"Claren," Trey said, then returned to his call. "Here's Rick. Thanks again. Great to speak with you."

"You take care, Trey, and travel well. Have fun tonight."

"Thanks." Trey was frustrated with her answer about joining the Agency but he had little recourse.

So now you're answering my calls? Huh, let it go. No doubt he thought he was helping.

Trey handed Rick the Comsat before heading to the bathroom.

"Hey, Claren. What's up?"

"I wanted to check in with you. He seems good but Jeni told me about your night. Is he really okay?"

"Yes, I think so. He hasn't wanted to talk about it much. I took him to the art museum and also to Dachau earlier today. Tomorrow we head out at 1100," Rick said.

"That is why I called. I'd like you and the *cub* to head to *Oslo* tomorrow instead. Something has come up."

"I see. What about Sami and the professor?"

"They can wait—it doesn't concern them, but the intel coming in so far is *undetermined*."

"Is there anything that we need to prep him on prior to *Oslo*?"

"No, it's a *routine debrief* but it will also be good to allow Parker to meet our new guy. Nothing heavy."

"Okay, do you want me *present*?"

"Yes, it will be better for him if you are there. They're expecting you guys tomorrow morning at 0900. Great work, everyone is pleased—he's surpassing expectations and your leadership is key."

"Thanks, but it's a team effort. We are all *determined*."

"Travel well, Rick. Take care of our *cub*." Then she ended the call.

Shit! What the hell is going on—there's a massive shift. Destroy the phone. Rick took out the encrypted SIM card before wrapping it in a hand towel. He then smashed the device several times. Rick peeked out the eyehole, then carefully opened the door. He quickly glanced down the halls in both directions. *No one. What's the breach, Claren?* She had alerted him to a high-security risk.

All officers learned early to have key words with their mentors that trigger a shift in assignment or breach in security. For Claren and Rick, they had several but one of their highest escalations was *undetermined*, and the connection phrase was *routine debrief*. He quickly pulled out paper and pen from the hotel desk. He wrote down her codes:

Cub, Oslo, undetermined, Oslo, routine debrief, Parker, cub.

His jaw tightened as he stared at the words. *What are you trying to tell me? Is it a location? Should I call Jeni? Shit, we're cut off till we decipher this and establish comms.*

Trey stepped out of the bathroom dripping wet from a shower. "What are you doing? Why did you destroy the phone?"

"Put on your running clothes. Now."

Trey got dressed as Rick pulled out a small walking map from the desk drawer.

"Claren called you *cub* again—she alerted me to a security risk. I need to get to a pay phone."

"I'm sure there's one in the lobby."

"No, it's a sophisticated, encrypted tool. She's so precise—it has to be here. Maybe a train stop or bus station." Rick scanned the map. "She kept saying Oslo. There's U-Bahn, Sendlinger Tor, Isartor, Munich Karlsplatz, and the Munich Central Station. There's nothing like Oslo."

Trey looked over his shoulder. "Maybe it's letters. O-S-L-O and not Oslo?"

"That's it—brilliant, Tiger. It has to be Sendlinger."

"What?"

"Letters—Sendlinger's abbreviation is SL. The SL between the circles, oSlo." Rick grabbed Trey and kissed his head. "You're my good luck charm."

Trey grinned.

"Let's go."

Rick took only the SIM card, cash, and GTI car keys. They ran the short distance to the Sendlinger Tor station and down the stairs into the underground. The station was packed with summer tourists.

"Stay close to me, Trey." Rick scanned the station for public phones. Through the mass of people, Rick spotted the first bank of phones. "There."

As they approached, the third one from the left started to ring with the familiar tone.

Rick grabbed the receiver. "Hello?"

"Rick, is Trey with you?" Her tone was dark and stiff.

"Yes." Rick frowned. "What's going on?"

"Ivan escaped."

CHAPTER 65
ESCAPE

van escaped? How the hell? A chill shot through Rick as Claren repeated herself. "When, Claren?"

"They never made it to Prague. There was some sort of accident. A truck driver found them—he thought they were all dead, but Parker is alive."

"When?"

"Last night—we're still getting details."

"Wait—so Ivan survived and then escaped? How—"

"I'll tell you what we know, but is Trey with you?"

"Yes. He's right here. Why?"

"We don't know all the details, but from the looks of things—Ivan's KGB."

"Are you fucking kidding—" *Of course, only a trained operative could have escaped.*

"Ivan took out two of our agents." She paused, then her tone grew stern. "Our intel was off. He wasn't a target for the Iranians or Iraqis. Much closer to home. Serbia."

"Milošević?"

"Yes."

Fuck! Rick gripped the phone. "How is Parker? Have you talked to him?"

"No. He's lucky to be alive—he's still in surgery."

"Where's Ivan?"

"We don't know."

What the fuck? Rick held the phone away and turned away from Trey. His tone deepened, "What do we *know*?"

"He killed both of Parker's men and took off in his Peugeot sometime between 0045 and 0300."

"He didn't head home to Hana?"

"No, we still have eyes on her in Prague. She's at their apartment. No sign of him." Again, Claren paused. "Rick, there's something else. At first we thought it was nonsense, but . . . I need you not to react."

Rick glanced over at Trey. The young man furrowed his brow, but Rick gave him a slight smile and nod. "What?"

"The truck driver said Parker kept repeating these words over and over. Then the doctor confirmed the same four words before they put him under for surgery—it sounds crazy but he apparently kept saying. 'Ivan. Munich. Zlobivých kluků.'"

"Munich I get but what's that last part? Czech?"

"Yes. *Naughty boys.* Plural."

Adrenaline shot through Rick as his mind raced. *Naughty boys in Munich. He knows Trey's not dead. Oh my god.* "He knows?"

"Yes."

"Hold on, Claren." Rick turned back to Trey.

"Is everything okay?"

"Yeah, I'll tell you in a minute." Rick pulled out a ten mark coin, handed it to Trey, and nodded to the newsstand. "Grab us some water?"

Rick waited till Trey walked away. "Who burnt the mobile? Is Frankfurt compromised?"

"I don't know, but I couldn't take the chance. There's a bigger problem. Jeni called, and turns out Catherine escalated the situation to the BND. They're pissed we played in their backyard without them."

"No doubt. Well, we may not have helped things at the pub in Nuremberg. Where's Jeni now?"

"She's at the station ops in Frankfurt."

"Has she uploaded the files?"

"Yes, before we got word from Prague. Why?"

"Do you think Ivan has seen them?"

"Doubtful, but it is possible."

What a shit show! Rick took a deep breath. "Walk me through it again—what do we know?"

"They crossed the border after midnight according to the records. We think Ivan used his leather harness and made a slip knot to take out the officer driving the car. They struggled, forcing the crash. Forensics thinks that Ivan broke through the back seat and strangled him in less than ninety seconds. Caused them to hit a tree over the border in a deeply wooded area near Bor."

"He waited. He knew."

"Exactly, he nearly severed the head from the body."

"Classic KGB."

"Textbook—not that we need more proof. After the crash, he killed the following officer in his car, but left Parker injured."

"He thought he'd bleed out."

"Yeah, we think he spoke to Parker—then left."

"Then the truck driver finds him and he repeats those words?"

"Yes. Thanks to Parker, we know what we know. They called me a few minutes ago once they identified him at Motol Hospital in Prague."

Rick closed his eyes. "They left us at the inn in Nuremberg 2230, driving northwest on the A6. They crossed the border at approximately 2355, which would put them on the E50 at the Bor cutoff at about 0100 or 0130."

"Yes, then the trucker reported the accident to his dispatcher at roughly 0240, but our team was not notified until Parker was airlifted and ID'd at Motol at 1400."

"Oh my god, Claren. He's had nearly twelve hours, placing him anywhere—back here in Munich, Prague, anywhere . . ." Rick immediately looked over at Trey in line to purchase the bottles of water.

"We can rule out Prague."

"How?"

"Jeni and the team were confirming possible locations in both Germany and Czech when the BND called. They got a hit on Ivan's tags. Logged at the border at 0420."

"Shit, he's in Germany. Why? Revenge?

"We're running scenarios—"

"No way," Rick interrupted. "There's no way he would try to take on us and the BND on their home field? Right?"

"We don't know. The incentive is strong, Rick. He may be rogue now and looking for revenge. It's simple, but clearly we don't know him like we thought we did. He isn't some low-ranking engineer with a fetish."

"No, but why Serbia?"

"We're working on that. Seems Ivan's a ghost—he doesn't show up in any of our collective KGB intel. Maybe Hana too."

"Damn it. So now what?"

"It's a delicate situation—POTUS cannot afford any leaks. I'm starting to get calls. Both sides are breathing down our necks."

"Whitehouse and BND?"

"Yes."

"That's why you shifted—buy us some time?"

"Thank god you figured it out."

Rick shook his head. "So Trey and I are what? Collateral?"

"Not you."

Her words shot down his spine. Rick glanced back at Trey.

"If you walk—"

"I won't leave him." Rick waited but she did not response. "Claren, I will not—"

"No one's asking you to. That's why we're OTR."

"So, what now?"

"Look, I need time but I *will* figure something out."

"Until then—what? We're on our own with a possible rogue KGB agent *and* the BND chasing him, me and a civ we *knowingly* put into harm's way?"

"I am thinking of solutions, but yes for now you're correct."

"Have you contacted Moscow or St. Petersburg for intel?"

"Of course—nothing yet but they're at least cooperating. The Agency is on high alert. We cannot risk an incident with Germany or Russia, in an election year no less. The media would have a field day with any part of this or Trey."

A bolt hit Rick. "That's it. That's it, Claren."

"What?"

"Trey. If Ivan's KGB—he's burned. Trey's his ticket."

"If he gets Trey, he's got intel to trade."

"Yup."

"The White House would panic. There's no way of containing this if it leaks."

Huh, like Mexico City. Shit! "I bet Ivan's counting on that."

"That's solid, Rick. You may be right, but if that's the case, you're gonna have to play with the BND."

Trey returned with the waters and stood by him. *Don't spook him. She knows I won't leave you, Tiger.* "Exactly, I'll tell Trey and we'll lay low."

"I'll tell Jeni. Glad that I went with my gut on this and bought us some time."

"Me too, Claren."

"Be safe. Lay low. Jeni will keep us updated but the BND will have all Agency field operations in Germany cooperating—including us."

"Right. So we have to make a choice."

"Yes. You don't have much time, and we are running out of options."

Trey tapped Rick on his shoulder, and Rick brushed him off. But Trey tapped again and whispered, "Rick, our friends from the pub." He nodded to the BND agents walking down the stairs toward the crowd.

"Claren, I've got to go," Rick said.

"Protect him, but contain this—"

Rick hung up the pay phone and scanned the station. The BND agents were looking around the crowd but clearly had not yet seen them. Rick took Trey's arm as they backed slowly toward the station newsstand.

"Follow me—stay close."

They merged into the flow of people up the stairs and into the open market set up near the medieval arch gate. Rick had them stop and pretend to stretch before starting a slow jog. *I've got to tell him. Really no other choice but to let the BND take us in—they'll have tons of questions.* He glanced at his watch. *Shit, we've probably got an hour at best. All our gear is at the hotel. They'll nab us in minutes if we go back.*

Rick observed the streets around them. *We're only like two or two-and-a-half kilometers from the US consulate.* "Let's cross, Trey." They stopped running and waited for the light to allow them to cross over to the street and the edge of the park on Königinstraße. They ran north along the river and stopped near the US consulate at the

Sportanlage Hirshanger Park. Rick instructed Trey to lie on the grass as they again pretended to stretch.

"What's going on, Rick?" Trey asked and then opened his water. As he drank, Rick paced around. "You can tell me—whatever it is."

"Ivan is missing."

"What do you mean *missing*?"

Rick took a knee beside Trey. "He escaped."

"What?" Trey's voice strained.

"Please listen."

Trey nodded.

For several minutes Rick took his time and explained what he knew of the situation choosing his words carefully and stopping short of the apparent murders of the CIA officers. "So, the way I see it. We really have two choices. Head back to the hotel and let the BND take us in, or—"

"Or what?"

"I'm thinking, we could try to head over there." Rick motioned ahead of them. "That's the US Consulate—we could try, but it could get really messy."

"Cause you're dark ops and I'm not supposed to be doing this?"

"Yeah."

"So if we go with the BND, what happens to Ivan?"

"They'll most likely want our help to get him. He's possibly looking for us."

"But if we go to the consulate, Ivan gets away?"

"Probably."

Trey shook his head. "No. No way did I do this to have to look over my shoulder for the rest of my life— Wait, tell me again what happened to the agents that took him back to Prague?"

Rick shook his head.

"Did he hurt them?"

Don't lie to him. This is his life too.

"Did he kill them?" Trey asked.

"Yes, this situation has escalated way beyond what we thought." Rick paused. "Look we don't know for sure —but we think he's KGB."

"Are you serious?"

"And if he is . . ." Rick shook his head. "We'll be forced to play their game. The BND will be running this."

"Okay, I think that I get it. We're safer working with them, right? The BND?"

"Possibly, but we're dark ops. Jeni will try to assist us from Frankfurt and Claren from Langley. But we're essentially on our own until Ivan's apprehended."

"You really think that he will come after us—for revenge?"

Rick shrugged.

"Why? What does he gain—why not just disappear?"

"Trey, I gave up trying to understand human behavior long ago. I try to think in terms of survival. Fight or flight. Look at this from his perspective. He has few options. He's killed two CIA officers—the whole world will be looking for him now. My guess is that in less than twelve hours, Israel, Russia, and Britain will be alerted. With Bosnia and Croatia in turmoil, he's cut off. Trapped. Whether he's active or not in the KGB, I guarantee you that his monthly trips to Germany were not sanctioned. He's burned. He knows his fate if his comrades find him first."

"What will they do?"

"Slit his fucking throat and Hana too."

"Geez." Trey lay back on the grass.

Rick took his right leg and started to stretch it.

"So then what?" Trey asked.

"He'll go down swinging. If he gets to us and blows our cover within the Agency, BND, or KGB, then he has intel to trade."

"Wait, so getting to *us* could give him a last option to get out?"

"Exactly," Rick said as he released Trey's right leg and motioned for the left.

"And the BND, they will want us as bait to lure him?"

"Most likely."

"I'm the liability here then—being a civ," Trey deduced.

"It will raise a lot of questions, but we can cover those together. I won't leave your side, Trey, but you have to keep cool and follow my lead."

"Will they all know I'm a civ and gay?" he asked quietly.

"Yeah." Rick sensed Trey's panic. *He's smart and knows that they might be biased, which means that they'd take risks with him cause he's gay, expendable—not on my watch.* "Hey, I know you're worried, but I'm here. Semper protege."

Trey nodded.

"And besides, you also have an advantage, Trey."

"What's my advantage?"

"Our training. They won't know—not the BND nor the other US agents. No civ has ever undergone your level of training—and *that* gives us an advantage." Rick smiled.

"So what now?"

"We run back to the hotel. Let the BND spot us. We'll allow them to bring us in."

"Where?"

"Probably their headquarters here in Munich. I know a few of their agents. Who knows, with any luck, Elise Diehl may be on the intake team."

"Is she cool?"

"Very. I've known her for years. She may help us, but it'll be a challenging game of revealing only what we have to to work with them and set the trap. Okay?"

"Okay." Trey's tone was uncertain.

"You can do this, Tiger. And think—next week you'll be in flight attendant school in Philly." Rick grinned, pretending to point to emergency exits and pull on an oxygen mask. "Coffee, tea, or me?"

"Jokes? Really? You're unbelievable, Rick Morgan," Trey said as they turned and began their slow jog back to the hotel.

They had only been in their room for three or four minutes when the knock came.

"Housekeeping."

Rick held out his fist to Trey. They bumped it top and bottom.

"We got this, Trey," Rick whispered. "Stay calm."

CHAPTER 66
BND

Ready or not. Rick turned the door handle. The force of the door knocked him backward as four large German agents burst through shouting in both German and English.

"Runter, Runter! Get down, Get down!"

They forced Rick and Trey down on the bed, handcuffing them behind their backs.

A woman spoke loudly. "Einfach mit unseren Gästen, Jungs. Easy with our guests, guys."

Wait, I know that voice. Elise? Rick tried to cock his head to see the woman.

"Rick, I am sorry to have to take you and your friend in this manner, but you need to come with us now."

The men pulled both Rick and Trey to standing.

"What the hell, Elise? What's going on?" Rick pretended to struggle a bit against his captor's grip.

"You guys are in danger. Your engineer has escaped. Let's go now—I'll explain."

The men pulled out black sacks.

"Hoods. Really, Elise?"

"We need to protect our colleagues. Besides you should have thought of that when you didn't include us in your plan." She nodded and her agents hooded them both.

In the darkness, Rick sensed that they led them down a stairwell and into a waiting van.

"Rick?" Trey called out with panic in his voice.

"It's okay, Trey. I'm right here. Don't struggle. We're okay."

Elise added, "Apologies for our methods, but you are safe now. Please relax and we'll explain to you and Rick once we are at our offices."

The van stopped and the four agents walked them from the van for several minutes in the darkness and then sat them down in chairs. They removed their hoods and handcuffs.

"Warten Sie hier. Wait here," one of them barked as they left the room. The fluorescent lights overhead were blinding as their eyes adjusted.

I bet we're in the Munich BND field offices in Pullach. The room was configured as a conference room but without windows. Along one wall was a large, all too familiar mirror running the length of the right-hand side of the table. *Interrogation room. Be cool—they're watching. Check in with him.*

"You okay?" Rick asked.

"Yeah. Where are we?"

"Camp Nicolas. It's kind of like Campus in Langley."

"Are we in trouble?"

"Not exactly. They're our allies. Elise and her team will no doubt explain." He nodded to the mirror. "But I think we're going to be here awhile."

They waited for several minutes. Suddenly the door opened and Elise entered.

"Guten Tag, Hübscher." She greeted Rick with a kiss on both cheeks.

"Elise, you look amazing. Life is good?" Rick said.

"Yes. Who's your friend?"

"Trey Carter meet Elise Diehl."

She kissed him on both cheeks too, leaving the scent of rosewater in the air.

"Rick, do you need anything?" Elise asked.

Rick looked in the mirror and was reminded that they were still in their running shorts and T-shirts. "A quick shower would be great, if we have time?" Rick asked. "But if there's no time . . ."

"No, of course." She turned to the mirror. "Bitte bereiten Sie die Herrenumkleide und die Duschen für unsere amerikanischen Gäste vor."

Trey turned to Rick and raised his eyebrows.

"They're getting the locker room ready for us."

Elise turned back. "Yes. We have about four or five hours to review the situation, agree on the plan, and engage."

"You need *our* help?" Rick asked.

"We need each other, Rick. He's extremely dangerous, former KGB." She glanced at Trey and back at Rick.

"He's fully briefed and has class five clearance. You can speak freely."

She again stared at Trey.

"I want to help. If I don't understand something, Agent Diehl, I'll ask my coach."

"Your *coach*, huh? All right, let's get you guys cleaned up so we can get started." She smiled. She placed a hand to her right ear and nodded.

"Oh Elise, can I get some ointment to clean his cuts? Ivan did a number on him," Rick said.

"Of course. Is he okay?" she asked.

"He'll be fine, but we need to keep them clean."

"You really okay, Trey? I saw the footage," she said.

"Yes."

Two of her agents accompanied Rick and Trey. After they showered, Rick knelt down and started to clean up Trey's two deep cuts and welts that were starting to scab over on both cheeks.

Rick glanced at the two agents. "Mein ganzes Training und das ist meine Aufgabe—deinen Arsch zu reinigen und zu verbinden."

They laughed and seemed to relax a bit.

"Guessing that joke's on me?" Trey asked.

"Yeah. All my training and this is my assignment—cleaning and bandaging your ass."

Trey laughed.

They dressed in their own clothes and returned to the conference room.

"Feeling better?" Elise asked.

"Much." Trey smiled.

"Good, please let me introduce my handsome Americans," she said to the two others in the room. "This is Rick Morgan, CIA and his civilian operative, Trey Carter."

Rick and Trey both nodded as Elise continued, "And these are my colleagues, Dr. Peter Schmitt and BND Agent Eva Hartmann."

The group shook hands while an attending agent brought in a speakerphone. They took their seats at the large conference table.

"Shall we begin?" Elise looked to Rick.

He nodded.

"I'm more than a little confused. You could have avoided all of this with a simple phone call. Rick, we go back what—five, six years? We knew about Ivan Dimitri as well—we've also been tracking him."

Obligatory reprimand—got it. Go for it, Elise, I'll play along. Rick waited for her to finish. "You know that I was following orders."

"So American—you're always pulling a Rambo and going it alone, with a civilian no less," she said, pointing to Trey.

"I'm not Rambo, but as you all must know by now, my team is *special.*"

"Unsanctioned and dark ops," Elise said with a bit of sarcasm. "We are quite curious to learn more about your 'team,' but perhaps later. Right now we have a deranged nuclear engineer who is former KGB to deal with."

"Fair enough. What's the plan?" Rick asked bluntly. "How can we help?"

"Now." Elise turned to Trey. "We have all seen the tape. I'm sorry you went through that. I hate to ask but are you willing to confront this psychopath again?"

"Yes." Trey glanced at Rick.

Rick saw the sadness on Trey's face. *Jesus, I'm sorry, Trey.*

"Really?" Elise asked.

"Yes, ma'am. I'll be fine. What do I need to do?"

"We have a plan, but first let me tell you what we know. Ivan returned across the border using a Serbian passport but with the same Czech plates on the Peugeot," Elise said. "We believe he's returning to Munich, and we *hope* that he is hunting you two or at least you Trey in one of our various homosexual clubs." She pulled a map from her file and unfolded it on the table between them. "We're thinking a gay discotheque here in Munich like this one: Club New York. He'll pursue you either there or in one of the other establishments. Our sources in the gay community tell us that tonight is a special night at the club, dedicated to the singer Donna Summer." She turned to Trey. "You know, Donna lived here in Munich for several years."

Trey looked puzzled. "I'd never heard of her until Rick."

Rick laughed. "Trey only recently became familiar with the work of Ms. Summer."

Elise shrugged.

"So what's the plan?" Rick looked back at the map. "Do we go out tonight and hit several clubs and bookstores in the open, hoping to attract him? Flush him out?"

"Yes, but we will have eyes on you and undercover agents monitoring."

"And *if* he takes the bait and we get near him—" Rick said.

"We'll take him into custody," she interrupted and turned to Trey. "Maximum security. He won't get away twice. Not in Germany."

The phone on the table rang, and Agent Eva Hartman answered, speaking softly. "I have Langley," Eva said. Elise nodded, and she placed the receiver down and pressed the speaker button.

"Hey, Trey. Hey, Rick." Claren's voice was clear and confident. "Elise, thank you and your team for taking care of my guys."

"Claren, how are you?" Elise said.

Rick turned to Trey and pursed his lips.

"Good, but I will rest easier when all of this has been quietly handled. Director Tibbins and I want you to know that we apologize for not seeking your assistance in the first place and now for showing up at your door with such a problem."

"I'm sure we can discuss it further after we capture the engineer."

"Of course," Claren said. "Elise, I reached out to our Moscow and St. Petersburg station desks. Ivan and Hana are confirmed, *both* are former KGB. I am faxing over the intel. We have eyes on Hana. We're monitoring her in Prague with our ops team."

"Are you bringing her in?" Elise asked.

"Not yet. We don't want to upset anything there or in Munich in case he has eyes on her as well. He wasn't due back until tomorrow night, so we have time."

"What is the jurisdiction for capture? I assume you will take him into German custody?" Rick asked.

"Yes," Elise said. "But if he and his friends in Serbia are trying to assist Mr. Milošević with weapons-grade nukes, then you can bet we'll be asking for your help."

"I can assure you that we'll be ready to support—anything you need," Claren said.

"Good, I don't need to tell you that the situation in Croatia and Serbia is a powder keg." Elise turned to Eva.

"We've been monitoring the situation for months. It's growing more dire by the day. War's inevitable." Eva's tone was serious.

"Maybe, but we're still applying sanctions," Claren said. "No doubt you've seen our disturbing intel. Milošević is killing non-Serbian ethnic Albanians and Croatians en masse."

"Bastard. And precisely why they want Ivan. Low-grade nukes. Genocide." Elise shook her head. "Goddamn it. How the hell did we not see this?"

"Elise, we agree. Our intel was off in Prague. We thought the Iranians, PLO, or Iraqis were likely going to approach Ivan. Instead, he was courting them right under our noses the whole time," Claren said. "Serbia."

Elise conceded, "You weren't alone there. We also thought that the Iranians were most likely to approach Ivan. So, we have a serious situation on our hands. Trey, can you handle another assignment tonight?"

All eyes turned to Trey.

"Yes, ma'am. I'll do whatever you guys need me to do." He turned to Rick, then back to Elise. "But may I make one request?"

Elise nodded.

"Can I please have my coach with me or near me?"

"Absolutely."

Dr. Peter Schmitt spoke up. "How long have you been working with the Agency?"

Great, now we hear from the shrink, right as Trey is agreeing to help. Don't spook him. Dr. Schmitt was the BND expert in neuropsychology and training.

Trey glanced at Rick, who nodded. *Don't hold back, Trey.*

"A month and a half," Trey answered.

Elise shot a look at Rick, and her expression was unmistakable. "Are you kidding me?"

Rick shrugged and turned to Dr. Schmitt. *Typical, no emotions— geez, like Doc M, stone-faced.*

"I'm a hard worker, and I think that I am picking it up," Trey said.

"Rick, this is *highly* unusual and most dangerous," Elise stated. "I cannot believe that *your* government would send a young, untrained civilian into such a dangerous—"

"Elise, you're right," Claren interrupted. "It is a most unusual situation, but I will say that we have a new protocol. I believe you will find our young civ is quite capable."

Rick stood and reached out to Elise. "May I please borrow your Glock?"

"What?" Elise snapped. "Why?"

"Please allow me."

Elise pulled out her Glock 17 from her back waistband and handed to him.

Rick took the gun and laid it in front of Trey. "They don't know you. Show them why they should trust you. On my count, three, two, one, go!" He held up his watch.

Trey took a deep breath and grabbed the Glock. He disassembled it into all thirty-four pieces in less than forty-five seconds.

"Hands up. Forty-five seconds? You must be nervous. Calm down, you got this. Three, two, one, go!"

Again, he took a deep breath and deftly reassembled the Glock in forty-two seconds flat.

Without looking at his recruit, Rick held out the clip while staring at Elise. Trey took the clip and loaded the weapon, returned it to the table for Elise, with safety on but barrel toward himself. "Your equipment, ma'am."

"Civilian, huh?" Elise narrowed her eyes and took back her Glock.

"Yes, ma'am."

CHAPTER 67
HUNTER

old you, Elise. Don't say anything and let her come to her own conclusion. Rick observed the three BND officers. Elise inspected her gun.

"Sure you're ready for this, Trey?" Elise asked again.

"Yes, ma'am."

Elise glanced at her two colleagues.

"Are you nervous or scared?" Dr. Schmitt asked.

"Yes, sir. I won't lie."

Rick heard Trey's Southern drawl grow stronger and knew that his recruit was tense.

"How do you overcome your fear in the moment and engage with the target?" Dr. Schmitt pressed.

"I sing."

"Sing?"

"Yeah, y'all all got trained for this and have years of experience. I don't, but my team believes in me." Trey turned to Rick. "When things get crazy, I tune it out and sing a song in my head."

"And what song are you singing now?"

"It's country. You wouldn't know it, sir."

"Try me."

"Garth Books."

"'Friends in Low Places'?" Dr. Schmitt asked.

"You know it?"

Dr. Schmitt sang the first line and caught the group off guard. Trey grinned.

Rick rolled his eyes as Dr. Schmitt turned to Elise and nodded.

She glanced back at Trey. "All right. Let's get our plan together."

Eva winked at Trey and smiled.

"We'll head out 1915 and start at Club New York, then the New Man bookstore, and we'll make our way back here, here, and here. Okay?" Elise asked.

"Those are all gay bars?" Rick asked.

"For the most part," Elise said.

"What about the other bookstore?" Eva pointed to three streets over.

"We can have Trey make a wide circle, hitting each one. We'll put you on wire and talk you through it." Elise looked up from the map to Trey.

He nodded.

"How will we cover him from here in such an open space?" Rick asked.

"We'll position teams here, here, and here. Rick, you and I will be mobile and cruise slowly through this area. Eva and her unit will hold back at Club New York and have vantage down the avenue. Agreed?"

I don't like being in the open—it's risky—but if we have teams on alert, I guess it's a calculated risk. Let her run the show. Rick nodded and carefully studied the locations on the map. "It's open but we'll have eyes."

"Yes, I thought that too, but is he likely to gamble so boldly?" Eva asked.

Rick shrugged. "We'll have to be ready."

By 1845, the group had agreed on their pattern and rotation. Elise and Rick would hold back while additional BND agents, mostly in their late twenties, assembled as Eva instructed them.

"You gotta blend in—it's a Saturday night. I don't want to see any equipment visible." Eva pointed to the handle of a Glock protruding from her agent's waistband. "You guys—it's Saturday night. Act like it. Be casual and call in anything even remotely suspicious—doesn't matter how small. You see it—tell us. We need all eyes and ears."

The group nodded and each was assigned their locations.

"They do look the part—jeans and leather," Rick commented to Elise. "It's good to see the support, but we don't want to spook Ivan."

"I know but we have to also think of public safety—our team will at least blend in better than if we had to use the city police."

"True." Rick turned to Trey. "We should go get ready."

Rick and Trey returned to the men's locker room along with a few members of BND. They picked out shorts and a shirt for Trey. After he dressed, he was fitted with a wire and earpiece.

"Can you see the wire through my shirt?" Trey asked Rick.

"No."

"Do I look all right?"

He's nervous. Clear the room and talk to him. Rick did not answer him but instead turned to the team and in German asked, "Guys, can you give us a minute? Alone?"

They left Rick and Trey.

"I don't like the wire," Trey said.

"I know, but they're running this. Besides, it will make it easier to guide."

"Yeah, I guess. Will you be in my ear?"

"Constantly."

"So this is it then?"

"Yeah."

"How am I doing with them?"

"You're doing great. Don't overthink it . . . Be yourself."

Trey nodded.

"Listen, no matter what happens tonight, I want you to know that I'll be there. I'm gonna talk you through it. Keep your eyes open and use our training."

"I know. 'Scan the crowd. Listen with my eyes and ears,'" Trey recited.

"And?"

"Semper protege."

"Exactly," Rick said. "Those aren't only words, Trey. They're my promise to you."

Trey again nodded.

"Do you remember our safeword?"

"*Takedown.* Why?"

"If you need me to break protocol and end this—I will. You say *takedown*. It's over."

"What about Ivan?"

"We'll get him and go home. In and out—but your safety come first tonight. You hear me? Come here."

He bear-hugged Trey. He didn't care if the Germans were watching.

"If things get bad, please get him. If I get hurt, promise me that he hurts worse."

"Shh—don't even think that." Rick pulled back but still held his shoulders. "Look at me. You're going to be fine. We got this. Say it."

"We got this."

Rick released his grip. They walked out of the locker room and were met by Elise.

"Ready, Trey?"

Not really but I guess so. Do I have a choice? Trey held his thoughts. "Yes, ma'am."

They reviewed the map and locations, then headed out in several vans to their drop zones. Rick rode with Trey in a black Mercedes sedan. Right before 2200, they were once again near Marienplatz.

"Ready?" Elise turned to Trey in the back seat. He exited the car.

Trey glanced back as Rick, Elise, and the two armed agents drove off in the sedan.

"Check, check. Trey?"

"Yeah, I hear ya."

Should've worn pants—it's kinda chilly but could be my nerves. Still, something feels odd—cooler. Guess it's the wind. Trey walked alone block by block around the city on foot for roughly two hours. He was guided by the BND to no avail. *No sign of Ivan, anywhere—this is impossible. Literally, a needle in a haystack.* He had been asked to enter into several gay bars and Club New York.

Trey looked around at the empty club. A bartender shrugged as he prepped for the crowds that might arrive. *No way would anyone be out yet—it's too damn early.* "Guys?"

"Yes, Trey. Go ahead."

"It's too early," Trey called out to the wire on his chest. "All these places are empty. Can we stop a minute?"

"Are you tired?"

"I need to get my bearings. This isn't how we'll find him. Can I please be me?"

"What do you have in mind?" she asked.

"I need a minute to clear my head."

"Okay. You want to break?"

"No, ma'am. Can Rick hear me?"

"Yes, he's sitting right here."

"Rick, if he's here and looking for me, then technically I wouldn't know it, right?"

"Yeah, that's right," Rick said. "What's your gut telling you?"

"He didn't spot me at the café or the bookstore. Not at first—he cruised me from the street. You always say that people show you through their actions, right?"

"Yeah, usually," Rick confirmed.

"We'll if he's here and looking for me—I bet he's been watching me this whole time—on the streets."

"What are you getting at?" Elise asked.

"This may sound crazy, but my gut has been telling me to slow down—stop looking and let *him* find *me*."

"Your call, Rick," Elise said.

Trey waited for an answer.

"Okay, Tiger. We go with your gut."

"Cool. I'm gonna retrace my steps a bit." Trey walked back to Sendlingerstrade toward Marenplatz. When he got close to the café, Trey stopped and stood staring across the street. He then sat down on a bench with a clear view to the café. *This is it—he saw me here.* Trey heart pounded, and he remembered those first glances from Ivan days prior. *Seems like forever ago now—why am I so nervous? Calm down. I need a song.* He turned to Cyndi Lauper. As if audible, he heard the eerily beautiful first few cords of "True Colors."

Give him a minute—he's the one out there on his own. Rick could sense the impatience from Elise's team members shifting in their seats.

"What's he doing?" Eva asked over the radio.

Elise shot a look at Rick. He raised his eyebrows.

"He's collecting himself," Elise relayed.

"Do we have time for this?" Eva asked.

"Yes, we're giving him a minute."

"Standing by."

Elise turned back to Rick.

Come on, Tiger, I can't hold 'em off much longer.

Suddenly Trey stood, crossed the street, and turned.

"Now what?" one of her agents asked in an exasperated tone. "He's on the move, repeat he's on the move."

Again Trey paused before walking the four blocks back toward the bookstore.

What are you doing, Tiger? Aha, the bookstore, of course. "He's going back to the bookstore—wait." Rick remained locked on Trey's every move. *You're getting too far ahead. What are you thinking? Come on, stay focused.*

Trey did not enter the bookstore but stood with his head lowered as if in quiet reflection, then headed toward Blumenstrass.

"Get closer please." Rick shot Elise a look. "He's too far ahead of us."

"Pull up a bit," she instructed the agent driving the sedan.

Trey turned left down Angertorstade and slowed his pace.

"It's too exposed." Rick pointed up at the curved buildings.

"Slow down," Elise instructed.

"I can't slow anymore," the driver said. "What's he doing?"

"Hold here," Elise said.

Suddenly Trey again stopped.

"Trey?" She called on the radio.

No response.

I don't like this—too many buildings and trees. We're too far from him. Rick took the radio. "Trey?"

Silence filled the car.

"Trey respond now."

"Can't." The clenched jaw response was unmistakable even over the radio.

"Why?" Rick asked.

"Being hunted." Trey's voice was barely audible.

"What? How do you—" Elise called out.

Rick held up his hand to her. She muted the mic. "What?"

"Don't spook him—trust him."

She nodded and turned back. "What the hell?"

Slowly, Trey turned around and knelt on the sidewalk. He stretched his arms out and began to sing aloud.

"'Have thine own way, Lord. Have thine own way. Thou art the Potter—I am the clay.'"

"Okay, Rick, we tried his way but I have to put a stop—"

"Fuck!" Rick yelled and pointed. "Look!"

The energy in the car surged as they all registered the now visible red dot on Trey's forehead.

"I'll be damned!" Elise said. "He's scoped—repeat: target has him in scope. Scan roof tops immediately."

"I have to get to him." Rick reached for his door.

Elise grabbed his arm. "Not yet—"

"He's gonna kill him, Elise!"

"Stop, Rick! We'll lose Ivan. Think about it. We don't even know where he is in all these buildings."

This is why I didn't want to green light us being in the open. Too many angles. Rick's mind raced. He turned back to Trey.

"You know I'm right." She loosened her grip on his arm. "If he was gonna take the shot, he would've. If keep our cover, we get him."

Shit, she's right.

CHAPTER 68
PROTECT

That's his scope. This is it—if I die, then I want the Lord to hear my voice. Instinctively, when Trey saw the bouncing red dot on the sidewalk, he reverted to his faith and sang.

"'Mold me and make me, after thy will. While I am waiting yielded and still.'"

How in the hell? He did it—in a city of a million. He found him. Rick remained fixed on Trey.

"Eagle teams report," Elise barked.

"Nothing."

"Negative."

"Nothing here either."

Each team reported.

She shook her head. "We have visual on his scope—where the fuck is he? I want answers, people. Keep scanning."

"Rick, what is Trey doing?" Elise asked.

"He's offering himself up," Rick said.

"Why is he singing? Has he lost it?"

"No. He grew up really religious. He's kneeling at the altar of his church back in Georgia—giving himself."

"What?"

"A living sacrifice," Rick said.

"So that's a hymn?" she asked.

"Yes."

Elise turned up the radio as Trey's voice echoed.

"'Have Thine own way, Lord. Have Thine own way.'"

Eva's voice interrupted. "Elise, come in for Eagle Team 1?"

"Go."

"We have visual on the target—repeat: visual on the target. Permission to take the shot?"

"Do you a clean shot?"

"Not clean. But we—"

"Hold for clean shot. Keep visual on target."

Rick's jaw tightened as he stared at Elise.

"We wait," she said sternly.

"Elise—"

"We *wait*. If he's gonna take the shot—there's not a damn thing we can do, but we have to get this son of a bitch." She clicked the radio. "On my call."

"Affirmative, on your call," Eva confirmed.

Trey continued to sing quietly as a few people walked around him. One person stopped in front of him.

"Get up," the man barked.

Trey raised his head. "Hello, Ivan."

He grabbed Trey, pulling him to his feet.

"Look!" Rick turned to Elise. "We fell for his trick. Decoy. His scope was fixed."

"Scheisse!" She immediately gave the call, "Geh! Geh! Geh!"

Rick bolted from the car in a full sprint, pulling the Glock from his waistband as he ran. He was sixty yards away, as they had held back to give space on the tree-lined side of the street to avoid engagement. *Damn it—we're too far! They should've listened to me.*

Rick heard Elise and her agents following behind him as her voice rang out in his earpiece.

"We're green. Repeat we're green. Do you have the target?" Elise called out. "Take the shot."

"Negative. The trees— We're repositioning. Repeat: negative line on target."

God, please help me. Rick? What do I do now? Do I fight back yet? Trey looked beyond Ivan and saw figures running toward them in the distance. Suddenly, a bus pulled into view. Ivan tightened his hold on him. *Where are we going? I can't see them now. Fight back, now.*

Trey jerked and then felt the metal rod. *Gun. Now what?*

"Don't resist," Ivan barked.

Suddenly Trey heard Rick in his ear. "He's right, Trey. Don't resist. Don't fight him—not yet. I'm coming."

Get here now—he's gonna shoot me. Trey stopped resisting and walked with Ivan down the street, away from the advancing team.

"What the fuck!" Rick did not conceal his anger as the bus pulled between them. "Move, move, move!" He banged on the side of the bus. *Find him—I can't see Trey.*

"Do you have the target?" Elise yelled into her radio as she caught up to Rick and pulled his shoulder toward the left flank of the transit bus.

"Negative. Repeat, negative."

As they circumvented the bus, the driver pulled away.

"Finally!" Rick shouted. *Where is he?*

When the sidewalk came back into view, Trey and Ivan had vanished.

"Where are they?" Rick barked. "We're exposed. Scan left." He and Elise immediately turned back to back, weapons drawn, observing all sides of the apartment building, trees, and street. "Anything?"

"No," she said.

"Target is moving north. Repeat: north," Eva said over Elise's radio.

Rick and Elise bolted up the street.

"Do you have a shot?" Elise snapped.

"Negative. Elise, there's a crowd. Wait . . . Where'd they go? We lost visual."

"Damn it!" Rick stopped. "Elise, wait."

"What?" She shook her head.

Rick clicked his audio button. "Trey, come in. Trey?"

CHAPTER 69
BLOOD

Where's Rick? Why isn't he already here? As they walked, Trey's mind raced. He stole a glance over his shoulder. *Nothing. Nobody. Rick?*

"Trey, come in. Trey?" Rick voice scratched through on his earpiece. *Respond. How without Ivan knowing? Click the audio on and off.* Trey carefully allowed his arm to slow and put his hand into his pocket. He felt for the wire and switch. *Got it.*

Click. Click.

"How did you find me?" Trey said aloud.

"Easy. You alone. Why?" Ivan asked.

"Trey, I hear you—repeat: I hear. Play along with him," Rick whispered in his ear.

"Yes. I'm sorry, sir. Are you gonna punish me?"

Suddenly, Ivan tugged Trey and they ducked down a driveway before the intersection with Destouchesstrasse.

"Where are we going?"

"Quiet!"

I ain't going any further. Rick, where are you? Say something.

Rick heard Trey's question to Ivan.

"Tiger, do you hear me? Clear your throat for me." Rick held his breath.

Cough.

"Is this your car? The blue one." Trey's voice echoed on the radio.

"Trey, do not get in that car. You hear me, do not get in that car," Rick barked.

"What is dis? Wire . . . I kill you now," Ivan snapped.

Screech!

Oh my god—where is he? Get to him. Rick paced and listened. The radio was silent.

"Elise, come in, Elise. Eagle team 2."

"Go for Elise."

"We have visual. Repeat: we have visual on them both—target has weapon."

"Where?"

"They're in the alley beyond a Chinese restaurant before Destouchesstrasse."

"We copy. Keep visual." Elise pointed two blocks away to Rick.

Rick took off in a full sprint. *Hunan Garden—that's it.* He darted across the street. *Get to him.*

As he rounded the corner, Rick stumbled to a stop.

"Hello, Agent. Is dis your faggot?" Ivan held a long blade to Trey's throat.

Oh fuck, stay calm. Try to reason with him in Russian. Rick put down his Glock and raised both hands. "Нет, пожалуйста, давай поговорим об этом," Rick pleaded with Ivan in Russian. "Put the knife down. There are teams all around us. You're surrounded."

Ivan tightened his hold and pressed the blade. Trey's eyes widened with panic.

"No, he's only a kid. A civilian."

"Civilian?"

"Yes."

"Bullshit," Ivan barked. "But you're not, Agent."

"No. I'm not civilian." Rick slowly took two steps forward.

"Ah, ah, ah . . . step back, Agent."

Rick did not move. "Please, a question for you, Ivan?" Rick stared intently at Trey. "Atacar ahora."

Ivan seemed confused for a split second before a lightning bolt of pain shot through his body. Trey gripped Ivan's testicles and squeezed with all his might as they buckled over together.

"Aarrgh!" Ivan screamed.

Trey let go of Ivan and twisted away from the blade. He jabbed his elbow deep into Ivan's rib as Rick had demonstrated in their training. The air from Ivan's lungs blew out loudly as he stabbed the air blindly and barely missing Trey's head.

As Ivan swung again, Trey dropped to the ground under his weight. Rick lunged and dove with full force, knocking Ivan over Trey to the ground.

Get up! Get him. Rick's adrenaline surged and he recoiled to his feet. *Fuck!* A burning sensation stung Rick left shoulder. Then his right thigh. *What the—*

Rick stumbled backward as Ivan raised the blade a third time.

Pop, pop!

Rick watched Elise fire short blasts at close range. Blood shot from Ivan's leg. Rick felt the cold bricks against his cheek. He closed his eyes. *Get him! Take him out, Elise.* A wave of nausea and weakness washed over him. *Stay awake. Trey!*

He opened his eyes and saw Trey on top of Ivan with both hands around his throat. His eyes grew heavy, and darkness sipped into his mind.

"Stop! Get back." Elise pulled Trey off Ivan as four agents pounced on him. Quickly with military precision, Trey watched them flip him over and cuff his arms behind his back. Two stood and pulled their weapons and one kneeled into his back.

Rick? Trey turned and saw the pool of blood surrounding them. "Rick!" Trey tore off his shirt and wire. He immediately tied a tourniquet on Rick's bleeding thigh. "Elise, help me!"

"Oh my god, medics—Eva get medics. Rick's been hit."

Trey held tight to his thigh as Elise assessed his shoulder.

"We need to keep him alert."

Trey leaned down. "Rick, look at me. Look at me!"

Rick opened his eyes, then closed them.

"No, no—look at me, Rick Morgan!"

He opened his eyes again.

"That's it. That's it. Stay with me. Stay with me, Rick. Don't you leave me, Rick Morgan. Don't you go anywhere."

Trey looked up at Elise. She nodded. Her hands were bloody as she held his shoulder.

So much blood. Oh God, please help him. Keep squeezing. We need help. Trey turned back to Elise. "Where's the ambulance?"

"They'll be here soon. Keep pressing," Elise instructed. "Rick, stay with us. Stay with us, Rick," she repeated over and over.

"Hey. Trey?" Rick whispered.

"What?" Trey leaned downward and strained to hear over the commotion as more agents arrived. "Tell me, what?"

"I, I will survive," Rick said.

"You better. Yes, you will survive!" Trey smiled through his fear.

Lights flashed and radios squealed loudly around them. Suddenly Trey was pulled back. He stood with Elise as medics took Rick. They strapped him to a gurney and whisked him to the awaiting ambulance.

"Trey?"

Trey turned to Elise. Her blouse sleeves were now red.

"We need to go. Come with me." She pulled him into the back seat and the door shut. "Buckle up."

Trey buckled his seatbelt as the swirl of lights around the car flashed. Agents got into the front seats and the sedan lunged forward.

"He's strong, Trey. He's going to make it."

Trey turned to Elise. He took her hand. She held his firmly.

It feels sticky.

He glanced down. Rick's blood was wet and glistened on them both as the city lights flickered. The car sped through the streets of Munich. Trey silently prayed.

God, please help him—please don't let him die.

CHAPTER 70
OUT

"I don't care—I'm not leaving." Trey's tone was deep and his voice cracked.

"I'm not asking you to leave—please take these scrubs and shower?" Elise stood in front of him in a crisp blue pant suit and white blouse.

"Sorry, I thought you were one of the orderlies—they've been trying to get me to leave. I'm not—"

"I heard." She motioned to the nurses' desk. "I hear you're pretty stubborn."

"Yeah, I can't . . . if he . . ."

"I know. I'm sorry I left but I ran home to get cleaned up."

"Have you heard anything?"

"No, but I think they think he'll be out of surgery soon. Let's get you cleaned up too—okay?"

Trey nodded. She guided him down the hall of the hospital and to a tiled bathroom with a shower divided by a white plastic curtain.

"I'll put these here." She placed the neatly folded blue scrubs on the chair outside the curtain. "You gonna be okay?"

"Yeah."

"I'll be right outside—I'm not leaving again. I promise." She stepped out.

"Thanks." He closed the door and stripped off his blood-soaked clothes.

Why was there was so much blood? Please be okay, Rick. Please God.

He turned the dial and the warm water washed over his body. The white soapy bubbles turned pink as he scrubbed the dried blood from his arms and body.

"Well, you look better." Elise smiled as he emerged from the bathroom in the scrubs. "The doctor is waiting for us—you ready?"

"Yeah."

Elise and Trey walked to the doctor standing at the nurse's station reviewing his notes.

"Hello, I'm Doctor Heilman—I'm the attending. You must be his friend."

"I'm Trey Carter." Trey nodded and then asked, "How is he?"

"Lucky—he lost nearly a liter. But we've been able to stop the bleeding and repair both wounds. Let's start with his—sorry, Schenkel."

"Thigh," Elise translated.

"Yes, sorry, my English is rusty. The blade nicked his femoral."

"That's why there was so much blood?" Trey asked.

"Yes. We repaired it and stabilized, but he'll need several days here to recover. The good news or how do you say—strange thing is how precise the cut was performed."

Trey shot Elise a look. She shook her head slightly.

The doctor continued. "Lucky for your friend the blade did not turn. It went in and out—cleanly. It does not appear to have damaged the bone or muscle. He'll be very sore but heal in a few weeks."

"What about his shoulder?" Elise asked.

"Ah, that's the tricky one. The blade—I assume the same one that inflicted the wound on his femur—did turn. We took our time and repaired each layer. The muscle and how do you say, Fleischgewebe."

"Flesh—tissue."

"Yes, tissue. Each layer, but—" He shook his head.

"But what? Will he be okay?"

"Ja, Ja. But we don't know if nerve endings were damaged. Time is needed."

"Thank you, doctor."

"Of course—we hope for good recovery."

They parted and went to his room. Rick was wired to several monitors and two IVs.

"I am guessing you'll stay here?" Elise said and motioned to the nurse wheeling in a rolling cot, with pillow and blanket atop.

"Yes, thank you."

"I knew. Listen, here's a phone. My number and Jeni's are programmed. She's on her way back to Frankfurt. If you need anything or if he wakes up—call me?"

"I will."

"I'll see you tomorrow."

"Where's Ivan?"

"Locked away—don't worry. Okay?"

Trey nodded and she headed to the door. "Elise?"

She turned backed.

"Thank you."

"Of course. Get some rest." Elise smiled and exited as the nurse unfolded the cot and arranged the bed for Trey.

"He's lucky." The nurse motioned to Rick lying unconscious in the bed.

"Yeah, that is what the doctor said. Should make a full recovery, we hope."

"And to have good friend." She smiled and placed a hand on Trey's shoulder. "Sleep now."

Trey nodded.

Forty-eight hours later, Trey was sitting by Rick's bed when he sensed a stirring. He leaned in and watched as Rick's eyes twitched and then opened.

"Hey." Trey tried to smile.

"Hey, Tiger."

"How you feel?"

"Beat up. Why so sad?"

"Rick?"

"That's my name, Trey. Ha."

Trey grinned slightly. "Easy—you've got a lot of stitches."

"How many?"

Trey shook his head and took his hand. "I don't know—over a hundred."

"Are we still in Germany?"

"Yeah."

"What day is it?"

"Tuesday."

"Did we get him? Ivan?"

Who cares—don't go right back into work. Always work. Trey kissed his hand. "Yeah, Elise's team has him."

"I don't remember all of it. You okay?"

Trey nodded. "Thanks to you."

"Who else is here?"

"Only me."

"Alone?"

"No, there's always a couple of Elise's agents outside."

Rick nodded. "How long have I been here?"

"'Bout two days, but you've been out of it. Elise and her team have been here a lot."

"Where's Jeni?"

"Frankfurt—she was here but had to go back there and then head to Langley."

"Is she okay?"

"Yeah." Trey squeezed his hand and stood. "You hungry?"

"Kinda."

"Let me go tell Hilda."

"Who?"

"Your nurse—I'll see if they can get you something." Trey leaned over and kissed Rick's forehead.

"What was that for?"

"Because you're okay."

By Thursday, Rick was feeling better and able to eat more. Trey was feeding him soup when the hospital room door opened and one of the armed agents posted stuck his head in.

"You guys have a visitor."

Trey nodded. Claren walked into the room. "Hey."

She took one look at Rick with Trey and smiled deeply. "I'm so grateful that you're both okay. I spoke to your surgeon, Rick. You are one lucky son-of-a-bitch."

Rick smiled at Claren and glanced at Trey. "Yes, I am." He pulled himself up in the bed and turned to Trey, "Can you give us a minute, Tiger?"

"Okay, but take it easy."

"Yes, Nurse Carter."

"I mean it—I'll tell Hilda." Trey left the room.

"He's devoted to you."

"He's a pain in the ass, but he's grown on me."

"Elise and Jeni tell me that he hasn't left this room for four days."

"No. He's unbelievable. I am lucky."

"That you are—surgeon said the blade nicked but didn't sever your femoral, and your shoulder was a fairly clean cut. You'll be sore for several weeks. How do you feel?"

"Ready to get out of here and go home."

"That's not up to you."

"Guess not. At least we got him. Where's he? Have you seen him?"

"No, nor do I plan to. He's in lock down in a maximum-security facility. We took in Hana in Prague. She claims to know nothing."

"You believe her?"

"No."

"Has the KGB claimed them?"

"They never *heard* of Ivan and Hana."

"Bullshit."

"Don't I know it." Claren shook her head. "Elise and the team are going to *forget* our earlier incidents in Nuremberg and Bor. For now, all this is contained. Jeni will get Trey to his training in Philly next week, and we have to get *you* home."

"Are we booked on flights?"

"He's booked commercial but you're getting a private medic flight, then straight to Walter Reed."

"Lovely—can't wait. I hear the food's terrific." Rick managed a smile.

She smiled.

"Does Trey know?"

"Not yet."

"Can I tell him?"

"Yes, it would be best from you. He needs to be on that plane tonight and you know our stubborn Tiger better than anyone."

"Is he free to go? Leave us?"

"For now."

He raised his eyebrows.

"He'll go to his Global training but—"

"Claren, he did what we asked him to do."

"Yes, he did. And—" she stopped.

"For now," Rick repeated her words.

"Yes." She squeezed his right foot and smiled. "We've been through so much, you and I." She rounded the bed and placed her hand on his forehead. "I'm so grateful that you're okay."

What the— Tears? No, Claren has never cried. At least never in front of me. Rick sensed her welling up. She then shocked him as she planted a kiss on his forehead.

She took a step back. "Tell anyone that I did that, and I will stab you myself."

They smiled at one another. He raised his hand and she took it in hers. After a moment, she squeezed it.

"See you on Campus. Take care, Rick." Claren turned to exit the room.

"Claren?"

She looked back.

"One day, can we let him go? Give him a way out?"

She nodded.

"Promise me?" Rick said.

"I promise."

Alone in the room, Rick thought about Claren's look—it had told him everything. *She promised but did she mean it? Can Trey walk away? Hell, can any of us ever really walk away? No one was ever really out—free to walk away. It's like we're all bound together—Claren included. Bound to the protocol.*

He thought about the Agency and his tenure. *I should call and check in on Jeni.*

A new thought popped into his mind. *Trey—I want to hold him. He's part of my life now.*

"Got you some juice." Trey returned alone. "Do you want any more soup?"

"No, I'm good. Listen, I talked to Claren and well I want to talk to you. Global's next week."

"What? Are you getting out of here?"

"Come here." Rick smiled and patted the bed beside him. Trey sat on the edge. "Our assignment is done."

"What's next?"

"Next, you go to Philly. Global Airways."

"What about you? Is that why Claren's here?"

"Trey, Claren rarely goes out in the field like this. She needed to show up and smooth things over with Elise's director, the BND, and our consulate."

"So that's it?"

"Yeah."

"When?"

"You're headed back tonight."

"What about you?"

"I'm on a military medic flight tomorrow. Your training starts on Monday. I will check in with you in a couple of weeks, but for now, this is where our time ends."

What? He's not welling up? Is he gonna blow up? Huh—nothing?

Trey sat on the bed and looked out the window. "I need to say something to you, Rick."

"Okay."

"I hope you know that I did my best. It was hard. You were a jerk those first few weeks." Trey turned to Rick. "But I . . . I love you. I know we're not lovers—I know that we both have to move forward but—"

"Shh, come here." Rick pulled him in and kissed him tenderly.

"Can I ask you something?"

Rick nodded with a raised eyebrow.

"What was his name?"

"Who?"

"The only man you've loved. Your Israeli?"

Rick froze and for the first time since the night at the lake, he let down his guard. "Baruch," he said, swallowing hard.

"I want to love someone like that one day."

"You will. One day when all this is done. You will."

"You think so?"

"I know so. Tiger, you are gonna to find the right guy. I hope that I get to meet him." He paused, as they smiled at each other.

"Yeah, so you can scare the shit out of him," Trey said.

"No, to warn him," Rick said with a wink. "Come here." He did his best to hug Trey with one arm. "Listen to Jeni. Okay? She'll meet you at Dulles."

He nodded.

"Now get out of here—I need to rest and you have to get cleaned up and get to Philly."

"See you, Rick."

"See you, Trey. Make me proud."

"I will," he said softly.

Trey walked out of the hospital room and was met by Elise and Claren.

"Trey, one of my team will take you back to Camp Nicolas, so you can get your things, and catch your flight," Elise said.

Trey nodded.

"Well, I guess this is goodbye. Thank you, Trey. We wouldn't have gotten him without you." She extended her hand. Trey ignored her hand and went with instinct—hugging her instead. She startled but melted into his embrace.

"You are not like any agent I've ever met—and that is a good thing," she said with a tight squeeze. She let go and they parted. "Don't let any of this change you, Trey—stay you. Okay?"

"I will. And thank you for all you did for Rick."

She smiled. "Goodbye, Trey."

Claren and Trey walked out of the hospital without speaking. As they approached the awaiting cars, she gently grabbed his elbow. "Hey."

Trey turned to her.

"You're worried about Rick—aren't you?"

"Yes."

"He's going to be fine. I promise."

Trey nodded.

"Trey? I'm proud of you, young man. You hear me?"

"Thank you."

"Now, you know everything you've experienced is classified—secret. Right?"

"Yes, ma'am."

"Good luck next week. Global's training will be tough—don't take it for granted. Do your best."

"I will."

"We'll be in touch." Claren gave his arm a squeeze and walked to her awaiting car.

Trey got into his car with the BND agent, and they drove away from the University of Munich Hospital.

"How long is the drive?" Trey asked from the back seat.

"About twenty or twenty-five minutes. Here's your stuff from the hospital." He handed a clear, plastic bag of blood-stained clothing over the seat.

"Thanks." Trey opened the bag and felt around the clothing. *Yes.* He pulled out his tiger head key ring.

Thank you, Rick.

Trey held it to his lips and kissed its inscription.

Semper Protege.

Dear Reader,

Thank you for reading Brian David Randall's *Demaris: Protocol*!

We know your time is precious and you have many, many entertainment options, so it means a lot that you've chosen to spend your time reading. We really hope you enjoyed it.

We'd be honored if you'd consider posting a review—good or bad—on sites like **Amazon, Barnes & Noble, Kobo, Goodreads, Twitter, Facebook, Tumblr,** and your blog or website. We'd also be honored if you told your friends and family about this book. Word of mouth is a book's lifeblood!

For more information on upcoming releases, author interviews, blog tours, contests, giveaways, and more, please sign up for our weekly, spam-free newsletter and visit us around the web:

Newsletter: riptidepublishing.com/newsletter
Twitter: twitter.com/RiptideBooks
Facebook: facebook.com/RiptidePublishing
Goodreads: tinyurl.com/RiptideOnGoodreads
Tumblr: riptidepublishing.tumblr.com

Thank you so much for Reading the Rainbow!

RiptidePublishing.com

ACKNOWLEDGMENTS

Special thanks to Rachel, Grace, Caz, and the entire team at Riptide Publishing for taking the chance on me as a first-time author. I also want to express my gratitude to the Maine Writers & Publishers Alliance, the Association of Former Intelligence Officers, and the writers in my life, Ron Currie Jr., Chris Bull, Dave Pallone, and the late Marvin Liebman for their nurturing support of my writing. Revisiting this dark fifteen months of my life in 1992-93 has been cathartic but extremely difficult at times.

When I walked away in November of 1993, I slammed the door shut and tried to move forward with my life. I came out of the closet fully and walked authentically in nearly all parts of my life, but without sharing details of the exact nature of my time with World Airways and the Agency. I am thankful for Dr. Roger Segalla for throwing me a lifeline in 2002. His counseling helped me sort out these conflicted feelings, memories, and emotions that I'd unsuccessfully buried. For many of us within the LGBTQ community, it can be painful to revisit darker periods in our coming out and struggle for equality. All of us have unique paths and struggles. In 2024, I am astonished how far we've come since August 1991 when, as a young man fresh out of Liberty University, I moved to Washington, DC.

Prior to Executive Order 12968, signed by President Clinton in August 1995, and "Don't Ask, Don't Tell," known homosexuals were not allowed to serve in national intelligence and our military. Those closeted risked everything if they were "outed." Friends ask me why I chose to write my story as fiction. The answer is simple. I did not want to "out" anyone either from their clandestine role or sexual orientation.

Fiction has also allowed me leeway for a fuller, more complete retelling after thirty years. In order to publish as a former, I was required to contact and complete the process with the CIA PRB, publisher review board. As part of those discussions, it is important to highlight that the CIA has had full equality for officers, operatives, and associates fully since 1996, including sexual orientation.

I am thankful for my inner circle: David Morris, Justin Burkhardt, Nick Gill, and Andy Smith—you are my posse, my "ride or die," and friends for life. Book one, *Demaris: Protocol*, is dedicated to my husband, partner, and best friend, Alex Beal. For more than twenty years, it has been my privilege to walk by your side.

Finally, to my assigned CIA officer represented within the series as "Rick Morgan." I've kept my promise and never taken one day for granted since November 9, 1993, Dubrovnik. I owe you my life and am grateful to share our story but most importantly your story.

Semper protege,

Tiger

ABOUT THE
AUTHOR

Brian Randall is a first-time novelist with *Demaris: Protocol*, book one of the Demaris Protocol series. He is an openly gay graduate of Liberty University. He lives with his husband of more than twenty years with their German Shepherd, Forest, in Portland, Maine.

X (formerly Twitter): @brian__randall

Web: www.demarisprotocol.com

Enjoy more stories like
Demaris: Protocol
at RiptidePublishing.com!

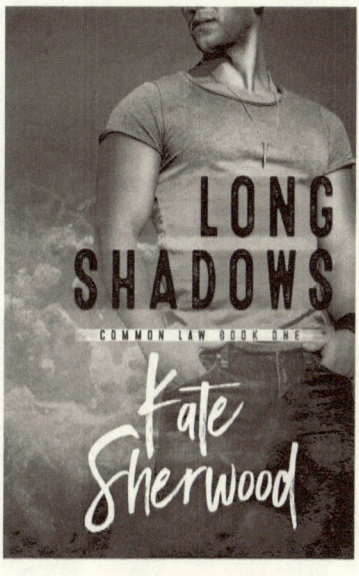

Long Shadows

Sometimes a bad decision is so much better than a good one.

ISBN: 978-1-62649-526-5

Anyone But You

Murder is one hell of a drag.

ISBN: 978-1-62649-891-4

www.ingramcontent.com/pod-product-compliance
Lightning Source LLC
Chambersburg PA
CBHW031019030726
47497CB00004B/928